Chris Nyst was born in B[...]
1953. Raised in Brisbar[...]
from the University of Q[...]
practice as a solicitor in B[...]
Coast. As a lawyer he has been involved in some of
Australia's most sensational cases. He is recognised as
one of Queensland's finest criminal law advocates, and
has been a regular speaker and guest lecturer on
criminal law and advocacy. As a writer he has made
prolific contribution to a range of legal publications.
His first novel, *Cop This!*, was published in 1999 and
received excellent reviews.

Chris lives with his wife, Julie, and their four
children on the Gold Coast, where he is a partner in one
of the region's largest law firms.

# GONE

# GONE

## CHRIS NYST

HarperCollins*Publishers*

# HarperCollins*Publishers*

First published in Australia in 2000
This edition published in 2001
Reprinted in 2001
by HarperCollins*Publishers* Pty Limited
ABN 36 009 913 517
A member of the HarperCollins*Publishers* (Australia) Pty Limited Group
http://www.harpercollins.com.au

**HarperCollins*Publishers***
25 Ryde Road, Pymble, Sydney NSW 2073, Australia
31 View Road, Glenfield, Auckland 10, New Zealand
77–85 Fulham Palace Road, London W6 8JB, United Kingdom
Hazelton Lanes, 55 Avenue Road, Suite 2900, Toronto, Ontario M5R 3L2
*and* 1995 Markham Road, Scarborough, Ontario M1B 5M8 Canada
10 East 53rd Street, New York NY 10022, USA

National Library of Australia Cataloguing-in-Publication data:

Nyst, Chris.
   Gone.
   ISBN 0 7322 6811 7.
   1. Crime – Australia – Fiction. 2. Mystery and
   detective stories. I. Title.
A823.3

Cover photograph: IPL/Peter Beavis
Printed and bound in Australia by Griffin Press on 50gsm Bulky News

7 6 5 4 3 2      01 02 03 04

*To my parents, who loved me dearly,*

*without qualification or condition*

# CHAPTER ONE

Bill's eyes snapped open. His heart was beating hard in his chest and in the darkness he could feel the cool of the sweat-soaked pillow at the back of his neck. There were demons that haunted Bill Keliher, and they were out and about tonight.

As he threw back his head he felt the whisky burn a purging path through his gullet, and he quickly pushed the bottle back into the glass. One, two, three straight down in quick succession until his breath began to settle and the tremble in his hands began to fade. He closed his eyes, tried to hide, but the demons were there.

"Where you off to, kids?"

"We're going to the beach."

"Hop in. I'll give youse a lift."

It seemed a thousand years ago, that hazy morning in the early days of the summer of 1965. It was another world, and Bill was another person. But he could not forget.

"Is this a real police car?"

"Sure is, mate."

Little Michael's eyes were like saucers, full of wonder. He was so soft, and precious and innocent, holding tight on to his little sister's hand, just as his mum had no doubt said he must. His first ride in a real police car.

Bitter tears seeped into Bill's eyes and he felt his heart begin to race again. There were so many things he wished he could change. He sucked in a settling breath, then poured down one more swallow.

*       *       *

Faye McCabe dragged the change bottle off the fridge and spilled some coppers into her open hand. She could feel immediately that Barry had snuck a few bob out. Not surprising. It was Saturday. He always did. Of course he always said he wouldn't, but he always did. And Faye didn't really mind. Barry worked hard pencilling for Horrie Niland every Saturday and he was entitled to a few beers and a quiet bet or two. Of course she always said he couldn't, but she knew he did.

She nudged the coins across her palm. Threepences, a couple of zacks, and big brown pennies. Soon they'd all be gone. Decimal currency was on its way. In a couple of months Australia would have the new American-style dollars and cents, and all these old familiar coins would be phased out. She played the television jingle over in her head: *In come the dollars and in come the cents, out go the pounds and the shillings and the pence*. It was all so modern and exciting. And daunting in a way. Faye closed her fingers and fondly caressed these old friends as she tried to think how many cents a shilling would be worth. Was it twelve? Or was it ten, or twenty maybe? All so confusing.

She opened her hand and looked again.

"Geez, look at that."

A farthing. She hadn't seen one in years. Halfpennies were rare enough these days, but a farthing was something special. Nineteen twenty-nine – wasn't that amazing? She hadn't realised that they were still making farthings right up until the twenties. Barry had probably picked it up in his change last night at the pub. This small reminder that she had finally trained her husband to empty his coins out into the jar was mildly satisfying.

"Michael, look. A farthing."

"Geez!" Little Michael was suddenly bouncing around her feet. "Can I have it, Mum?"

"We'll see, darl. I might just put it up for now."

Faye had a strange uneasy feeling as she held the little coin between her fingers. It was as though familiar friends were leaving them for ever, and she would miss them. She put the farthing down on the laminex and decided to put together a collection of imperial currency for posterity. All her life people had been telling her that you can't hold on to the past, but Faye was an old-fashioned girl, and a hoarder, and she never could help that.

\*    \*    \*

"Do you want me to get a bobcat out here, Bill?"

"No, mate. For all we know we're looking for chopped-up body parts, and they could've been here thirty years. We've got to take this nice and gradual."

Besides, the department probably wouldn't spring for the cost of getting a bobcat up here for another wild goose chase. The nearest town of any size was Grafton, and that was a good hour and a half away. Bill pushed the shovel in and turned over the first sod, thankful that the soil was soft and sandy. Wally Messner joined in, and the two detectives fell into sync with a rhythmical beat that was somehow almost comforting. Neither really wanted to find what they were looking for. Unearthing the remains of long-dead children was a most unpleasant prospect, and each was happy to have the other for company.

Bill Keliher had worked with Wally Messner on and off for nearly twenty years, originally in Darlinghurst in the early eighties, when Wally had first joined the coppers, and later for the Armed Robbery Squad, and then Homicide. He liked to think he'd taught the younger man a thing or two, and right now it was good to have him at his side, turning sods and puffing steam into the cold morning air.

They'd been on the go since sparrow's fart, checking everything there was to know about the old bloke. So far they had turned up nothing but a couple of ancient dishonesty convictions dating back before the war and a string of drunk charges in the sixties and the early seventies. It looked like Herbert Lancelot Montgomery had lived most of his life in much the same way as he eventually died, alone and friendless. The records showed that he joined up in forty-three, saw combat in North Africa and later in the Islands, and was demobbed in forty-six. He seemed to have hit the diesel pretty badly back on civvy street, as most of his known addresses were old flop-houses in the inner city and the Cross. Finally he showed up out here in the bush, back in the mid-sixties. He'd wandered around these parts ever since, half-dero and half-hermit hillbilly, too much of a drop-kick weirdo even for the hippies and the alternative-lifestylers who had made this area their own. Apparently in the seventies he had been welcomed and then affectionately ignored as a kind of off-beat oddity. But for the past fifteen years he had rarely been seen, except on pension day when he would come to town looking like Robinson Crusoe and leading around an old cattle dog with only marginally more mange than him, buy up a few provisions and then disappear again into the bush. Back to this little shanty, hidden in the clearing of the scrub, a one-room shed with an underground rations cellar, an outhouse and a rust-spotted watertank. The wreck of an old pre-war jalopy, its once bright red paint now cracked and faded, was propped up on the boundary fence, the only sign of any automation on the property.

Montgomery didn't sound much like a child-killer. Just a broken-down old pisshead, a casualty whose statistic hadn't made it into the record books. Ordinarily Bill wouldn't have bothered following up the call. There had been so many, just as he'd expected. Each anniversary of the disappearance of the McCabe children brought new leads. Every ten years they were inundated, and in this the thirtieth year it seemed like a cruel deluge sent to drown them. Some were genuine attempts to help, others oddballs with misguided theories, and some sick crackpots amused by sending coppers down dry gullies. Every passing year brought new stories. Every story brought another lead. Every lead might just be the crucial one. The anniversaries reminded Bill Keliher that the public had not forgotten the hapless McCabe children, could not forget them. Just as Bill could not forget.

The old woman had sounded tentative, reluctant, ashamed perhaps to think ill of the dead, particularly her own flesh and blood, lost to her so long and now found, a lonely mostly decomposed corpse discovered by a bushwalker who had chanced upon the humble cabin in the wilderness. Her older brother had never been the same after the war. At first he'd gone back to his old job at the hardware store, but he couldn't seem to settle. He was always arguing with the customers. Not like him at all. Then he started missing days and coming late to work. The owners had to let him go, and he moved out of home soon afterwards. He disappeared then, and though he turned up unexpectedly at home after a couple of years and stayed a day or two, he wasn't the same person that his family knew, and everyone was more or less relieved to see him go again. After that he became a kind of phantom in their lives, never mentioned in conversations but somehow always present, like an embarrassing indiscretion that everybody sensed but no one wanted to confront.

There were no suspicious circumstances. Herbert Montgomery was an old man; the only thing remarkable about his death in the context of the life he had lived was that it had been so long in coming. It seemed he had hoarded enough memorabilia in his shanty for the police to trace him back to a Mrs Enid Beatty, his younger sister and only living relative. So they delivered to her his scant possessions, the sum of his life boxed up in a carton no bigger than a small TV. An old photo of their mother at the beach at Portsea, and another one of Rex, a family pet that she had long-since forgotten; his army discharge papers, and a medal, an old rifle, a compass and some pots; his First Holy Communion certificate of all things; some magazines and newspapers; old photographs of people that she didn't recognise and letters from people she had never heard of. Funny, but it made her cry to see old Rex again. It was all so long ago.

And then there was the scrapbook. Old and yellowed, rolled, creased and flattened out again, it lay underneath the magazines at the very bottom of the box. She could see from the bulging wrinkled pages that it had been someone's labour of choice, tended lovingly and carefully maintained. When she opened it a chill ran right through her ageing body.

She recognised the clippings immediately. All Australians knew the smiling faces of Michael and

Catherine McCabe, frozen for ever in the collective consciousness of a nation as two beautiful happy children captured sitting on the back stairs of the modest house that had been their home – until they had disappeared, almost thirty years ago to the day, never to be seen again.

She turned the pages over, and with each turn the faces were still there, recurring in a file of yellowed clippings that chronicled the entire tragedy. The initial disappearance, then the search, the police investigation, the parents' heart-wrenching appeals, the endless speculation, the new leads, the theories, one thing and then another, year after year for decades. Each story had been saved, cut out and carefully pasted.

"Well, ma'am, it was a big story at the time of course."

Old Montgomery wasn't on his Pat Malone in having a morbid fascination with the McCabe case. Bill Keliher had been fielding calls like this for thirty years, and he knew better than to get excited about a few old news clippings.

"But he was there at the time they disappeared."

"What?"

"He lived near there. Not at Brighton Bay, but just inland a bit, at Yelgarabbi."

She went quiet then, and when she started up again Bill could hear a waver in her voice that made her sound like she wanted to get something off her chest. A lot of people lived with little secrets they were dying to offload. Bill Keliher knew that as well as anybody.

"There was an incident when he was young. We kept it very quiet."

It seemed Herbert Lancelot Montgomery had disgraced himself somewhere around the age of sixteen. Flashed his old fella at his seven-year-old cousin. Maybe it was worse than that; Bill wasn't sure. It was hard to prise any real detail from the old girl. Family secrets like this one tended to get locked up pretty tight. But Bill knew that secrets like these held the answer; one day a family's shame would turn the key. Kids don't just disappear without a trace. Someone sees. Someone knows. Someone fears. Someone suspects. Someone cannot bear to think it could be true. Secrets are buried, but in their grave they writhe and bubble and ferment.

"We'll go up there and have a gander, ma'am."

Bill felt sorry for the woman. There was so much that she couldn't understand about her long-lost brother, things that confused and worried her, perhaps that burdened her with guilt and terrified her that she might have to share the shame of some secret sin. He wanted to absolve her, put her mind at rest, relieve her of the burden.

"We'll have a look. I'm sure it'll all check out okay."

"There's . . . there's a grave up there."

"A grave?"

"Up on the back boundary. Maybe not a grave. There's a patch up there, as though something's buried. And there's a cross."

Murderers don't often bother with a decent burial for their victims but there was no mistaking the nature of the plot they found up on the southern boundary of the property. Whoever had been buried there was honoured with a Christian cross, and the site had been maintained and, until recently, visited regularly. Someone ought to check it out. And that meant Bill Keliher and his partner Wally Messner needed to roll up their sleeves and dig.

Missing-person files were usually hopeless soul-destroying cases that no one wanted to get stuck with. One day a teenage kid has a barney with his parents and he walks out in a huff. And that's it. He disappears without a trace. Or some sheila takes off, leaving her old man with a tribe of snotty-nosed kids and a head full of questions that he can't answer. She's not on drugs, she's not in trouble, she's just gone. No enemies, no one that wants to harm her. It makes no sense. It doesn't make the newspapers and it doesn't raise an eyebrow. No blood, no weapon, probably no crime. Just tragic human loss. They were hollow, endless, thankless cases best avoided at all costs. No promotion attached to them, no job satisfaction, no interesting challenge; just disillusioned, heartbroken families wondering why, and how, and if. And what if.

The McCabe file had long since turned into one of them, a case that could only sap your enthusiasm and identify you as a failure. Thirty years ago it was Australia's biggest story and every copper in the job wanted to put his hand on the brief. The leads were there, plenty of them. The tall thin man spotted chatting with the children at the beach; the car, the note, the sightings. It was so solvable, the answer seemed just around the corner. Only the best and most ambitious were assigned to the McCabe case then, and they were privileged to be involved. But as the months rolled into years, the confident predictions disappeared, the press statements stopped, and the old information began to be recycled. The fruitless, repetitious, boring detective work turned into frustration that seeped from the McCabe file like ooze from a festering sore. It had become one of those losers. A no-go file that would give you nothing and take you nowhere.

Eventually, the penny dropped and people began to walk away. This might have been Australia's biggest case, there might have been some leads. Once. But after thirty years it had become just like all the rest – a riddle that would never be unravelled, a mystery that would never be solved. Everyone believed that now. Everyone but William James Keliher. He knew that no secret could ever be buried so deep that sweat and toil and tears wouldn't eventually bring it to the surface. Some day it would be there, suddenly. It would burst into the daylight in all its horror, just as it had burst into his consciousness a thousand times before, wrenching him sweat-soaked from the terrifying visions of his restless sleep.

This one will come up, Bill Keliher told himself, as he pushed the shovel down into the sandy soil. And he was going to be there when it did. He had to be. It was his secret.

Things were different for Wally Messner. He hadn't been there from the beginning. He came along much later, long after the glory and promotion once associated with the McCabe brief had gone. Bill had plucked the dusty file out of the 'too hard' basket and toiled alone for years before Wally Messner showed up and said he'd lend a hand. He was interested, that's all, and he could see that Bill could use some help. So he had pitched in and helped, and he'd been helping ever since. Every time a new lead wanted to air their family's dirty linen, or unload a bit of gossip that they'd once heard in the pub or over the back fence, Wally had been there. And when it came to turning over old stones and exploring dry gullies, Bill knew just what a lonely job it could be. Another shovel was always welcome.

In over thirty years of service Bill had made a lot of good mates in the job, but Wally wasn't one. Wally was a good man, solid and reliable. But he had an abrupt manner and little conversation beyond his fascination with horse racing, not Bill's cup of tea at all. They were an odd couple thrown together by a common case, and both men knew it. Willing partners, but not friends.

As they grunted and puffed together in the early-morning light, Bill wondered what it was that kept Wally in this thing, that gave him the energy to keep on backing up, one fruitless lead after another, up one blind alley and then down the next.

"Argh shit!"

The two policemen fumbled for their handkerchiefs and pressed them to their noses as an acrid stench burst from the ground. Bill's heart began to thump in his chest. They had found something.

"Can we, Mum? Please?"

Michael had perfected the subtle art of gentle persuasion in a way that only a nine-year-old can.

"Please?"

He was already dressed in his new shorts and striped T-shirt, and the rolled-up towels and swimmers bundled in his arms announced that he was ready to set off. Faye's irritation melted at the sight of her determined little boy, his zinc-smeared nose peeping out from beneath the broad-brimmed hat. It was all meant to reassure her that he had thought of everything. He had his sandals on for the one-mile walk to the Loxton Park swimming baths, because he knew Mum would insist that they had something on their feet. He had his little sister dressed up in her bathers and a sundress so Mum didn't have to organise her, and he'd even made sure she had a hat on because he knew his mother wouldn't want her getting sunburnt.

Faye smiled and shook her head. He was such a little soldier. Captain Michael. Poor little Catherine was destined to be organised and pushed around all her life. Organised and pushed around, but loved and cared for too. Michael idolised his baby sister, and Faye knew that her little girl would always have her champion and protector to look after her.

"Well, if you're going to go to the pool, I want you back home by lunchtime, all right?"

"Ripper!"

13

Michael was already scurrying around, shuffling his sister towards the door.

"Twelve o'clock sharp, Michael. Back here for lunch. All right? I want you to get stuck into those chores of yours this afternoon."

Faye McCabe walked her two beautiful children to the front gate of their home and farewelled them with little kisses. Kisses that meant nothing, that were so fleeting and so devoid of any urgency that eventually, with the passage of time, Faye would come to wonder whether she had kissed her children at all that day. She would always tell herself she had, because she couldn't bear to think otherwise. In truth, she would no longer remember anything of those little kisses. But she had done. She had kissed her children, and then stood briefly at the wooden gate and watched the two most precious people in her life walk hand in hand, chatting idly to each other, down the quiet country road, and out of her world for ever.

A piece of Faye McCabe left her that day, and in its place there came a cruel relentless torment that pursued her and accused her, every waking hour of her life.

\*     \*     \*

"Righto, Barry. Tell us again what you did that day."

Vince Donnelly felt bad about it, but he had to ask the question. None of the police sitting in the stuffy little office at the rear of the Brighton Bay police station believed for a moment that Barry McCabe was in any way responsible for the disappearance of his children, but right now he was the only one they had who looked remotely like a suspect. And as painful as it might get, it was up to Vince to ask the ugly questions.

"Well?"

Barry looked up from the chair like a big dog that has just been belted with a rolled-up newspaper. They could all see he didn't want to talk about it. But Vince had a job to do, and this was part of it. So far the kids had been gone eleven days without a trace and, although no one was letting on officially, the horizon was already looking very bloody blank. That's why they had brought Vince in. As one of the state's most experienced detectives, it was his job to turn it all around. And that's what he was going to do.

"Come on, Barry, we haven't got all bloody day."

Young Constable Bill Keliher could feel a bitter lump rising in his throat as Barry McCabe cast his glassy eyes around the room as if looking for support, then finally sucked in a deep breath and blew it out.

"Like I told the other detectives, Inspector, I knocked around at the tip for about an hour, and then I slipped down to Barrons Landing till lunchtime, then I headed home."

"What were you doing at Barrons Landing?"

"Just went down to wet a line."

"Were you with anyone?"

"No. Me and Alby Astor have got a spot down there. We keep it quiet like. Alby's been away so I just slipped down meself, see if I could jag a couple."

"Don't you take the lad with you?"

It was one question too many and a part of Vince hated himself for asking it. But another part reminded him that two kids were missing and every day that passed reduced the chances of them showing up alive; that ninety per cent of these ugly little crimes turned up a dirty penny in the family; and that if anything was going to crack, someone had to turn the pressure up. Barry McCabe's eyes filled with moisture as he quietly shook his head.

"Well, Barry, do you or don't you?"

"No."

It came out a feeble whisper that shamed them all. A couple of detectives shifted uncomfortably and looked down at the floor. Bill Keliher squirmed in his chair, wanting desperately to step in and tell them all to pull up and leave the bloke alone.

"You didn't tell your missus you were going fishing?"

"No."

"Why not?"

Barry McCabe was a big raw-boned dairy farmer's son with twice the strength of any man in town. He'd seen his tough times as well as good and he had earned himself the respect of those who knew him. But right now he was beaten. He was groping for an answer, not to the question Vince had asked him, but to all the questions he had asked himself these past eleven days, the same ones that turned over and over in his head, that writhed around and gnawed at him even when he tried to sleep. He'd been everywhere, looked everywhere, asked everyone, thought of all the things the kids might want to do, where they might go. There had to be something he had missed, some little detail he had overlooked, some penny that would eventually drop and suddenly the answer would be there. His two big hands were locked together and his glassy eyes were staring blindly at the realisation that this was a problem that the sweat of his brow could not resolve. Bill Keliher could see his agony. It was like watching a bullock that has given all it can straining against an overwhelming load.

"Well, Barry, why not?"

Bill pushed the chair back and strode towards the door. He heard it swing closed somewhere back behind him but he saw nothing and he knew nothing until he stepped out onto the front verandah, heaving deep breaths of the sweet fresh morning air. His head was spinning. He was frustrated, and ashamed, and angry, and bewildered.

Bill knew that Barry McCabe knew nothing. No one who had been there from the start could question that. Interrogating him like this was about as much use as flogging that poor beaten beast to death just because it couldn't move the load another inch.

The two McCabe children had left their home in Bentley Street just after nine o'clock. Their father had been gone a half hour or so, and they had promised their mum they'd be back home from the public baths by lunch. She had taken three shillings from the jar – that would be plenty to get them in and pay for soft drinks. Young Michael wore grey King Gee shorts and a red and green striped T-shirt, sandals and a straw hat.

His little sister wore a pink sundress with a floral pattern over lime-green swimmers. She had white patent sandals on her feet and a cane sun bonnet with a navy band. They had walked hand in hand the short distance to the corner and then turned right into the Point Road, and disappeared.

Faye McCabe watched them to the corner, then went back to her ironing. As she put the coin jar back up on the fridge, she felt for the little farthing. It was gone, and she tried to think what she had done with it. Had that little wretch Michael got his hands on it? She'd ask him later. At about ten she did a load of washing and she was still hanging out the clothes when her neighbour Shirley Wyatt dropped in for a cup of tea and a chat.

By the time Shirley left, it was around midday, and Faye expected that the kids would be home soon. She made up some sandwiches and started on a cake. Before she knew it, it was getting on for one. Still no kids. She popped the cake into the oven and walked to the front door. No sign of them. Her watch showed right on one o'clock and now Faye was feeling quite annoyed. She had expressly told Michael that she wanted them home for lunch, and she had too much to get done to be standing around waiting for them to come dawdling home in their own time. Where was Barry anyway? How long does it take to run a load down to the tip? He had said he might just check the crab pots on the way back, which probably meant that he was still down there, hours later, wasting time as usual.

The day was starting to get warmer. Standing at the

front door in the direct sunlight Faye McCabe was hot and bothered. Where were those kids, for heaven's sake? She puffed a strand of hair back from her sweaty brow, looked at her watch again for emphasis, then stepped out from the threshold. As she neared the Point Road she was gathering momentum, preparing to let loose an earful to her children as they wandered idly back. She came around the corner and drew a breath, ready to let fly.

But as she made the turn she stopped and breathed out gently. Ahead of her the Point Road stretched out a half a mile to the horizon bathed in the early summer haze. They weren't there. She squinted into the distance but still there was no one. Faye set her jaw and shook her head. Little beggars!

She sat at the kitchen table tapping her foot. As soon as Barry got back she would send him up to Loxton Park to bring them home. And then they'd catch it. This was the last time Michael would be going to the pool on his own. If he couldn't show enough responsibility to be back home when he was told, then he wouldn't be going, and that was all there was to it! Where the hell was Barry anyway?

Faye got started on the icing, but she was all thumbs. The kids were all right, she was sure. They were probably playing tag in the wading pool, or sitting on the grass talking to their friends, oblivious to the time, not giving a minute's thought to lunch. The more she thought about it the more annoyed she was with Michael. He should know better. Catherine would be starving by now.

By two o'clock Faye had been down to the corner twice more, and she was starting to get worried. Perhaps there'd been an accident. The littlies were very closely supervised at Loxton Park, but what if Catherine had gone over to the big pool? What if she had taken off her floaties? Faye was nervously paging through the phone book looking for the number for the Loxton Park baths when Barry finally came in, ready to triumphantly announce the morning's catch. He didn't get too much out.

When Barry McCabe got down to Loxton Park at around ten past two, he spoke to Arthur Gaskill on the gate. He told Arthur he had pulled a half a dozen good-sized jew out of the river earlier on, and that he wasn't staying for a swim, he'd just dropped by to pick up the kids. Arthur didn't recall having seen them, but guessed they'd be somewhere over with the other children playing on the grassed area. Barry said he'd just slip in and grab them.

It had never once occurred to Barry McCabe that his children wouldn't be there. He had always known that they'd be safe and well, giggling and playing with their little friends. He'd frown and gently remonstrate with Michael, and then they'd beg to stay, and he'd refuse, warning them that Mum would kill them all if they weren't home in two minutes flat. They'd go on and on and eventually he would compromise and get them an ice block to take home.

As Constable Bill Keliher stood on the verandah of the Brighton Bay police station remembering that fateful day, he could still see the shock in Barry McCabe's eyes when he first saw him in the station at about eight o'clock that night. He was sitting in the back room by the sergeant's desk, stunned, uncomprehending. By then, strange, seemingly inconsistent facts had started to emerge.

The children had dropped in at Bernie Malley's shop on the Point Road that morning. Michael bought them both an ice cream, and then splashed out a bit and bought a family block of Cadbury's. Bernie wasn't sure that Faye and Barry would approve so he asked if it was to take home, which Michael said it was. No one seemed to have seen them at the pool, but several people saw two children fitting their description playing on the swings in the park opposite the surf club down at Shaggy Head. It was a good three miles from Loxton Park, too far for them to have walked. At around eleven thirty Mr Harry Lewis and his wife Marjorie, up from Melbourne for a holiday, saw the same two children on the beach just north of the surf club. They were with a man who looked to be in his late twenties. Nearly an hour later several other witnesses, mostly early-season holidaymakers, remembered seeing the two children with this man. They seemed very friendly, 'running and chasing each other' on the beach, 'flicking each other with their towels' and 'wrestling playfully' in the shallows and on the beach. Some recalled this man as having light brown hair, others blond, but all agreed that he was tall – perhaps six two, six three – and gangly, painfully thin, but sinewy and muscular. He wore only skimpy bathers and was very tanned. Just after one o'clock, little Michael went into McKay's Cakes and bought three pies, two sausage rolls and three lamingtons, and paid with a one-pound note. He had left home with three shillings in his pocket.

At around half past one, Robert Allen, a trainee with the Post Office, saw the children sitting on the seawall eating something, sandwiches perhaps, or cakes. They were with a man who was dressed 'just normal, sort of thing – long strides and a shirt'. He was eating too. Robert didn't take much notice; he saw the kids there and assumed that they were with their dad.

Bill Keliher had not known Barry McCabe well before the children's disappearance. They'd said hello, and now and then they'd have a word or two about the weather, or how the fish were running, but otherwise they hadn't had much contact. But Bill didn't have to know him well to know he wasn't hiding the children. If you wanted to know about the enormity of this tragedy, you needed only to look into the eyes of Barry McCabe.

The morning of that third day seeped back into Bill's brain. He could still hear Barry's hoarse half-whisper in his ear as he eased a cup of tea into the big man's hands.

"Jesus, Bill, what sort of mongrel would do this? They'll be terrified by now. Little Cathy's only four years old. She'll be frightened to death staying out all night. Who'd keep two little ones away from their mum like that?"

Bill's thoughts were jolted by the sound of heavy bootsteps on the verandah's wooden boards. Vince

Donnelly stopped beside him and opened up a bag of Drum.

"You're Keliher, aren't you?"

"Yes, sir."

"Played in the front row for Balmain."

"Yeah."

"I was there for nearly ten years."

"Yeah, I know."

"Long time back of course." Donnelly was nodding as he rubbed a little wad of tobacco between his callused palms. "So what was all that about in there, Keliher?"

"Nothing, Inspector. I just needed some fresh air, that's all."

"Is that right?" Donnelly rolled the cigarette in one hand as the other delved into his shirt pocket for his matches. "How long have you been in the job, son?"

"About eighteen months, sir."

"Is that right, eh?" He licked the paper, ran his thumb along the edge, and lit it up. "Bastard of a case this one."

"Yes, sir."

"No one should do this to two little kids, should they?"

Bill swallowed and looked up at the older man. "No, sir."

"No. But someone has, Keliher. Someone has." Donnelly's tone was brusque and callous by design. "And it's our job to find him. And hopefully bring those two kids home. And you know something, Keliher?"

"What's that, sir?"

"We will. We'll find whoever done this. We'll turn over every bloody stone and shine a torch up every bloody bum we need to till we do. 'Cause you know, son, every question has an answer. And it's our job to answer this one. And if we have to hurt some feelings, or put some noses out of joint, that's a shame, but that's the way it is. We're gonna find whoever took these kids. Whether it's just some deadbeat round the place or it's the local bloody reverend, or even if it's their father or their uncle or their maiden bloody aunt for that matter, we'll get 'em. If we keep our minds on the job and we stick to it, we'll get the bastard. I don't care if it's the Archbishop of bloody Canterbury, son, we'll get 'im."

\*　　\*　　\*

Even in his early sixties Peter Rosenthal was still a handsome man. Tall, slender, immaculately groomed, he had a striking presence that made Wally Messner uncomfortable. Those intelligent blue eyes were sometimes so incisive and intense they made Wally feel transparent.

"So, a comprehensive search was conducted of the property, was it?"

"Oh absolutely. Yes, Judge. Yeah, too right."

"Keliher showed no sign of cutting corners or just going through the motions, as it were?"

"Didn't seem to, Judge, no."

"All right."

The distinguished chairman of the recently

established Juvenile Crimes Commission was still scanning Detective Sergeant Messner's brief report on the search of Herbert Montgomery's house. Occasionally he would murmur something quietly to himself as those clear eyes darted back and forth across the page.

"A dog?"

"Yes, Judge, yeah. Montgomery had an old blue cattle dog that used to follow him around for years apparently. Thing must have died. He had it buried out the back. Had a cross and the whole works. Obviously when his sister's gone up there she's seen it and immediately figured it was a grave like. Which it was of course, but she's thought someone was buried there. Like, not a dog, a person, sort of thing."

"Mmmm." Peter Rosenthal was once again absorbed in the report. Nineteen years at the bar and another sixteen on the bench had trained him well to dissect the written word and digest it quickly. So far there seemed nothing much remarkable about Keliher's approach to the investigation. Routine leads were to be followed in a routine fashion. Nothing was ignored. There was no sign of prejudice or predilection, no special knowledge evident.

"Couldn't have been in the ground too long, 'cause it stunk to high heavens when we dug it up."

"Mmmm."

Wally Messner may as well have been talking to himself, and in a sense he was, just trying to relieve his own discomfort at having to sit silently, waiting for the chairman's questions. Peter Rosenthal was oblivious to him, still evaluating the repercussions of the document in his long white hands.

"All right, Sergeant Messner," he said eventually, as if woken from a trance. "That's excellent." He folded the report and placed it on the desk in front of him. "That all seems to be in order. Given our intelligence regarding Senior Sergeant Keliher, we'd like to continue to have an overview of his investigation. Of course, that's not to say that there's necessarily any substance whatsoever to the concerns that have been raised about him. We merely want to keep an eye on it, that's all."

"Yes, Judge. I understand."

"Good." Peter Rosenthal shifted forward in his seat, thereby announcing that the conference was over. He slipped open the desk drawer. "Your efforts are appreciated."

Wally Messner reached across and gratefully received the sealed white envelope.

# CHAPTER TWO

"I just loved him so much!" His face was buried in his bony hands, still covered in coagulating blood. "He was beautiful!"

"Not any more he's not," Morrie Fleet muttered to himself as he climbed out of the police car. "Righto, Suzie. Watch your scone." Morrie put one fat hand on the suspect's head to manoeuvre it safely through the doorway as he pulled him roughly with the other.

Suzie Q, born Ernest Richard Garner, had just cut his lover's throat.

"You sit down there and have a blow while we get things organised, all right?"

Morrie positioned Suzie against a chair on the back wall of the day room and eased him into it, then followed Bill Keliher towards the door.

"Sergeant Keliher!" Suzie blurted suddenly. "I loved him so much!"

Bill tried to give a reassuring nod. "Yeah, mate. I understand."

Love means different things to different people. To some people it's hearts and flowers; to some it's lust; and to some it's a self-effacing need to give and keep on giving. Suzie's love was something else. It was a dark love that turned suddenly. It was an unforgiving love, with sharp and dangerous edges. It was the kind of love that coppers knew about. The kind that came out of the night with knives, and guns, and broken bottles. The kind that saw homes broken and kids battered. The kind of love that leaves cadavers lying on the lounge room floor and blood painted on the walls.

"You just relax now. Can I get a cuppa for you?"

Suzie's ugly face began to melt with gratitude, his chin began to tremble, and thick black mascara tears rolled down his cheeks. "Oh ta, Sergeant."

Christmas time in Darlinghurst was never uneventful, and the early hours of Boxing Day 1982 were so far running true to form. A uniform patrol car had been pulled up in the street at around three a.m. by a male juvenile, known locally as Doris, who claimed that Suzie Q had gone berserk with a bread knife and had tried to kill young Doris and Suzie's live-in boyfriend Garry Willet. When the uniforms arrived at the old converted terrace down behind the Cross, Suzie was sitting disconsolately on the front step cradling the bread knife in his blood-stained hands. Inside on the lounge room floor lay the semi-naked body of Garry Willet, drug addict, pornographer and pimp, his throat cut through. One more slice and Suzie would have had his head right off.

Ernest Richard Garner hailed originally from Melbourne. He was born at Flemington in 1945 and lived there until 1966, when he ran away to Sydney and began living as a woman. Around about the same time, he changed his name to Suzie Q and moved into Kings Cross, where he walked the streets to cater for the fags and weirdos. He had a little bit of form for drugs, and a couple of minor convictions for dishonesty, but until now everyone had figured he was harmless.

When Suzie staggered home that morning, he found his flatmate entertaining Doris on the lounge room floor. Garry Willet had been showing more than passing interest in the fresh-faced boy for weeks, and the sight of them together in the house finally set off something in Suzie's brain. He took hold of a fire stoker and hit Willet twice, fracturing his skull and dislocating his left elbow. As Willet staggered to his feet, Suzie struck again, breaking both the radius and ulna in his left forearm. He then walked calmly into the kitchen, picked up a bread knife and came back swinging. Doris bounded out the door just as the real carnage was getting underway.

"That bitch Doris! This is all his fault!"

Suzie dissolved again into a blubbering heap as Morrie Fleet carefully aligned the carbon paper in the typewriter and took another sip of coffee. Bill stood back, waiting for the interview to start and wondering how long all this would go on. He was tired of Darlinghurst, the freak shows and the tragedies. As he looked at Suzie's shaven legs and the discoloured knuckles of his big bony hands, and watched him sobbing bitterly like a little boy who'd caught his finger in the door, Bill Keliher felt empty. Suzie Q had committed murder and would soon go to gaol for life. He had just reached perhaps the lowest point in his pathetic life. Who would be crying now for Suzie? Someone must be. He must have been someone's special child once. Where had he come from? What went wrong?

"Come on, mate, you'll be okay." Bill laid a comforting hand on Suzie's shoulder without thinking. Morrie Fleet stopped tinkering momentarily and looked up quizzically, but Bill ignored him. "Why don't you have another cup of tea."

Suzie sniffed, and then produced a tissue from nowhere apparent and wiped his eyes.

"Thanks, Sergeant."

For the next two hours they proceeded with the interview of Ernest Richard Garner in relation to the wilful murder of Garry Gordon Willet. The whole ugly tale was told and retold in fine detail, and almost faithfully recorded in two-finger fashion by Morrie on the typewriter. It was a tale Bill Keliher had heard many times before in one form or another. A tale of crazy violent acts that leapt from nowhere to devastate the lives of human beings, all painstakingly recorded for future court proceedings. It was a surreal process that involved formally documenting in measured rational language bizarre events that were beyond the bounds of comprehension. Between sipping tea and waiting patiently for Morrie's typing to catch up, Bill and Suzie discussed the blow-by-blow details of the last moments of the life of Garry Willet. Suzie's emotions ebbed and flowed, but he got through it, as people always did. The most distressing part for him was that they called him 'Ernest' or 'Mr Garner' in the interview, and not 'Suzie'. But he could see why; there were no hard feelings. No judge or jury would ever understand how things really were in Darlinghurst.

As Morrie pulled the last page from the typewriter and was shuffling the others into order, Suzie Q slumped down in his chair, talking to himself, working hard to try to justify his actions to the only person who was still interested in listening.

"He was an evil man. He had it coming. All those young boys. They were just children."

Morrie handed Bill the ordered pages of the Record of Interview and Bill rattled off the standard questions to the suspect, who gave all the right answers. Was he willing to sign a copy of the interview (he was not obliged to do so)? Yes. Did he give the interview of his own accord? Yes. Was any threat, promise or inducement held out, et cetera, et cetera. Between his answers, Ernest Garner continued pouring ever-mounting invective over his late boyfriend.

"He was sick. He'd have sex with them while I was in the other room."

Bill really didn't want to know. "I'll get you to sign just there on the bottom of each page."

As he took the pen from Bill, Suzie continued. "He was always trying to find new kids." He stopped and glanced dramatically over his left shoulder and then moved forward in his chair as if he were about to share a secret that was for Bill's ears only. He shaped to speak but didn't, as if he'd thought better of it. He straightened up and put the point of the biro to the page but then stopped again and looked straight into Bill's eyes. He sat silent for a long moment, then moved so close that Bill could smell the odour of stale alcohol and cigarettes on his breath. And then he whispered something that Bill Keliher had been waiting and dreading to hear for the past seventeen years.

"He had the McCabe children."

Suzie's eyes were wide now, conspiratorial, waiting for the right reaction.

"What?"

"Him and another bloke. Years ago. They had them right here in the Cross."

"What other bloke?"

"A creepy guy. Sick guy. They say he was with the Brethren."

Morrie Fleet rolled his eyes. In eleven years in Darlo he'd heard every bullshit story there was to hear from every halfwit, ratbag, pothead and weirdo that God had ever put breath into. If he had two bob for every time he'd heard some dickhead fantasise about the so-called Brethren, he'd be a rich man. It was one of those macabre urban myths that seemed to spring out of nowhere and circulate for ever with not a shred of credible evidence to support it. This one seemed to have held particular appeal for the drag queens, shirt-lifters, carpet-munchers, kiddie-fiddlers and other assorted deviants that Morrie dealt with every day. It had its genesis in the mid sixties, when the dismembered bodies of two young women and a fifteen-year-old boy were found in bushland outside Burnie in Tasmania. A small-crops farmer by the name of Van Duren was lumbered with it, and came up with a bizarre story about some weird group he called the Brethren, who he claimed had done the actual deeds and had forced him to dump the bodies for them. Two of the victims were from around Sydney and the third was from country New South Wales; they'd all disappeared separately over a period of about three years. The oddest thing was that there was some evidence to suggest that they had all died at about the same time, which was roughly when, according to Van Duren, they were delivered to him in petrol drums stacked on the back of an old Ford ute. Of course, he gave no registration or other reliable information on the ute and no satisfactory description of the driver, and his explanation of his supposed tie-up with this mob he called the Brethren was so patchy and uncorroborated that it was quickly identified as bullshit.

As police probed into the background of Van Duren, there soon emerged a vivid picture of a disturbed individual. He had a history of petty crime and mental illness, and was known for flights of extraordinary fantasy. His estranged wife, who had fled with her children to Western Australia, told of sexual abuse and brutal violence sometimes linked with semi-religious rituals. Van Duren had apparently developed a fascination with the occult and built some kind of weird altar in the old shack on his Burnie property. From his infrequent forays into the community, neighbours in Burnie recalled a belligerent character given to threatening behaviour and spontaneously violent outbursts. He was given a wide berth by the locals. There was some evidence that he had been in the vicinity of at least two of the disappearances at the relevant times, and there was no doubt that he fitted the profile of an abductor perfectly. His claims that the murders were the work of someone else didn't hold much credence with the coppers at the time, although it was suspected that Van Duren must have had some help. So they humoured him with his stories about the so-called Brethren; he was charged with the murders, but told that if he could come up with some evidence to support his claims there might be something in it for him. He didn't, and within a week he'd necked himself at Risdon Prison, which Morrie reckoned was about the best possible result. Good riddance.

But for some reason the legend of the Brethren had survived. It was regularly recycled – mostly by sexual offenders trying to buy a deal, or loops and nutcases who had nothing better to do but waste police time – and bobbed up from time to time with different variations, right through until about the mid seventies. Idle speculation had linked the mythical Brethren at one stage or another with most of the unsolved disappearances that occurred during that period, and almost invariably had been subsequently proved wrong. In the early seventies one so-called investigative journalist claimed that the Brethren did exist – or at least had existed for a period in the mid to late sixties – as a loose and highly secretive grouping of individuals in several states who shared a common interest in various sexual deviations and traded their own pornographic literature and criminal and sexual liaisons. He claimed it had all started with a close-knit party set of academics at a Melbourne university who had livened up their get-togethers with LSD and young hairless boys. According to the journalist, most of them got out or grew up, but a few actually went on with it, and linked up with others interstate. They were mostly well-educated men – academics, doctors, lawyers, maybe even politicians – who all had too much to lose to go out and get their jollies on the street. So they traded within their own ranks and they paid top dollar for what they wanted, which was cheap thrills and priceless secrecy. They bought anonymity and protection from their suppliers and, according to the journo, from the police.

Morrie hated journos, mainly because they told bullshit stories that encouraged drop-kicks and weirdos like Suzie Q.

"It's true," Suzie said, as he drew with one finger on the desk in front of him. Little flakes of the dried blood of Garry Willet dropped onto the blotter as Suzie's long bent finger traced across it, leaving the outline of a symbol. Morrie recognised it straight away. It was a Christian cross with a capital B framed into the lower right-hand corner – supposedly the emblem of the Brethren.

"Wake up to yourself, dickhead!"

There was something sick about a drag queen murderer telling lurid stories about two long-lost kiddies, and Morrie Fleet wasn't going to cop it. He had worked on the McCabe investigation on and off; he had swum neck-deep in the frustration of it all; he had read all the stories and the statements. He had grown impatient with the speculation and the theorising, and could no longer tolerate such idle gossip. "Just fuckin' shut up and sit there till we get this paperwork done up, right?"

Bill Keliher was a decent bloke, a simple good-natured country boy who'd come down from Glen Innes to play football and ended up a copper. His big square freckled head and burly frame had earned him the nickname Boof, and like most blokes in the job Morrie Fleet had a lot of time for him. But Bill's preoccupation with the McCabe case was well known, and Morrie was pleased to see that his harsh words had snapped his partner out of his momentary trance; Bill was now busily collecting together the pages that Suzie had scrawled his signature onto. He shuffled them into alignment and, mumbling something about the stapler, headed for the door.

"They sent a letter to his parents."

Morrie Fleet looked up from his typewriter. Bill Keliher was frozen in the doorway.

"What letter?" Morrie started quietly.

"It was a letter that the little boy had written."

"Did you see this letter?"

"I didn't read it, but Garry told me about it word for word. It was so sad. He said he was looking after his little sister but she was frightened and she wanted to go home."

Morrie Fleet turned and looked at Keliher standing in the doorway. The letter that was sent to the McCabe parents had never been made public and had remained a closely guarded secret even amongst police ranks. The few who knew of it did not know the contents unless, like Bill and Morrie, they had been involved in the investigation. But Ernest Richard Garner knew about it and, unless he was guessing, he even knew what it said.

"Did you see the kids?"

"No, but they had them somewhere around here. Garry told me. He was an evil bastard!"

The kids had been gone almost five weeks when the letter turned up in the McCabes' mailbox. Barry heard his wife call out something incoherent and found her sobbing uncontrollably on the front step, sprawled beside the torn envelope on the porch and still clutching desperately to the one-page letter. When he read the contents he felt as though his brain was going to explode. He wanted to run somewhere, hit someone, tear something apart. But who, and what, and where? He recognised young Michael's careful handwriting that had always pleased his teachers and made his dad so proud of him.

*Dear Mum and Dad, We are okay. We are with a man who says we can come home if you do what he says and do not tell the police anything. I am taking good care of Catherine. She is frightened and keeps wanting to come home. So could you please do what the man says so we can come home soon. I miss you. Michael.*

Faye McCabe had to be sedated by the family doctor, and although Barry declined any medication there was a strong smell of whisky on his breath by the time the police investigators commenced their interview. Both parents were confident the handwriting belonged to their son, and initial comparisons with samples of Michael's schoolwork seemed to confirm the match. The envelope was postmarked Sydney, and had been processed through the local post office. Neither parent could remember anything that gave any clue as to what the kidnapper's demands might be. Barry McCabe had automatically called the local police, and Bill Keliher and his sergeant immediately contacted the detectives who arrived within the hour. After questioning Faye and Barry they concluded that the kidnapper intended to make contact later to communicate his demands. They didn't tell them that secretly they feared that he might be watching, waiting to see if police became involved before attempting to make further contact. They immediately put the whole investigation under wraps.

"What about this other bloke?" Morrie Fleet was testing Suzie Q's story as gently as he could.

"Ooh, gee. Peter, I think. Yeah, Peter."

"Peter what?"

"Gee, I don't know, Sergeant. But he was a freaky guy. Real tall and thin and cold looking."

The blood had drained from Bill Keliher's face. He

was hovering over the elongated oddity sitting at the desk in front of him as though he didn't know whether to throttle him or hug him. Morrie could tell from his vague, absent look that he was struggling. He laid a hand on his partner's shoulder.

"You all right, Bill?"

"Yeah, mate."

Morrie pulled his notebook from his pocket and scribbled the details they had been told so far. Whether or not Suzie Q was bullshitting, he knew something, and it was more than anyone else had come up with in the past seventeen years. And that meant he would have to be closely questioned about the activities of his ex-lover. It was going to be a long night. They were going to have to turn him upside down until they had wrung every last drop out of him. But in the meantime there was something that had always troubled Morrie.

"Did they follow up that letter at all?"

"Oh, no way!"

"Why not?"

"They were too scared to. The cops were on to the letter straight away."

"How did they know that?"

"Don't know. I think someone tipped them off."

"Who?"

Suzie Q suddenly looked sadder and more frightened than he had since his first cup of tea two hours ago. His eyes filled with moisture and a black tear dribbled down his cheek.

"Don't know," he whispered. "Don't know."

# CHAPTER THREE

Faye McCabe lived alone in a small but comfortable apartment overlooking the Ocean Beach at Manly. From the modest lounge room windows she could see the beautiful blue ocean that spread to the horizon. She could feel the liberating breezes. As she caught sight of the Ford swinging into Ocean Road and drawing to the kerb she took a deep breath and braced herself.

Faye had come to Sydney looking for her two lost children, so long ago that it seemed another lifetime. It was a time so shrouded in pain and doubt and fear and confusion that it hardly seemed her life at all. It was a vague memory, a notion of what she'd left behind. For a time she had wandered lost, searching the face of every child, suspecting the look of every stranger. Every siren, every door-knock, every ring of her telephone pierced her to the soul. Every walk to the mailbox had been a journey filled with horror and with hope. She had ventured to the edge of the abyss, and she had teetered there alone, so long.

But Faye had survived. Somewhere she had found the strength to start again, to carry on. She had come to Sydney to find her children and eventually she had found herself. She had finally learned to walk away. But as she saw the door of the Ford swing open, she knew that she was about to be pulled back.

"Hello, Bill."

The smile on Faye's gentle face was warm and wistful, and made Bill Keliher feel suddenly awkward. He was back again, still with no good news. Everyone knew there would never be good news now, only news; and Bill wasn't even sure that he had news.

"Hello, Faye."

Her eyes were clearer, somehow stronger. It was close to six years since he had seen her, but if anything she looked younger, more contented. She must be forty-five. She looked good. Bill flashed on a vision of her standing in the front yard of the old house in Bentley Street, young and healthy, her auburn hair cut to the shoulder and blowing gently in the fresh sea breeze. The hair was cropped short now and was a deeper red, but the same curves were there and her natural beauty had survived it all.

"Come in, Bill. It's good to see you."

He knew it wasn't true. She'd seen more coppers in the past seventeen years than anyone should have to see in a lifetime. He hated himself for coming here, putting her through all this. But he had no choice, he had to do it, for more reasons than he could ever tell her.

"As I said on the phone, I was hoping you might be able to have a look at a couple of photographs for us."

Her face was suddenly fragile, vulnerable. He laid the manilla envelope on the coffee table and they sat opposite each other, saying nothing. He could see how she was struggling to keep it all together, how determined she was to handle it. But she'd been through so much. Bill had watched her and Barry wait through those first few days, hoping beyond hope that their precious children would suddenly reappear, gasping with some tale of having got lost in the bush and sniffling with relief to have been found and to be home. He had tried to offer reassurance long after everyone knew it was a lie. He had joined the emu parades and the searchers scouring the sandhills and the bush, the river banks and the parks. He had felt the parents' agony as the police divers dragged the river and patrol cars cruised the streets of nearby towns with loudspeakers that announced unemotionally, "Police are looking for two missing children, a boy aged eight and his four-year-old sister." At first the whole nation had held its breath waiting for an outcome. Congregations prayed for a miracle as locals checked stormwater drains and underground tanks. Eager volunteers converged on the seaside town, searching all isolated locations and unoccupied sheds and premises, and as their ranks swelled into the hundreds, hope diminished by the day. Eventually the empty search became too horrible for people to keep living with. The volunteers went home and the public moved on, leaving Faye and Barry with their unsolved riddle.

The children had been gone six years when Barry went off the headland at Bonny Point. He'd been drinking way too much for months, according to his mates down at the Anglers Rest, and it was only a matter of time until he had an accident. Ever since he and Faye had separated he'd been hitting the bottle pretty hard, and that night was no different. He'd had his favourite photo out again, but his old mates made allowances. They remembered, and they understood.

"That's typical of Michael that one, isn't it? That's him exactly. That's his smile. Remember? And he's got Cathy by the hand. Always looking after his little sister. Remember that? He was always looking after her, wasn't he?"

His car went straight off the end of Bonny Point Road, and it didn't stop till it hit the rocks at the bottom of the headland. No skidmarks, no screech of brakes, no nothing. He'd had a skinful, and it was a dark, winding road. It could have happened to anyone in his condition. But no one was surprised when it happened to him. And no one asked the question, and no one blamed him, no matter what the answer was.

"How has your life been, Bill?"

The photograph was still in the envelope on the table between them, untouched. He wished he could get up and walk out of her life, leave her in whatever peace she might have found. Almost involuntarily he reached across the table and he felt his hand touch hers. It was soft and cold. It was the first time he had touched her in a long long time.

"I'm good, Faye. I'm good."

She smiled again, that same sad sympathetic smile that was for both of them – for their loss, as well as hers. They talked again as friends, and more perhaps; he about his sons, Mark who was already nearly as tall as his father, and Paul who had just joined his brother in the senior school, and about his wife Joan's illness which now was hopefully behind her; and she about her new life and her work at the City Mission, and how she hoped to change the kitchen in the flat some day, and the great joy the ocean views gave her. They talked for the best part of an hour, the envelope lying unopened on the table there between them. They talked about everything unimportant and important in their lives, except for two lost children. And eventually Faye made him aware by the look in her eyes and the tone of her voice that it was time to talk about the reason he had come to see her.

"They're just photographs of a guy who may or may not be a suspect, Faye." She nodded and looked down at the envelope. "We just want you to have a look and see if the face means anything to you."

As soon as Faye McCabe slipped the photographs of Garry Willet from the envelope, Bill could see that at last they had a real connection and a real suspect. After seventeen years, they'd just stepped off the starting blocks.

\*     \*     \*

Ernest Richard Garner, alias Suzie Q, was getting special treatment at the prison. He had his own slot and all the cigarettes and magazines he needed. And he was in and out of the block every five minutes. To the other inmates it could mean only one thing: Suzie was a dog.

It was true. Ernest Garner was 'a reliable informant' and the police were doing all they could to keep him in cotton wool, because right now he was their best and maybe only chance of cracking the McCabe case. Faye McCabe had instantly recognised the face of Garry Willet as that of the odd-looking young man who had taken a caravan at Bonny Point for almost two months at the end of 1965. Barry had suspected him of having something to do with the break-ins at the unoccupied holiday houses out on the point; Barry was always going on about it, and she even thought he might have spoken about the man to Bill or to the sergeant. The stranger was a scruffy-looking type, and Faye was fairly confident he had been friendly with one or two of the local boys, but there again she wasn't positive of that. The one thing she was certain of was that this was the same man, and that meant that Garry Willet had been at the scene of the crime not long before it happened, which made Ernest Garner's story even more compelling. The next step was to identify his mate, and that meant turning Willet upside down. Vince Donnelly wanted him checked out top to bottom.

"I want to know every wart and freckle, every skeleton, friend, relative and lover, every pie he had his finger or any other digit into, every hole he ever crawled down, every mate he drank piss or smoked drugs with or whatever else it was he got off on. This other grub is in there somewhere and if we look hard enough we'll find him."

The little group had been hand-picked, mostly experienced detectives who had shown an interest in or at least a willingness to stick with the McCabe case, plus one or two young blokes who were too green to recognise a loser when they saw one. Young Wally Messner, who had worked with them on the Garner case, was the only other one from Darlinghurst, but Bill knew them all. Vince Donnelly was getting on now, and there was a kind of desperation in his voice that hinted why he hadn't cashed in the super and put his feet up years ago. The McCabe case was the one that got away, and it had become everything to him. Donnelly had organised Bill's transfer back to Sydney in the early seventies so he could be part of the team and they'd worked on and off together ever since. There was not a cop alive that Bill had more respect for than Vince Donnelly.

"Bill, can I see you a minute?"

As the team dispersed to get started on their designated tasks, Bill followed Vince into his office, a little tingle of apprehension in his stomach.

"Bill, you were stationed in Brighton Bay in sixty-five, weren't you?"

"Yeah."

"You must have come across this Willet up there, surely?"

"I don't remember him. Not from the Bay. First I knew of him was in the Cross in the mid seventies."

"But he was up there on Bonny Point for nearly two months. You must have come across him."

"Not that I remember."

"Didn't some of the locals complain about him?"

"Not to me they didn't, Vince."

"You sure, Bill?"

"Yeah, mate, yeah. I'm sure."

Vince gently nodded his head in the thoughtful way Vince did.

"Fair enough."

They say confession is good for the soul. Defence lawyers love to scoff at the suggestion that anyone would voluntarily admit to policemen the often terrible dark secrets of their soul. Why would anyone gratuitously admit to anything that was going to land them in the slammer? It was a good question, one that Bill had often asked himself. But as he walked out of Vince's office, there was a part of him that wanted to turn round and walk right back in there, to sit down and have a long yarn with Vince Donnelly about the McCabe case.

It took less time to come up trumps than any of them had dared to hope. Queensland police records on Willet showed up a 1971 summary conviction for one count of gross indecency, jointly charged with one Robert Arthurson. Crosschecks with other jurisdictions turned up a 1977 shoplifting blue for Arthurson in northern New South Wales. At that time Arthurson had also been charged with possession of a false driver's licence in the name of Alan Arthur Roberts. And the name Alan

Arthur Roberts bobbed up again in the Victorian records as an alias used in 1978 by a drink-driver by the name of Robert Allen, date of birth 15 February 1943 – the same name and date of birth as the young postal worker who'd claimed to have seen the McCabe children sitting on the seawall with a man he took to be their father. Within twenty-four hours, Vince had the watch-house records up from Melbourne and the photographs confirmed it. Robert Allen was the missing bum buddy of the late Garry Willet.

By the time Suzie Q arrived at police headquarters, he knew there was something serious happening. The three detectives who had picked him up from Long Bay had been more than usually tight-lipped and tense. He was led into a room where Vince Donnelly was waiting, looking drawn and saying nothing. As Detective Fleet pushed Suzie down into a chair, Donnelly opened up a folder and placed it carefully on the desk in front of him.

"All right, Mr Garner," he commenced in a low growl. "I want to know if you see anyone you recognise."

The fear in Suzie's eyes was immediate. There were twelve photographs neatly arranged on the identification board, but he was looking at only one face. They all saw it instantly and waited, breathless. Ernest Richard Garner was big enough and ugly enough to realise what he was getting into.

He grasped at the cropped hair that hung over one ear and tugged at it nervously as if willing it to grow so he could draw it like a veil across his face and hide from the eyes that now studied him so closely. Suzie was a girl inside a man's body. It didn't matter what she saw in the mirror, she knew how these men looked at her and what the world thought of her. They didn't see her pretty face, only the ugly lump in her throat and her bony, masculine hands.

If Ernest Richard Garner identified the McCabe kidnapper, he would be the main witness to a crime that had burned itself deep into the national psyche. Kids didn't walk to school alone since the McCabe children had disappeared; people didn't leave their doors unlocked. The kidnapper had released a dark and sinister demon that still walked Australian streets. People didn't talk about it any more, but they knew it was out there, a real-life manifestation of the boogieman they had created to keep their children indoors and away from strangers. The McCabe kidnapper had stolen more than two children: he had carried away a quality that had made life in the sixties different from the way it was today. Ernest Garner understood what was at stake. And he understood that if he put his finger on the kidnapper, the eyes of the whole country would turn on him – an oddity, a low-life freak who would be guilty by association, a murderer who had kept the nation's darkest secret for over fifteen years.

"Manslaughter." Garner blurted out the word almost before he thought of it. "I want my charge dropped back to manslaughter."

"We can do that."

Vince Donnelly hadn't taken his eyes off Garner for a second.

"And I want some credit."

Donnelly nodded. They were about to hit paydirt.

"You've been around, Suzie. You know the deal. We tell the judge it was a crime of passion, spur-of-the-moment stuff, alcohol involved, no premeditation. Garry wasn't exactly a model citizen. We tell him that without your help the case probably never would've been solved, et cetera. Bloke with shaved legs is going to do time tough enough without being a Crown witness so you should be given special leniency et cetera, et cetera. Discount for an early plea. Who knows what you might get it down to. Whatever it is, we'll make sure you do it easy. You'll get your own slot in a secure protection unit, the whole deal."

Ernest Garner looked around the room at the row of intense eyes bearing down on him. His head was spinning with a thousand different thoughts. His hand was trembling lightly as he laid his bony finger on the photograph of Robert Allen.

Ernest Garner was given his own slot in a secure protection unit, and all the magazines and cigarettes he wanted. He was in with other dogs, some kiddie-fiddlers, a couple of bent coppers, and some general protection inmates. It was a good deal.

And so it should have been. He hadn't just given them a pigeon, he had given them the proof. Donnelly played hardball, and concessions had to be wrung out of him. Murder back to manslaughter was one thing, but Ernest Garner had wanted a short sentence or at least a positive recommendation from the Crown, and

Donnelly wasn't giving anything away. Garner had had to dig deep, dredge through his memory for something concrete they could use to pin the bastard. He came up with a conversation in the flat at Surry Hills during which Allen told them all about the kidnapping: he had met the children on the Point Road walking down to Loxton Park; he had said he would drive them to the swimming pool, but then talked them into coming to the beach with him; they'd had a swim and then he'd told them he had rung their parents and their mum had said that it was okay for them to come to his house for something to eat; he had hidden them somewhere – he didn't say where – before bringing them to Sydney.

It wasn't much, but it was enough. In a case like this one – where every living soul that was ever likely to find his way onto a jury would desperately want to bring down a conviction – it was enough. It was a full confession of the offence of kidnapping and maybe even enough to convince a willing jury to infer murder. And that meant it might be enough to convince Allen to tell them the whole story.

Garner rarely used the yard. After muster he preferred to stay cooped up in his cell where he would read and play with his hair while the others got what daylight and fresh air they could. That's what he was doing when they last remembered seeing him that afternoon. They didn't see the warder who unlocked the unit gate and they didn't see the two men who entered shortly afterwards. One had a faded image of a strange-looking Christian cross tattooed on his thick right forearm.

The arm coiled around Garner's throat and closed quickly in a vice-like grip that left him gasping for air. His mouth no sooner opened than a rolled-up sock was pushed between his teeth and jammed in so hard and deep that he was gagging from the pressure against his throat. The blood was bursting in his face and his eyes were bulging as they darted about wildly, searching for some understanding. He could see bits of another man fumbling with the chair and then standing on it and looping something through the light fitting in the ceiling. Suddenly he was being lifted, hoisted up towards the light.

Suzie Q was powerless. She didn't struggle. It was no use. She knew now where she was going, and she knew why. Her pretty eyes filled up with tears as the belt was slipped around her porcelain-white neck.

# CHAPTER FOUR

As Bill followed Vince and Morrie down the metal stairs onto the Coolangatta tarmac, he could already see the compact shape of Frankie Box behind the glass wall of the airport terminal. Frankie's grin was spread from ear to ear. There was nothing he liked better than a visit from the boys.

Detective Sergeant Francesco Vagianni was better known as Frankie Box. He was the son of an Italian cane-cutter from north Queensland and he had all the class you could expect from a spaghetti-eater raised on Queensland rum. Bill couldn't help but smile when he saw Frankie waiting there for them; he was a good bloke and a good cop.

"What's this, the Sydney mafia moving in? Just as well I was out here on the lookout." Frankie had Bill's hand in a clamp and was shaking vigorously. "How the fuck are you anyway, Boofhead?"

Morrie Fleet was grinning at his old mate, but Vince Donnelly didn't seem to get the joke.

"Oh, Frank, have you met the boss? Inspector Vince Donnelly – Frank Vagianni from the Gold Coast CIB."

Frankie grabbed Donnelly's hand as if it were going to get away.

"How are you, Vince? Mate, don't look so stressed. I got good news for you boys."

He was right, it was good news. And as the New South Wales detectives sat around the table in the day room at the Broadbeach station with the Queensland boys, they all tried to work out where it left them. News of Ernest Garner's suicide had come through from the prison less than an hour before they were due to fly out to Queensland, and the trip had been a pretty sombre exercise. Without Garner they had no confession and therefore no case, unless Allen decided to make a clean breast of it, and that was most unlikely. Any bloke who'd had the front to make a bullshit statement to the coppers at the time, and then sit on something this big for seventeen years, was hardly likely to come up with a case of the guilts now. But Frankie's news changed everything. While Bill and the others had been in transit, the fingerprint bureau had phoned through their results.

The letter that had been sent to the McCabes way back in sixty-six had been carefully preserved right from the outset. In later years, when the technology had been developed, police had lifted three sets of adult prints from the letter and the envelope. One set on the letter matched the prints of Faye McCabe. Until now the other two sets had remained unidentified.

"The prints on the envelope are Allen's." Frankie

let it sink in for a moment. "It's a dead-set positive match-up."

The smiles that spread around the group stemmed more from relief than anything else. The news of Garner's death had knocked them back almost to square one, but now suddenly they were right back in the game. If they had nothing more, the fingerprints would get them home. The fact that Allen had been at the scene when the kids disappeared, together with his prints appearing on the note, added up to a fair circumstantial case. That was all a jury was going to need for this one. And with any luck, once Allen knew his prints were on the envelope he might just drop his bundle and wrap it up for them with a nice neat confession.

"I don't want to have to frig around with any messy extradition."

Vince was right. The Queensland boys had tracked Allen to a beach shack on the esplanade at Burleigh and the plan was to swoop on him at first light the next day. But if he burred up and had to be arrested there in Queensland, they couldn't take him down across the border into New South Wales without a formal extradition order from a magistrate, and that could take time. In a case as big as this one, there'd be lawyers jumping in before they even had him in the jurisdiction.

"Relax, Vince." Frankie Box looked confident. "I'm a warm Italian guy. Bobby's gonna love me. I'll just ask him to take a friendly drive with me down across the border to Tweed Heads."

Frank had booked Bill, Vince and Morrie into a motel at Coolangatta. All they had to do was get up in the morning and be at Tweed Heads station by about six thirty. In the meantime Frankie and the Queensland boys would drop in at Allen's flat and introduce themselves. Once they got to know each other better, Allen would gladly accompany them down to the Tweed to have a chat with the New South Wales detectives.

"We'll tell him nothing till he gets there. Then youse can drop it on him. Hopefully he'll shit himself and spill the beans."

"What if he won't make the trip?"

"Relax, Vince, will you. I'm telling you, he'll love me."

"I don't want him knocked about."

"Please, I'm not that kind of guy."

Vince looked uncomfortable about putting Frankie Box in charge of his best ever chance of solving the McCabe case. But options were in short supply. Vince was out of his jurisdiction and one way or another the Queensland blokes had to be brought into the loop. Even if he went with them into Allen's flat, any questioning would have to be done according to the Queensland rules.

They dropped Vince back at the motel at about half past eight. By closing time Morrie Fleet was starting to talk shorthand in the public bar of the Port O' Call Hotel. An hour later, Bill and Frankie Box were propping up the long bar in the Fan Club, telling lies and watching Morrie and some of the young blokes making dills out of themselves up on the dance floor.

"Looks like he's got a tight arse, that inspector mate of yours."

"He's all right, Frank. It's just that this one means a lot to him."

"You too, Bill."

"Yeah, me too."

Frank Vagianni had been in the job for about ten years. In that time he'd done a lot of work with Bill and Morrie, either when they came to Queensland to pinch someone or look into something, or when Frank fluked a junket down to Sydney to extradite a grub back from the big smoke. They were good blokes and they always put on a good time for a copper out of town. And like any good Italian boy, Frank always made sure he reciprocated. But Bill was a good copper and Frank knew that too. In the morning, after all the piss had been drunk and all the molls were bedded down, Bill would do his job, no risk. And no job meant more to Bill than the McCabe case. Frank had heard the older man talk about it more than once, when he was in his cups and maudlin, vowing he would some day get the bastard, make him pay. Frank had two kids of his own. They lived with their mother but they were everything to Frank, so he knew how this McCabe thing had got under everyone's skin and made them ratty. But for Bill it was something else again.

Bill Keliher pushed his heavy frame up off the bar. "I'm going to take a leak."

As he stepped through the crowd towards the gents Bill could feel the effects of having matched it rum for rum with Frankie Box for the past two hours. His head was thick and the music was beating strongly in his brain. As he stood shoulder to shoulder with the punters at the trough and stared at the wet stainless steel, his mind was drifting. Tomorrow he would come face to face with Robert Arthur Allen once again. Tomorrow they would know the truth. As he lumbered to the door and pushed his way back into the darkness of the club, Bill's heart began to race a little. Visions of dead children flashed before his eyes and he felt his stomach turn. He barged blindly through the throng, no longer careful, his heart now beating strongly and sweat forming on his forehead as he bumped young men aside and trudged towards the exit. The bright lights of the foyer and then the coolness of the night on his sweat-soaked neck revived him slightly. He lurched down the front stairs and sucked in the fresh air to clear his thoughts. Tomorrow was the day that Bill had been waiting for for seventeen years, and he dreaded its arrival. He dreaded the thought of sitting in another interview room listening to vile secrets, uncovering the unspeakable and the unthinkable. Where would it all lead them? Would they discover the whole truth? He pictured little Michael sitting in the front seat of the car, still holding tight on to his little sister's hand, and then an obscene vision of his murdered body lying ravaged in a shallow grave. He squeezed his eyes shut and saw them all, all the dead and the damaged and the violated he had seen paraded through his days and nights. Until now the McCabe kids had not been there. But tomorrow they would be.

"You all right?"

Frankie Box was sitting on the bench next to Bill, his elbows resting on his knees.

"Yeah, I'm all right." Bill looked across and saw a kind of understanding in his eyes. "Too much of that bloody awful rum, that's all."

Frankie straightened up, suddenly more cheerful. "You Sydney blokes are just a mob of big sheilas, aren't you? Can't stomach a little drop of the old medicinal Queensland rum."

Morrie Fleet and the younger blokes were now straggling down the front stairs as Frankie Box leapt to his feet and broke into song. "You might look fancy in the gym / You might give the bag a lickin' / But if you can't fight on rum / Then man, you must be chicken."

Bill Keliher fell in spontaneously with the laughter and applause. The demons had departed and only the pleasant dullness of his brain played with his thoughts.

"Let's go down to Amy's and see what she's got for us."

\*    \*    \*

The knock on the front door was loud and persistent. The idea was to get the suspect to open up before he was properly awake and before he'd had time to collect his thoughts.

"Robert Arthur Allen?"

"Yeah, that's right."

"I'm Detective Francesco Vagianni from the Broadbeach CIB. We'd like to have a yarn with you."

"About what?"

"About whatever you want it to be about, Robert. Mind if we come in?"

It took eight minutes for the detectives to come up with a bag of grass that Allen claimed to know nothing of. He couldn't think who might have left it in the spare bedroom or when or how it could have got there. Frank played it all low key. They had some information that someone was dealing drugs from this address so they were here to check it out. But they couldn't see much here to suggest dealing and no one was going to get too excited about one bag of dope. They probably wouldn't even bother charging him with it. They'd just get him to do a quick interview back at the station denying any allegations about dealing so they could put a report in to the boss showing they had followed up the information and it had come to nothing. That way they could close the file. They'd probably do it at the Coolangatta station because the Tweed coppers wanted a quick word with him as well.

"About what, do you know?"

"No, mate, wouldn't have a clue. Some old shit, I think. Probably just some outstanding traffic warrants."

On the way down to Tweed Heads, Robert Allen sat quietly in the back seat of the police car alongside a young detective, looking blankly out the window at the passing scenery. In the rear-view mirror Frank glanced at him from time to time, wondering if he had any inkling of what they had in store for him when he got down to the Tweed. If he did, there was nothing in his face that gave him up. It was devoid of all expression, seemingly relaxed, as if he were going for a Sunday drive in the country. Maybe he did have some old traffic fines unpaid in New South Wales and figured it would be quickly sorted out; maybe he was dumb as dogshit and had never even contemplated that the day might come; or maybe he was just a cold, conniving bastard who knew how to hold it all together. Whichever way, he was in for a rude shock.

When Vince Donnelly and his two offsiders walked into the interview room and closed the door, the blood drained out of Allen's face. The expression didn't change, but it was three shades lighter as Donnelly stood silently in front of him. Morrie Fleet planted one plump buttock on the corner of the desk and Bill Keliher pulled up a chair in the corner. He hadn't seen Robert Allen in a long time. The man had not aged well. His hair was prematurely grey and thinning, and his suntanned face was marked and lined with wrinkles. As Bill waited for Vince Donnelly to start, he could feel his own heart pounding in his chest, racked with anticipation of what would be revealed and what concealed.

"Remember me, Robert?"

"Yes."

"I've come to tell you it's all over, son. We know the truth, the whole story."

Allen showed no emotion. "I don't know what you're talking about."

"Yes you do, son. Yes you do. You know precisely what I'm talking about. I'm talking about the McCabe kids. And I'm telling you right now, I don't want any more of that bloody bullshit you've been feeding us for the past twenty years."

Allen's jaw dropped open as though he was about to say something, but he didn't. He was thinking, and Vince stepped in quickly to make sure he didn't start thinking in the wrong direction.

"We know you picked the kids up on the Point Road and you took them to the beach. You told them you'd rung their mother and she'd said it was okay for them to come home with you. We know all of that. We know about how you brought them to Sydney and how you and Garry Willet sent the letter. We know it all. We've got a witness who's going to testify against you."

Allen shook his head. He was still thinking. "No you haven't."

There was something in the tone of the reply that instantly told Donnelly that this man knew about the death of Ernest Garner. It was confident, assured, almost gloating. Somehow he already had the news that Vince himself had received only a few hours ago. One corner of the suspect's mouth was curling slightly into the start of what seemed to Vince to be a knowing smirk. He didn't wait to see it. Seventeen years of anger and frustration suddenly exploded, and before he knew what he was doing he was flailing wildly at the suspect, who was now hunched forward covering his head with both arms.

"You vicious little shit! You killed them, didn't you! You arsehole!"

They were mainly only slaps and weren't doing too much damage. The others watched him sadly. You could see Vince wasn't in the habit of dishing out a flogging to his suspects; he was obviously a little rusty. If ever he was going to start, this was the right bloke. Bill Keliher was quickly on his feet, but he let Vince thrash off a bit of steam before he laid his hand on the older man's shoulder.

"Steady on, Vince. Take it easy."

Donnelly stepped back, panting heavily. He looked slightly embarrassed and paced one way then the other before he turned to the door. Robert Allen had now straightened up with an insolent half-smile on his face.

"You've got nothing on me, shithead."

It was truculent and disrespectful and the kind of talk that Frank Vagianni didn't like to hear from low-life grubs.

"Hey, Bobby."

As Allen turned his head, Frankie hit him with a short right that came from nowhere and blew him completely off his chair and back into a crumpled heap against the wall. Pound for pound, Frankie packed more wallop than a Sherman tank.

"Watch your mouth, eh pal? You put another hole in your manners like that and I'll put a hole in you."

Allen wasn't travelling all that well, but he was still conscious and he looked curiously unflustered. That was no mean feat for someone who'd just taken a short right from Frankie Box. Frankie sized him up. He didn't look like a bloke who was about to drop his bundle.

"Morrie, why don't you and Vince go out and grab a cup of coffee. Bill and I'll stay in here with Bob and get better acquainted."

Vince was already out the door.

"Listen, Boxhead, we don't want him knocked about. All right?"

"Morrie, please! You know I'm not that kind of guy."

\* \* \*

With two cups of steaming coffee in his hands Morrie carefully stepped his way up to the table in the day room where Vince was sitting, his head propped up by his palms.

It happened to them all at some stage. Eventually there came a time when you'd done too many hours' overtime or had gone out too hard, or the stakes had been too high or the grub too slippery or too half-smart. There was always going to be a breaking point in this job. It was just a matter of when and where you reached it, and how badly you fucked up when you did. In the scheme of things this wasn't all that bad.

"You all right?"

"Yeah."

Vince cupped the coffee in his hands and stared at it in silence for a long while.

"He knew Garner had gone off," he said eventually.

"You think so?"

"Too right he did." Vince finally lifted up the cup and took a sip. "How would he know that?"

"I don't think they've even notified the rellies yet."

"That's what I mean, Morrie. Outside the prison we're the only ones that know. How the hell did he find out?"

Bill Keliher appeared at the door to the day room, closely followed by Frank Vagianni. They ambled to the table and sat down without saying anything. Vagianni laid his notebook on the table and flicked through the pages until he found his place.

"Here's how it went." He put one finger on the page and read from his notes. "When you went out for coffee, Mr Allen said to Bill, 'What are you hassling me for anyway?' and Bill replied, 'Because your fingerprints were positively identified on the letter that was sent to the parents of the children.' Allen appeared shocked at this, and I said, 'How do you think your prints got on that letter, Robert?' He replied, 'How do you reckon?' I said, 'Did you send the letter to the McCabes?' He said, 'It was all Garry's idea. He wanted to get money for the kids.' I said, 'Did he take them or did you?' He said, 'I did, but you'll never prove that now. It's all too long ago.' I said, 'What did you do with the children?' He replied, 'What children? Do you think I'm stupid? You find the bodies and I go for murder. I'm not saying nothing more.' We sought to question him further but he declined to answer any further questions."

Vince Donnelly didn't look too happy. His chin was buried in one hand. They all sat awaiting his response. Eventually he nodded slowly.

"It's probably enough for kidnapping. We've got the fact that he was at the crime scene when they disappeared and Willet had been there twelve months previously. We've got his prints on the envelope and his claim it was Willet's idea to send the letter. And we've got a direct admission that he took the kids. If we pin him on the abduction, a judge will put him in for life anyway."

Frankie looked across the table at Bill Keliher.

"Done."

Bill took him by the hand and shook it firmly.

"Done."

# CHAPTER FIVE

Young Constable Mick Fletcher heard the trouble coming. Mid-week mornings in the Tweed Heads station were usually pretty quiet and, as was customary, this morning it was just Mick and Phil Bartrim sharing front desk and court duties. Phil was out back serving tea and toast to the boys in lock-up when Mick heard the burbling putter of something sickly chugging along Bay Street on no more than three cylinders out of four. When it pulled into view in front of the police station and drew into the kerb Mick raised his eyebrows.

"Jesus, what's this?"

The big old Mark 10 Jaguar had seen better days, but it still looked like there ought to be a chauffeur sitting in the front seat. The British racing-green duco was all original and, despite a dented panel at the rear, the overall impact was so august as to make Mick anticipate the arrival of someone important. He was wrong.

The engine closed down with a rattle and a bang, and the man who stepped out of the driver's seat was no chauffeur. He was tall and thin and gangly, with a crop of spiky, messy hair, and trendy glasses that made him look like some sort of off-beat musician or pseudo-intellectual. His stove-pipe trousers and the shirt sleeves rolled up over his forearms gave the impression he'd been through the wash and all his clothes had shrunk on him. But for all his odd appearance he stepped out onto the street with an air of confidence and even arrogance. He was holding something rolled up in his right hand which, once he'd dusted his shirt sleeves back down, proved to be a crumpled suit coat which he pulled on and straightened out before he pushed one hand into the pocket, produced a pack of cigarettes, and lit one up. He dropped the match onto the road without a second thought and, leaning on the Jaguar, looked around him north and south as if sizing up the town.

Mick Fletcher watched the long-limbed stranger stride sanguinely across the double lanes and up the wooden stairs.

"Morning, Constable."

"Yes, sir, can I help you?"

Mick Fletcher wasn't in the habit of calling people sir. It just came out.

"I'm looking for the prosecutor." He sucked hard on his cigarette and flicked the ash onto the floor that Mick had swept not two hours earlier.

"Yeah, well I'm it this morning."

"Oh right. I'm Eddie Moran. I'm here for this Maxwell bunfight."

Aaron Maxwell had been charged with unlawful assault occasioning actual bodily harm. He had appeared himself before the magistrate and entered a not guilty plea when the matter was first mentioned back in March, and so the court had listed it for hearing, but Mick had figured that, like most matters of this kind, it would be sorted out before it got to trial. He'd arranged for the complainant to come in, and he had the arresting police on standby just in case, but he doubted any of the witnesses would be needed. When the blood was running hot and everyone was still full of righteous indignation, the defendant always pleaded not guilty and set the matter down for trial; but eventually tempers cooled, and the prospect of a formal trial before the beak was a lot more daunting than a punch-up in the pub, and inevitably, when trial day came around the defendant would have second thoughts and the plea would change to guilty. This one was no different, a neighbourhood dispute gone bad: two blokes out back of Cudgen forever blueing over the back fence, until finally a son of one of them decides to jump the fence and sort it out once and for all. Things had escalated from there, and the young bloke, a footballer, copped a wooden stake right through his left hand, but still had enough in him to pick the stake up and brain the complainant. It was just an ugly dust-up really; if it hadn't happened on the other fellow's property, the son probably wouldn't even have been charged, but after staying overnight in the Tweed Hospital the complainant had insisted. About a month ago Maxwell had brought a cross-complaint for the same charge against the neighbour. It was filed by some firm of solicitors up in Surfers Paradise called E.C. Moran & Co.

As Mick shook hands with Eddie Moran over the front desk, he couldn't help but think this bloke was going to cause him trouble. He was young, maybe twenty-five or twenty-six, but he acted like he owned the joint, and Mick had an uneasy feeling in his stomach.

"So is this one going ahead?"

"Of course. Why wouldn't it?"

Moran had the charge book open on the desk and was carefully studying it. If Mick was going to turn this one round into a plea of guilty he was going to have to do a little bit of massage.

"There's probably some room to move on bodily harm."

Moran wasn't biting yet. He had pulled a piece of folded paper from his pocket and was now copying notes of something in the charge book, looking for all the world as though he was preparing for a fight. Maybe he just hadn't got the message. Mick decided it was best to spread his cards out on the table straight away.

"I'd say if your bloke pleads to the assault, I could probably talk the boss into dropping bodily harm."

Moran bounced upright as though someone had just kicked him in the bum.

"What?" He looked uncomprehending. "You're not suggesting Maxwell would plead guilty to this shit?"

Mick Fletcher was suddenly on the back foot, grasping for excuses.

"Well, you know ... "

"We couldn't possibly plead guilty to any of this. The whole thing's a bloody outrage, even you should be able to see that. This complainant's a maniac! A danger to the public! I don't know who he knows in the police down here but the very fact that my fellow's been charged over this is absolutely scandalous!"

Mick Fletcher felt his hackles rise. Maxwell had belted his next-door neighbour black and blue, and to suggest that there was something untoward about the fact that he'd been charged was way out of line.

"Mate, he put the bloke in hospital for a couple of days."

"It's probably a good thing he did. At least it's stopped that maniac from attacking some other poor innocent passer-by! Have you got some particulars for me?"

"What?" Mick was struggling for an appropriate retort to Moran's last ludicrous assertion, but the lawyer had already changed his tack.

"Particulars! Don't you know what particulars are?"

"Yeah, of course I know what particulars are."

"Well, where are they? We're entitled to them, you know that don't you?"

"Yeah."

"How long have you been prosecuting, Constable?"

"Since February."

"Since February?" Moran rolled his eyes and shook his head in feigned exasperation as Mick Fletcher cursed himself for having answered the question at all. "Well, this is a very serious charge, Constable. I want some particulars."

Mick was determined to put up some sort of a fight. "Well, you should have the facts sheet, that's got all the details on it."

"They're not particulars, Constable! I want particulars! Do you understand what I'm talking about?"

"Yeah."

"All right then. I'm going next door to see my client. When I come back, I'd appreciate it if you would have some appropriate particulars for me."

With that, Moran stuffed the folded sheet of paper back into his pocket and disappeared in the direction of the courthouse. Phil Bartrim had come back from the cells and was standing in the back doorway with a little pile of plates in both hands and cups hanging off each thumb.

"Jesus," he gasped. "Who was that arsehole?"

When Edwin Cassius Moran stepped onto the wooden floorboards of the small verandah of the Tweed Heads courthouse, his client Aaron Maxwell sprang to his feet as though he'd been called to attention. The little he'd seen of his lawyer so far made him jumpy.

"What the fuck are you wearing?" Moran opened.

Aaron looked down at his T-shirt. Even upside down, the 'Born to be Wild' emblem looked all right to him.

"What?"

"You are fucking joking, aren't you?"

Aaron was not the smartest bloke on earth, but he could tell this joker was trying to have a go at him. It occurred to him to take the shithead by the throat and shake him once or twice, but then he remembered what the coach had said: he was to behave himself and do everything the lawyer told him. Aaron really wasn't sure about the bloke, but he'd been recommended by the bigwigs in the club administration (and they had a vested interest in keeping their star forward on the paddock) so he must know something.

"Get home now and put a decent fucking shirt on. Make sure it's got a collar." Moran wasn't waiting for an answer. "And have you got that five hundred?"

"No, I have to wait until the bank opens up at ten."

"Well, you know the rules – no dough no show. I'd suggest you come back via the bank."

As Aaron Maxwell plodded off to find his car, Eddie Moran was sizing up the situation. Maybe Maxwell had the money and maybe he'd be back with it. If not, Eddie had spent the best part of an hour driving down from Surfers Paradise for nothing. Unless . . .

As Eddie Moran charged back into the station, Mick Fletcher was slumped across the desk with pen and paper.

"How are those particulars going?" Moran demanded as if he had a right to know.

"Yeah, they should be finished in a minute."

"Right." Moran turned on Phil Bartrim who was minding his own business sipping coffee from his favourite cup as he read the morning paper. "Constable, have you got anybody in the cells today?"

"Yeah," the constable responded, somewhat tentatively. "There's still four blokes in."

"All right, I'll fill in as duty lawyer for the morning."

As Bartrim led the way to the watch-house cells, Eddie Moran was trying to do his sums. Legal Aid didn't pay too well for appearances as duty lawyer, but four inmates probably meant at least a couple of bail applications; and if Maxwell didn't come back with the money, he could stretch it through into a second hour which at least would make the trip worthwhile.

"One bloke doesn't have to front," Phil Bartrim droned as he turned the key in the main gate. "He's been remanded down to Grafton on an old kidnapping blue. He's just waiting for the van to transport him."

The Tweed cells had been built a long, long time ago. They hadn't been designed for comfort or privacy, nor with the convenience of inmates and their legal counsel in mind. The walls were made of stone, the floors were bare cement, and the doors and windows were just openings with heavy bars that shut out visitors but welcomed the winter winds. Eddie Moran leaned against the bars as his newest clients approached him one by one, like the faithful queuing for confession. As the third one left him, he reviewed his notes: two fine defaulters and a drink-driving plea. Even Eddie would have trouble stretching this into a second hour. He needed at least one more volunteer. Over by the far wall, number four was huddled, his arms wrapped around his legs, his head buried in his knees. This must be the one on kidnapping.

"What about you, buddy? You okay?"

There was a cackle from the far end of the holding pen and a gap-toothed, tattooed inmate advised, "You wouldn't want to get too close. You might catch something."

Moran ignored it. "You all right, pal?"

As Robert Allen looked up to respond, Moran could see even from a distance that the man had copped a beating. His cheeks were puffed, his lower lip was swollen and his left eye was nearly closed.

"You look like you could use a lawyer."

When Eddie Moran strutted back into the police station, Mick Fletcher proudly handed him a carefully crafted set of particulars. The lawyer snatched them from his hand and immediately began to read; he didn't seem the least bit grateful.

"Mmmm," he murmured as he studied them, then added, "Is this it?"

"Yeah," Mick answered weakly, sounding more apologetic than he would have liked.

"All right." Moran was already on his way back out.

"Yeah, hang on a second." Mick Fletcher wasn't going to let him off that easy. "What about your cross-complaint. I wouldn't mind some particulars of that."

"What?" Moran looked deeply insulted. "Are you serious? We're not giving you particulars!"

Mick Fletcher wasn't sure if he'd missed something.

"Well, why not? We're entitled to them."

Moran recoiled theatrically, then slapped his notes down on the counter, cocked one eyebrow and stared quizzically at the prosecutor, apparently astounded by the man's impertinence.

"Your complainant's a madman, Constable! He's a thug! Surely you don't seriously think I'd consider for one moment trusting sensitive details of my client's case to a dangerous maniac like that?"

Mick Fletcher was still groping for a logical response as Moran turned on Phil Bartrim, who up till now had been content to sit behind his desk and watch the show.

"While we're on the subject of particulars, Constable – who bashed that prisoner in the holding yard?"

Phil Bartrim froze like a rabbit in the headlights.

"Well?"

Phil wasn't going to handle this too well, so Mick jumped into the breach.

"We don't know."

"Was he beaten in the watch-house?"

Phil Bartrim suddenly found his voice again. "No bloody way!"

"So he was like that when they brought him in?"

"Maybe." Phil looked uncomfortable. "He didn't look that flash, but it was late. And it was dark like, you know."

"I want him examined by a doctor immediately."

Mick Fletcher couldn't wait to answer this one. "Sorry, mate, no visitors in the cells."

"The man has been seriously assaulted. I want a

doctor in to see him straight away and his injuries fully documented. You organise it immediately or I'll bring it to the attention of the magistrate and have him make a formal order."

"Like I said, Mr Moran, no visitors."

Moran grunted disdainfully at the two policemen. "We'll see," he snapped, then turned and left.

"We'll see all right, you dickhead," Bartrim cheerfully guffawed as soon as he was safely out of sight. "Old Freddy White wouldn't give you the shit out of his bum, you arsehole!"

Frederick White, Stipendiary Magistrate, was a naturally conservative man. It was not that he intended partiality. He had great respect for the British justice system which demanded equal time and weight to both ends of the bar table. But he had been raised in a disciplined God-fearing family that had survived hard times and knew the value of hard work. He had started as a junior counter clerk and studied nights to finish school and get ahead. He'd clung to his position in the public service all his life because he knew it offered job security and some future for his family. Frederick was a government man. He was tight-fisted, tough, and some would even say mean-spirited. And he was not the type to warm to the likes of Edwin C. Moran.

As events transpired, the trial of Aaron Maxwell commenced before His Worship shortly after ten o'clock as listed. Mr Moran, solicitor, appeared for the defence and very quickly managed to turn the whole proceedings into something of a shambles. Through cross-examination of the first police witness, he raised a genuine doubt about the actual positioning of the boundary line between the complainant's property and the defendant's. Though probably of little relevance, this seemed to attain disproportionate significance in everybody's mind, particularly after Moran's constant assertions that the complainant had been a trespasser on the defendant's property when the first assault occurred and ought to have been charged as such. The problem was exacerbated when Moran made it clear, early in the cross-examination of the complainant, that the injury to the defendant's hand had seriously prejudiced his potentially lucrative fledgling football career, and these proceedings were really just a dry run for the major damages suit that would soon follow. From there the proceedings deteriorated into something of a slanging match, the animated cross-examination of the complainant consisting of little more than tireless abuse and repeated insults hurled by the defence lawyer. Freddy White eventually tired of warning him to tone down his behaviour, hoping instead that the less he interrupted the sooner the whole performance might be over. By the time the mid-morning adjournment was called and Mr White SM stomped off to his chambers for a soothing cup of tea, the complainant was exhausted. When Moran came up with an offer in the tea room – that if the prosecution dropped the charge, his client might withdraw his cross-complaint and agree to relinquish any right to damages – it seemed too good to be true. The complainant grasped it with both hands, and to Mick Fletcher the opportunity to get rid of Moran once and for all was almost irresistible.

When the prosecutor advised the court that the complaint and cross-complaint had been withdrawn and asked that both charges be dismissed, it was all Freddy White could do to suppress a rare smile from the bench. As he delivered the pronouncement ("The charges are dismissed and both parties are discharged") and turned to ask the final question ("Any further matters, Constable?") before adjourning for the day, he was already warming to the prospect of a relatively stress-free afternoon. The dawning smile faded on his lips as Moran returned to his feet.

"There's another matter I need to raise before Your Worship."

Moran moved straight into his application. Robert Allen, who had appeared before the court the previous afternoon to be remanded in custody, was currently an inmate of the Tweed Heads watch-house awaiting transport to Grafton Gaol. While performing duty lawyer services in the watch-house earlier that morning, Moran had made certain observations of the prisoner which suggested he'd been beaten. Moran had requested of the police that the man be given medical attention but that request had been refused, and he now requested that the magistrate direct that appropriate arrangements be put in place immediately.

This all sounded very messy, and Freddy White wasn't about to get mixed up in it.

"Well, that's a matter for the police, Mr Moran. They control the watch-house. There's nothing I can do about it."

He hardly had the words out of his mouth before Moran had thrown a dilapidated leather briefcase up onto the bar table and was rustling and delving into its contents. He emerged with several photocopied sheets of paper from which he proceeded to quote copious authorities and high-minded judicial pronouncements regarding treatment of prisoners and suspects and the power of the courts to intervene and exercise some supervision where the interests of justice so required. He became more animated as he went on, to the point where Mick Fletcher started to become concerned that he might actually know what he was talking about. Fortunately Freddy White remained unmoved. Tweed Heads was still a long way from the Privy Council, and Freddy wasn't about to let some insolent young pup dictate to him.

"Yes well, that's all well and good, Mr Moran," he groaned when the lawyer finally drew a breath. "But I'm functus officio so far as Mr Allen is concerned. He's already been remanded to Grafton and there's no current proceeding before this court that allows me to exercise any jurisdiction in his case."

"Then I'm making an instanter application for bail to this court on his behalf," Moran shot back without a second's thought, and he promptly sat down at the bar table and began scribbling notes onto a foolscap pad.

Freddy White glared down at the young solicitor, who totally ignored him. Mick Fletcher kept his head well down as the silent seconds ticked away, disturbed only by the sound of the lawyer's biro scratching feverishly on the page.

Finally the magistrate growled reluctantly to the prosecutor, "All right, Constable, have the prisoner brought in."

What followed was a piece of high farce in which the parties (apart from the applicant's solicitor) went lamely through the motions of an application for bail. In reality, both the prosecutor and the magistrate were aware from the outset that there was no living possibility that Mr White SM was ever going to give a moment's thought to granting bail to Robert Allen. He was on a very serious charge (and, as the police had charged him, he was no doubt guilty). He'd been dealt with yesterday and remanded in custody without even asking to be bailed, and now he was back before His Worship thanks only to the impertinence and obstinacy of his ill-mannered lawyer, whom Freddy White now intended to put right back in his place.

"Bail refused. Remanded in custody," Mr White announced with gusto and with not a little relish once the show was over. "Is that all, Mr Moran?"

"Not quite, Your Worship." Moran was for once civil and restrained. "I renew my application to Your Worship for a direction regarding medical attention."

"Application denied!" boomed White. "Is that all?"

"No, Your Worship," replied Moran politely. "Would Your Worship please record your observations of the prisoner's condition here today."

Freddy scowled and shook his head. This was all too much.

"Mr Moran, I have no power to mark the record with observations of that kind!"

Moran looked up, appearing somewhat nonplussed. "Oh, I'm not suggesting Your Worship mark the record. I'm merely requesting that Your Worship commit your observations to writing so as to avoid any unnecessary embarrassment to Your Worship upon trial of this matter in the Supreme Court."

"What?" Freddy didn't like the sound of this. "What's the trial of this matter in the Supreme Court got to do with me?"

"Well, in the circumstances, Your Worship, I'd anticipate Your Worship will be a witness."

Mr White SM propped back in his chair and slapped his two hands firmly on the bench. "A witness? Are you trying to threaten me, Mr Moran?"

"No, of course not, Your Worship." Moran looked sincerely shocked by the suggestion. "But Mr Allen's injuries will no doubt be relevant to certain issues in the trial, and since it now appears unlikely that there will be any independent medical evidence of his injuries then that seems to make the three of us here today the only witnesses. A person of Your Worship's eminence of course will carry particular weight. In the circumstances, it would seem to me prudent that Your Worship make written notes now so as to avoid any credibility or similar issues arising under cross-examination at the trial."

He made it sound almost logical, and Freddy White

was suddenly concerned that this young popinjay might be maverick enough to go through with it. His eyes narrowed as he sat silently, trying to work out just what defence counsel was really up to. Moran stood at the bar table, responding to his hostile gaze with a demure respectful disposition, until eventually White was stumped. He looked over at the prosecutor, who immediately looked down at the floor. Then he looked back at Moran, who returned the look enquiringly.

"Well," the perplexed Mr White eventually responded, "I'm not qualified to comment on the man's medical condition."

"That's true, Your Worship. Certainly it would be preferable to have a doctor see him."

White let out an involuntary growl and glared over at Mick Fletcher. This was all his fault. "Well, Constable, what's the problem about having the prisoner examined by a doctor anyway?"

Mick Fletcher made an effort to reply, but the writing was on the wall. He raised some half-hearted minor hurdles which he immediately proceeded to dismantle to accommodate His Worship's wishes. He wasn't sure that a doctor would be immediately available but the police would make enquiries and no doubt something could be organised. The facilities for visits in the cells were limited, but arrangements could be made to allow the doctor to examine Mr Allen in an office in the police station. Something would need to be worked out regarding the doctor's remuneration. Suddenly an air of cooperation permeated the discussion and it seemed nothing was too difficult. As a relieved Mr Frederick White SM finally rose from the bench that afternoon, Constables Fletcher and Bartrim were busying themselves with the arrangements to have Robert Allen medically examined.

Before they took the prisoner back to the cells he was courteously allowed a private moment in the courtroom with his lawyer.

"Can you lay your hands on some money for the trial?" Moran was already puffing on his first post-court cigarette.

"I think so."

"Good." He flicked a card from his shirt pocket and pushed it into Allen's hand.

"Call me if you do."

With that, Edwin C. Moran turned to Mick Fletcher and signalled that he was all done.

"Thanks, buddy," he said brightly. He sucked a last lungful of smoke, dropped his cigarette onto the floor and ground it underfoot, and then swaggered out the door.

# CHAPTER SIX

The trial of Robert Arthur Allen was scheduled to commence in Sydney in the June sittings of the Supreme Court. The presiding judge was to be the recently appointed Mr Justice Peter Rosenthal, a man of excellent legal pedigree. At forty-eight years he was a relatively young man who had a reputation as a brilliant mind with a balanced, open outlook. Undoubtedly he was wasted in crime; his skills would have been put to better use in the commercial-causes jurisdiction, where he had mostly practised at the bar. But all the judges had to take a turn in the criminal courts and no one was keen to do the McCabe trial which had the potential to be a long drawn-out affair. When the time came, Peter Rosenthal agreed to sit without complaint or hesitation, just as those who knew him at the bar would have expected of him. He was a disciplined, no-nonsense sort of man who got things done.

But as the commencement of the trial drew near, Rosenthal was privately expressing trepidation to some of his colleagues. Ever since Allen had appeared to face the charge in the Local Court at Grafton, the McCabe case had burst back onto the front pages of Australia's newspapers, and now the media frenzy was reaching fever pitch. The committal hearing had reopened all the old wounds, and there were soon unprecedented scenes of local townsfolk picketing the courthouse, waving banners and shouting slogans, baying for the blood of the accused. The heart-rending accounts of the parents of the children were played and replayed, fuelling the fire of a growing mob mentality. Lawyers were posing serious questions about just how far the press could be allowed to go and the extent to which the coverage had already eroded any prospect of a fair trial. The situation had escalated to the point where the Crown was happy to concede a risk of bias in the Grafton area, and agreed to move the trial to Sydney where the bigger pool of prospective jurors would reduce the risk of prejudgement. But no one could seriously believe that any juror drawn from any town or city in Australia would not have seen the media coverage and formed a view of the accused. It placed a heavy onus on the court to ensure that the essential tenets of the justice system were preserved; the presiding judge would need to battle against the tide of public opinion – and perhaps his own personal predilections – to ensure the jury strictly observed the presumption of innocence and the requirement of proof beyond a reasonable doubt. It would be difficult for any judge, and for the relatively young and inexperienced Justice Peter Rosenthal it shaped as a daunting task.

For his part, Vince Donnelly was still not pleased. He had a kidnapping brief with 'murder' printed on the back page, but no body and no story. What they had would get them to the jury, and any jury in the land would convict Allen without thinking. But for Vince, putting Robert Allen behind bars was not enough. His job was to bring home the kids, and he couldn't. Their mother still went to bed at night wondering what had happened to her children and where their little bodies lay. She had no grave to lay the flowers on and nowhere for the tears to fall. And something else troubled Vince: Robert Allen wasn't in this alone. He'd been in Brighton Bay throughout those first few weeks; the coppers had been all over him and anyone else who'd been within cooee of the scene, and they'd turned over every log and leaf in town. Wherever those kids were at that time they weren't in the Bay, so someone other than Robert Allen must have had them. There was another one, maybe more, and only Allen knew who they were.

But he wasn't telling. He was a cold-hearted little bastard who they couldn't seem to get to. Vince had put the facts in front of him: the notebook evidence together with his presence at the scene and his prints on the envelope would sink him, sure as shit. That meant he'd wear the whole thing on his own, even though he probably had help. Even if he beat a murder charge, kidnapping carried maximum life; and on the strength of what was in the notes, and his total failure to cooperate, the judge would give him the lot – he'd have murder in the back of his mind and he'd hand out a life sentence. And unless Allen coughed up the story, he'd never get parole. Never. He'd die in gaol. Either the crims would fix him up for what he'd done to the kids or, worse still, he'd survive for the next thirty or forty years until he finally fell off the perch. Either way he'd do it tough. But it didn't have to be that way. He could tell his story. No one starts out to kill two kids; something must have gone wrong – there must be some story to tell. Whatever it was might just get him manslaughter and maybe something less than life, or at least parole, eventually. In the meantime Vince could guarantee protection.

Allen didn't even look like he was interested. Whatever the story was, it must have been too terrible to tell. Either that or it involved someone he feared more than any prison cell.

*　　*　　*

Faye McCabe was spared the agony of being present at the committal hearing. The Legal Aid office was happy to accept her statement uncontested, and although there was some brief cross-examination of the police officers, the hearing was concluded quickly and without the need for most of the witnesses to attend.

She had tried hard to avoid any of the press coverage, but from the moment of his arrest Robert Allen seemed to appear on every page and every channel. It was always the same photograph: a recent watch-house image taken under bright lights and alien conditions, the strained face of a man accused. Faye had managed not to look at it closely, no more than a glance before she wrenched her eyes away, determined not to have her peace destroyed, not to be dragged back into sleepless nights filled with terrifying visions, or loving dreams that ended brutally with the truth that came with waking.

But now, as she sat opposite Bill Keliher and looked at the photograph between them, she could see another man, a younger man from another world and another time. The face was lined and weather-beaten, but it was the same face. It was the young man who had brought the telegram to Mrs Marchant when her son was killed all those years ago. The same young man whose eyes had filled with moisture as she sat sobbing on the front verandah; who had come next door to tell them that the poor woman was upset; who had stayed to see if he could help; who had cared, apparently.

"Yes, I remember him." The terse edge disappeared from Faye's voice as she slid the photo back across the desk. She sounded almost relieved. "He wasn't from the Bay originally, I know that. But he worked at the post office for a year or two, I think."

"Did you ever see him with the kids?"

"No, I don't think so. Only at the front gate, if they were out there when he was dropping off mail. Michael would talk to anyone, Bill – you remember how he was." The word 'was' seemed to stick slightly in her throat. She looked over Bill's shoulder to where Inspector Donnelly was standing, then back to Bill, and the tears gathered in her eyes. Bill held her gaze and smiled back at her.

"I think I only ever saw the man once or twice. He was a bit odd, I suppose. Very quiet, perhaps a bit effeminate, I don't know. But he was pleasant sort of thing, polite, you know." Her hand crept feebly across the desk and dragged the photograph back towards her. As it came closer she stared into the emotionless eyes of Robert Allen, and asked the question she had asked herself a thousand times of a thousand different faces. Was this the man? Was this the monster who had robbed her of her children, her family, her life, her sanity? The face looked sad, disconsolate, defeated, almost incapable of the horror that someone had visited on Faye McCabe.

"We'll get him, Faye, don't worry." Bill Keliher was leaning forward in his chair and the deep tone in his voice was somehow comforting. "We'll put him away."

She looked into his eyes and Bill understood. The fate of Robert Allen was irrelevant to Faye McCabe. She was searching, had been searching for the past seventeen years, for the fate of her children, not for Robert Allen. She longed only for the peace that truth would bring, and the truth remained a mystery. She had to know what Bill Keliher couldn't tell her.

\* \* \*

"Your mate finally hit the tin, but he hasn't left us too much time to get this thing cranked up."

Eddie Moran was chewing gum and bouncing one foot below the desk as he skimmed the Crown outline of facts. He was annoyed, that much was obvious. Eddie liked to get things right, and coming in at the last minute didn't help.

"All right," he said eventually, pushing his chair away from the narrow wooden desk and rocking back against the wall. "You've got a shitload of work to do, pal, and you're going to have to get started straight away. I'll tell you what I want from you in a minute. But before we get down to exploring the minutiae, I want to look at the big picture. Right?"

Robert Allen nodded silently. He looked pale and weak and it was not at all surprising. He was still recovering from surgery, and propped up against the brick wall of the prison interview room he looked likely to collapse at any moment. Allen had copped some special treatment from the remand-yard heavies, and it made Eddie's eyes water just to think about it. A short length of garden hose with barbed wire stuck inside it, lubricated with axle grease, and shoved straight up the clacker. The garden hose came out okay, but the barbed wire that it left behind would have been extremely painful. There was always someone somewhere who wanted to play judge and jury, and the rock apes on the inside had already found his client guilty.

"Are you guilty?"

"No."

"Good start. What was your relationship with Garry Willet?"

"I'd met him once or twice."

"Horseshit, pal!" The front legs of Moran's chair slammed onto the cement floor and he was now leaning forward on the desk pointing an accusing finger. "We haven't got time to fuck around with sensibilities here. Now we both know that you and this clown Willet were more than just pen pals, so let's cut the crap!"

Allen's eyes rolled slightly in his head as though he had gone faint. Eddie didn't care. He had got his money up-front as a retainer, so even if the bloke keeled over dead he would still get paid. He had no time or inclination to start tap-dancing around the issues. They were a week out from a trial and right now they needed to move forward.

"I'm gay, Mr Moran," Allen said eventually. "That doesn't make me a paedophile, or a kidnapper, or a murderer. I'd no more harm two little children than fly in the sky."

"Yeah, well I'm afraid it's not going to make you Mr Popular with the jury either. Were you and Willet an item?"

"At one stage we were. Garry had a wide circle."

A clever line occurred to Eddie but he decided not to touch it. "Did you and Willet send the letter to the parents?"

"No." Allen hesitated. "I mean, Garry might have, but I don't know anything about it."

"Why would the other guy – the dead guy, what's his name, Garner – why would he have told the cops that you and Willet were in it together?"

Allen closed his eyes and shook his head. Curiously he seemed to be gathering strength as they went. "He was a nutcase," he said emphatically, and from what

Eddie had seen of the photographs of Garner he wasn't inclined to argue the point. "Suzie – that's what he called himself. He was a drag queen. He was insanely jealous of anyone who got close to Garry."

If Garry Willet were alive today he probably could attest to that. So far Allen's answers made some sense. It was time to drop the big question and watch for the reaction.

"So how would your prints get on the envelope?"

Allen looked his lawyer straight in the eye.

"I don't know. I've got no idea."

It was an interesting answer. Eddie had never thought much of the fingerprint evidence. So far as he could see, it didn't prove a thing, not in the circumstances of this case. Robert Allen had worked in the very post office that had processed the letter. Eddie had checked the records, and Allen had been at work on the day the letter had gone through. It was hardly surprising that his fingerprints might turn up on the envelope. As far as Eddie was concerned it was non-probative and highly prejudicial. He might even have it withheld from the jury. Whether or not he did, there was an obvious innocent explanation for the fingerprints which the police hadn't thought of, and apparently neither had Mr Allen. It occurred to Eddie that a guilty man probably would have found it straight away.

"Did you tell the police you took the children?"

"No, of course not."

"They say you did."

"They're lying."

Another good answer. Straightforward, to the point. Minimalist. That's how Eddie liked it. He flipped open his folder and clicked down his biro.

"Okay, what happened?"

Allen sucked in a deep breath and blew out, as if preparing himself for an unpleasant task.

"Well, it started with the older bloke, Donnelly. He was accusing me, saying they knew I'd taken the children. He reckoned I picked them up on the Point Road and took them down to the beach, and that I told them I'd rung their mother. I don't know where he got all this from – Suzie, I guess. Anyway, I didn't know any of that at this stage, but this Donnelly is saying they know this and they know that and he claims they've got a witness to it all. And I know that's bullshit 'cause it never happened, and I say so, and he just goes berserk. He was belting me and kicking me, and then the other guy, the little swarthy-looking guy, he got stuck into me as well."

"Vagianni?"

"Yeah, that's him. The Queensland guy."

"Okay."

"So then they all left the room except Vagianni or whatever his name is and the tall bloke."

"Keliher."

"Yeah, Keliher. So then, when the others were gone, Vagianni takes a handful of my hair and lifts me up out of the chair and gets his face up real close to me and says, 'All right, cunt, there's two ways we can do this. Either we can beat the story out of you or you can just tell us the truth right now.' And at that stage I thought, these guys are crazy, and I just clammed up. I wasn't going to say another word. So he kept threatening me for ages and hitting me around the head and then eventually he stopped and said, 'Fair enough, shithead, have it your way.' I remember that really clearly because they both walked out and left me there for about ten minutes and I thought maybe they were going to leave me alone. But then they came back in and Vagianni had his notebook out and he started reading what he'd written, and then he said something like, 'There you are, that's how I remember it – you got anything you want to add?' And I just said nothing and they walked out."

Eddie scribbled his last note and drew a line across the page. It was a good start. They had an explanation for the informant and the fingerprints, and they had a story to tell about the so-called confession, complete with medical corroboration of a belting. Eddie Moran had himself a case. He leaned back in the chair until it dropped against the wall behind him in the poky little room. He was chewing again now, grinding gum between his teeth and stretching it out with his tongue. Allen stood impassively against the other wall, a sorry-looking figure who had copped about as much as most men could take. But he wasn't beaten yet. He had a cold stare to match Eddie's and he held his gaze until the lawyer looked away. Strange cat. Murderer? Who knows. Come to think of it, who cares. Eddie had a fee already in the bank. And Eddie had a case.

Frank Vagianni had a hangover. He had been in the Cross most of the night drinking bourbon, which was not his drink. Now he was paying for it. He had been at Sydney city headquarters since about seven, straight from the Cross. This was to be the first day of the McCabe trial and the whole team had been given strict instructions by Vince Donnelly to be there bright and early – at least Frank had managed one out of two. They had been through their statements umpteen times until at last Vince had found something else to worry about; he was off with the uniforms trying to organise an exhibit that someone had just realised was still at Darlinghurst and would be needed by the Crown later in the day. So he was out of Frankie's hair.

"Allen's got himself another lawyer."

Frank had his head down on the desk and was in the early stages of sweet slumber. The voices in the background hardly registered.

"Yeah? Who's he got?"

"Some young bloke, a solicitor from the Gold Coast."

"What?"

"Yeah. Apparently he's going to do the trial himself, without a barrister."

"What? You're kidding!"

"Yeah, mate, no bullshit. I just heard it from the Crown."

"The bloke's mad! What's his name?"

"Moran or something like that, I think."

"Moran? That'd be right! He'd have to be a fuckin' moron."

"The Box'd know him. Hey, Box! Box!"

The mention of his name stirred Frankie slightly and he grunted recognition.

"You know this bloke Moran?"

"Huh?"

"You know some young solicitor from up your way by the name of Moran?"

Bang! Frank Vagianni was suddenly awake.

"What?" He spat the word out with such rancour that the young detectives stopped in their tracks.

"Moran. Do you know him?"

"That fuckin' prick! Do I fuckin' know him!"

\*   \*   \*

Eddie Moran made sure to time his arrival at the courthouse perfectly. He didn't want to get there too early or too late. It was one of those lovely situations where his client was in custody so they couldn't get any shots of the accused, which made the lawyer star of the show. But if he didn't make it easy for them, the slack bastards were just as likely to rely on archive footage of the police investigation and the committal hearing. Journos were a lazy breed and television cameramen were worst of all, so he couldn't really count on them being there before about nine forty, even with a case as big as this one; and by about nine forty-five or ten to ten, some of the more anally retentive scribes would be wanting to start heading in to make sure they didn't miss the kick-off. So there was an optimum window of opportunity between twenty to and quarter to. He would arrive at about eighteen minutes to, and get out of the taxi on Elizabeth Street about fifty metres from the main entrance. That would give them every chance to get him as he walked towards the courts.

Eddie Moran was twenty-five years old. He had been out of university a little over two years, and although he already had a reputation on the Gold Coast for terrorising country magistrates, this was his first jury trial and his first client charged with anything more serious than bodily harm. When the McCabe children disappeared, Eddie was a boy of barely eight years, doing his best to survive the second grade. The event came and went without his knowledge, a piece of ancient history he learned years later, an unsolved crime that seemed to hold undue significance for reasons unexplained. The anguish of the parents, all of them, meant nothing to him, then or now. So as the taxi turned into Elizabeth Street, the roadblock up ahead took Eddie by surprise. It covered the whole street and footpath and stretched for fifty metres either side of the Supreme Court. He could see immediately it was there for the McCabe kidnapping trial.

Eddie bit off a little piece of thumbnail and bounced his left foot on the taxi floor. What the hell was going on? There were television vans parked everywhere and at least three hundred people on the pavement. This thing was bigger than he had thought. He could see some banners in the crowd and there was some sort of altercation going on near the main doors to the court. Some people were calling out and others were pushing lightly, trying to move through the front doors of the complex, but most were merely standing around, waiting for something unapparent.

"This'll do me here."

Eddie stepped out onto the footpath at the edge of the crowd and put his briefcase down. Then he pulled a Camel from his pocket and lit up. Maybe he'd bitten off a little more than he'd intended to. His heart was racing and he sucked so hard on the cigarette that his head was lightly spinning. Eddie had never done a Supreme Court trial before. Fuck it. How hard could it be? He sucked again, picked up his briefcase and stepped out. It was time to crash or crash through.

"Defence lawyer! Coming through!"

Robert Allen's stringbean solicitor nonchalantly nudged his way through the far extremity of the vast crowd. The cry went up quickly, and suddenly journalists, cameramen and sound gaffers were pushing out from the inside, wading through the mob in far more vigorous and practised fashion towards the approaching lawyer. At close range Eddie could see only hostile faces, which he did his best to treat with due disdain. At first they crowded close to him, shuffling begrudgingly to one side as he inched forward sucking on his cigarette and breathing where he pleased. Then as the shouted complaints and instructions of the cameramen filtered through, people started to stand back and size him up. Presently the sea parted, until eventually Eddie was looking down a line of faces on each side and striding towards the media, who were still jostling through the last remnants of the parting throng. Eddie could feel the distrust and disapproval of the crowd. Everybody hated him. Just the way he liked it.

Squeezing into the courtroom itself proved difficult even with the assistance of the bailiffs. There were people crammed into every corner and no one was too eager to surrender space to anyone. When Eddie had finally edged his way into the ribbon of free space around the bar table, he straightened himself up and threw a scornful glance across his shoulder. All he could see were small-minded people clinging to the collective comfort of a lynch mob. He scowled his contempt at them and then swung his bag onto the bar table.

"Johnny Rotten. That's what they call him up there."

Frank Vagianni was standing so close in the packed courtroom that Bill could smell last night's nicotine and alcohol.

"Does he know what he's doing?"

"Mate, he's a fuckin' goose!"

The Deputy Director of Prosecutions, Mr Mark Bolster QC, was prosecuting. Mr Paul Dorrington of Counsel was his junior. Next to Dorrington at the bar table sat Paul Burrows, a senior solicitor with the Director's office, and on the end of the line a young clerk was arranging books and folders on the table. As Moran dropped insolently into his seat alongside them they looked across as one, and he ignored them.

The judge entered with the usual announcement, and quickly made his mark before the crowd had even settled. "Mr Bailiff, I want this courtroom cleared of anyone who doesn't have a seat. There's a public gallery for those that wish to follow the proceedings but I won't have people standing in the corridors, or anywhere else for that matter. Please attend to that immediately."

There followed a brief period of pandemonium during which the bailiffs summarily despatched the unseated and unwanted before the courtroom was restored to order. As the last bailiff resumed his position, a reverent hush fell over the gathering in anticipation of the judge's next instruction. Peter Rosenthal spoke civilly and quietly but with unmistakable authority.

"Ladies and gentlemen, before we begin I want to make a few things clear. This is a court of law and this is a criminal trial. The liberty of one of our fellow citizens is at stake and it is the duty of each of us to ensure that the proceedings are carried out appropriately and with due decorum. Those members of the public who wish to participate will remain at all times within the public gallery and will be expected to conduct themselves responsibly. I will not tolerate any inappropriate gesture, comment or outburst that might in any way influence the impartial deliberations of the jury. I remind all of you that our system of justice embraces certain fundamental principles, which apply to the accused in this case just as they apply to each and every one of us. They dictate that he is to be considered innocent of any wrongdoing unless he is proven guilty beyond any reasonable doubt. I have also been made aware of the provocative treatment of this matter in the media to date. I take this opportunity to caution the ladies and gentlemen of the press that, should anything they say or write infringe the rules that circumscribe the proper reporting of these proceedings, I have powers to punish contempt of court. Please understand that I will not hesitate to use them if that becomes necessary to ensure a fair trial."

It was a good start. Eddie couldn't have said it any better himself, and it was the perfect platform for the jump that he was about to take. If the judge was going to go making little speeches about justice and the like, he would be in no position to refuse the application Eddie intended to make as soon as the jury was empanelled. He looked back at Allen standing in the dock. Even in an atmosphere as dangerous and alien as this he seemed to show no fear, no emotion at all.

The jury was marched in and called up one by one. On the first run through, Eddie challenged all of them, just to show them that he wasn't going through the motions and he expected them to perform if they got the job. The process dragged over an hour and by the time Allen was arraigned and the prosecutor had run through the list of anticipated Crown witnesses, Rosenthal was talking about the morning-tea adjournment. But Eddie had an application to push through, and he wanted Rosenthal's ruling before he forgot the lovely little justice speech he'd made that morning.

"I ask that Your Honour conduct a voir dire into the circumstances of the alleged confession."

A discreet rumble ran through the press benches. A voir dire hearing meant that the judge would be asked to determine in the absence of the jury whether the confession had been obtained by means unlawful or at least unfair. The proposal promised a juicy slanging match and usually some fireworks. The journalists were already warming to the prospect.

"Mr Moran, I haven't read the lower-court depositions. Is there a confession of the offence by the accused?"

"No, Your Honour."

"Then I don't understand your application."

"There is an alleged verbal confession said to have been recorded by police in the form of notes in an officer's notebook. It's uncorroborated in any way and we say it's a complete fabrication."

Eddie was a great believer in the value of primacy and recency. Make your big point early, and make it clear and unambiguous.

"Yes." Rosenthal was thinking. "But surely the question of whether or not the confession was made is a matter for the jury, not an issue for me to determine on a voir dire."

"I'm not asking Your Honour to determine that issue. Mr Allen was savagely bashed by the arresting police immediately prior to the alleged confession." Another rumble sprang from the press bench and ran throughout the courtroom. "I'm asking that Your Honour rule on the unlawful behaviour by the police affecting the admissibility of the alleged confession."

Mark Bolster QC was on his feet immediately, scoffing in a most condescending fashion: the 'solicitor appearing for the accused' had obviously confused the principles applicable to the reception of evidence on a voir dire to determine the voluntariness of a confessional statement. The procedure was appropriate where it was agreed that a confession had been made but the defence challenged whether it had been made voluntarily or claimed it had been induced by threat or promise or actual violence or some trick or other unfair tactic or inappropriate behaviour. The starting point was an acknowledgement that the confession had been made. How could His Honour be asked to rule that a confession which was said not to have been made had been made involuntarily?

Bolster had a tendency to speak apparently authoritatively and often pompously on subjects that he hadn't looked too closely at, and this was a case in point. The inherent logic of his argument appealed to him, so much so that he went on at some considerable length, and the more he spoke the more dismissive he became of the whole basis of the application. Unfortunately for him he was quite wrong, and in the circumstances Eddie was happy for him to take as much time as he chose to establish his credentials as one who was willing to put his mouth firmly into gear without first engaging his brain.

Eddie Moran liked to win, and he already knew that meant being well prepared. He had the relevant case law already photocopied in duplicate and, when Bolster finally sat down, he slid one copy along the bar table towards him and handed the other to the judge. Rosenthal digested it quickly and efficiently.

"Well, Mr Bolster," he said dryly, looking up from the page, "there certainly seems to be a basis for the application."

Bolster looked a little flushed as he peered up over his glasses. "Yes, Your Honour. I won't take the matter any further."

It was always good to put the first blood on the floor. Eddie kept his head down as he waited for the judge's ruling.

"All right, we'll take the morning adjournment now and when we come back we'll commence the voir dire."

Frank Vagianni was on his third cup of strong black coffee when Moran strode into Christie's on Elizabeth Street. The sight of him swaggering into the little café made Frankie gag and splutter, which in turn provided some delight to Morrie Fleet, who could always see the funny side of things, particularly when he wasn't expecting to be the next witness on the stand.

"Jesus, Box. You love that bastard, don't you?"

"Yeah, Morrie, like my bloody piles."

At the far end of the café, the lawyer had slapped a note onto the counter and was waiting to be served when the proprietor Tony Penisi spotted him.

"Hey, Eddie. How you doin', man?"

"Hey, Tony. How are you, buddy?"

"Long time no see, man. Where you been?"

"I'm living up in Queensland now, Tony. On the Gold Coast."

"Woa! Surfers Paradise, eh?"

"Yeah, pal, that's pretty close actually."

"Yeah? You a surfie now are y'? Hey?"

"Yeah, that'd be right."

Tony was quickly into full swing, pouring coffee and mouthing off, which was what he did best. Moran absorbed it with good humour and general disinterest as though he had heard it all before and was accustomed to it, and demonstrated the good sense not to try to match the jibes. While Tony prattled on, the lawyer pulled a soft pack from his pocket. He lit up a smoke and turned to lean back against the counter, sizing up the café and its clientele. When his view reached the table where the five detectives sat, he nodded his acknowledgement. A couple of them nodded and then looked away, but not Frankie Box. When Bill looked up from his coffee, the Box was staring at the lawyer, who was still standing with his back against the counter at the opposite end of the café, calmly and coolly returning Frankie's stare. They looked like two gunslingers in an old-time movie, ready for the draw. Morrie Fleet was close to cracking up and was working hard to keep it all together, for Frankie's sake. Bill quickly put his nose back in the coffee cup.

Tony came to the rescue with a long black in a takeaway container. As Moran paid, he turned and nodded brazenly to Frankie and his friends, then stepped out into the street. He was no sooner out of sight than Morrie's hilarity burst its banks.

"Shit, you love that bloke, don't you!"

Frankie's Latin blood was up and it took him several glances at Morrie blubbering beside him before he finally got the evil look out of his eye and broke into a half-smile. He hadn't had much to do with Moran but he'd seen enough of him to know he was a half-smart, jumped-up little shit. He came from Frank Vagianni's patch and sooner or later Frank was going to put him right back in his place.

"I think I know this bloke." Bill Keliher was talking to himself as much as anyone. "He played for Balmain Juniors when I was helping out with reserve grade. He's Digby Moran's youngest lad."

"What?" Morrie had stopped laughing. "Digby fuckin' Moran?"

Digby Charles Moran had been around since Adam was a lad. He'd run half the inner-city pubs at one time or another, and so far as anyone recalled he was the first one to have topless barmaids of a lunchtime. You could always lay a bet with Digby if you needed to, and like every other publican in town he'd steer you in the right direction for a trollop if you asked him, but all in all he ran a clean show and he caused no trouble. The beer was always cold and it was on the arm for coppers in any one of Digby's pubs. He was a widower, and his three sons had been raised mostly by the housemaids and the bar staff, particularly the older two, Dennis and Jamie. They were good kids and top sportsmen. Jamie had turned into a pretty handy lightweight in the amateur ranks and Dennis had actually taken a couple of state titles as a cruiserweight. They had both played first-grade rugby league at one stage or another and they still had pubs in town. But there was quite a gap to the youngest son, and by the time he had reached school age his old man was travelling well enough to shunt him off to a flash boarding school, so no one had seen as much of him as he was growing up. A few years later, Digby had taken up an offer to manage a pub up on the Gold Coast, and the young bloke had gone with him.

"Digby Moran. He's a fuckin' old urger if ever there was one." Frank Vagianni was unimpressed. Things were different up in Queensland and Frankie wasn't saddled with affection for the good old days. "I nearly pinched him for receiving about twelve months ago." Frank was deep in thought. "So that's his shithead son, eh. Good."

*   *   *

There was nothing very subtle about Eddie Moran's cross-examination of Frank Vagianni. It was crude, abusive and calculated to get right up Frankie's nostrils.

"You bashed him, didn't you, Mr Vagianna?"

"That's Vagianni."

"Whatever. You bashed him, didn't you?"

"No I didn't."

"Yes you did."

"I didn't."

"You bashed him and then you verballed him."

"No I didn't."

"I put it to you that you did."

"Well I didn't."

"You did. You know you did, don't you, Detective?"

"No I didn't."

"You're lying about the whole thing, aren't you?"

"No I'm not."

"Yes you are. You're lying right now."

"I'm not."

"Yes you are. You're nothing but an inveterate liar. Isn't that true?"

"No it's not."

"Yes it is."

"No it's not."

"It is."

"I object!"

Thus far Mark Bolster QC had shown more patience than most would have and the judge didn't need to hear the grounds of his complaint.

"Yes really, Mr Moran," groaned Rosenthal. "I think you've made your point, haven't you."

The young lawyer didn't miss a beat. He moved to his next point so quickly that the judge wasn't sure if he had been obeyed or just ignored.

"Did you see Mr Allen in a bruised and battered state in the Tweed Heads police station that day?"

"I certainly did not."

"Not at any stage?"

"Not at any stage."

"You didn't send him out of that police station with bruises all over his face?"

"Certainly not."

"And it follows from what you've told us that he didn't have any bruising when you first came into contact with him that day?"

"Not that I saw, no."

Moran snatched up a one-page document from the bar table.

"Well, he didn't have 'a marked swelling and tenderness to the right orbital region with visible draining of blood into the right eye socket', did he?"

"No."

"Not when you first contacted him that day and not when you eventually parted company with him?"

"No."

"Well then how the hell did he come to have those injuries when he found his way into the watch-house?"

Bolster was quickly back up on his feet.

"I object to this, Your Honour! There is no evidence that the accused had any such injuries in the watch-house or elsewhere."

Moran leaned across and insolently slapped a copy of the medical report down on the bar table in front of his opposing counsel. Then he truculently glared back at the judge.

"The morning after Allen was lodged in the Tweed Heads watch-house he was examined by a Dr Robert Elms at the request of Mr White SM, the Stipendiary Magistrate who remanded him to Grafton. My learned friend now has a copy of Dr Elms' report. The doctor can be called in these proceedings if required. Now,

Vagianni, why don't you explain to us how these injuries seem to have materialised from thin air."

For the second time in two minutes, both Peter Rosenthal and Mark Bolster felt vaguely sidelined by this impudent young man. But in his own rambunctious way he had answered the objection and made out a basis to proceed. The fact that he had now apparently moved on without waiting for a ruling seemed somehow inappropriate, but since there was nothing much to challenge his right to do so, both men sat back and listened as Frankie Box appeared to become more and more unsettled. Vagianni was an experienced witness and there were plenty of easy answers to the question; ordinarily he could have come up with them in his sleep, but he was now so angry with Moran that he was starting to make some elementary mistakes.

"I don't know."

"Well I do. It was you, wasn't it? You and the other policemen bashed him, didn't you?"

"No we didn't."

"Yes you did."

"We didn't."

"You did. You know you did, don't you?"

"We didn't."

"You did."

"I object!"

It went on that way for longer than it should have, with Moran intermittently establishing a point which he would then follow with a tirade of what was little more than crude abuse directed at Vagianni, who became increasingly agitated and unsettled, until the considerable patience of the judge and the prosecutor had been yet again exhausted; at which point Moran would simply move on to another point and repeat the whole exercise. It was rough and highly unpolished stuff, but the members of the press gallery were entertained by it, and the witness quite enraged, while the judge seemed curiously powerless to curtail the whole performance. Moran stepped his way through each of the findings outlined in the medical report, treating each one as a separate peg on which to hang another inflammatory attack on Frank Vagianni, who was so intent on matching the young lawyer's impertinence with his own brand of intimidating response that the overall impression was of a witness defending a vulnerable position in a way that showed him more than capable of threatening behaviour. As the exercise progressed, even the judge, who had at first seemed to be irked by the defence counsel's robust style, seemed to become more interested. By the time Moran cast the doctor's report to one side, Rosenthal was sitting forward on his chair, studying the witness's demeanour.

"So once you'd finished bashing him you verballed him, didn't you?"

"I don't know what you're talking about, Mr Moron."

"That's Moran."

"Whatever."

"You verballed him, didn't you?"

"Don't know what you're on about."

"Well what don't you understand, witness? You know what a verbal is, don't you? It's a police expression referring to the practice of fabricating confessions by suspects, isn't it?"

"No, it's a figment of the imagination of lawyers trying to get their guilty clients out of trouble."

"Whatever it is, it's what you did, isn't it? You fabricated this so-called confession recorded in your notebook, didn't you?"

"Why would I do that?"

"You did, didn't you?"

"No I didn't!"

"Yes you did. You know you did."

"I didn't."

"You did!"

"I object!"

The point was suddenly all over and Moran was on to the next one before Bolster had resumed his seat.

"You say these notes are an accurate record of the conversation with Mr Allen?"

"Absolutely."

"Word perfect?"

"Yep."

"And they record the whole conversation?"

"Every word of it."

"How long after the conversation were they written up?"

"Can't recall really. Within a short time, anyway."

"And you remembered the conversation word perfectly when you came to write the notes?"

"Yep."

"How's that?"

"I got a good memory, that's how."

"Is that so?"

Frank Vagianni returned the lawyer's sceptical glare with a wry smile.

"Well, you read the notes out a few minutes ago in evidence in chief. With your memory you should be able to repeat the whole conversation for us now word perfect, is that right?"

The smile quickly disappeared. Frank Vagianni wanted to cross the courtroom and plant one firmly on the lawyer's chin, and it was all he could do to keep himself in check. As he shifted in his chair and rolled his eyes and shook his head, he looked so volatile that Bolster jumped to his feet.

"Well really, Your Honour, this is a bit unfair in my respectful submission. It's one thing to recall a conversation in the relative calm of a police station – to be asked to recite it under the stressful conditions that pertain in court is quite a different exercise."

Moran was leaning one elbow on the lectern, eyeing Bolster with an insolent snarl.

"If my learned friend wants to help Mr Vagianni with his evidence, why doesn't he just jump into the witness box with him?"

It was a comment so grossly disrespectful of the Deputy Director of Prosecutions that it delighted the press gallery, while everyone at the Crown end of the bar table recoiled in horror. Mr Bolster QC was stuttering in search of a response. Judge Rosenthal was frowning angrily and looked about to intervene when Frank Vagianni stepped in.

"No, actually now I think about it, I wrote the notes contemporaneously."

"Contemporaneously?"

"Yeah."

The judge and the Deputy Director both looked a little miffed, as though they felt they had been ignored again, but the cross-examination rolled on regardless.

"So did the accused sign the notes when you finished writing them?"

"Nup."

"The notes are unsigned?"

"No they're not."

"The accused didn't sign them to confirm their accuracy?"

"No, but I signed them, and so did Sergeant Keliher."

"Why didn't the accused sign them?"

"He jacked up when he realised he'd put himself in."

"But you didn't even ask him to sign them?"

"Yes I did."

"Well where's that in the notes?"

Frank Vagianni looked down at the notes and back again. The set of his jaw suggested extreme anger, and he glared back at the lawyer with a look that confirmed it. His eyes darted back and forth to the notebook several times before he came up with an answer.

"Says right there we tried to question him further but he declined."

"Doesn't say anything about asking him to sign the notes."

"Well I did and he declined."

"Sure?"

"Yeah."

"Positive?"

"Yeah."

"You just omitted to write that down."

"No, that's what's meant by what I wrote."

Frankie was poking the notebook with one stubby finger.

"Yeah? Let's see that notebook, witness."

Moran was not even looking at the witness. He had one hand extended in the general direction of the box while he scanned his notes on the lectern. There was something so arrogant and demanding about his stance that Frank Vagianni would have preferred to throw the notebook at him. As the bailiff delivered it politely to Moran, the lawyer curled his lip and held it up with two fingers, as though he might catch something from it.

"Why is this taped up, witness?"

"The pages that are relevant to this investigation are available for inspection. The rest of the notebook has been covered over and taped up."

The pages preceding and following the notes of the conversation were bound together and covered with brown paper and adhesive tape, in order to maintain their confidentiality. It was a standard procedure, followed almost invariably in such proceedings, and no one could recall it ever being challenged. But the young lawyer didn't seem to understand all that. The witness had barely completed his answer as Moran commenced to tear away the tape, causing an explosive rattling of chairs at the far end of the bar table as Bolster leapt to his feet.

"Your Honour, I object!"

Vagianni had been waiting for a chance to jump onto the front foot and he now barked at the lawyer with renewed authority.

"Those notes contain confidential police information which is not for public consumption!"

"Yes, thank you, Mr Moran!" Rosenthal stepped in, eager to control this unpredictable young man. "I don't think it's appropriate that any irrelevant material be unsealed."

"Well I don't concede that it is irrelevant, Your Honour."

For the first time since the circus had begun, Moran was standing resolute and upright at the bar table with both hands anchored firmly to the lectern in an orderly fashion, looking both respectful and determined. He waited quietly for Rosenthal's response.

"As I understand it, Mr Moran, that's what the witness has said. Is that the position, witness – that the covered material is not relevant to this trial?"

"Yes, Your Honour."

"Yes, well there you are, Mr Moran, that's as I had understood the evidence."

"But I don't concede that it's correct, Your Honour."

"Well, the Crown's not relying on anything other than the conversation in the open notes. That's right is it, Mr Bolster?"

"Yes, Your Honour." The smug look on Bolster's face attested to his view that the young solicitor was way out of his depth. "The other notes simply have no relevance to these proceedings."

"In my submission they are relevant, Your Honour, whether or not the Crown relies on them." The histrionics and the posturing had finished for the time being and Moran now looked a serious lawyer seeking to advance a structured argument. "They assist to confirm the timing of when the notes of the alleged confession were written in the notebook. The officer claims the notes were written contemporaneously with the interview, which took place on the twenty-third of January this year, 1983. By looking at the dates of the entries in the notebook that precede and follow the relevant notes, one might better determine whether the notes were in fact written at the time and date alleged. The defence has a legitimate forensic purpose in determining that issue, and therefore in accordance with accepted principles it is appropriate that the whole notebook be available for inspection."

It was a serious argument and it soon had Bolster, his junior Peter Dorrington and their instructing solicitor Mr Burrows frantically paging through texts and scurrying back and forth to the court library for the relevant case law, as Moran proceeded to expand upon his argument with detailed reference to supporting High Court authority. His method was concise, accurate and effective, his understanding of the legal principles clear-minded and precise. For the first time since the voir dire had begun, Peter Rosenthal felt comfortable, considering and dissecting established legal principle advanced in a sensible, dispassionate fashion. The questions that he posed to the defence counsel were answered with no embellishment or misinterpretation of judicial statements, just factual and reasoned comment on the applicable authorities. As the discussion proceeded Rosenthal found himself drawn irresistibly to the defence position and ultimately agreed that it was appropriate that the sealed portions of the notebook be inspected, although initially only by himself, to establish whether the defence might have a legitimate interest in seeing the rest of the notes.

"The notes immediately preceding this interview are dated the twenty-second of January this year," Rosenthal announced as soon as he had removed the first seal.

So far so good. Frankie Box was trying to remember what jobs he had written up in the second half of the notebook as the judge removed the second seal and looked quizzically at the pages that followed the Allen interview.

"Yes," he said eventually. "I'll allow the defence access to the notebook."

The bailiff dutifully delivered the notebook into the waiting hands of Edwin C. Moran. As soon as Eddie had scanned the pages, he reverted to his rabid self.

"Sixteenth of November last year, Mr Vagina. You're a bit ahead of your time, aren't you?"

"That's Vagianni."

"You're a bit ahead of your time, aren't you?"

"I don't know what you're talking about."

"Don't you? Well I'll tell you what I'm talking about. How is it that a conversation that supposedly took place in November last year appears in your notebook after a conversation that you claim occurred more than eight weeks later?"

"I was probably just a bit slow writing them up that's all."

"What?"

"I obviously didn't write the conversation up until much later."

"Are you serious, Detective? Surely you're not serious?"

"Yes I am. I'm deadly serious."

"Witness, the November notes start: 'As we spoke I recorded the defendant's answers in my official police notebook.' It purports to be a contemporaneous record of the conversation."

Vagianni looked like he had just regurgitated a bitter mouthful of last night's bourbon. He badly wanted to be rid of this obnoxious lawyer.

"Well, I don't know, I must have just written them out of sequence somehow."

"What? How could you do that?"

"Yeah, I think that's what I done. I just left a gap and wrote that November stuff towards the back of the notebook."

"Are you serious?"

"Yeah."

"You can't be."

"I am."

"Why would you do that?"

"I felt like it, that's why."

"Are you serious?"

"Yeah."

"You can't be, witness. You can't possibly be serious."

"Yeah well I am, so learn to live with it."

"You seriously expect us to believe that story, do you?"

"Yeah I do."

"You can't possibly think that anyone would believe that drivel."

"Gee, well I'd be bitterly disappointed if you didn't, Mr Moron."

"Is there something wrong with you, witness?"

"There'll be something wrong with you if I come over there!"

"Is that right?"

"Too bloody right it is!"

"Your Honour, I object!"

\*   \*   \*

Bill Keliher had been sitting in the corridor outside the courtroom for what felt like an inordinately long time. Morrie and the other boys had started up a game of euchre in the witness room; Bill was scheduled to be second witness in the voir dire, so there hadn't seemed to be much point dealing him a hand. But as the morning disappeared and the clock started ticking down towards the luncheon break, Bill had to wonder what was taking all the time. Theirs was a relatively simple piece of evidence, which Bill had rehearsed so many times he could say it in his sleep. The defence would challenge the notes as a fabrication because they weren't signed by the accused, but how long could that take? Everyone expected they would allege Allen had been belted; but again, how many different ways could you say that? What was taking Frankie so much time?

When the door finally opened, Frank came out grinding his back teeth and muttering obscenities. Bill wanted to ask him what was going on, but the bailiff was standing at the doorway awaiting the next witness, and in any event Frankie looked temporarily incapable of any coherent response. As they passed in the corridor he growled and shook his head in such an angry fashion that Bill felt a little flutter in his stomach. He steeled himself for what he felt sure would be a hostile reception.

\*   \*   \*

"Yes, just a couple of matters, Sergeant," Moran commenced politely once the short evidence in chief was over. "Firstly, these notes. Do they accurately record the conversation?"

"Yes."

"The whole conversation?"

"Yes."

"And you were present throughout?"

"Yes."

"Whenever Detective Vagianni was with Mr Allen, you were present?"

"Yes."

"And Vagianni faithfully recorded every question and every answer?"

"Yes."

"Except at the end where the notes simply say, 'We sought to question him further but he declined to answer any further questions.'"

"Yeah, well that was just something like 'Are you willing to answer any further questions?' and Allen said no he wasn't, so we didn't bother writing that down verbatim."

"But that's all it was, just 'Are you willing to answer any further questions?', answer 'No'. That was it?"

"Yeah, pretty much."

"And otherwise everything was absolutely accurately recorded?"

"Yeah, that's right."

"Vagianni didn't ask the accused if he wanted to read the notes, or sign them to verify their accuracy?"

Bill Keliher sensed trouble, but there was nowhere he could think to hide. He held the notes in front of him wondering what the right answer was.

"No, it doesn't look like he did really, no."

"Did you?"

"No, I didn't."

"Why not?"

"Pardon?"

"Why not? Why didn't you ask him to verify the notes of the conversation?"

"How do you mean?"

Suddenly, without warning, the rabid dog was off his chain again. Moran slammed his brief folder onto the bar table and boomed at the witness.

"How do I mean? Are you kidding, witness? How do I mean! You get a confession to a crime that's been unsolved for nearly twenty years and all you've got to prove it is some handwritten notes, and you don't even ask the suspect to confirm their accuracy! That just can't be right, can it? Why didn't you ask him to verify the notes?"

"I don't know really."

"Yes you do!"

"No, I don't think I do."

"You do, witness! Don't lie! You know very well the reason you didn't ask Allen to read those notes! You didn't ask him because you knew he wouldn't verify them because they were nothing but a complete fabrication!"

"They're not a fabrication."

"Yes they are! They're rubbish!"

"No they're not."

"Pure drivel, aren't they?"

"No."

"Nothing but complete swill!"

"Well, I must object, Your Honour." Bolster's voice was tentative, but Moran had been building such a head of steam that it was time to intervene and say something, no matter what it was. "I'm not sure that any of this is relevant in the current voir dire proceedings. I can see how it might bear on the jury's determination of whether the accused confessed to the crime, but how does it relate to the issue of whether the confession was voluntary?"

"It doesn't," snarled Moran, turning a page of his notes as though he had almost worked the rage out of his system. "Mr Keliher, there's just one more thing I want to ask you. You were aware at the time you interviewed Mr Allen that police had lifted latent fingerprints from the letter and envelope that were sent to Mr and Mrs McCabe in February 1966, weren't you?"

"Yes."

"The handwriting on the letter was identified by the parents as Michael McCabe's, wasn't it?"

"That was their strong belief, yes."

"If someone's prints were found to be on that letter, that would be a pretty damning piece of evidence, wouldn't it?"

"Yeah, I think so."

"Well, you did a print comparison against Mr Allen's fingerprints, didn't you?"

"That's right."

"And they matched the latents on the envelope."

"That's right."

"So Allen's prints were on the envelope."

"Yes, they were."

"But they weren't on the letter, were they?"

"No, we haven't got a positive match-up for the letter yet."

Moran closed his folder on the lectern and paused briefly for effect.

"Then why did you tell Mr Allen that they were?"

"Pardon?"

"Why did you tell the accused his prints had been discovered on the letter?"

"Well, I meant the envelope the letter came in."

"But that's not what you said, is it?"

Bill Keliher was fumbling with the notebook. "I'm not sure. I think I said the envelope, didn't I?"

"No you didn't, witness. According to your evidence, you told him that his prints were on the letter."

"Did I?"

"Yes you did, witness. And that, I suggest, is a very significant departure from the truth." Moran looked up at Rosenthal and paused briefly while the judge soaked up the point. Once he was sure he had, the young lawyer added, "I have no further questions for this witness."

*　*　*

"Confessional evidence can constitute proof of the highest calibre in a criminal trial." Peter Rosenthal had a troubled look on his face. Every eye in the hushed courtroom was upon him, waiting for his findings on the issues that had been raised in the voir dire over the past two days. The journalists were busily scribbling in their notebooks, hoping for a sensation that might be tomorrow's story. At the back of the court, the police were sitting forward on their seats, anticipating every word. Mark Bolster QC and the prosecution team were huddled in together at the bar table as though they were trying to pack a scrum. In the dock, the accused Robert Allen sat bolt upright, his face expressionless as usual, while in front of him his lawyer was hunched over, chewing gum and bouncing one foot below the table.

"A free and voluntary admission of guilt by an accused person is a strong statement against interest, capable of constituting proof beyond a reasonable doubt. However, a confession will be excluded from the purview of the jury where it is found to have been involuntarily obtained, or induced by some behaviour so improper or so unlawful as to call for its exclusion as a matter of fairness to the accused. Unless such circumstances are demonstrated, the evidence must go before the jury whereupon it is a matter for the members of the jury to decide whether they are each satisfied on that evidence to the requisite standard.

"In this case, the defence claims that the accused was beaten by police such that if the confession was made, which is denied, it cannot be said to be voluntary, and must therefore be excluded. At this stage of the proceedings, the onus of proving voluntariness is on the prosecution and the standard required is proof on the balance of probabilities. That is, the prosecution must prove that it is more probable than not that the accused admitted his guilt voluntarily. In my view, the prosecution has discharged that onus to the requisite standard.

"The police officers who interviewed the accused and dealt with him at the Tweed Heads police station on the twenty-third of January this year all gave evidence that the accused was well treated at all times. Detectives Keliher and Vagianni swore that the challenged conversation occurred spontaneously, and certainly without any officer having in any way assaulted or manhandled the accused. Each of the police officers was extensively and at times vigorously cross-examined about the events surrounding the confession. Neither was shaken from his story that the admissions were made voluntarily and without any assault or other misbehaviour by police.

"I accept the defence evidence led from Dr Robert Elms, a general medical practitioner practising in Coolangatta. Dr Elms gave evidence that on the afternoon of the twenty-fourth of January he examined the accused at the Tweed Heads watch-house and found him to have recently sustained injuries which in the doctor's opinion were consistent with a moderately heavy beating. As I have said, I have no hesitation in accepting Dr Elms' evidence in that regard. However, each of the detectives who dealt with the accused on the twenty-third of January has sworn that he bore no signs of any injury whatsoever when he left the Tweed Heads police station on the evening of that day. Evidence was called from watch-house staff to the effect that no injuries were noted on the accused when he was received at the watch-house and no complaint was made by the accused. In the circumstances, I am left to conclude that when the accused was lodged in the watch-house he did not have the injuries which Dr Elms discovered on examination the following day. The watch-house book which was produced and tendered in these proceedings shows that there were a number of other inmates in the watch-house throughout the evening of the twenty-third of January and the morning of the twenty-fourth. None of those inmates was called to give evidence but it seems to me at least possible that the accused was assaulted by one of them after he was lodged in the watch-house by the arresting police officers. Given the nature of the charge faced by the accused, it is not inconceivable that one or more of those inmates may have harboured animosity towards him. In any event, I consider the possibility that the accused was assaulted in the watch-house far more likely than the proposition advanced by the defence that trained police officers, sworn to uphold the law, acted in flagrant contravention of the law to beat a confession out of the accused and then conspired to cover up the fact by giving perjured evidence in these proceedings."

Mark Bolster QC could feel the tension starting to drain out of his chest. Defence counsel could rant and rave and jump up and down all he liked about bashings and unsigned notes and whatever else – once the jury heard that Allen was right there when the McCabe kids disappeared, and that his fingerprints had showed up on the letter sent to the parents five weeks later, they wouldn't have a moment's doubt about the notebook evidence, and they'd be falling over each other to get back in to bring down that guilty verdict. If Allen decided to give evidence about the bashing it would make it all the worse for him; the Crown would get leave to cross-examine him about his criminal history and then everything the jury were suspecting about him would be confirmed in all its glory. Gross indecency, offensive behaviour in a public place, and indecent dealing – all charges that to the jury would mean just one thing: Allen was precisely the sort of pervert who would snatch two kids. From that point nothing would turn this case around in favour of Robert Allen. Certainly nothing his impertinent young lawyer was ever likely to do or say. Mark Bolster had been around a long time and he had done a lot of jury trials. He could see that young Moran had some ability, but he could also see that his abrasive manner was going to get his client nowhere with a jury, especially in a case like this. Next to Robert Allen, Edwin Moran was going to be the most hated man in that courtroom. In fact, from what Bolster had seen of his performance so far, it was possible Moran might just edge his client out. He certainly wasn't going to win any popularity contests, and he was about as likely to get Allen a sympathy verdict as he was a babysitting job.

The confession was central to the prosecution; without it there was no chance to get any of the Garner–Willet connection in, and the fingerprints were way too thin to stand on their own. Moran would argue that the evidence was such that no properly instructed jury could be satisfied of the accused's guilt beyond a reasonable doubt, and Bolster would have a difficult time resisting such a challenge.

But now it sounded like Rosenthal wasn't going to buy the induced-confession argument. And that meant it was all over bar the shouting.

"Thus, as I have said, I am of the view that the prosecution has satisfied the onus which it bears to demonstrate voluntariness on the balance of probabilities. I therefore reject the defence application to have the alleged confession excluded from the jury's consideration as involuntary."

Bill Keliher could hear Vince Donnelly beside him breathing out a long deep sigh. He had seen the McCabe case eat away at Vince all these years. It had him beaten. Bill knew that, and he figured that Vince knew it too, even though he would never admit it, not even to himself. Otherwise he wouldn't have gone with Frankie's notebook, not in a million years. They all knew they had the right man, and finally their frustration had turned to desperation.

Frank Vagianni looked at Bill through the corner of his eye and flicked a sneaky wink. Once they got the notebook past the judge, they were home and hosed. The jury wasn't going to be the least bit interested in giving a grub like Allen the benefit of any doubt, and they weren't likely to give a square root that the coppers might have touched him up to get a confession. Frank looked so happy with himself that Bill couldn't help but smile a little, and he bowed his head to hide it. This was it. They were coming home with a wet sail.

"I turn now to the exercise of discretion."

Vince Donnelly's eyes bounced open and peered up at the judge through a furrowed brow. Suddenly the tension had returned.

"Where the defence can demonstrate on the balance of probabilities that a confession or admission of guilt has been obtained by police through some behaviour which is so illegal, improper or inappropriate as to render it unfair to the accused to allow the prosecution to rely upon it, then a trial judge should exercise his discretion to exclude the evidence from the jury's consideration. It is in this respect that the evidence has caused me particular concern."

The detectives lined across the back row of the public gallery were all staring at the judge, as if their concentration alone could determine every measured phrase he articulated.

"It is common ground that the admissions made by the accused to police at the Tweed Heads police station on the twenty-third of January this year were immediately preceded by a statement made by Detective Keliher to the effect that the accused's fingerprints had been found on a letter sent to the parents of the missing children. According to the evidence of both Detective Keliher and Detective Vagianni, the accused asked them why they were hassling him and Keliher replied, 'Because your fingerprints were positively identified on the letter that was sent to the parents of the children.' That statement was untrue. Fingerprints of the accused were found on the envelope in which the letter was enclosed, but not on the letter itself. The discrepancy was of course a most significant one, since the presence of the accused's fingerprints on the letter would have been very much more inculpatory of him than was the true situation. In making the statement, Detective Keliher clearly intended to impress upon the accused that the case against him was a compelling one. In so doing he misstated the facts in a way which was so fundamental and crucial that one must conclude that he thereby intended to mislead the accused or, on the construction most favourable to him, made the statement careless of whether he thereby misled the accused or not. In either event, it is in my view clear from the evidence that it was that misstatement that induced the accused to make the admissions relied upon by the Crown."

Vince Donnelly didn't wait to hear the judge's ruling. He rose slowly and quietly to his feet and made his way past the others to the courtroom door. Bill could see his face, drawn and pale, as he shuffled past them.

"In the circumstances, I am of the view that it would be unfair to the accused to allow the prosecution to rely upon the alleged admissions. I therefore allow the application and in the exercise of my discretion I exclude the evidence of alleged admissions made to Detectives Keliher and Vagianni."

Mark Bolster QC was ashen-faced as he rose to his feet. Peter Dorrington and Mr Burrows were both whispering feverishly at him and no sooner was he upright than he bent down again to get a closer earful.

"Would Your Honour pardon me a moment?" he flustered before stooping once again, and eventually straightened up to add, "I wonder if Your Honour would allow the Crown a brief adjournment to consider its position?"

The conference that ensued went on for almost an hour, but its result was a foregone conclusion. No matter how much any of the police wanted to fight on, without the confessional material the Crown had no case. Mr Bolster QC explained it in as many ways and as diplomatically as he could, but it all added up to the same proposition: if they proceeded with the case they would lose. Allen would be acquitted. At the close of the prosecution case the defence would eventually apply for a 'no case' ruling and the judge would give it to them; he would have to, because without the confession there was no case. And if he ruled that way, he would have to direct the jury to acquit the accused, which meant that Allen could never again be tried for the offence. Once an acquittal had been entered, that was it. He couldn't be brought back again. The alternative was for the Crown to discontinue the proceedings, ask for the return of the indictment and endorse it nolle prosequi, thus ending the trial there and then but leaving the way open to recharge Allen if and when new evidence became available.

The mention of new evidence to the detectives sitting in the conference room was like talk of planning a major new offensive to battle-wearied troops. But there was no alternative. When the prosecution team returned to the courtroom, the detectives were conspicuous by their absence.

*   *   *

The young man with the odd-looking glasses and unruly hair was standing on the steps of the courthouse surrounded by cameramen and journalists. On the television screen he looked extremely thin, but he moved and swaggered in a robust way that made him seem quite powerful.

"My client has maintained his innocence from day one. Day one!"

As Faye stared blankly at the television screen, her fingers were idly running over the handful of coins cupped loosely in her palms. They were cool, pleasantly round, and somehow comforting. She had retrieved them days ago from the sealed-up box in her old suitcase in the spare room, and now, for how long she was not quite certain, she had sat holding them, caressing them, remembering.

"Today's decision is nothing less than an absolute confirmation of Robert Allen's presumed innocence of any wrongdoing whatsoever!"

The lawyer was poking an accusing finger at the camera. He looked angry and determined. None of it meant anything to Faye. She looked down at her hands. A florin, some shillings, two threepences, a halfpenny, three sixpences, and two brown pennies. Worn, familiar. Old friends from another lifetime. She had put them all aside for her beautiful children. To help them to remember. She had told herself that she would give them to her children one day. And she would, one day. But not today.

"If the police really are interested in solving the McCabe case, then the first thing they need to do is acknowledge that Robert Allen is not the culprit.

There's absolutely no credible evidence that he was in any way involved. And that means the real culprit is still out there!"

The moment he stopped talking the lawyer was besieged by voices competing for attention.

"But isn't it true that there is nothing to stop the police from recharging your client?"

He was snarling now, glaring at someone off-camera. "Mate, are you listening to anything I've been saying? Are you keeping up with all this or what? Robert Allen has been discharged, all right? Get over it! The question you need to ask is not whether my client can be recharged but who really did kidnap the McCabe children."

Suddenly the television screen had changed, and there they were. The voiceover was talking about 'the McCabe children', which had become a cold and distant term that referred to a heinous crime, an unsolved mystery, a police investigation – concepts that were clinical, impersonal. Ideas that were comfortable, manageable. The female voice was reciting the forgotten facts of the case, but Faye didn't hear them. She was looking at the photograph on the screen, the old black and white snapshot of the McCabe children. She was looking at the faces of her children. She was remembering.

It was a warm day in September. One of those spring days in the Northern Rivers when the summer haze makes an appearance just to remind you that it's on its way. She remembered looking out along the Point Road all the way to Bonny Point. It was so clear you could see the pandanus leaves rustling on the headland. It was such a pretty day that she couldn't even try to keep the kids out of the water. Barry was away as usual, but she soon had the inflatable pool out on the front lawn and was puffing away at it as the kids played with the garden hose.

Bill was a magnificent-looking man in those days. She could still see him jogging up the Point Road, a blue navvy singlet stretched across his barrel chest, his broad shoulders swathed in perspiration. She had felt embarrassed, perhaps a little guilty that part of her had thought to set the pool up here in the front yard in the hope that she would see him. As he came nearer, his suntanned freckled face drew into a broad smile and then a laugh which put her instantly at ease.

"You look like you're hard at it, Mrs McCabe."

She pinched the mouthpiece and sat back, trying to look as composed as possible as she brushed a lick of hair up off her forehead.

"I'd say I've still a bit more puff than you, Constable Keliher."

He returned a cheeky grin that made her blush, and then in one leap bounded across the fence.

"Well, let's see, shall we."

He was standing over her as she half sprawled on the grass, his naked legs and shoulders glistening with sweat. She looked up at him and felt her pulse quicken. Suddenly, without warning, she surprised herself with a seductive little half-smile. Bill grinned broadly and then dropped to his knees and placed his big hand over hers.

"Let's have a go at this thing."

He soon had the pool in both hands and was blowing to inflate it, interrupted only by the need to answer Michael's non-stop questions, and to duck Catherine's erratic waving of the garden hose. Faye had repaired to the house and made him up a sandwich and a lemonade, just to thank him for his kindness. As she watched him dodging Catherine and fielding Michael's questions on the front lawn, she blushed to think about that half-smile. There had been something happening between them for a long time now. Where had it come from? She was a married woman. It was something that she hadn't known was in her and she had been shocked by it, and at the same time excited. The sound of his easy laughter as he avoided the hose floated through the window and made her smile.

He had stayed for an hour or more, playing with the children, and then they had sat together on the front verandah, talking openly and warmly, like good friends. And after he left she had sat and thought about him and sometimes smiled as she remembered how charming he had been. She sipped lemonade and watched the children running around the pool, in and out, splashing and giggling. And as she sat and watched her happy children playing in the front yard of their home, she told herself that her children were the only thing that mattered in her life, and nothing should ever interfere with that. She was a married woman and she had a family. She had two beautiful children whom she loved more than life itself. She would never do anything that would put their happiness in jeopardy.

As the afternoon sun began to throw long shadows across the front yard, Faye rounded up the children, wrapped them in towels and deposited them with milk and biscuits on the back stairs in the fading warmth of the western sun. It had been a good day. Michael had his arm around his baby sister and was patiently instructing her on how to dunk her biscuit in the milk. Ordinarily Faye was not a camera person, but she just had to catch this moment.

"Say cheese!"

"Cheese!"

They were both looking at their mother, grinning broadly with smiles that said that they were home and safe and happy, and they always would be.

And now, in the small living room of her comfortable unit overlooking Manly beach, their mother was looking back at them, framed on the television screen. They were still her perfect, lovely children. Just as she remembered them. Just as they would always be. She looked at their grinning faces and she smiled, a sad inconsolable smile. As her vision blurred beneath her tears she murmured just one word:

"Sweethearts."

The picture on the television changed, and Michael and Catherine McCabe were gone.

# CHAPTER SEVEN

Bill had had too much to drink that night. But then, why shouldn't he? He was fifty-seven years of age, he had no wife to tell him what to do, and no one to impress. He had the night off work, there was nothing on TV, and he'd had a shit of a day – 29 December 1995. Thirty years to the day.

He sat in his poky little one-bedroom flat in Surry Hills and poured himself another Scotch. The grave had piqued their interest for a while, but after all that digging they'd come up with nothing more than the half-decomposed remains of a mangy old dog. Herbert Montgomery may well have been haunted by the memory of the McCabe case. But then he wasn't the only one.

When Bill had got back to the station around midday, his desk was littered with a daunting pile of messages deposited by the bemused clerks who had been fielding calls all day. They were too young to understand the significance of the anniversary; all they knew was that the calls were strange, and the callers stranger, throwing up weird theories about a piece of ancient history. The day's phone notes were stacked on top of those that had been coming in all week in the lead-up to the anniversary, and when Bill saw them he realised why he had decided to head off to the hills at daybreak. With one hand he scooped up roughly half of them and held them out to Wally.

"Split you."

Wally took them dutifully and turned to leave as the young clerk leaned in through the door and added one to Bill's pile.

"Oh, there was one more," she quipped. "Called herself Catherine McCabe. But she didn't leave a return number."

As Bill poured himself another Scotch, he thought about how tired he was of the nightmare that came back into his life every year. His sons had never known an entire Christmas with their father at home. He mostly chose to work the Christmas–New Year stretch; it was the silly season for anyone connected with the McCabe job, and there were always leads to follow up. And even when he was at home his mind had been somewhere else.

It had been no life for Joan. They first met when he had come back to Sydney, trying to forget and just be a young bloke again. Joan had helped him. She was what he'd needed then. She was brash and up-front and she knew exactly what she wanted. She overwhelmed the big country boy with her brazen personality and her voluptuous, insatiable body, and he immersed himself in both. It still excited him to think about the first time he had bunned her, spread-eagled across the bonnet of a police car in the car park at headquarters. She had just hitched up her skirt and perched her bum up on the bonnet and pulled him on. She was a wild young thing. Who would ever have thought that they'd tie the knot? They'd done well enough together, all things considered. She'd been a good mum to the boys and she'd looked after all Bill's needs. But Bill wasn't the bloke for Joan, if one existed. She was driven and she needed more than Bill would ever have to give her. Her dalliances had started early in the marriage, and although he played the outraged husband well, the truth was that when they were sliding on each other's naked flesh in the darkness, his fingers were always on another body and his mouth was kissing other lips. It all would have ended bitterly but for her illness. That had forced them to rethink things. By the time the doctors had finally given her the all-clear, they both understood how fond they were of one another and how much they owed each other, and that they weren't meant to be together. Joan went to university and found herself a new life and a new man, and Bill was glad. And now he was alone again.

Vince Donnelly had retired in eighty-four. The Robert Allen trial had more or less finished him. He hung around to cope with all the post mortems that the department had insisted on, but ultimately it was clear that even if Allen was right for it they didn't have the goods on him. Everything that could be done was done: every known associate was spoken to, every lead was covered, all the clues revisited and re-evaluated. If there was something on Allen, they just couldn't find it. And all that did was confirm that Vince Donnelly had fucked up big-time. After a lifetime in the force and a career that had made him a living legend as a police investigator, old Vince bowed out a loser, beaten by the McCabe case. He died not more than five years later.

And so the file had landed in the waiting arms of Bill Keliher, the only one who'd been there from the start. Bill wasn't giving up. He would die with this one if he had to. He had no choice.

*"Where you off to, kids?"*

*"We're going to the beach."*

*"Hop in. I'll give youse a lift."*

Bill Keliher threw back his head and drained the glass. There was so much he wished he could change. The whisky swirled around inside him and numbed his brain. He could see Faye standing on the verandah of the hall, bathed in the swinging yellow light of a single bulb that swayed gently overhead, waved by the summer-evening breezes, back and forward. Her dress was fluttering lightly in the warm air, pressed against her abdomen and thighs, accentuating every feature of her body.

"Sorry, Faye. Sarge says he's going to have to sleep it off in the lock-up. You can pick him up tomorrow morning."

It wasn't the first time Barry McCabe had got himself into a dust-up at the local hall. As usual, he and the others had started drinking pretty early and by the time the meals came out they were in no mood for eating. By ten o'clock most of them were looking the worse for wear and by eleven they had all stopped making much sense. Bill Keliher had watched them standing round the keg, guffawing, and arguing about sport, and trading fishing stories, and he had a fair idea where things might end up. Deep down he hoped they would, and they did. Someone who'd been getting on someone else's nerves shoved someone else and spilled his beer as well as someone else's, and from there it erupted and kept going until the police finally broke it up, by which time the sergeant had copped one on the chin, and Barry McCabe and a couple of others were lying about in a state of semiconsciousness. It meant that Bill's social evening was interrupted and by the time he got back to the hall most of the single girls were gone, but that didn't worry him. He hadn't come there to see them.

"I'll walk you home if you like."

She'd left the kids next door with Mrs Marchant so she and Barry could go to the parish ball, and now she was alone for the night. They both knew what was going on. It had been happening for months, and the harder he tried to stop it the more she was there in his thoughts. He would sometimes jog along the Point Road on his morning off in the hope that he would see her walking to the shops, and if he timed it wrong he would turn at Loxton Park and run back again, and back and forth, until he was exhausted, and eventually he would come upon her quite by accident and exchange pleasantries, and then he'd walk with her, and they would talk and she would laugh that beautiful infectious laugh of hers. She felt the same way as he did; he could see it in her eyes when they 'chanced' upon each other in the street, or she came into the station to enquire about lost property or the state of the roads. He could see it now as she stood beneath the swaying yellow light.

"I'd like that."

They walked back along the Old Point Road and when they got to the lookout they sat down together on the headland and watched the big yellow moon dancing on the waters off beyond the breakers, out on the horizon. And Faye told him all about herself: how she had grown up in the Bay; how she always dreamed of leaving but knew she never would; how she and her friend Trudy had made plans to go one day, to London maybe, or even Paris. She had met Barry at age seventeen, and Trudy had sailed for London three weeks after they got married right there in Brighton Bay. Trudy still wrote from time to time, last time when she was back in London working for an advertising company. It all sounded so exciting. She'd even seen the Beatles.

"I know I'll never get there now." Faye arched her slender eyebrows and smiled softly. "And that's okay I guess." Even in the moonlight he could see the wistful yearning in her eyes as she looked out to the horizon. "It's just that sometimes I think that life could have been so different."

There was something in the moment that moved him. He reached across and touched her lightly on the cheek, and her eyes closed gently. He turned her face to his and smelt the fragrance of her as their lips touched for a moment and then parted and then came together tenderly. As he held her in his arms for the first time, it felt so right that all the doubt and the guilt were instantly swept aside.

And even now, sitting in the lounge room of his Surry Hills apartment, drinking Scotch from a chipped beer glass, Bill Keliher could smell the perfume on her neck and ears and shoulders. He sat completely still and closed his eyes and breathed her in. How many times had he woken from erotic dreams, still stiff, his heart quickened by the thrill of it, surprised to realise that it was she who had so pleasantly disturbed his sleep? She whom he had touched so briefly, she who had lost so much, she who had suffered so. And the guilt sickened him and soured him so that he could no longer feel aroused, only ashamed.

The shrill ring of the telephone burst into Bill's consciousness, wrenching him back to the here and now. He put the glass down on the coffee table and groaned to his feet, cursing aloud the insistent ringing. As he snatched up the receiver he heard his voice gruffer than he had intended it to be.

"Hello?"

There was a hollow silence on the line, and Bill felt it straight away. Someone was there.

"Is that you, Constable Keliher?" It was a thin, childlike whisper.

He hadn't been called 'constable' in nearly thirty years.

"What?"

There was another silence.

"Hello?"

"I still remember you."

"Who is this?"

"It's Catherine McCabe. Don't you remember?"

Bill Keliher had a sinking feeling in his chest. It was a sudden emptiness, not yet panicked as fear so often was, but dark and foreboding and filled with dread.

"What are you talking about?"

"I remember you." It was a child's voice, innocent and unaffected. "You drove us to the beach in your police car."

The statement struck him like a pick handle to the face. No one knew that. No one.

"Who are you? Who told you that?"

"I want to go home, Constable." It was soft, pleading, pathetic. "Please take me home."

Suddenly the panic rushed in, unheralded and screaming.

"You bloody sick bitch! Who are you? What do you want from me?"

The blood in his eyes and ears was set to explode and his chest and throat were heaving wildly. He saw nothing and knew nothing, and he punched short, sharp grunts into the silence on the other end of the phone. Then he stopped, his breath suspended, listening. Think. Observe. Detect. What was happening? What did he hear? What should he ask?

Now there was a new sound on the line. Still faint, unclear. A soft gurgling sound. Weeping? A child weeping? Bill Keliher was frozen in the pain of his memories and his guilt. He listened silently to the whimper of a small child on the line, and his big eyes filled with tears and gently closed. Finally the demons had come to meet him face to face.

\* \* \*

"Jesus mate, you look like you've seen a ghost!"

Morrie Fleet never changed. He was always trying to take the mickey out of someone. He'd jumped the force in ninety-two and scored himself a plum job with Telecom in charge of its investigations branch, and he was doing pretty well. He had himself a pretty secretary and a fancy-looking office and a big desk, but he was still the same old Morrie. That's why Bill knew he could count on him.

"I need a favour, Morrie."

The smile faded on his old friend's lips. He could see that Bill was serious. "Sure, mate. What's the problem?"

"I've been getting calls."

"From who?"

"That's what I want to know."

Bill wasn't saying much. They'd been friends a long time, but being a copper teaches you there's some things you don't need to know, and some things you don't want to tell.

"You want a trace put on?"

"No. They've stopped. I want to get back through the records. Find out who was making them."

"You want historical records?"

"Yeah. There were about a half a dozen over two weeks, all to my home. I can give you pretty exact times."

Morrie's old friend Bill Keliher looked haggard, as if he hadn't had much sleep. If he was that fired up about these calls, it meant there was some big trouble on the other end of the line – blackmail maybe, or an irate husband, or someone from the past come back to square things up. All things you could use a mate to help you with.

"What's the secret, Bill?"

Bill set his jaw and shook his head. If he could have told a living soul, Morrie would be it. They'd been together in more scraps and down more gullies hand in hand than anyone he knew. He'd shared his first day at Darlinghurst with Morrie, he'd stood back to back with him at Blacktown when the bikies played up merry hell, and together they'd turned over every bar and brothel in the Cross. There weren't many secrets that he kept from Morrie. But there was one.

"Just a secret, pal, just a secret." He slapped a piece of paper on the desk. "That's the number at my new digs. It's a flat in Surry Hills. The date and approximate time of each call are there as well."

Morrie picked up the paper and skimmed the details.

"Sorry mate, we can't do it."

Bill Keliher's eyes narrowed. "What do you mean you can't do it?"

He was in worse shape than Morrie had thought. Whatever this thing was, it had him by the balls.

"I mean we can't do it. Telecom doesn't keep those kinds of records on incoming calls."

"What?"

The response was loud and belligerent. Anybody else might have taken offence at the tone, but Morrie Fleet had had his share of working in the kitchen when the heat was fairly up. Bill Keliher was under pressure and he needed help.

"Let me run it through the computer, see if they come up as outgoing calls on the records of a known offender. Okay?"

It took Bill a few seconds to process that information in his head. His old friend waited patiently.

"Yeah, okay Morrie. Thanks."

It went without saying that the job was confidential; Morrie would have to handle it himself, and that meant it might take a little time. As it turned out, he got back to Bill sooner than either of them had expected. He didn't say much on the phone but he sounded jumpy, and this was the first time Bill could remember Morrie sounding jumpy. They had to meet; no, it couldn't be in Morrie's office, or the station. Bill didn't like the sound of it.

As he walked along the busy footpath, Bill was turning over all the possibilities. Morrie must have found something in the known-offenders records. So someone was going to try and turn him over. Someone had found out the truth and now they figured it was payday. How did they know? Someone must have seen him. But why hadn't that come out at the time? As he trudged blindly through the crowd, he relived the agony of those first few weeks, waiting for someone to come forward, waiting to be asked for an explanation, to be exposed, discredited, humiliated. Perhaps it was the car. Bill had always worried about the car. Maybe someone had tested the police car.

As soon as he turned into the coffee shop, he spotted Morrie, half obscured behind a menu, looking comically clandestine.

"Well?"

Morrie looked gaunt. He seemed to have something to say but didn't want to say it.

"Bill, I don't know what you've got yourself into here, but I want you to know that if you need help from me you've got it."

Bill didn't have time for any of this shit.

"What's the story, Morrie?"

He had no call to snap at Morrie like that, not in the circumstances, and Morrie wasn't going to cop it.

"Murder's heavy shit, Bill."

"What are you talking about?"

"You know fucking well what I'm talking about!" The two men were face to face and Bill could see the passion in the other's eyes. Morrie was angry, and he was also disappointed. "I'm talking about Bernie Radovic and whoever put a bullet through his brain last week!"

"What?"

The well-known Sydney bookie Bernie Radovic had been found dead in his luxury penthouse on the Gold Coast on 12 January. It was a professional hit, and those who knew Bernie Radovic and the circle he had moved in weren't a bit surprised.

"I don't know anything about that job. They pinched Lenny Fiske for it."

"Yeah, and they're still looking for whoever paid Lenny to get the job done."

Morrie had his nose right out of joint. Bill had come out of the blocks too hard at him. He hadn't meant to, but he had.

"What's that got to do with me?"

Morrie Fleet looked straight into the eyes of his ex-partner, sizing him up. He'd known Bill Keliher in enough tight corners to be able to read him just a little. Bill was looking back at him, searching for an answer. Morrie had no doubt the big bloke was trying hard to hide something, but maybe this wasn't it. He held his gaze as he dropped the answer on the table.

"The calls to your place all came from Radovic. They're on his phone records, every one of them."

It was red-hot news to Bill Keliher, that much was certain. He weighed it once, then twice, then again, and every time he ran it over in his mind it made no sense at all. Morrie waited for a long time before Bill eventually spoke again in a bewildered kind of half-whisper.

"Can you make them disappear?"

It was a big ask from a bloke who wasn't even pretending to put Morrie in the know.

"Possibly."

Bill Keliher grabbed his friend's fat hand and held it tightly.

"Morrie, you've got to trust me on this one." His voice was firm again, unfaltering. "I never had anything to do with Radovic. Someone's trying to do a number on me. It goes a long way back and you don't want to know about it. I don't know what it's got to do with Radovic but I need to find out. And it's not going to help me to be a suspect in a murder blue."

Morrie was embarrassed, sitting in a coffee shop holding hands with an ageing flatfoot. The big bloke was obviously desperate. Morrie had got out of the force to put this sort of stuff behind him. He had another few years to go before he started looking at retirement, and the last thing he needed now was to get himself tied up with something shonky.

"Bill, you know me, mate. I'm no saint. But I . . . "

"You know me too, Morrie." Bill's hand was clamped tight as a vice. "Murder's not my go." He held Morrie's gaze. "Can you make it disappear?"

They'd known each other twenty-five years. They'd been through good times and bad times together, watched each other's kids grow up, and shared the odd beer as their marriages fell apart. They'd had a lot of fun together and a few tears too, and they'd both laid their careers and more on the line more than once to back each other up. They'd done some things that were best left unmentioned and some they both were pretty proud of. Bill Keliher was a good copper and a good man.

"Sure, Bill. Yeah, I can make it disappear."

Bill wrapped his two big paws around Morrie's hand and shook it firmly. "I've got to talk to Lenny Fiske."

"I don't think you'll be doing that, mate. He's got himself a lawyer."

"Yeah? Who?"

"Moran."

# CHAPTER EIGHT

The uniformed police were on the scene within minutes. They'd got the call from a hysterical neighbour downstairs and several all-night revellers at one of the trendy al fresco restaurants in nearby Tedder Avenue. It's not every night you're disturbed in the wee small hours by the sound of automatic pistol fire. Not even in the ritzy cocaine corners of the Gold Coast's flashy Main Beach.

There was shit and disaster everywhere. Before they got to the front security doors, they could already see in the darkness the blobs and spatters of black blood slopped across the pathway. Even at that stage it looked like a murder scene. The clean white tiles and the walls in the common stairwell were dotted with bright crimson spots that led an ugly trail towards the penthouse unit, and at intervals along the way small unidentifiable bits of what looked like human tissue had been thrown or spat onto the floor and walls. The front-door handle to the unit had taken two, maybe three shots from what had to be at least a .45, and the door itself had splintered from the handle. Someone had been real keen to get inside.

"Jesus!"

In life, Bernie Radovic had been no oil painting. He was a big, knuckle-dragging Yugo with a head like a robber's dog. And the bullet that someone had put through his right eye certainly hadn't improved his looks. The fresh-faced constable pushed the front door open and found himself looking at his first real live dead man. The bookie was staring straight back at him through one glazed eye and an empty socket filled with crusted blood and splintered bone. He was slumped back in a squat against the wall, his thick arms draped on either side of him, palms upwards, as if he were still asking the question: What the fuck happened?

On the deep, white carpet was more of whatever it was that had been littered on the stairs, fleshy dabs of blood and spittle, but now mixed with something else that looked like bone perhaps, or maybe plastic.

"Get outside and suck in a couple of deep breaths. And then call CIB and tell them we've got a homicide down here."

The young bloke's face was chalky white, and the last thing his sergeant needed was a fresh chunder in the middle of a murder scene. It wouldn't be the first time. As he followed the black-red dabs along the narrow hallway the sergeant had a sickly feeling there was more to come. He wasn't wrong.

The door to the main bedroom was ajar. The bookie's

girlfriend was still huddled in the corner, curled up in a ball like a little child hiding from the scary things that come out after dark. Her head was slumped into the corner and the sergeant was grateful that he couldn't see her face. Only a mat of singed hair caked in crusted blood and ragged tissue. It wasn't neat, but it was only one shot, put in just behind her ear and up into the brain. The gun held up so close that the scalp was powder-burnt around the wound, a patch of hair blown clean away. Whoever pulled the trigger was a cold bastard who knew just what to do and how to do it.

As he waddled back down the hallway the old sergeant tried to take everything in. Murder scenes were almost always like this – a jigsaw puzzle emptied out onto the kitchen table. You could see the pieces everywhere but nothing seemed to fit together, and nothing made sense. But the longer you looked at it, the more it would. The hallway seemed clean, except for a few small bits of splintered wood scattered on the carpet. No blood. No grubby fingerprints, no scuff marks. The cream-coloured walls were clean, the gloss paint on the skirting boards still glistening, unblemished. Nothing on the cornices or ceiling.

The lounge room was a different story. There the pieces were splayed out in a confusing jumble, challenging the foolhardy and the inexperienced to come play with them. But the old sarge had been around too long for that. He squeezed the flattened notebook from the back pocket of his trousers and started scratching out some notes.

'1.37a.m. 12.1.96. Unit 9, 25 Pacific Avenue, Main Beach. Bernie Radovic.'

The sergeant had no trouble recognising the deceased. Radovic was a Sydney bloke but he was back and forth to Queensland regularly and the coppers kept an eye on him. Even for a high-profile Sydney SP bookmaker he moved in some very dodgy circles. He had too much money for his own good and he liked to splash it around when he came up to his holiday unit on the Gold Coast. When Radovic was in town, you could catch him seven nights a week poncing around the trendy bars and restaurants of Main Beach, shouting drinks and tucker for a tribe of putty-nosed rock apes or bleach-blonde glitterati who looked like they were putting more up their noses than in their mouths. It was no surprise that Radovic had found a sticky end.

The sergeant made a list, starting at the door. Wood fragments and spent cartridges on both sides. The first minute blood spatters on the doorjamb just inside. The damaged ceiling above the entrance way, a gaping hole big enough for some grub to drop straight down from the ceiling cavity into your lap. Blood spots and spatters everywhere, and then a pool, right there in the middle of the room. Someone had bled like a stuck pig there all right, but who? Not the sheila rolled up in the bedroom; her end had been quick, and relatively tidy. The sergeant walked back to the bookie and took a closer look. The only wound he could see was the ugly hole straight through his ugly dial, and he certainly hadn't gone anywhere after that. Someone had spilt claret by the cupful on that carpet, and they hadn't stopped around to give a statement to the coppers.

As the sergeant turned back to the door, some pieces fitted neatly into place. Beside the pool was a patterned smudge, where someone or something had been lying. And then the trail of deep splotches leapt out at you, like footprints in the snow. There amongst them was something red and pink and white, caked in crusted blood. It could have been a little piece of the pet pooch's surprise treat, fresh from the butcher's shop and ready to be buried in the backyard garden. But it wasn't. It was one of those sickening little jigsaw pieces that made part of you say, 'Jesus, I don't want to know.' He squatted down to take a closer look.

It was a piece of something from a human body, about the same size as a book of matches and swathed in a thick red coat of half-coagulated blood. But there was something hard and shiny there. Bone maybe, but not bone. With the end of his biro, the sergeant gently lifted up one gooey corner. Leaning forward, squinting for detail, he could see yellow, black and silver. Two ageing, sculptured teeth, fixed into a plastic denture plate.

＊　　＊　　＊

"Mate, I was just in the wrong place at the wrong time. Dead set."

Eddie Moran had not laid eyes on Lenny Fiske in about four years. The last time they had spoken was at Long Bay Gaol, straight after Lenny had drawn six years for a robbery at Hurstville. But as Eddie watched him now across the narrow desk in the Silverwater Remand Centre, it could have been a hundred years ago. Lenny looked like an old man. With his top dentures gone and his upper lip scarred and mangled, his face was folded up in a grotesque mask, and he spoke with a lisp that would have been laughable had the subject matter not been so serious.

"I run into Radovic down the Broadie Pub one afternoon and he asked me to drop up and have a yarn with him. Said he might have a job for me."

It had taken police no time at all to trace the shattered denture plate found in Bernie Radovic's unit back to Lenny Fiske. And when you moved in Lenny's circles you were never hard to find. The New South Wales police picked him up in a safe house south of Sydney, doped up on grass to kill the pain of a slowly healing bullet wound to his face. He was in Silverwater awaiting extradition back to Queensland on a murder charge.

"Dead set, I didn't knock the bloke."

The .22 slug had gone straight through his top lip and hit the upper denture plate, the deflection splitting his tongue right down the middle. Lenny never had been known for his honesty, but now he really was talking with a forked tongue. The swelling had subsided, but the tear had healed badly, leaving a lumpy ridge of scar tissue that had him struggling with his words.

"I never even seen the sheila at all. Didn't even know she was there."

Lenny's story was simple. He'd responded to Radovic's invitation and gone to see the bookmaker at about nine thirty that night.

"He was already three parts cut. Mate, you know them Yugos. Love their piss."

As Radovic poured the vodkas into Lenny, he explained why he had asked him up. Seemed he had been travelling a little rough at the track, and owed a lot of money to the punters. Someone had put a contract out on him, and he wanted Lenny to stand up for him.

"I'd done a little bit of debt collecting for the bloke, and he knew that I was well respected round the town."

"Collecting from who?"

"Oh, just blokes. It's a while back now, mate. I can't remember names or nothing."

The stone interview rooms at Long Bay Gaol were old and poky, and getting someone's story in those cells had always been an intimate affair. But here at Silverwater the rooms were tall and wide and wooden, so spacious that it seemed like every lie would echo up into the ceilings and sneak out through the walls and windows. Eddie was going to have to let this part of the story grow on him.

"I got full and passed out on the lounge room couch."

According to Lenny he didn't even hear them enter. He woke up to the sound of a gunshot in the lounge room, and there was the bookie slumped against the wall with the shooter standing over him. And then he turned on Lenny and fired. One shot in the face. When Lenny came around he was choking on the blood collecting in his throat. He rolled over on all fours and spat a ball of blood and denture plate out onto the floor.

And then he looked around. It didn't take him any time at all to realise this was no place for Lenny Fiske to be found. The front door had been shot in and there was a gaping hole up in the ceiling. And Bernie Radovic was looking unquestionably dead. Lenny still had two years left on his parole, and in such circumstances a dead body could mean nothing but bad luck. So he dragged himself into the kitchen, wrapped a tea towel around his face, and staggered out into the street. Half passing out, he drove to a mate's place out at Nerang where they cleaned him up and filled him full of Scotch and Panadol before shipping him out to a safe house the next day.

And that was it. That was Lenny's story. Simple. No names, no pack drill. Just as you'd expect from Lenny Fiske. It didn't explain to Eddie why anyone would expect to wring a gambling debt out of Bernie Radovic by putting a bullet in his brain; or why, after taking all the trouble to line up what was a pretty expert-looking hit, they would be so sloppy as to overlook the fact the place was full of visitors and then leave Lenny with only a speech impediment to stop him talking; but those were little details that he would no doubt clean up later.

\*　　\*　　\*

The prosecution, on the other hand, had a different theory. It went like this: Lenny Fiske and some as yet unknown mate of his had been hired to pay a visit to the bookie. The block where Radovic lived was pretty well secured, so Lenny and his mate had come in through the downstairs unit, the occupants of which later reported that a window overlooking the garden had been forced. The two men had then let themselves out into the main stairwell and proceeded to Radovic's apartment on the second floor. Outside his unit they removed a ceiling access panel and one of them went up into the ceiling cavity. He was to crawl into the space above the bookie's unit and then drop down and open up the front door for his mate. Unfortunately, both being as dumb as dogshit, they had not reckoned on the difficulty of kicking out the gyprock ceiling panels, and by the time the first guy had got down into the unit he'd made such a racket that the bookie was waiting for him when he landed. A struggle had ensued inside the unit, causing gunman number two outside to decide to shoot his way in through the door. (Hence the damage to the front-door lock – which, Eddie noted, remained conspicuously unexplained by Lenny's story.) The second guy burst in at decidedly the wrong time, because by now the bookie either had the gun, or had wrestled it into a position such that Lenny Fiske walked straight up to the wrong end of the barrel, and copped one down his throat.

"That's the theory, huh?"

Detective Senior Constable Sasha Kelly sat in the witness box of the Brisbane Supreme Court and eyed her cross-examiner with palpable resentment. Her distrust of Eddie Moran was profound. One of the new breed in the service, Kelly was a serious young professional who had worked hard to crack the boys' club within her own ranks, and she had seen enough of Moran to recognise the kind of consummate chauvinist that had made her rapid rise such a constant battle. And Moran had a reputation as a special kind of show pony who lived a flashy lifestyle on the Gold Coast and saw himself as some sort of legal megastar, flitting around the country making appearances in high-profile cases just to keep his media star shining.

"That's the way we believe it happened, Mr Moran."

Eddie Moran nodded thoughtfully and looked around the courtroom, as if enormously impressed.

"That's a good theory, Senior." He gave another thoughtful nod, just for effect. "Yes, very impressive, really."

A mild wash of amusement lightened up the courtroom, and Sasha Kelly felt her stomach turn. Moran was playing to the crowd, and the journalists grinned mindlessly as they sensed the Eddie Show winding into gear. A full press gallery for what was a sadly routine murder case: the reporters had no doubt been organised by Moran himself, lured by the promise of some empty stunt that was unlikely to advance his client's case but would probably get him on the front page of the papers. They were hanging on his every word, and Moran was revelling in it. He was the complete showman, a real grandstander, the kind of strutting peacock that Sasha Kelly despised. While police worked hard to stem the tide of human tragedy and make the streets a safer place, Moran reduced the whole process to a circus in which he took the starring role. In her relatively short career as a detective this was her first case against him, but she knew his type too well. All bluff and bluster, histrionics, without substance. They came out swinging, playing to the jury (or the worst of them, like Moran, to the press), but rarely laid a punch.

"I'm glad you're so impressed, Mr Moran."

"Oh, I am. I am."

Eddie hesitated, smiling at the witness. She was very cute. Her hair was pulled back tightly and the buttons on her blouse were fastened right up to her neck. All designed to make her look as tough as shit, Eddie figured. Too bad it didn't really work. He could see the faint outline of her bra pressed up against the blouse, and he couldn't help but fantasise about her long hair hanging loose around her face and those bra straps sliding off her shoulders. It felt good to be undressing a police witness as the whole court waited, wondering what brilliant strategy he was hatching. The smile broke into a grin.

"But listen, lady, these theories are just that, right? Just sort of speculation – an attempt to infer a possibility from the available facts?"

"I would say a probability in this case, sir."

Decision time had come. The senior constable was ready for a fight, and Eddie had to work out whether he was going to give her one. The Crown had a solid-looking theory that made Lenny Fiske seem very guilty, and they had laid it on the table early. No doubt Detective Sasha Kelly had helped them dream it up and was proud of it. The question was, was now the time and place to put it to the test?

One consideration was that this arresting officer was a seriously top-looking sort, and arguments with such individuals were to be avoided where at all possible. He didn't have to challenge this theory now, head-on. He could do it bit by bit, chipping away quietly at the evidence, and then later highlighting the weaknesses of the theory in his address. That would save him putting the delightful Ms Kelly offside, and who knew what opportunities might develop for him down the line. But then again, she was a copper, and even Eddie Moran had some standards. In fact, not only was she a copper, but it seemed to Eddie she was a half-smart one who had jumped to one or two conclusions that were way out of line. She was working hard to put Lenny Fiske back into the slammer for a permanent stretch, without even considering what would be plain and clear to see if she just took the time to look.

Lenny had come up hard. He was regarded by those who knew him as a lovely bloke. Mention his name in Sydney to the right people and you'd always get the same report: "Lenny? He's a lovely bloke!" That didn't mean it was true, but that was his reputation. Born in a terrace down behind the Paddo hospital, he had grown up on the city streets. His mum had died in childbirth and he'd been raised by his grandmother. By all reports she was a hard case who drank rum with the wharfies and could give points' start to any of them in a fist fight, as long as she was in any kind of shape. The story was that Lenny loved her dearly, as he was entitled to: she was all he had. And no one ever said a nasty word about her, out of respect for Lenny, and their own wellbeing. When he was fifteen, some drunken hoon decided to neutralise her formidable left hook with an empty bottle; he cracked her skull open and threw her body in the harbour. So the welfare put young Lenny in a boys' home. The police couldn't find the bloke who topped his gran, but Lenny did, and when he came out of the home he paid the hoon a visit, which the hoon did not survive. There was a lot of sympathy around the town for Lenny at the time. A life stretch for a kid of seventeen was a tough break. But Lenny didn't whinge; he copped it on the chin. No stories, no explanations.

So Eddie Moran would have been happy to upset Detective Kelly to help out Lenny Fiske. But there were other serious considerations. The press were here in numbers and they were waiting for a show. They'd be half asleep by morning tea, and most wouldn't make it back after lunch, so if Eddie was going to get his picture in the paper he'd have to make an early run. The best way to do that would be to finish this witness quickly and then try to wring a few concessions out of the police forensic officer. The press loved to see those scientific types get all tied up in little knots and have to admit things that they didn't really want to. And Eddie always felt it made him look particularly clever when they did.

"Well listen, possibility or probability, it doesn't amount to proof beyond reasonable doubt, does it?"

A nice motherhood statement to park the theory for later reference. Then move on to the next witness. No need to upset the beautiful Detective Kelly, just move on to the forensic stuff and put a show on for the journos.

"I don't think there is any other rational hypothesis available on the proven facts, Mr Moran. So in my view this theory is proven beyond reasonable doubt."

"What?" Didn't this sheila realise it was Eddie Moran that was supposed to be making the motherhood statements around here? "Are you serious?"

"Yes, sir. There is no other way to explain the physical evidence found at the scene than on the basis that Leonard Fiske was one of the killers and he was shot, either intentionally by the deceased Radovic, or inadvertently by his accomplice during a struggle with the deceased."

She was just warming up. This little lady was spoiling for a fight. Maybe she didn't realise that this was the Eddie Show and Eddie was the star. But more likely she did, and she didn't care. She had a bullshit theory that she liked a lot, and she was more than happy to take Eddie head-on to prove her point. She was young and ballsy and determined to show everyone that the shonky lawyer was full of shit. Just the kind of witness that Eddie Moran loved.

"You're not serious, are you?"

"Yes, I am."

"You can't be."

"I am."

"You're not."

"I am."

Not the slightest hesitation in her voice, not a hint of self-doubt or wavering confidence. Eddie liked her style; she reminded him of him. Except she hadn't done her homework. Mighty little science but a mighty lot of dash, as the Banjo would have put it. And still she was happy to put Lenny Fiske back in for life. She deserved a touch-up for that; and here she was drawing a line in the dirt and challenging Eddie Moran to step over it.

Of course there was danger in stepping over, inviting comment from a witness who would undoubtedly take any opportunity to steal the spotlight and make Moran-style statements designed to drive the wooden stake through Lenny's story. Percentage play dictated that Eddie shouldn't let himself be drawn into this confrontation. It would be safer to keep his cross-examination focused strictly on the facts, and deal with the speculation and theories in his final address when the witnesses would have no chance to challenge what he said. But what the hell. He had never been a percentage player. Eddie ran on instinct.

"You're seriously asking this court to believe that the incident had to have happened according to this half-baked, jumped-up theory of yours?"

"I object!"

The prosecutor Bruce Parforth was still trying to get his beer gut up above the bar table.

"Withdrawn. I'll let the jury work out for themselves that it's half-baked and jumped-up."

"Well, I object again!"

Parforth had no sooner slumped back in his chair than he was struggling to climb back to his feet. But Mr Justice Ransom was more than happy to relieve him of the effort.

"Mr Moran!"

The whole courtroom started at the sound of Ransom's bark. Even Des the bailiff stirred momentarily from his slumber. Eddie appeared not even to notice.

"Yeah, all right. I won't mention half-baked and jumped-up again. All right, witness, let's have a closer look at this theory of yours and see what we're to make of it, okay?"

As Eddie leafed nonchalantly through his notes, everyone was watching Ransom, waiting for the judge to snap. He had steam coming out of both his ears; if looks could kill, this would have been an ex-lawyer. But Ransom had been around too long to take the bait. He had seen Moran play this game before, and he knew that to take the matter any further now would only give this shyster an opportunity to play up further to the jury.

"Let's see now," Eddie finally continued, after giving His Honour every opportunity. "How does it go? One intruder comes in through the ceiling while the other one – this is supposed to be Mr Fiske, is it? – waits outside the door."

"Yes," Kelly answered confidently. "We believe that the plan was for Mr Fiske's accomplice to gain entry first, and then open the front door to admit the accused."

"Really? Okay, and the first part of the story goes like this, doesn't it? Both deceased persons are asleep when the first intruder enters."

"They were both in night attire, and the bed was

turned down. The light was out and the bed had been slept in."

"Yeah yeah, all right. Whatever." It warmed Eddie's heart to see the witness squirm at his irreverence. "But at any rate you reckon the deceased Radovic is awoken by the noise of the first intruder trying to break through the ceiling. Is that it?"

"That's right."

"What noise?"

Eddie was trying to look as puzzled as he could, partly for the benefit of the jury and the press bench, but mainly because he knew his theatrics were getting right up the nose of Senior Constable Kelly. She burred up immediately.

"The noise of him attempting to kick the ceiling panel out."

Eddie's feigned surprise at the venom in her voice not only entertained the audience but further aggravated Sasha Kelly.

"Yeah? So what, does this wake up his girlfriend?"

"That we can't be sure of."

"Oh, right. We've found something you can't be sure of." Eddie loved the opportunity to slip in a cheap shot. "But the rest is absolute, is it? Set in stone? Right?"

"The rest is clearly provable on the facts."

She was angry, so angry she was not about to compromise. Now Eddie had her where he wanted her.

"Clearly provable. All right. So Radovic is awoken by the noise of an intruder repeatedly kicking at the ceiling panel, and he gets out of bed and goes to investigate."

"We have statements from two neighbours that the lights in the deceased's unit went out at approximately ten p.m. —"

"Yeah, yeah, that's all right, Senior." No doubt Kelly was proud of her Sherlock Junior handiwork, but Eddie wasn't about to let her step into centre stage to tell the world about it. "I'm just trying to get the story straight, all right? He hears the kicking noise, gets up and goes out to investigate. Is that it?"

"That's right."

"Did you inspect the panel that was knocked out of the ceiling?"

"Yes."

"The edges had been cut almost right through with a sharp blade, probably a Stanley knife. Isn't that right?"

"Yes."

"Presumably cut through by the intruder before the panel was knocked out of the ceiling?"

"Yes."

"In that condition it would have popped out with no more than the lightest tap, wouldn't it?"

"I don't know that I'd be inclined to agree with that, Mr Moran."

"Not asking you about your inclinations, Ms Kelly. Just putting a reasonable proposition to you. You'd expect that panel to pop out very easily, wouldn't you?"

"Maybe."

"And it didn't have the slightest damage to its surface, suggestive of any hard blow of any kind, did it?"

"No, sir, I don't believe it did."

"Well, I go back to my earlier proposition. Isn't it more likely that it was popped out with no more than a light tap?"

"No."

Eddie loved this answer. It was dumb, dumb, dumb. This was nothing like a winning point for Lenny Fiske, it was just a little bit of minor tinkering. Radovic could have been woken up by anything. The sound of the cutting of the plaster panel; a goon bumping around in his ceiling cavity; maybe he got up for a piss; or maybe he just couldn't sleep. It didn't matter. It was a point not worth debating. But Kelly had come up with her theory and she was going to defend it, and maybe help Eddie to turn nothing into something. Police witnesses who were not prepared to concede the plainly evident were always a big bonus.

"Surely it is."

"No, it's not."

"It is, isn't it?"

"No."

"Maybe?"

"No."

"No? Fair enough. Well, the panel's there, I suppose. We can all work it out for ourselves."

Every eye in the jury swung over to the table where the panel sat in clear view. Four neatly cut out edges, sliced through to allow it to be popped out easily. Eddie remained silent for a moment as they soaked it up. Detective Kelly tried hard not to, but eventually she shot a telling glance at the exhibit. When she quickly looked back to the lawyer, Eddie met her with a half-smart smirk, raised his eyebrows at the jury, and continued.

"Whatever you reckon, Senior."

One or two of the jurors were quietly snickering along with the press.

"So let's see. Where does this fancy theory of yours go from there? Oh yes, having been woken by this thunderous battering on the ceiling panel, the deceased comes into the lounge room and engages the intruder in a violent struggle. Is that it?"

"We believe so, yes."

A hint of hesitation. Evidently Detective Kelly had realised this dog could bite. But Eddie wasn't going to let her back away.

"Yeah, well you believe so beyond any reasonable doubt, don't you? That's what you told us earlier. Beyond reasonable doubt. You're not wanting to resile from that already, are you?"

"No."

"No. All right, well don't be shy. You're convinced beyond any reasonable doubt that all this happened exactly according to this theory of yours?"

"That's right."

Another great answer, and Eddie loved it. He had verballed her a little on the question, and if she'd had more brains or more experience she would have pulled him up. But she was obviously short of a gallop and Eddie was happy to take advantage.

"Right. So we've got this violent struggle happening in the lounge room between the deceased and the first intruder, and this goes on for so long and is obviously making so much noise that the accused, who's still outside, decides to shoot his way in through the front door. Is that it?"

"That's right."

"Yeah well, I think we've got some photographs of that lounge room area here, haven't we?" Eddie was enjoying this. He took a long time to flick through the photographs on the bar table in front of him, knowing just how irritating he was being. "Hmmm." He studied the three photos he'd selected as though he were profoundly puzzled. "Listen, you police don't tidy up the crime scene before you photograph it, do you? I mean, you don't sort of straighten things up and throw the Mr Sheen over the furniture before you start clicking away, do you?"

The witness remained silent as Eddie continued to study the photographs, waiting for an answer. Eventually, with perfect timing, he peered up through his eyebrows.

"Do you?"

"No."

"No, I didn't think so. See, have a look at the crime scene photos, will you. Exhibit eight, Your Honour."

Des the bailiff dragged himself up from his chair and begrudgingly delivered the exhibit to the witness.

"Have a look at photos number nineteen through to twenty-one. Those photos show the relevant part of the lounge room, don't they, just below the hole in the ceiling, and next to the front door? That's where you reckon this violent struggle is supposed to have occurred. Is that right?"

"Yes."

"Yeah, that's what I figured. But what I can't understand is, if you look at those photos you can't see the slightest sign of any struggle."

Kelly was studying the photographs cautiously, reluctant to make anything but a carefully considered observation.

"You can't, can you?" Eddie was pretending to be struggling with this new conundrum. "See, the photographs show that there's a floor rug just there, laid on a tiled floor. Those things slip about pretty easily. But that rug looks like it's just been laid, doesn't it? Like it's not even ruffled. Hardly looks like it's been walked on, does it?"

Kelly was studying the photographs as if it were the first time she had seen them.

"I mean, that carpet hadn't been superglued to the floor or anything, had it, witness?"

"No."

"No, I didn't think so. And that very tasteful artificial cherry-blossom shrub there – is that what it is, a cherry blossom, is it?"

"I'm not sure."

"No, well it probably doesn't matter. Whatever it is it looks a pretty delicate thing. And yet it doesn't seem to be damaged in any way. There's not the slightest sign of any disturbance to that shrub, no bent or broken branches, none of those leaves or blossoms dislodged or anything like that?"

"No."

"That'd be pretty surprising if you had two grown men locked in a death struggle and wrestling all over that general area, wouldn't it?"

"Not impossible."

It was time to get tough. "I didn't say impossible, did I, witness." He locked her in a silent, disapproving stare that lasted just long enough for maximum effect. "It's you that's talking 'beyond any reasonable doubt', not me. Remember? I said it'd be pretty surprising. And it would be pretty surprising, wouldn't it, witness?"

Kelly looked down at the photograph, long enough to let Eddie have another chop.

"Wouldn't it!"

Kelly's pretty face was flushed with a look which told everyone in that courtroom that she hadn't factored in the undisturbed appearance of the scene.

"Maybe."

"Yeah, maybe." Eddie laced his voice with all the mock disdain he could muster. "Maybe very surprising, I suggest."

"Maybe."

Good answer, baby. Things were going well. It was time to move in for the kill. Stay tough. Stay mean. Eddie was studying the next photograph, nodding slightly as if to confirm that he had found exactly what he knew he would. Every eye in the room was on him, waiting for his next move. Eddie loved it.

"Look at photograph number fourteen, would you, witness." He slapped his copy loudly onto the bar table and tapped impatiently on the lectern as Kelly sifted through the pile in front of her.

"Got it there?"

"Yes."

He shot a quick glance at the press bench. They were all still there, and mostly still awake.

"In the foreground of that photograph we can see, can't we, a number of small pieces of debris, lying there on the carpet just inside the front door to the unit, and then at various points leading into the hallway?"

"Yes. That's right."

"Now, it's a bit hard to see what they are in that photograph, but some of them are in fact pieces of splintered wood, aren't they?"

"Yes, I believe there were some pieces of wood from the doorjamb in that vicinity."

"Yeah, that's right. Pieces of the doorjamb, and the door."

"I think so, yes."

"Splinters of wood blown away from the door-lock area when, according to your theory, Mr Fiske is supposed to have shot his way in through the front door?"

"That's right."

"To help his mate who is fighting with the deceased over the gun?"

"That's right."

"And as he bursts in he is shot in the face, either intentionally by the deceased, or accidentally by his mate in the struggle?"

"Yes. That's right."

"Well, if Mr Fiske was one of the assailants, that would be the only way one could possibly account for his injuries. Isn't that right?"

"Yes." The answer came out weakly, with no hint of her former confidence. She was waiting for a knockout punch, and her apprehension was infectious. The jury were sitting up attentively, and the whole courtroom seemed to be suspended in anticipation. Time to pause for dramatic effect, thought Eddie, and he stretched the silence till he couldn't stretch it any longer.

"But Mr Fiske wasn't one of the assailants, you see. And I suggest to you that the physical evidence found at the scene makes that very, very clear."

"I disagree." Now she had got a bit of strength back into her tone, so Eddie moved quickly to take up the challenge.

"Well then, have another look at that photograph, witness. You can see in the background there the front door is partly ajar, but we can still see the area around the damaged door handle and the doorjamb, can't we?"

"Yes."

"And that whole area is heavily bloodstained, isn't it?"

"Yes."

"Yeah. It was heavily spattered with the deceased's blood when he was shot at point-blank range in the immediate vicinity of that front door."

"Yes."

"But the blood-spattering from the male deceased's wound was confined to that front-door area and the adjacent jamb and wall. True?"

"Yes."

"In other words, he was shot in that immediate area near the front door where his body was found, and he bled there, and only there."

"That's right."

Eddie paused again. He had to get the next bit exactly right. This was the real cruncher. It wasn't much but it was the best, maybe the only thing Lenny Fiske had going for him in this trial so far, and Eddie had to maximise the impact. He couldn't afford for Sasha Kelly to stuff it up for him. For a tiny fraction of a second he cursed himself for being such a mug lair, but he was in too deep to turn back now.

"Photograph sixteen shows a piece of debris in the foreground of the photo which, according to the sketch plan, is approximately four-point-three metres from the front door. Correct?"

"Yes."

"That piece of debris is in fact a fragment of splintered wood, is it not?"

"Yes."

"Yes. It was one of the larger fragments that you police found in the unit."

"Yes. That's right."

"It's numbered thirty-eight on the exhibit register and it's described as a fragment of veneered ply measuring roughly eight centimetres by three centimetres. Correct?"

"Yes." Her voice was cautious, on edge, up on her toes and ready to dance.

"And it was found to correspond with the damaged area around the locking mechanism of the front door of the unit. By that, I mean you police were able to ascertain that it was a piece of the front door that had been blown away by the force of the bullets being fired from outside into the door."

"Yeah, but that's not surprising." Kelly sounded comfortable now. She knew the point and she was going to demonstrate her expertise. "That lock was shot away by a point-four-five calibre. That's a heavy-gauge pistol. Fired at point-blank range like that, you'd expect the debris to carry easily over that distance."

From Kelly's answer Eddie knew she hadn't seen what he was coming to, and that felt good.

"Oh, absolutely. Absolutely. This was a piece of the door blown clear down the hallway by the gunshots fired by one of the two assailants as they entered that unit."

They both knew that he was going somewhere, but only he knew where.

"Yes. That's correct."

Kelly's answer came out cautiously, begrudgingly. Whatever point it was he hoped to make, this was the platform for it, and she steeled herself to counter. This was the way that Eddie loved to play the game, coming out of nowhere so they knew you were going to do it to them but they didn't know how. He savoured the moment silently as the jury awaited his next move.

"That piece of wood, Detective Kelly." Eddie's voice was quiet, almost conspiratorial. "It tested positive for blood, didn't it?"

"Yes. In fact it was quite heavily bloodstained."

"Mmm. Yeah, that's right. Heavily stained with Mr Radovic's blood, wasn't it?"

"Yes, of course. Because it had been blown away from that area of the door that was spattered with the deceased's blood."

"Exactly!" Eddie slapped the lectern so hard to emphasise his point that Des nearly tumbled off his chair. "Spattered with the deceased's blood when he was shot at point-blank range and died instantly!"

Kelly looked bewildered, like a cat frozen in the headlights. What the hell was Moran on about?

"Yes."

"Yes, that's right. And what that tells us is that Mr Radovic's blood was on that door before that second gunman shot his way into that unit. He was lying dead and his blood was all over that door before the second gunman shot the lock away, blasting bits of the blood-soaked wood down into that hallway. That's what it tells us, doesn't it, witness!"

"I'm sorry, I don't follow you."

"Don't you? Well see if you can follow this one, witness. If you want to talk about reasonable doubt, I suggest there's one thing about this case that we can be satisfied of beyond any reasonable doubt, and it's this:

if Mr Radovic was dead on the floor with his blood painted all over that front door before the second gunman blasted his way in, he certainly wasn't locked in any struggle with the other gunman, and he didn't shoot anybody, intentionally or by accident. Did he?"

Kelly needed time to take it in, but Eddie wasn't giving anything away.

"Did he!"

"No."

"No. And that means your half-baked, jumped-up theory just doesn't square with the cold, hard, proven facts, does it?"

This time Parforth didn't bother to object. His Honour scowled but didn't say a word.

"Does it!"

Kelly's cheeks were flushed.

"No."

"No. And it also means that, like Mr Radovic and his girlfriend, Lenny Fiske was a victim of this crime, not the perpetrator. He didn't shoot anyone. He was brutally gunned down by one of those unknown intruders, just like Mr Radovic!"

Eddie wasn't waiting for an answer.

"No further questions, Your Honour."

He dropped back into his seat, his face awash with all the feigned disdain that he could muster.

# CHAPTER NINE

It's one thing to discredit the Crown theory for the crime, but in a murder case you have to do a lot more than that to get a points decision. The accused has to come up with his own story, and it has to be at least halfway plausible.

So far Lenny Fiske had made a reasonable job of doing that. It was simple and uncomplicated, which reduced the room for error. Lenny visits Radovic to talk about a job. Benign enough. Radovic tells him he's being threatened over debts owed at the track. That was good: it gave a motive to a lot of other suspects. He wants Lenny to act as his bodyguard. Not so good, although not fatal. The jury would ask themselves what particular talent it was that qualified Lenny as a potential bodyguard; a reputation as a strongarm wasn't the best thing in a murder case, but it could be explained. Lenny gets full and falls asleep. One look at Lenny and they'd have to accept that. When he wakes up, there's the murderer and bang – Lenny cops one in the face. There was no doubt that someone had shot him, and Eddie had established that it couldn't have been Radovic. So then Lenny bolts. That was where they were going to have some problems. John and Mary Citizen were going to find it hard to fathom why an innocent man who'd just been shot would see the need to scarper before the police arrived and put himself in snooker in a safe house while his face grew back together. But that was a relatively minor problem. They'd get over it.

It wasn't the best yarn in the world, but it was possible. Maybe it required a leap of faith but it didn't ask the jury to suspend all rationality. Until the fingerprint evidence arrived.

Eddie had taken a full statement from his client, and Lenny had described to him in detail all his movements on the night. How, when he arrived at Radovic's residence in answer to the invitation, he parked his car out the front, under a street light. He went in, large as life, straight through the front gate. And when he left, he went out the same way. After the murderer had gone, Lenny came to in the lounge room and, holding his face together with one hand, he dragged himself down the stairwell, through the front gate and down the road to his car. The trail of blood confirmed this: spots and smudges down the stairwell, heavy droplets out into the front garden, then more further west down Pacific Avenue. Eddie had walked the various police witnesses through it, tracing Lenny's route of exit out through the front door into the front garden and then to the point beneath the street light. It demonstrated that his car probably had been where he said it had, somewhere out front for all to see, not hidden away in some back street where you might expect a would-be assassin to deposit it. It was a small point, but they didn't have too many points so it was one worth making.

Then, on the fourth day of the trial, the prosecution sprang the fingerprint evidence on the defence. The scene of crime investigators had lifted latent prints from the downstairs unit where someone had come in over the rear balcony and gained entry to the complex by letting themselves in through the balcony door. There were several prints on the railing of the balcony and two on the inside of the front door. All were unidentified but one. A partial palm print on the balcony had been matched conclusively with the palm print of Lenny Fiske.

"So you tell me, Lenny. How'd it get there?"

Eddie Moran had just finished publicly humiliating Barry Parforth over his 'monumental incompetence' at having introduced this evidence at such a late stage of the proceedings, and he still had a little venom left to work out of his system. Eddie didn't like being embarrassed in the middle of a murder trial.

"If you went in through the front door, how come your prints are in the downstairs unit?"

Lenny looked characteristically unshaken, but in the circumstances perhaps a little too unshaken even for Lenny Fiske.

"I doubled back around." He had the story ready. There was no hesitation or falter in his voice. "I got out into the front garden, then I thought I heard voices on the footpath, so I decided to go out over the back fence instead. I got to the downstairs unit and I walked through the garden there. I was feeling pretty groggy so I put my hand up on the railing to steady meself."

Eddie had been warming himself up to give his client a good savaging. He hadn't expected Lenny to come up with any explanation, and certainly not with one so prompt and tight as this. It took the wind out of his sails.

"Why didn't you mention this earlier?"

"Forgot. I was pretty groggy at the time."

He was well rehearsed. Somehow he must have anticipated the possibility that they might come up with a print from the balcony. Either that or someone had told him about the latent prints even before his lawyer knew. Maybe it was something Eddie didn't want to know about.

"All right. We'll run it. Trouble is it's basically a new story. Parforth'll get a lot of mileage out of the fact that you've never mentioned anything about this before."

There was a brief silence while Lenny pondered whether to let out a little more information.

"I think I did."

"When?"

"To the Sydney coppers, I think." Fiske had a shifty look about him, like a cat with a canary in its mouth. "Ask Keliher."

"Bill Keliher?"

"Yeah. He maybe might remember."

Bill Keliher had been waiting around the courthouse for the past three days. He had some insignificant bit of evidence to give about the charge being read to Fiske at Silverwater and him consenting to be extradited. It was completely uncontentious and could easily have been admitted without Keliher being called, but Eddie had assumed that Keliher was up on the usual junket that brought New South Wales police to Brisbane – to give uncontentious evidence on insignificant issues so as to justify four days all expenses paid on the piss with the Queensland coppers. Keliher was called that afternoon, and he gave his uncontentious, insignificant evidence. There was nothing in it for Eddie to cross-examine him on, and he wouldn't have bothered getting to his feet had he not had clear instructions from Lenny Fiske to ask the question.

"Inspector Keliher, did you talk to the accused at all about his movements on the night of the murders?"

Keliher screwed his face up as though it was all unexpected.

"Oh, only very briefly, Mr Moran."

This was dangerous territory, asking a police officer who so far had done them no harm whatsoever what conversation he might have had with Lenny about the murder. It was an open invitation to Keliher to trot out a confession, and Eddie didn't like it one bit. He glanced over at his client. Lenny's expression told him that his instructions hadn't changed.

"What did he tell you?"

"Just that he'd met Mr Radovic at some hotel on the Gold Coast and he invited him to come to his unit ..."

It was all consistent with Lenny's story. Keliher was walking through it in a matter-of-fact fashion, regurgitating every detail of the defence. Lenny had told him all about it, how Radovic wanted him to be his bodyguard because there was a contract on him, how he'd had too much to drink and fallen asleep, and then woken up to be confronted by a gunman. It was a lovely little statement of the defence case coming from the mouth of a police witness and Eddie held his breath as each new sentence fell out, waiting for the bombshell that would sink them. It didn't come.

"He said he didn't know what to do. He had a couple of years left on his parole and if he was found at a murder scene he might get breached. So he just panicked and took off."

They'd come through it with a clean bill of health. Keliher had Lenny giving the whole story right at the outset within hours of his arrest. It was very useful stuff. He hadn't mentioned one way or the other whether Fiske had claimed to have backtracked around the rear balcony, but Eddie wasn't going to spoil it all by asking one question too many. As it was the story was intact; if Eddie asked and Keliher said that Lenny hadn't mentioned anything about the rear balcony, it would just confirm that it was all a recent invention. Eddie wasn't going to take that chance.

"Thank you, Inspector." He ignored the glare of his client and hurriedly sat down.

"Oh, and there was one more thing he said," Keliher added with some urgency. "He claimed that when he was leaving through the front garden he thought he heard some people on the footpath and he doubled back through the garden at the back."

The penny finally dropped. Keliher was delivering the goods for Lenny Fiske. He'd been paid off. Eddie looked straight at him, trying to take it in. He had always known Keliher as something of a plodder, capable of cutting corners here and there, and sometimes stuffing up, but not corrupt. He'd never known him to take a sling, and he'd never heard it said of him. But here was the evidence, clear enough.

"Is that so, Inspector?"

"Yeah, he was sort of steadying himself on the balcony rail there."

Eddie heard a murmur at the other end of the bar table. Sasha Kelly was whispering feverishly to Parforth. They didn't like this one bit. And neither did Eddie. He liked to win, but not this way.

"Your Honour, I've got no further questions for this witness."

\*　　\*　　\*

Lenny Fiske beat the Radovic murder blue. Eddie took a lot of bows as usual, and the newspapers were full of it for a week or so. The job hadn't paid particularly well – all Lenny could come up with was the five grand that had been somewhat mysteriously deposited in cash in his account three days before the hit – but Eddie had done it for the profile, and the result brought lots of that. As for Lenny Fiske, it didn't help him much. His parole had been revoked when he was charged and he went straight from his acquittal back to gaol to wait for the next meeting of the Parole Board to regrant him parole. Two weeks later he was murdered in a scrap at SDL. Someone put a shiv right through his neck and he bled to death in the exercise yard. By the time the warders found him, no one could remember what had happened.

Fiske's murder sent the press into a new frenzy, and once he was dead and gone and unable to sue for defamation, they were able to retry him in the media and quickly find him guilty. That gave Eddie lots of scope to become outraged and go public to remind everyone that his client had after all been acquitted of the crime. And that served to reinforce the notion that Eddie Moran was a very clever lawyer who had won the Radovic murder trial despite his client's guilt.

Eddie had been doing television interviews all week. When the call came through, he was sitting in his office with his feet up on the desk watching replays of his interview on *This Day Tonight*.

"There's a gentleman in reception who'd like to see you."

Kirsten was a tough chick who always sounded like she didn't give a shit. Which was true, but she made sure that when she spoke to Eddie she sounded like she gave even less of a shit than she really did. Eddie's ego was seriously out of control, and she saw it as her role to do whatever she could to cut him down to size.

"Has he got an appointment?"

Eddie knew he didn't have an appointment, but he also knew that rhetorical questions got right up Kirsten's nose and so were worth the exercise.

"No he hasn't got an appointment, shithead!"

Eddie loved it. He sucked back on his cigarette and blew a line of smoke rings out into the room. He should have sacked her years ago. But she had a great body and he was determined that one day he'd get her in the sack. And he loved her attitude. She was all attitude. Eddie pointed the remote and flicked the television off. Outside his window the sky was blue, the sun was shining, and down below the young girls were parading on the beach of Surfers Paradise in nothing but their string bikinis. Did Eddie really want to see a new client on a day like this?

"What's his name?"

"I don't know."

"Why don't you ask him?"

"Why don't *you* ask him?"

"What does he want to see me about?"

"What am I, Encyclopaedia Britannica?"

Eddie blew a couple more smoke rings. He really should have sacked her years ago.

"Tell him to take a seat. And fix him up a cup of coffee. I'll be with him in a minute."

Eric Pohl was a distinctive-looking man, the kind you don't forget. Sitting in reception with his macchiato on his knee he looked like the admiral of the fleet. His silk shirt and pure-wool reefer jacket were immaculate and his tie matched the handkerchief that ballooned from his breast pocket. Eddie hadn't seen him in nearly fifteen years, but he remembered his sallow features and his cold handshake. He hadn't lost the coiffured hair but it was shorter now, which made him look only marginally less creepy. He still had the Gucci suntan though; at his age it looked ridiculous.

"I wanted to talk to you about the Leonard Fiske case."

"Seems everybody does these days."

Eddie dropped into a chair and stretched his legs. Whatever Eric Pohl had to say to him he could say in reception.

"I was wondering what you're doing with his file."

"What's that supposed to mean?"

Pohl glanced self-consciously over his shoulder and then settled into the chair opposite. He wasn't comfortable talking in the reception but Eddie obviously wasn't going to ask him in.

"Do you have it here?"

"Of course I do. Why?"

"I'm doing some research for a book about the case. I was hoping I might have a look at Mr Fiske's file."

Last time they had met, Pohl was a professor of literature and history at some Melbourne university. So maybe it was true. But Eddie didn't buy it.

"It's privileged. No one looks at Mr Fiske's file unless Mr Fiske says so. And I don't think that's going to happen."

"Mr Fiske is dead."

"I noticed that."

"Surely privilege doesn't still apply now that he's dead."

"Sorry, pal." Eddie wasn't in the mood to argue points of law with Eric Pohl. "You're out of luck."

"I could make it worth your while."

Pohl was a repulsive piece of work. But he had lots of money, and that made him worth talking to.

"How much worth my while?"

"Well, you tell me."

"Ten grand."

"That's a lot of money for some research."

"There's a lot of file."

"All right, ten thousand. It's a deal."

Eric Pohl was sitting back with a look of self-congratulation on his ugly face. He had reckoned that for the right price he could always buy the services of Edwin C. Moran. The last time Eddie had seen that smug smile was in his first little office in the back of Broadbeach. Pohl's old friend Robert Allen had been charged with kidnapping two kids and had met Eddie Moran at the Tweed Heads watch-house. Allen was convinced that Eddie was the right man to defend him, so Eric Pohl had gone there to settle on a fee for Allen's defence. Eddie had taken a punt and named a figure that he'd thought was a lot more than the job was worth, and Pohl had said, 'It's a deal.' And then he had sat back with that same self-satisfied look on his dial that was in front of Eddie right now. Eddie wasn't interested any more.

"I'll think about it."

Pohl looked genuinely surprised. "I thought we had a deal."

"You did, didn't you."

He stood up stiffly like a man affronted, with his macchiato in one hand. With the other he produced a business card which he pushed under Eddie's nose.

"Here's my card. Give me a call when you're finished thinking."

Eddie took the card in one hand. It read 'Doctor Eric Pohl, Professor of Literature and History', with his faculty address and phone number. All written in gold leaf.

"You know what, pal?" Eddie slipped the card into the professor's macchiato. "I think I won't."

Pohl's long face sagged and his lip curled into a caustic scowl. He wasn't used to being declined, much less insulted. He set the coffee down, turned on his heels and sashayed out the door like a pouting prima donna.

"Way to go, Eddie!" Kirsten was sitting at reception with a cheesy grin. "That guy is like a bigger creep than even you!"

For once in his life she almost had him stumped for words. Eddie shook his finger thoughtfully at his wise-guy secretary.

"You know, I think I should've sacked you years ago."

"Yeah right."

*　　*　　*

It seemed as though everyone was interested in the story behind the murder of Bernie Radovic. And why not? It had everything. Gangsters, sex, drugs, intrigue.

To begin with, anything that hinted at an exposé of dirty dealings on the Gold Coast was always going to make good copy. The glitzy beachside tourist strip had a reputation for raunchy and sometimes shady goings-on. Although they flocked there for their holidays every chance they got, respectable Australians loved to look down on the morals of the gaudy tourist mecca. Add a high-profile Sydney SP bookmaker with links to underworld figures and previous convictions for pornography offences, mix that up with speculation about his appetite for designer drugs and the flashy company he kept with some of the Gold Coast's ritzy social set, and you had yourself a first-class story. It even had a femme fatale, a mysterious woman who found herself in the wrong place at the wrong time. Emma Ronson, the bookie's girlfriend who ended up dead on the floor of Bernie's penthouse, was remembered only as a dark-eyed beauty who rarely socialised and was quietly spoken and withdrawn when she did. But she was beautiful, and Radovic had been besotted by her from the day they had met, not six months prior to her death.

Even in its execution the assassination was bizarre. Lenny Fiske, a previously convicted killer, the hitman who dispatched Radovic. Who had sent him? Why? And what of his accomplice who had escaped scot free? Was he the one who had shot Fiske at the scene? Had he arranged Fiske's brutal reception at the prison? It was a real-life mystery being played out on the front page of the newspapers.

Ron Morris had a copy of the Melbourne *Age* spread out across the floor of his spare room. He had been trying to read bits and pieces of it as he finished off his push-ups. His arms pumped with mechanical precision. One after another. He didn't count; he tried not even to think about it, he just kept pushing. The newspaper was there to take his mind off it. The *Age* had done a two-page spread on the story, most of which Ron had already heard, but it still made interesting reading. His arms were shaking as they began slowly to grind to a halt. The pressure in his face was building. He stopped reading; he could concentrate only on pushing now, nothing else. Big drops of his sweat plopped down onto the page in front of him. He was grunting hard with each extension and he could feel the muscles in his back and neck locking up, faltering as they reached exhaustion. He kept on going. Push it. Hard. Keep going. His teeth were clenched with exertion, his eyes bulging in his head, his arms quivering violently before collapsing under him. He lay face-down on the soggy newspaper, sucking breath into his screaming lungs. It felt good. Ron Morris was strong, determined, able to survive. You never knew when you would have to fight for your very life.

He had a shower, combed what little hair he had, and put on a good pair of slacks and a long-sleeved shirt. He was expecting company. A policeman from St Kilda had rung to say that some Sydney detectives would like to come and talk to him about Sandra Hershey's case. He was pleased to do it. He desperately wanted them to nail their man.

It had been over twenty years since the attack on Sandra Hershey. It had destroyed her life. She was the first victim of the maniac who became known as the Ether Man. They had never caught him. But now, hopefully, the police were set to charge someone, and they wanted Ron's help to do it. He was looking forward to it.

Ron and Sandra had been friends. She was still in her final year at school then. She was buxom and pretty and so outgoing that everyone liked her. Ron was three years older, already a working man, but he would sometimes walk her home from the bus stop and she would flirt with him. She never flirted after the attack.

Ron was the one who had found her, her naked body scratched and twisted in the bottom of the ditch down by the park. She was unconscious then, the acrid smell of chloroform still pungent on her face and body. He raised the alarm immediately. By the time the ambulance and police were on the scene she was whimpering and writhing in discomfort.

Ron told the police what had happened. It was dark, but he could just make out the figure of a man coming from the trees beyond the oval. A big man carrying something on his shoulder. Ron had started to walk down towards the park. He didn't know why, it was just an impulse. And, as he had, the man had stopped and then crouched down as if to hide himself. Ron had kept walking, cautiously, straining to make out the figure in the darkness. Then, when he was quite close, probably no more than thirty yards away, the man had appeared from the darkness of the storm drain and strode away across the road towards the east; when he got to the corner, he had broken into a run and disappeared. But Ron had seen him clearly in the street light, a big man with brown hair. He was certain he would recognise him if he laid eyes on him again.

Since then he'd seen a thousand photographs but he hadn't identified anyone. He was confident today would be different. The Sydney police had been utilising all the latest technology to close in on the culprit and now they had someone firmly in their sights. All they needed was a positive identification from Ron Morris to confirm it.

\* \* \*

"Okay, Ron. As you know, I'm Detective Wally Messner and this is Sergeant Peter Farrow. For the purpose of this interview could you please state your full name for us."

The tape recorder on the coffee table whirred softly as they completed the formalities. In many ways it was just another interview; but in one way it was completely different. Wally was there to ask a witness to identify a very special suspect. If he did, all hell was going to break loose.

Wally Messner had the photo board clasped firmly in his sweaty hand. He hadn't prepared it himself. Someone from the Juvenile Crimes Commission had arranged the three lines of four mugshots, each roughly fitting the description Morris had given.

"All right, Ron. In a minute I'm going to turn this board over and you'll see that it contains a number of photographs, twelve in all, that show men of similar age and description. I want you to take your time and have a good look and see if there's anyone there you recognise. Okay?"

Wally Messner turned the board over and placed it on the coffee table. Before he had the time to take his hand away, Ron Morris dropped a heavy finger on photograph number seven.

"That's the bloke. That's him right there. Number seven."

Wally had a jittery feeling in his stomach. "Are you sure?"

"Absolutely one hundred per cent positive. I've been waiting twenty years to see that face again. That's him all right. That's the bastard."

\* \* \*

Wally Messner placed the photo board face-down on the boardroom table. Scrawled on the back in Ron Morris's untidy handwriting was his confident assurance: *I am able to positively identify the man in photo 7 as the man who I saw leave the park. I am 100% certain.*

"He went straight to him," Wally Messner sighed. "It's one of the strongest IDs I've ever done."

Peter Rosenthal was deep in thought. "You taped it?"

"Yep."

The chairman flipped the board over and looked at the photograph of Detective Inspector Keliher.

"All right, it looks like we have our culprit. But I don't need to tell you how messy this will be, so we don't move before we have all the evidence we can muster. Understood?"

The eight detectives sitting round the table nodded silently.

# CHAPTER TEN

Bill Keliher slipped the Fiske file from the cabinet and headed straight back to his office. He closed the door behind him and dropped the file on the desk. There wasn't much to it – copies of the notebook entries made by the officers who had picked Lenny up, a couple of statements that they'd sent up for the Queensland brief, the extradition papers, internal memos about air travel and accommodation. The usual stuff. It was a Queensland blue so anything of any interest would be on their file up there. The New South Wales coppers had just picked him up and passed him on.

Bill was leafing through the pages to make sure there was nothing he had missed. He wanted to get the file back quickly before anybody knew he had it. So far no one had asked any questions about his relationship with Lenny Fiske or his evidence at the murder trial. Lenny's death was big news even in Sydney, and Bill couldn't understand why the Queensland coppers weren't crawling all over everyone who'd had anything to do with him. So far he hadn't heard a peep. He wondered what they'd try to make of his visit to the gaol. Bill had his answers all rehearsed for when the questions came.

He'd known Lenny Fiske for years, pinched him on some petty stuff at least a couple of times. Over the years Lenny had slipped him a little bit of information here and there. Everyone was red hot for whoever had put Fiske up to the hit, and Bill knew that Lenny wasn't talking to the Queensland coppers. So when he came up for the trial he thought he might pay Lenny a visit just to see if anything came of it. You never know.

Bill tried to trace his movements over in his mind. When he first got to the Arthur Gorrie Remand Centre outside Brisbane, he had filled in an official visitor's pass at reception. He had scribbled his name and origin on the form in a way that he hoped would be illegible. Then he had turned on the charm at the front desk and chatted up the lady issuing the passes so she wouldn't look too closely at the writing. He had showed her his police ID but he wasn't sure whether she had entered any of the details in the system. She had punched something into the computer as she laughed and joked with him, but maybe she was just bringing up Lenny's details to check on his location in the prison. Maybe all they had on Bill was the scribbled pass. They wouldn't make much sense of that. Maybe the Queensland coppers didn't even know about his fireside chat with Lenny Fiske.

When Lenny first walked into the interview room he'd looked decidedly on edge. Bill didn't blame him.

He'd have been told only that he had a legal visit and he probably expected to be talking to his lawyer. Instead he had one of the coppers who was trying to put him in for life.

"Hello, Mr Keliher."

"Hello, Lenny."

"To what do I owe this rare pleasure?"

"I'm hoping we might help each other out."

Bill started out by assuring Lenny that he wasn't wearing any wires. What was said was between them. He turned his pockets out and put the contents on the desk. Then he put his briefcase up and turned it upside down. Lenny could sift through the papers all he liked – there were no bugs and no tapes. This was just between the two of them. Lenny sat back with a bemused expression on his face. No cop had ever grovelled to him like this before.

"I don't know who put the hit on Radovic."

"I don't give a shit about Radovic, all right? I know you shot him, Lenny, but I don't care. I don't give a fuck whether you go down for it or not. You want to defend it, good luck to you. Go your hardest. He was a fucking grub anyway."

Lenny Fiske was smart enough to know that these days they could fit an interception transmitter in the eye of a flea's dick, so he wasn't necessarily convinced by Keliher's emptying his briefcase. He could have a bug anywhere. But this was different. No copper he knew would talk like this into a tape about the murder victim. He'd always thought of Keliher as a straight shooter, and right now there was a kind of desperation in his voice that had Lenny interested in what he had to say.

"I want to know who put the contract out and why. And I want to know about the girlfriend."

"What about the girlfriend?"

Bill had struck a nerve. He saw it straight away. There was something that was troubling Lenny even more than the fact that he was sitting in a prison facing two murder raps and waiting to be put away for life. Lenny wanted to talk, and this was the time for Bill to level with him, at least a little bit. He told him that someone had been getting calls from Radovic's phone. The calls were from a girl and she had sounded young. Very young.

"There was a kid in there!" Lenny blurted it out as though he had been holding it in his mouth so long he had to take a breath. His eyes were wide open and intense. "There was a fucking kid in there, man!"

"Where?"

"In the unit, man! In the fucking unit!" Lenny buried his face in his hands and let out a painful groan. "They took her with them. They took the fucking kid."

"Who? Who took the kid?"

"The other guy." His voice was frail and broken. "And whoever organised the hit, I guess. I don't know."

"Where did they take her?"

Fiske looked up through bloodshot eyes, tears rolling down both cheeks.

"I don't know, man, I don't know. I didn't even fucking see her. But I heard her, man." He shook his head and dropped it back into his hands. "She was screaming. Poor little kid, man, she was fucking terrified."

It came out in bits and pieces. It was a story that he had been waiting to tell someone. When you come up the way that Lenny had you don't talk to coppers and you tell your lawyer only what he needs to hear. But a secret like this one was too much for Lenny Fiske. The only person who had ever meant a thing to him was his gran, and he couldn't bear to think that he had helped to execute a defenceless woman. The guilt of it stung him more than any bullet in the face, and every night since it had happened he had lain awake listening to the frantic screams of the woman and the sobbing of the child.

Once Lenny had composed himself a little he was surprisingly forthcoming; within an hour Bill was confident he had as much of the truth as Lenny knew. He had got a call on his mobile a few days before the twelfth from some guy who'd said his name was Steve. This guy Steve wanted to meet and talk about a bit of scratch, so they met on the beach front at Narrowneck. Steve was a big guy with a bald head, looked to be in his late forties, but Lenny didn't know him. He said he had a job to roll Radovic. The bookie was said to be carrying some serious money which he had in deep snooker; exactly where, he wasn't saying. But he owed enough around the town to make someone very interested in relieving him of some of it. That was Steve's job. All he wanted Lenny to do was stand guard outside the front door. Radovic had some pretty heavy mates and he didn't want any of them running in on him. Steve would supply him with a piece just in case there was any trouble, but there wouldn't be. All he had to do was stand out front and stay out of the way. The job paid five grand, regardless of how much they pulled out of there. Lenny knew something of this Radovic and figured that he had it coming. And jobs were hard to find, so five pianos wouldn't go astray. They got into the complex by breaking into the downstairs unit and then walking through to the central staircase and up to Radovic's place. Steve went up through a manhole in the stairwell area and into the penthouse through the ceiling. He had a .22 pistol fitted with a silencer. Lenny first realised there was something not quite right when he heard just one shot – ping – then something falling heavily against the door. It sounded like someone had gone down. Then he heard a woman scream. Steve had never mentioned anything about a woman. It was a terrified, piercing, agonised scream – he'd heard it in his head a thousand times since then. He heard a door slam and then more screaming. This wasn't Lenny's go. There was murder going on inside and Lenny wasn't interested in killing women. He rammed the door with his shoulder but it was rock solid. Inside he could hear someone else trying to force another door. And then he heard the little kid. He heard her crying and calling out to her mother. "Mummy, Mummy, please don't let him hurt me, please!" He put three or four shots straight in through the front-door handle and then kicked it open.

There was a reception waiting for him. In the darkness he could just make out Steve's big frame in front of him holding out the pistol. And then bang! When he woke up Radovic was on the floor beside him with one through his noggin, and the girlfriend was in the bedroom in a similar condition. The kid was gone.

"He never said nothing about no women and kids."

Bill Keliher believed every word of it. The police hadn't yet told anyone that they'd found Lenny's palm print on the downstairs balcony – they were going to play that trick at the last minute. So Lenny didn't know about it, but his story explained why it was there. He hadn't set out to kill anyone but on his own account he'd go down for murder, and that meant he was going in for life.

"I hope you're not running that as your defence."

"Don't be fucking stupid!"

They went through his story to the lawyer and then Bill filled him in on the surprise evidence that was coming and helped him work up a response. Eddie Moran was not to be told anything about their little chat. Lenny just had to make sure he asked the question and Bill would give him the right answers.

Just as Bill was set to leave, Lenny recollected one last detail that he hadn't mentioned.

"That bloke Steve had a tattoo on his right forearm."

"Can you describe it for me?"

Lenny plucked Bill's biro from the desk and pulled a piece of paper across in front of him. He drew a diagram of the tattoo and turned the paper round for Bill's inspection.

As Inspector William Keliher sat in his office at Sydney city headquarters, he thought about that strange insignia. He slipped the folded paper from his pocket and flattened out the page in front of him. Lenny Fiske had drawn a Christian cross with a capital B framed into the lower right-hand corner. The last time Bill had seen that emblem it was traced out in dried flakes of the blood of Garry Willet.

\*　　\*　　\*

Kirsten Foster was no dummy. She hadn't had much education but she had a brain and she had some go in her. She'd known Eddie Moran most of her life. He and her big brother Terry used to box together with Jim Kelsy at the city gym. Eddie always treated her like dirt, but then Eddie treated everyone like dirt. He called her Slick, for reasons she never could fathom. When she turned fifteen she left school and did a typing course, then moved out to Parramatta where she got a job working for a tyre company. By the age of nineteen she was married to a dirty low-down rat called Trevor Ellowe. Trevor was a real hunk, but he was never any good. He was a junkie and a scam merchant, and when he'd spent everything that Kirsten had, he went out and tried to steal from everybody else. She loved him and she wasted ten years of her life with him, but the best thing Trev had ever done for either of them was to get himself killed in a car crash in the Cross one night.

Kirsten got some money for it and she gave him a fancy funeral and an undertaker that made Trev look better than she'd seen him in a long time.

So she came to Queensland to start a new life for herself, and she ended up working for Eddie. By then he was a big star. Everyone knew Edwin C. Moran, lawyer to the rich and famous. But she knew he was still just Eddie. He was an arsehole, always had been. He couldn't help himself. But he gave her a new job and a new start when she needed it. He was okay.

Still, she wasn't going to take shit from the likes of Eddie all her life. She had one more term to go to finish her matriculation and then she was off to university. She'd worked hard to get this far, and nothing was going to stop her now. Every Wednesday night she had dinner in the mall in Surfers and then she came back into the office and worked on the computers doing research for her assignments through till midnight or whatever. She didn't mind the late nights. She was a late-night girl.

It was about eleven when Kirsten got up to make herself a cup of coffee. She was fiddling with Eddie's fancy new cappuccino machine when she heard something in the outer office.

"Eddie? Is that you?"

There was no answer but she heard a shuffle near the storeroom that made her start. Someone was there.

"Eddie?"

Suddenly the lights went out. Everything was black and Kirsten was groping and stumbling in the darkness.

She could hear someone moving close to her and her heart was pumping blood into her face and ears. She tried to scream but couldn't – all that came out was a breathless whimper.

Then she saw him in the blue light of the darkness, a tall black figure striding towards her. She saw his arm go back and then his fist come forward, slamming flush onto her cheek and splintering the bone around her eye. Everything went blank as she crashed back against the chairs and desks and down onto the floor. Then she was being lifted up again. He had a handful of her hair and was dragging her upwards until he lined up another punch that slammed into her face. They came again, one after another, as her vision mercifully disappeared behind her streaming blood and lapsing consciousness. She came to as she was being dragged clear of the broken chairs, sliding freely on the thick warm film of her own blood on the marble floor. It was like a dream now and she watched with a detached horror as he lifted one heavy boot and smashed it down onto her leg. She could hear the bones snap but she felt nothing.

As her eyes opened she was lying with her face flat on the cold hard floor. She could hear the rasping of her own breath as the blood gurgled in her throat. He was standing near her at the filing cabinet, leafing through the contents with a casual precision. He found what he wanted and started to remove the folders one by one as she coughed a spray of blood onto the floor. He looked down at her and then he stooped and took her by the throat. She was being lifted, her eyes seeing nothing but his huge hand and the curious blue pattern on his forearm. A cross, a strange Christian cross. Her eyes rolled back and took her to the sanctuary of blackness.

When she woke up in hospital, she could feel the pain everywhere even through the drugs. She eased her eyes open in the subdued night-time lighting of the ward. She was breathing gingerly, the breath still rasping in and out, as her eyes slowly found their focus. Beside the bed, Eddie Moran was sprawled untidily over two chairs with his head back, snoring lightly. He had eaten all her chocolates and his crumpled shirt and jacket were strewn with crumbs from the chip packet open on his lap. She watched him in silence. He was a mess. He looked a little bit like she felt. There was ash in the water vase and a cigarette stubbed out on the 'Thank you for not smoking' card.

Suddenly Eddie snorted, grunted, and opened up his eyes. He sat there looking at her for a long moment while his brain stretched into shape and she smiled feebly back at him. Eddie sucked in a reviving breath and moved forward in his chair.

"How you going, kiddo?"

"How do I look?"

"Fabulous."

They talked in whispers for a while until her eyes began to close as the drugs and the exertion dragged her back down.

"That guy, Eddie," she murmured through her slumber. "I think he took the Fiske file."

"Take it easy, Slick. We'll talk about it later."

"I didn't tell the cops that."

She was talking in her sleep. Eddie pulled his chair forward and laid his hand gently on her forehead and stroked her soft hair in time with her breathing.

"You know what, Eddie? Sing to me."

Not many people knew that Eddie Moran sang. He'd been singing since Kirsten was a little girl, and he'd always had a sweet, sweet sound. When Eddie played his guitar and sang the blues, she couldn't hate him any more.

"Yeah? What'll it be, Slick?"

"Anything by Tommy Waits."

Eddie tapped his knee and eased into a soft rendition of 'Heart Attack and Vine'. As he finished the first verse and slapped time through into the second, Slick half opened one bruised eye and smiled contentedly.

"I love you, Eddie."

"I'm telling you, I'm going to get you in the sack one day."

She smiled again and closed her eye. "Not today, Eddie. Please."

She was a tough chick. She'd pull through.

Long after she'd gone off to sleep he watched her in the dim light, feeling sick with anger. This wasn't just a break-in. This was a warning. Someone was trying to convince Eddie that it wasn't in his interests to be too smart, or to ask too many questions or go telling any tales about things he might have heard. Whoever it was didn't understand jack shit about Edwin C. Moran.

# CHAPTER ELEVEN

The Claw was strutting around the ring, rolling his arms and growling at the frenzied crowd like a demented gorilla off its medication. The dissidents in the back three rows and the motley crew in the bar area were peppering him with obscenities, but packed in around the ring the true believers were bellowing the chant: "Maul-er! Maul-er! Maul-er!" Each time the Claw leaned on the ropes and roared at them, they erupted in a crescendo of cheers and hoots, then settled back to "Maul-er! Maul-er Maul-er!" Bob Scully was on the microphone going through the usual mindless routine of how the Claw had taken on all-comers and hospitalised them all, how many feared he must be unstoppable, how this bout with the Mauler was to be the true test of his supremacy, and so on and so forth. Every few words Bob would suck in some air and catch his breath then launch into another barrage of his gravel-throated spiel; he'd eaten too much of the Peking duck before the show and the trousers of his dinner suit were getting smaller every day.

*   *   *

"Okay, Frankie, let's get out there!"

Frank Vagianni flexed his muscles in the mirror and tried to put some real venom into his snarl. He clawed his hands and bared his teeth and summoned all the terror he could for nine thirty on a Thursday night. The frenetic chant was reaching fever pitch outside as Frankie huffed and puffed and growled into the mirror. He was running through the routine in his head. He would do the stomp around the ring once and then get up on the second rope to salute the faithful. Then Tom would take him from behind in a backward Frankensteiner. The crowd loved it when the Claw played dirty pool, and Frank and Tom had agreed that Tom should get down and dirty straight away. Just how long Frank would stay on the deck they'd play by ear, depending on how the punters were reacting. By the sound of all the chanting going on out there this mob wasn't going to need too much encouragement. Bob Scully would put a couple of two counts on him before they worked their way up to a ropes routine. Tom would put him down in two or three coathangers and then Frank would recover with a reverse whip. Tom knew to give him plenty of room because Frank's knee was still a little dickie and he didn't want to throw it out again.

"Maul-er! Maul-er! Maul-er!"

Frank breathed out, and his gut slumped over the edge of his trunks. It was going to be a tough night.

Even the grunts and hollers of the ugh-boot set outside couldn't seem to lift him. He was in top shape for his age, but at nearly forty-five it seemed to get a little harder every time. How the hell had he let Boris talk him back again?

It wasn't hard to answer: three hundred for a half an hour in the ring. Boris Levsky had been doing the championship wrestling nights at the RSL for the past five years and the money had been good for Frank. His private investigations business paid the rent and alimony, but serving process for solicitors and the odd traffic-accident investigation for a damages action were never going to bring in the big bucks. At his age he was lucky to be asked, but then Boris owed him big-time. And anyway, he'd been working out in Levsky's Gym so long he practically had shares in the low joint. The Masked Mauler was a real crowd favourite almost from the jump. Frankie loved to ham it up, and the mask gave him the anonymity he needed to still show his face in public in the daylight. The Frank Vagianni Private Investigation Agency bought Frankie's bread and butter, but championship wrestling had put some gravy on his lamb chops. And Frank liked his gravy.

He had been out of the police force now since eighty-nine when that dirty filthy Fitzgerald Inquiry mob had stuck their noses in. Ever since those blokes showed up, things had gone steadily downhill for Frankie. He still couldn't believe the fuss they'd made, all over the proceeds of the Waterworld armed robbery.

It wasn't as though Frankie hadn't done a top job on

the bust. Within an hour of the robbery they had the two bad guys and all the loot. You can't do much better than that. Frankie had tailed them all the way into Surfers while Bertie Pratt was hanging out the back window of the getaway car taking potshots at the coppers like a cowboy in a B-grade matinee. Bertie was out on licence from a murder blue already, and at nearly sixty years of age he didn't have too much to lose. If they caught him he wasn't going to see the light of day again. And Frankie caught him.

When they ditched the car down in the Cascades and took off into the mangroves, Frankie followed them. Bertie and his mate opened up down on the riverbank but Frank waited for his chance and then got hold of the young bloke and kicked the shit out of him. The good thing about crims was they were all too dumb to realise their bullets would eventually run out. The other coppers got Bertie as he dragged himself back up the riverbank covered in mud and midges, but Frank was the big hero.

Talk about being a rooster one day and a feather duster the next. The Waterworld job was the start of all his woes. Bertie and his mate had two big plastic bags with about eighty grand in them. On the way back to the station the young bloke said they'd had a tip-off that it was all black money that hadn't gone through the cash registers and no one at Waterworld would want to put his hand up for it. That started everybody thinking.

That morning the uniformed boys had pinched 'Fair Deal' Freddie Staines, an old pickpocket who worked all the race meets and football games along the east coast. Freddie was in for questioning over a lorryful of hot Armani suits, but he had a pocketful of cash and he kept saying he had to get to the track that afternoon to put the lot on the nose of some hot tip. Now Freddie was an old lag and he wasn't in the habit of talking to coppers; in fact he wouldn't even tell the dentist what tooth to pull. But this horse was such a good thing that Freddie couldn't bear the thought of his not getting on, and he started offering to hold his hand up for the suits if they let him out just long enough to get down to the track and lay his bet.

He promised to come straight back to the watch-house but everyone agreed that wasn't on. They also agreed that he obviously had some red-hot mail. So they did a deal with Fair Deal Freddie: he gave them the name of the horse, and they promised to get his money on.

It was a rank outsider listed at fifteen to one – too good to miss. So they talked about it and decided that since nobody wanted Waterworld's black money they'd call it ten instead of eighty. That left them seventy to play with. Even if they could get odds of ten to one, Freddie's tip would pay them around seven hundred big ones when it came home. Split between the five detectives in the know, they'd come up with nearly a hundred and fifty thousand each.

They didn't quite get tens but they were still looking pretty good, until someone announced that one of the uniforms – a junior constable by the name of Sasha

Kelly – was claiming that the bag she had been asked to lodge in the exhibit office didn't contain all the Waterworld proceeds. She had been at the scene when the getaway car was recovered and she had distinctly seen the detectives taking two large plastic bags stuffed with cash out of the vehicle. Before she created any fuss she rang the accountant at Waterworld and he confirmed that two bags of cash were taken from the safe totalling about eighty grand.

Everyone went into a tight scrum. Someone had a quiet word with Sasha Kelly about whether she might have been mistaken, but she was playing Serpico and there was definitely no shifting her. There was nothing else for it – they'd have to put the money back. Problem was that it was already in the bookies' hands. So they hosed down Sasha Kelly and waited for the starter's gun. Everyone was sweating bullets and no one more than Fair Deal Freddie, sitting in front of a transistor radio in a closed interview room, surrounded by five very agitated coppers with their balls out on the line.

The nag came home by a nose. Freddie Staines fainted and had to be laid out on a table in the day room to recover. The boys picked up just over six forty. Even after the Waterworld cash went back, there was over a hundred in it for each of them. Constable Sasha Kelly looked a bit surprised when they announced the bags had been located, but what could she say?

Frankie put his share of the winnings in a tin he buried in the backyard and put it down to the perks of the job. He picked up a bravery commendation from the

Commissioner for a pinch well done and he took plenty of slaps on the back. It was all looking sweet.

It started to go bad at the committal. Out of the blue the Waterworld accountant comes up with the news that the cash is from the Queen's Birthday weekend takings and has been sitting there for the best part of the past twelve months. Only trouble is, the serial numbers on the notes recovered from the robbery show that a swag of them are recent issues that weren't in circulation twelve months earlier. All hell breaks loose, with the defence trying to wriggle out from under and the coppers doing backflips trying to explain what might have happened. Eventually they got through it, and Bertie Pratt and his accomplice both went down. And it would have ended there, if it hadn't been for the Fitzgerald Inquiry.

When Fitzgerald got the job in eighty-seven to root out corruption in the Queensland police force, he hand-picked his so-called untouchables and Miss Serpico Sasha Kelly was top of the list. She soon reopened the old Waterworld file and next thing they were crawling all over Fair Deal Freddie's peace of mind. To his credit Freddie held firm, but the same couldn't be said for all the coppers. It only took one of them to roll over; he bought himself an indemnity from prosecution and next thing Frank Vagianni and the others were all in the gun. The Police Union's solicitors dropped them when they were declared corrupt, and when the Special Prosecutors' Office laid charges they were all suspended. It was a tough time.

They all beat the blue eventually, but by the time it was over the money was all gone and Frankie's name was shit. There was no place for him in the post-Fitzgerald force, that much was clear enough. He stayed around long enough to make it look respectable and then he cashed in the super and said goodbye.

So now Frank was serving process for solicitors and putting headlocks on the Claw. It wasn't what he'd really wanted out of life, but it was a living.

"Maul-er! Maul-er! Maul-er!"

The crowd were chanting wildly as Frank strode out of the dressing room, and by the time he had arrived ringside he was finally starting to feel a little bit pumped up. Through the eye-holes of his mask he could see people all around him jumping up and down and waving their arms madly as he pulled himself up onto the stage. There was something about it all that he still loved. It was exhilarating, and Frank couldn't help but get swept up with the moment. He had planned to climb through the ropes as usual, but the showman in him got the better of him. Frank climbed up on the corner-post and growled at the crowd. They went crazy, cheering and applauding as he held his arms up in a victory salute. Frank was feeling bulletproof as he leaped off the post down into the ring.

He forgot about his dickie knee. As the Masked Mauler hit the canvas, his knee twisted under him and he went down grimacing in pain. The Claw looked perplexed. He stomped around the ring a couple of times circling his prostrate opponent, who lay there holding one knee and groaning, "Shit! Shit! Shit!" Then the Claw seized the moment. He dropped down on top of Frankie and pinned him to the canvas. The crowd called foul, and booed and hissed at this unfair attack on an incapacitated man. It was great stuff, and Bob Scully had been in show business long enough to know exactly what to do. He dropped on two knees and slapped the canvas.

"One-ah! Two-ah! Three-ah!"

It was all over. The Claw had won the bout unfairly and the whole crowd went berserk. They were yelling and screaming and stamping their feet in a display of universal outrage. Meanwhile the Claw was milking it. As the ring attendants carried the hapless Mauler back to the dressing room, the Claw stomped around the ring waving his arms and hurling abuse and generally doing everything he could to maximise the fury of the incensed crowd.

"Frankie mate, I loved it! You were fabulous!"

Boris Levsky was beaming. The big grudge match had turned into a boil-over and the Gold Coast public obviously wouldn't rest until they saw the Mauler get his chance to mix it with the Claw in a fair fight. Outside the crowd were roaring wildly and Bob Scully was on the microphone already talking up a rematch. It was beautiful.

Frank looked down at his puffed-up knee. It was an old football injury and he knew from experience that it would take a couple of days to come good. He did up the buttons on his shirt and stuffed the last of his gear back into his carrybag. He was going home to knock the top off a cold one and try to forget about today. As he struggled with the zip, a phone started ringing somewhere near the bottom of his bag. He dragged his gear back out and fossicked for his phone. This hadn't been his best day ever.

"Hello."

"Frank, it's Eddie Moran."

"Eddie, how are you, mate?"

"Good, buddy. But I need your help."

"You've got it."

Frank Vagianni didn't forget friends or enemies. Eddie Moran was Frankie's friend. When the solicitors had run dead on him and even his old mates had disowned him, Frank had realised it was time to get himself the biggest arsehole in the game. So he got Eddie. Eddie Moran was with him till the bitter end, giving cheek to everyone in sight and fighting like his life depended on it. Even when the money had finally run out, Eddie hung in there, mainly because by then it had got personal. He hated the Special Prosecutors even more than they despised him, which was no mean feat. If it hadn't been for Eddie, Frank Vagianni would have lost everything.

"We had a break-in on Monday night."

"Anything missing?"

"Yeah."

"What can I do?"

"It's sort of a long story. Did you see the news tonight?"

"No. What news?"

"I think you better have a look at it."

# CHAPTER TWELVE

TOP COP ON SEX CHARGES. The headline was spread over every newspaper in the stand. Frank grabbed a copy of the *Courier* and slapped two coins on the counter. He was looking at the shocked expression on the face of big Bill Keliher, flanked by fresh-faced young detectives frogmarching him through the media scrum. It was a still-shot of the same scene he'd watched the night before on the late-night television news. Inspector William Keliher, one of New South Wales' most senior and respected police detectives, twice decorated for bravery in the field, a man with thirty-two years' exemplary service, had been charged with sixteen sex offences and was being paraded before the frenzied media like a Christian on his way to meet the lions.

Frank could still see the footage of big Boofhead Bill, frightened and confused, squinting in the brightness of the arc lights, trying to keep his head up as he was bumped and jostled through the crowd. 'Police Inspector William Keliher is tonight behind bars, charged with multiple counts of kidnapping, abduction and sexual assault following one of the state's longest running and most closely guarded crime investigations. A joint task force comprising senior officers of the New South Wales police force and the Juvenile Crimes Commission today closed the net on Keliher after an investigation spanning nearly thirty years.'

Frank Vagianni had a hollow feeling in his chest. He had slept fitfully all night, the pain in his swollen knee somehow a symptom of the dark shapes and melancholy mood that permeated his dreams. He hobbled gingerly to Charlie's on the mall and laid the newspaper down on a sunny table.

"Just coffee, mate."

Peter behind the counter waved acknowledgement. When Frank was in the mood, they always had a busy time keeping the toast, eggs and baked beans up to him but this morning he obviously wasn't hungry. He was slumped heavily over the table, studying his newspaper.

'Last night Assistant Commissioner John Ockenhausen praised the efforts of the crack eight-man squad that used the latest forensic techniques including DNA profiling and computerised information systems to bring the investigation to a conclusion.'

Frank couldn't believe it. He'd known Bill Keliher for longer than he could remember and he had more respect for him as a copper and a bloke than just about anyone in the job. How could Boof Keliher be a sex offender? Frank traced back over all the times they'd had together, busting crooks, out on the drink, sitting around courthouses, working long nights trying to stitch up the bad guys. It made no sense at all.

It was hard to work out from the newspaper story exactly what was alleged against him, but as Frank could understand it there had been three series of attacks on females, some as young as fifteen, in and around the Sydney area. The first offences occurred in the early seventies in the Harbord area and took place over a period of thirteen months. Young girls were attacked after dark on their way home from work or school, drugged with chloroform, stripped and raped, then dumped unconscious on the footpath. Bill Keliher had been stationed nearby at Manly, and the attacks had stopped around the time he was transferred into the city. In the mid eighties the attacks commenced again, same modus operandi, and they recurred at various locations in the inner city for about another two years. Then they stopped again. The latest offences were said to be relatively recent, but the article gave no further details about them. It simply said that detectives had been able to link the crimes together to expose 'the bizarre picture of a Jekyll and Hyde character who by day was a well-respected police officer and family man, and by night a vicious criminal who stalked the city's streets'.

Sex was a strange thing. It was impossible to predict what might make a man want to take his dick out of his dacks. But this was very heavy stuff. This was loony-tunes territory. When you knew a bloke the way Frank thought he knew Bill Keliher, surely you had to have noticed something.

"Like the headline?"

Eddie Moran arrived at the table with a cappuccino in one hand and a doughnut in the other. Only Eddie could eat doughnuts at this hour of the day.

"So what's this theory of yours?"

"I've told you about your mate Bill's little stunt with Lenny Fiske. My guess is he knew more about why Lenny went to see the bookie than the rest of us did. Maybe even more than Lenny." Eddie took two chomps of the doughnut and washed it down with coffee. "After that goon belted Slick, I went up to the prison and snuck a look through Lenny's visitor records. Big Bill went to see him just before he delivered the now-famous little bit of bullshit that let Lenny off the hook. Now either he got paid for that or he did it for some other reason. My guess is the latter." Moran poked one finger at the headline on the table. "I think Mr Keliher is a man with a lot of skeletons in his closet, and he didn't want any getting out."

Frank looked hard at the lawyer. Eddie could be an obnoxious prick when he wanted to. "Bill Keliher's no rapist."

"Don't put your last dollar on it, Frank." Eddie was leaning forward in his chair building up a head of steam. "They've got fingerprints, ID, even DNA. Billy-boy was a closet deev." Frank was annoyed, despite himself. He could see what Moran was up to, trying to stir him up, get him defensive, make him want to disprove all this. "He stuck his neck out a long way to spring Lenny on that murder charge. Now there's someone else who wants to know how Lenny beat that blue, and he wants to know bad enough he's willing to send a leg breaker in to stomp all over Slick and lift Lenny's file. And he knows that something shifty has gone on because he's obviously not too worried about yours truly running to the cops. So whatever happened between Keliher and Lenny Fiske, Eric Pohl knows something about it."

"So what?"

"So what? So it just so happens Eric Pohl is an associate of a known sex offender by the name of Robert Allen, who Keliher tried to stitch up for the McCabe kidnapping. With no small assistance from you, I might add. And now Keliher's up on kidnapping too. What a coincidence!"

Eddie stuffed the rest of the doughnut in his mouth. He was starting to enjoy the sound of his own voice, but Frank didn't want to listen to it any more.

"What do you want from me, Eddie?"

"I want you to find out what's going on, Frank. I think all these boys are into something they shouldn't be, and people are getting hurt just so they can keep their little secrets. I want to know what their secrets are."

"Keliher's not a rapist, and he's no kidnapper."

"You believe what you want to, Frank. I'm not interested in Keliher. I want this Eric Pohl. I'm going to nail him for what he did to Slick. And I'm going to nail the animal he sent in to do the job."

Frank sat silently processing the information. He didn't like the sound of it. Revenge was a messy motive for any sort of business, and lawyers running private agendas were a complete disaster. On top of that, every way you turned on this one you might see Frank's old friend Bill Keliher, and that was one thing he didn't want to do. If it was true, Frank didn't want to be the one to prove it. But then again, maybe it wasn't.

"Well, Frank? Are you in?"

"I'll think about it."

Frank didn't really think he would, but as it turned out it was all he seemed able to think about all day. He started the morning going through his unpaid accounts and trying to reconcile his bank statements, but it was no good. His mind just kept on wandering. Bill Keliher was a gentle giant, an ordinary bloke with kids of his own. He worked hard, liked a beer, was dedicated to his job. How could he be some sort of night stalker? Frank thought about the lurid tags the press were already bandying about. 'A Jekyll and Hyde.' 'A master criminal who lived a double life.' 'Police officer by day, rapist by night.' Boof Keliher? A sex fiend? How could it be? When they went to Amy's for a free root, Bill usually spent the whole time downstairs playing pool. Was that it? Did he have some kind of problem? Frank kept thinking about the bloke in England they called the Yorkshire Ripper. Supposedly he didn't even remember any of the crimes he had committed. Was Bill some sort of nutcase?

According to the papers, they had fingerprints and DNA on him. There were sixteen charges spread over nearly thirty years. Sixteen. One or two might be bullshit, but sixteen? With that kind of smoke there had to be some fire. Even if he wasn't right for them all, there was more to Bill Keliher than Frank had ever seen.

By ten thirty Frank had to get out. He didn't exactly have clients beating down his door and he needed to clear his mind. He closed down the office and headed over to Levsky's for a work-out. It was hopeless. The place was full of knockabouts and ex-coppers who all wanted to talk about Boof Keliher. They'd seen it on the TV and they'd read about it and they'd thought about it, and they couldn't believe it. Of all the people that might qualify as a deviate rock-spider Bill was the last. By the time Frank dragged himself out of there he had done a lot of talking and not much else, and he left with a feeling that something wasn't right. Anyone can fool some people all the time, but Bill was universally well thought of, even by blokes he'd pinched at one time or another.

Frank was depressed. He'd always known that black was black and white was white, and if you kept your eyes open and one ear to the ground nothing much would pass you by. He had sat through all the social-worker profiles and the psychological mumbo jumbo and the defence-lawyer bullshit, but he had always been able to work out why people did what people did, and that had made him a good cop. He could work a bad guy out before they worked it out themselves. Or so he had thought.

Frank got back to the office just after twelve. If there were no messages stuck to the door, he'd head back home, pick up a carton on the way, and spend the afternoon watching the fights on video.

"A lady dropped in to see you."

Paul, the gay guy who did therapeutic massages down the hall, was hanging by one arm from the doorjamb.

"Who was she?"

"She didn't give a name but I said you'd probably be back in by one. She said she'd come back then."

"Fuck!"

Paul had seen Frank cranky more than once and he didn't need to hang around. Frank huffed and puffed a bit but eventually felt silly pacing up and down the empty hallway and retreated to his office. He had forgotten the two stubbies that were still sitting at the bottom of the fridge but when he found them he felt much better. By the time he heard the knock on the outer office door, it was a more mellow Frank Vagianni that climbed out from behind his desk.

"Hello, Mr Vagianni."

The handsome fifty-something woman held her hand out to him confidently. She was too elegantly dressed to be a client. Either his ex-wife had a new lawyer or this sheila was in the wrong place. Frank took her hand and shook it.

"Frank."

"Yes. Frank." The troubled look around her eyes turned quizzical. "Don't you remember me, Frank?"

Before she had the question out his brain was already putting some pieces into place. She was familiar to him. He knew her pleasant face, her gentle manner. He knew her well.

"Hello, Faye."

He'd never called her Faye before; she was always Mrs McCabe. But Frank had come a long way since then. He had nothing to be proud of in the McCabe case, but he had nothing to be ashamed of either.

"I spoke to Morrie Fleet last night. He suggested that I call you."

The news about Bill Keliher had first broken in the Sydney press in the late afternoon and was sent around Australia. The detectives on the case had timed the arrest to meet the preferred four p.m. deadline for the television stations to have their story in the can for the six o'clock news. Those that were quick enough had snippets in their late-afternoon bulletins, and the radio stations had it as their lead on the five p.m. news and every hour after that. The story had leapt out at Faye from the radio, alleging everything but explaining nothing. Her brain had lurched from shock to confusion, the questions hardly formulated before they were replaced by new, even more frightening ones.

She had been that way for almost an hour. And then she saw him, lead story on the television news. He was older now and greyer, still a big man but dwarfed by his surroundings. When she saw his face she clutched her mouth and gasped for breath. The answers came. This was the same Bill Keliher she had always known.

"There's been some sort of terrible mistake." The

words crept feebly from her mouth at first, but she recovered quickly. "Bill Keliher didn't do these things."

Frank Vagianni's face was blank, devoid of all expression. She could see he was listening, but was he hearing her? What did he know of Bill Keliher? Had he seen the man's soul? She had.

"Someone was trying to blackmail him." Her voice had real strength to it now. "I don't know why. But it had something to do with that bookmaker who was murdered. Radovic. And I think these charges are tied up with it."

As soon as the news was over, she had telephoned Morrie Fleet. Since Vince Donnelly's death he was the only other one she'd stayed in touch with. Morrie was a mess. It took him all of two minutes to cave in and tell her about the meetings they'd had. Bill was going to talk to Lenny Fiske and the next thing Morrie knows Fiske is acquitted, and then he's murdered and the press is full of crazy speculation about what Radovic was up to. And now Bill had been charged, and anyone who knew Bill knew that he was one of God's own gentlemen.

Morrie's ranting confirmed what she was already sure of in her heart. Bill Keliher was no kidnapper and no rapist. He was a good decent man who had lived her grief with her and had remained faithful to their love for thirty years.

"Morrie faxed me these and said to give them to you. He said if anybody knows you've got them, it means his job."

Frank Vagianni took the pages in his hands and studied them. They were the outgoing telephone records from the bookie's penthouse for the six weeks prior to his death. He ran through them carefully, looking for recurring numbers, patterns, anything familiar.

Faye McCabe sat silently waiting, wondering what was going through Bill's mind right now. She remembered those nights before the dreadful tragedy, when she had gone to him and they had held each other. She could still smell the skin on his face and neck, feel the gentle touch of his broad hands on her body, hear his deep voice whispering in her ear. For a time she had felt reborn, believed again that she might one day walk to the horizon, live her dreams. But the mornings always brought guilt, and the shame of her betrayal. And as much as he had become everything to her, she knew that he couldn't be. She had a role that lived above her dreams, transcended her desires. Her children loved their father. Her life with Barry had devolved into breakfast on the table and cold beer in the fridge, but when he was home he loved his children, and he made them happy. That was all that mattered. Bill had talked crazy, desperate talk, about running away together, making a new life. But it wasn't her life that mattered, it was her children's. In the end she broke it off, cruelly in a way, but mercifully. He couldn't understand, or didn't want to, and those weeks were heartbreaking for them both. And then the children disappeared and everything went crazy. But even in the depth of her despair she knew he was still there somewhere, and he cared.

Frank Vagianni looked at Faye McCabe across the desk. She of all people had cause to doubt Bill Keliher. She knew Bill had been there when her kids had disappeared; she knew what people were saying about him now. Her kids were still missing after thirty years. In the past twenty-four hours she must have asked the question. But if she had, she wore the answer clear enough in her expression.

"Can I get a copy of these?"

The tone of Frank Vagianni's voice told her that he believed Bill Keliher was innocent.

"Frank, I want you to get him a lawyer. The best there is."

"That's easy." Frank lifted up the phone and punched in the numbers.

"Okay Eddie, you got me. I'll help you to pin Pohl."

"Good."

Moran sounded like there had never been any doubt about it. Frank hated that.

"But on one condition, Eddie. You act for Bill Keliher."

He could hear Eddie sucking on his cigarette and blowing out the smoke. "That's a bit messy isn't it, Frank? What happens when you find out he's guilty?"

"I wouldn't tell you anyway."

"I already know he's guilty, Frank."

"That's never stopped you before, Eddie."

"No, I don't suppose it has."

\* \* \*

Elizabeth Nichols was waiting nervously in the reception area. She had tried for over ten years to put the nightmare of her abduction behind her. She was barely out of her teens when it happened, a young woman she remembered now as happy, carefree, confident. It wasn't really so. She had always been uncertain of herself, a nervous, lonely child who was struggling to cope with her adulthood. The hideous attack had devastated her. Physically she had recovered well enough in time; the scars sickened her, but the wounds had healed. It was the memories that still haunted her, stalking her like that maniac who had attacked in the darkness all those years ago.

"Thanks for coming in, Elizabeth. I'm Wally Messner. This is Sergeant Peter Farrow."

Elizabeth followed the two officers to an interview room – closed and windowless, with stark fluorescent lighting, one table and three chairs. It aroused unpleasant memories and she wrung her hands as the two detectives arranged their paperwork. They had caught someone, a policeman who had attacked not only her but many others. It had been on the television and in all the newspapers. He was a psychopath of some kind, a sort of split personality who pretended to be helping people and upholding the law but was just a vicious animal, the animal who had attacked her, leapt at her from the darkness and taken away her life. They had him now and he would be punished, locked away so that maybe some day Elizabeth could walk in a city street at night, or sit in a darkened cinema, or sleep untroubled by the noises of the night. He had been identified already, but they wanted her help too. She was one of the few who had seen the face of the attacker – only briefly in the darkness, but she had seen it – and the memory was in her mind for ever. It was hard to recognise him from the news footage, but he was more than ten years older now; all she had seen on television was a fleeting glimpse of an older man being jostled through the crowd. Detective Messner would show her a photograph taken of him at the time. She would recognise him instantly, she knew she would.

"All right, Elizabeth, now I'm going to show you a board that contains twelve photographs of twelve different men who should all be roughly the same age and fit the general description of your attacker. What I want you to do is take your time and look carefully at each of the faces, and just tell us if any of them look familiar. Okay?"

Elizabeth felt her heart quicken and the hairs on the back of her neck tingle. In a second she would be looking at the face of the monster who had savaged her. The panic of that night rushed into her stomach. She could feel his iron grip crushing her resistance, pinning her arms against her body; she could smell the chloroform clogging her throat and mouth and nose.

"I think I'm going to be sick."

She clutched at her mouth and waited helplessly as the wave of nausea engulfed her, incapacitated her, and finally subsided. One of the officers was holding a glass of water out in front of her, and she took it and sipped, until she felt her nerves gradually relaxing.

"I think I'm ready now."

"You right?"

"Yes. Thank you."

"Sure?"

Elizabeth nodded purposefully and braced herself as Detective Messner flipped over the white board to reveal the photographs of the twelve men. She was relieved to survive the initial shock. None of them leapt out at her immediately. She was grateful for that. Her recognition would be more gradual, less brutal. She would study each face, one at a time. They were arranged in three lines of four, all big men, muscular, brown or sandy-coloured hair, square jaw. Just as she remembered him. But now as she went through, she couldn't find him. He looked so different on the television, so much older, stressed and under pressure, not like the faces in these photographs. There were several that could be him.

She went through them one more time. She knew he was there. They had already caught him. One of these photographs showed the man that had attacked her and all the others, and the police were relying on her to help them put him away. All she had to do was find the right one and the monster would be locked away. He was one of them, she knew he was one of them. Which one was he?

"Number one looks sort of familiar."

It was a bad start. They had Bill Keliher right there smack bang in the middle of the photo board at number seven. She didn't need a map to find him.

"Yeah. Anyone else?"

"Ah, number three?"

Maybe she did need a map.

"Right. What about further down? Take your time. Go through each row carefully. Do you see anybody further down? Maybe in the second row there at all?"

"Gee, I don't know. They're all so similar."

The frustration must have showed on Wally's face. Peter Farrow stepped in to ease her through the process.

"Yeah, that's okay," he said cheerily. "You've been through the top line. See anyone in the second line that looks familiar?"

"Ah, five maybe?"

"Yeah, right. Now, anyone else there in that line?"

"Gee, not really."

"That's okay, Elizabeth, take your time. Would you like another sip of water?"

"No, I'm right thanks."

"Okay, just take your time there. Anyone else you see there in line two?"

"Well, I'm not sure. Number seven maybe?"

"Number seven. Good. Okay. Good. Now what do you recognise about the man in number seven?"

"Well, I'm not really sure."

"But you recognise him as the man that attacked you anyway."

"Ah, well ... "

"You've picked him out as the one anyway, so I suppose we can say you've just generally recognised his whole overall appearance as being like the attacker."

"Yes, I think so, yes."

"That's good, Elizabeth. Excellent." Farrow snatched the card from her before she had a chance to change her mind. "All right," he said, turning it over, "I'll get you to write number seven on the back of the board and just sign it for us."

"Is that him is it?"

"Sure is."

"Oh, I thought so. It's just that they all look so alike."

"Yeah, that's okay. That's fine."

"I mean, when I look at them now, they're not really alike, I suppose."

"That's okay." Farrow was all smiles. "Just write there something like 'I recognise the man in photo number seven as the one who attacked me', and maybe, you know, if you're ninety per cent certain or ninety-nine per cent or whatever, just write that in, and then just sign it for us on the bottom."

With great relief and a feeling of small triumph, Elizabeth Nichols turned the photo board over and wrote on it: 'I am 100% certain that the man in Photo 7 is the one who attacked me.' As she signed her name she felt a great weight lifted from her shoulders as though she was finally about to be released from her own dark prison.

# CHAPTER THIRTEEN

"Yeah, yeah, I've heard all that shit. I've read all the newspapers, pal. I just haven't seen any evidence!"

Bruce Parforth hated dealing with Edwin Moran. He was a rude, obnoxious pig, and had no idea how to behave. The prosecution of Inspector William Keliher was a plum brief and Bruce had felt greatly honoured when the Director had entrusted it to him. But it all seemed to turn a little sour when he heard that Moran would be defending. And now, standing on the chequered tiles outside the number one Sydney Local Court, he knew exactly why. Moran was a complete boor. He had asked Bruce what the Crown case was and Bruce had summarised the particulars the police had given him; that was enough to launch Moran into his full routine.

"Evidence, pal, evidence! Not press releases, not bullshit! Evidence! You know what evidence is, don't you?"

"Yes." Bruce wished he hadn't answered that.

"Good! Let's see some! If all you're relying on to oppose bail is the supposed strength of the Crown case, then you better have some evidence of what it is. I want someone in the box!"

Moran was headed off in the direction of the cells before Bruce could even counter. He always had to make everything so difficult and unpleasant. This was just to be a mention. Bail had already been refused once; it shouldn't even be an issue here. If Moran wanted to get bail, why didn't he make an application to the Supreme Court? Bruce had intended to come down today just to give the court a time frame as to when the police brief would be completed and when a committal-hearing date might be set. It was to be short, straightforward and uncomplicated. The press would photograph him on his way in and his way out, and none of it would do his reputation any harm, and then he would go back to his office and get some work done. But Moran had to make a chore out of the whole thing. He had given Bruce no notice of any proposed bail application and now he was threatening to object to any statement from the bar table summarising the Crown case. Bruce could put one of the detectives in the box to give evidence on information and belief, but that meant Moran would cross-examine him for sure about every facet of the Crown case and turn the whole thing into a circus for the press. And if Bruce didn't put someone in the box, Moran would announce to all the world that the Crown had no evidence at all.

"The Crown's got enough evidence to sink a battleship, pal." Eddie Moran was staring intently

242

through the glass at his new client. "So you better come up with a few answers pretty bloody quickly."

Bill Keliher stared blankly back at him from the confines of the tiny interview room. He had heard so many threats and so much tough talk in the past week that he was numb. The lawyer wasn't making any impact. Soon he would be taken up into the courtroom to be the centre of attention once again. In his lifetime he had seen a thousand people marched up the creaking stairs into the old wooden dock. Wretched, miserable people. Guilty people.

"Why would anybody want to set you up for these charges?"

Moran was scowling at him insolently, deriding him, taunting him. Bill didn't care.

"I don't know."

Moran threw his folder into the corner of the narrow desk that separated them on either side of the glass partition.

"Sorry, pal, not good enough!" He pushed his face towards the glass until his mouth was almost touching the speaking grille. "You and your mate Radovic were spending a shitload of time together on the phone." His lowered voice was harsh and accusing. "I want to know what he had to say to you."

The stark fluorescent lighting was reflecting off the glass, obscuring Bill's vision of this new interrogator. He felt strangely detached. His mind had struggled with so many questions in the past few weeks; it was now exhausted, beyond fear, or hope, or even comprehension.

He slowly shook his head then silently buried his face in both hands.

Moran straightened up in his chair, the interrogation over, his voice resigned for now.

"You won't get bail. The Crown's got a very strong case, and right now we've got no answer to it. I'll see you up in court."

He picked up his folder and walked out.

\*　　\*　　\*

"The Crown's got no fucking case at all and you know it! This man should be on bail!"

Bruce Parforth cringed. Trying to have a confidential defence–prosecution discussion with Moran in the foyer was impossible. When he chose to he would without warning trumpet wildly self-serving and invariably inflammatory announcements for all to hear. They echoed throughout the tiled foyer area, to the great amusement of the press who were straining their ears anyway to pick up what they weren't entitled to. Bruce had told Moran that although he had one officer from the investigation team with him to instruct, that officer couldn't give reliable information about all aspects of the investigation; separate tasks had been divided up and allocated to nominated personnel, and since the brief was yet to be compiled, the only one who could give any sort of reliable overview of the case was the officer in charge of the investigation. And Senior Sergeant Messner wasn't here. Moran didn't seem to understand, or didn't want to.

"This is a complete stitch-up!" That announcement made, he thankfully reduced the volume. "If you oppose bail solely on the strength of the Crown case, I'll be objecting to anything short of reliable evidence from someone with a first-hand hold on the investigation. If I don't get that, I'll be assuming that all the press talk about fingerprints and suchlike is a complete beat-up, and I'll be making the point loud and clear in open court."

"I don't think there are fingerprints actually." Parforth said it sheepishly, and immediately regretted it. "I think the media got that wrong."

It was something that had been worrying Bruce all morning, ever since Moran had opened his performance. The Police Commissioner had publicly announced that the investigation team had conducted fingerprint and DNA comparisons and had come up with a strong scientific case against the suspect. That was all true, but although a conclusive DNA match-up for Keliher had been made, linking him positively to the crimes, as yet no prints had been positively matched. The journalists had jumped to that conclusion on the basis of the Commissioner's ambiguously phrased statement. It was just an error by the press and did not detract in any way from what was clearly still an overwhelmingly compelling prosecution case, but Bruce knew what Moran would try to make of it.

"What!"

He bellowed it throughout the foyer, and Bruce braced himself for the barrage that he knew was about to follow. To his surprise it didn't come. Moran took him by the arm and led him away from his associates to a corner in the shadows of the overhanging arches. Finally, he spoke in a conspiratorial whisper.

"Do you know how that's going to sound if it comes out in court today? The Commissioner won't be here. You're going to be the one left trying to explain in front of the eyes and ears of the world what was and wasn't said about those fingerprints."

It was true. It was probably irrelevant but it was true. Bruce didn't like the sound of it.

"Listen, Bruce." Parforth felt Moran's hand on his shoulder. "My bloke's copped a real shellacking in the press so far. If we've got to go in there and argue bail, I'm going to have to square that up." Moran didn't have to paint a picture for Bruce Parforth. He'd seen the Eddie Show before. "Keliher'll get bail. If he doesn't get it here, the Supreme Court will give it to him no question. He's been thirty years a copper for fuck's sake. No priors, exemplary record. All you can hang your hat on is the strength of the Crown case, and the coppers haven't even turned up to support you. It's outrageous, buddy. I wouldn't put up with it if I were you."

It was true. If they wanted Bruce to challenge bail the least they could have done was provide him with a decent brief. Why should he have to go in there and explain what the Commissioner did or didn't say with Moran trying to make a liar out of him? How did he get to be an apologist for arresting officers who hadn't even bothered to turn up?

"I'm telling you, buddy, you shouldn't be expected to run off the hospital passes these coppers are serving up to you. If I were you I'd be speaking to someone with a bit of sense. Someone with some clout. We could work out a consent agreement with appropriate conditions. There'd be no need to call any evidence. The whole thing'd go through in two minutes flat."

Bruce Parforth was thinking. He looked out into the foyer where a phalanx of journalists watched them intently.

"I'll get some instructions."

Bruce left his clerk to hold the fort while he made a beeline to the office of the Juvenile Crimes Commission. Peter Rosenthal had agreed to see him urgently and when he arrived he was shown straight through.

"Why are we opposing?"

Rosenthal had always had a reputation for coming quickly to the point. Bruce tried to give him a concise answer:

"Strong Crown case."

"No, that's a factor that the magistrate should take into account in considering our opposition," the Commissioner replied urbanely. "But why are we opposing? He's not likely to abscond. Are we concerned he'll re-offend if granted bail?"

"Well, we could argue that."

Rosenthal dismissed the comment with obvious distaste. "Are we concerned that there's any real risk of the defendant re-offending at this stage?"

"Probably not, really."

Rosenthal nodded thoughtfully. Keliher had an unblemished record. There was nothing to suggest he might abscond or threaten prosecution witnesses. He had a stable history and ties in the jurisdiction. The charges were serious and the evidence in support of the Crown case was strong, but it was unlikely that the case would be tried for many months. He was probably entitled to be bailed, and even if the magistrate refused him now, a Supreme Court judge would undoubtedly be disinclined to keep a man with his background in prison when so far nothing had been proved against him. Peter Rosenthal had no wish to see the man suffer more than was absolutely necessary.

"See if you can get them to agree to a residential condition and to report daily to the city station. He'll also have to surrender his passport and refrain from leaving the state."

When Bruce Parforth relayed the proposed conditions back to Moran, Eddie agreed without hesitation. He didn't wait around to discuss any of the details. He marched straight into the court and started organising courthouse staff and uniformed police to have the matter brought on promptly. Within minutes Keliher was being bought up the internal stairs into the dock amidst a hum of murmurings throughout the public gallery. The mention then proceeded, with the prosecutor outlining the proposed schedule for delivery of a copy of the brief to the defence and the anticipated timing for the listing of a committal hearing. When the magistrate enquired if there was to be an application for bail, Parforth seized the initiative, advising that the Crown position was that it would not oppose bail being granted to the defendant, subject to various stringent conditions. He felt that sounded appropriately grave and underscored the Crown's position that the charges were serious and the Crown case was a strong one.

Moran added nothing. He listened while the prosecutor listed out the proposed conditions and when His Worship asked if he had any comment, he said demurely, "We're happy with that."

"Very well," the magistrate announced, "I find that the applicant is a suitable candidate for bail and I grant bail subject to the following conditions." He listed them one by one, writing them onto the record as he went. A condition that he return to live at his current place of residence and not live elsewhere without the prior written approval of the Director of Public Prosecutions. A condition that he surrender any passport held by him and not apply for any further passport during the currency of the bail order. A condition that he report daily to the officer in charge of the Sydney city station.

"Finally," the magistrate concluded, writing as he spoke, "the defendant is not to leave the state of New South Wales."

Eddie Moran was quickly to his feet.

"I take it, Your Worship, that that's except for reasons directly related to the preparation of his defence."

The magistrate stopped writing and looked down at the prosecutor.

"What do you say about that, Mr Parforth?"

Bruce Parforth looked blank. He hadn't anticipated any qualifications. Eddie took advantage of the silence to advance his argument just a little.

"I mean, his legal team is based in Queensland, Your Worship."

"Yes, well that seems reasonable, doesn't it, Mr Parforth?"

Parforth was still thinking. But yes, it didn't sound unreasonable.

"Yes, Your Worship."

The controversy had passed and the magistrate looked pleased.

"Very well. Not to leave the state except for reasons directly related to the preparation of his defence."

Eddie Moran was back up on his feet.

"And of course the residential condition and the requirement to report would not apply while he's interstate."

"Yes, of course."

Bruce Parforth wrote it down. It looked all right on paper, and seemed reasonable enough. It didn't matter anyway. It wasn't going to make a bit of difference to the bail. But still, he wasn't happy. He couldn't help but feel that Moran had somehow done him down.

\* \* \*

Frankie Box was feeling nervous as he waited in the laneway area behind the cells. Predictably, Eddie Moran had disappeared immediately the court adjourned, taking half the media contingent with him up the footpath. But they'd all returned and were now waiting with the mob of angry relatives and concerned citizens milling on the footpath. This one had brought them all out, not just the families and friends and the people who lived in the areas that had been terrorised, but the cop-haters and the do-gooders and the just plain crazies. They had been well enough behaved before the bail decision, but now they were working themselves into a frenzy. Frank was going to have to move Bill out of there as quickly as he could. The police had let him wait here in the restricted area to collect him, but sooner or later they were going to have to run the gauntlet. How the hell did Eddie manage to get out of all of this?

Suddenly the door clanged open and Bill Keliher stepped out. Frankie hadn't seen him in the flesh in years. He looked dazed and drawn, but it was good to see him.

"G'day, Boof."

Keliher's big chin quivered as he took him by the hand.

"Box!" He wrapped his other hand around Frankie's and shook it vigorously. "Frankie Box!"

They stood there shaking hands as tears glistened in the big man's eyes. There'd been no warning. One minute he was being processed through the watch-house as a sex offender and the next thing he was standing face to face with Frank Vagianni, whom he hadn't seen since they were coppers chasing crooks together. Frank had known the big bloke would be coming through that door, but when he saw him standing there it instantly felt like old times, as if the past eight years hadn't happened. They shook each other warmly by the hand and Frank smiled so much he couldn't stop. He broke into a laugh, and then he laughed so much he cried. He grabbed Bill in a bear hug and cried. He had told himself he wouldn't embarrass Bill like that, but he couldn't help it.

"You all right, Frank?" Bill said eventually, still trapped in Frankie's hug.

"Yeah mate, yeah, of course." Frank wiped his eyes and grabbed Bill's bag. "I've got a hire car straight out front."

As they walked towards the footpath the crowd spotted them.

"Rapist!"

"Animal!"

"Filthy pervert!"

"Crawl back under your rock, you disgusting creature!"

The words rang in Bill's ears. Frank moved the bag into his left hand and clenched his right into a weapon. Two young constables were nervously standing by on the footpath as Frank pushed out through the gate and tried to stare down anyone that was near him. He wasn't going to take a backward step. The crowd moved awkwardly around the two men striding out towards the street, wondering if they should do something more precipitous, more direct. As the television cameras moved in, some seemed to gain extra courage and became more vocal, but still they kept their distance as the threatening form of Frankie surged ahead followed closely by his ward.

When they got to the car, Frank left Bill at the kerbside to go to the driver's door. This seemed a signal to the more belligerent to move a little closer. The closer they came the more agitated they got, until eventually they were jostling and pushing Keliher up against the passenger side of the car. Frankie fumbled with the key and then paused momentarily to hurl a tirade of violent abuse and threats at the main antagonists, much to the delight of the television crews. As he finally turned the key and flipped the central locking, he looked up at the waiting face of Keliher. It wasn't scared. It wasn't even angry. It was patient, resolute, determined. Bill Keliher wasn't giving up. He was biding his time.

As Frank pulled out from the kerb, scattering the cameramen in various directions, he heard Bill heave a deep sigh.

"Relax, mate. It's all over."

"For now."

"Yeah, mate. For now."

They drove in silence for a while, threading their way through the city. Eddie had a flash room in the Marriott, but in the interests of conserving costs he had booked Frank into a dilapidated motel out at Manly. The plan was that Frank would take Bill back to the motel to freshen up and Eddie would join them there later for a conference.

"We'll need to get started straight away, Bill. If we're going to beat this thing you're going to have give me some facts to work on."

Bill Keliher lowered his head wearily. "Not today, Frank. Not yet."

They drove on some more in silence. It had been a stressful day and there were things bouncing around in Frankie's brain that were going to drive him crazy if he didn't get them out. Finally he had to say it.

"You didn't do it, did you, Bill?" He looked over at his old friend. "Tell me you didn't do it."

Bill Keliher looked back at him, his eyes unflinching. "I didn't do it, Frank."

Frankie Box believed it. "Then we need to get started straight away."

"No." His voice was quiet, but determined. "Not yet. There's someone I've got to talk to first."

\* \* \*

The photographs of Elizabeth Nichols were not pretty. Her attacker had bitten the nipple clean off her left breast, leaving an ugly gaping wound that turned even Eddie's stomach just a little. The missing part had never been recovered, presumably washed down the storm drain into some river for the fish to eat.

Elizabeth Nichols had ventured out too late one night, all alone. She had been dragged from a dark footpath into bushes where she struggled briefly with a tall man, clean-shaven, with dark hair under a black beanie. She could confidently identify the man as

William Keliher. He had pushed her hard against a tree and punched her violently in the stomach. As she gasped for air he thrust an acrid-smelling rag into her face. She was pinned there face to face with him, looking straight into his frenzied eyes, until she eventually, mercifully, lost consciousness. After she woke up, life wasn't quite the same.

The attacks described in the prosecution brief were all violent, swift, and brutally efficient. Eddie had been through all four folders and now he had them splayed out on his desk as he wandered back through the contents. Similar stories repeated throughout the various complainant statements. Young girls walking home alone, attacked suddenly and savagely, dragged into darkness and knocked out with chloroform, then stripped and raped, their bruised and ravaged bodies unceremoniously dumped for later discovery by some shocked passer-by. The photographs of Elizabeth Nichols added a new element. The mutilation of her body gave compelling evidence of a dangerously sick mind.

The ever-helpful Bruce Parforth had explained to Eddie that the Keliher brief essentially fell into three parts, corresponding with the three series of attacks. There were a total of sixteen offences arising out of attacks on eight separate complainants, all of whom had been abducted, violently assaulted and raped. Although there had been many more women attacked, these were chosen as representative because the facts of these cases were so similar as to allow the Crown to present them as a series of attacks by the one offender. All sixteen offences would be proved against Keliher by three methods: direct identification evidence by witnesses who could place him at the scenes of some of the crimes and identify him as the offender; DNA evidence obtained from a blood smear found at the scene of one of the most recent offences, which conclusively identified him as the attacker; and the 'similar fact' rule, by which the assailant's guilt of one offence would be enough to infer his guilt of another 'strikingly similar' offence. If Parforth could convince a judge to apply the similar fact rule, all he had to do was prove that Keliher had attacked one of these women, and that would be enough to qualify as proof that he'd attacked them all.

There was some identification evidence in five of the eight cases, but Eddie was already confident that only two of the five were likely to cause them any trouble. The other three had written only weak equivocations on the flip side of the photo boards – 'Number 7 looks familiar' or 'The one in Photo 7 has similar features'. Their statements all contained the confident assertion: 'I recognise the defendant as the man who attacked me that night'; but Eddie knew that their own handwritten note on the photo board was the true barometer of how they would perform in court, not the hopeful summary typed by a policeman. Only two had written strong assertions in their own handwriting: Elizabeth Nichols and Ron Morris. They were likely to present a real challenge, particularly Morris. Elizabeth Nichols had seen this man under difficult conditions – it was dark, she was under attack, her face partially covered by the rag. Maybe Eddie could do something with her. But Morris had seen the man in the illumination of a street light walking from the scene. He claimed to be one hundred per cent certain. He would be difficult.

The identification evidence was potentially compelling, but the clincher was the DNA. Witnesses could get it wrong; sometimes they even lied. But the telltale bits and pieces that you left behind along the way were pretty hard to argue with. To be fair to him, Keliher had been tidier than most: in nearly thirty years he hadn't given them so much as a fingerprint. He'd obviously been very careful, mindful to leave no identifying clues; he must always have worn a condom, because there had been no semen, nothing. All he'd left were bruised and ravaged bodies and the smell of chloroform. Even the victims' clothes were gone. Until 1995, when he attacked Melissa Smith, an eighteen-year-old kid. She was grabbed from behind and dragged backwards, a vice-like grip around her throat and her face covered with a foul rag. She didn't know what hit her and within minutes she became the final victim. But before she lapsed into unconsciousness she clawed at the arm that held her, and she remembered feeling the warm slippery blood under her chin.

And now things were different, procedures more efficient. The police had DNA technology. Samples of the foreign blood found on Melissa Smith were taken, stored and later tested against the DNA of Inspector William Keliher. The match-up was positive.

Eddie Moran yawned and ran his fingers through his tousled hair. Acting for a guilty man was one thing, but if what was in this brief was true, this Keliher was a special kind of fruitcake, and he was somehow of interest to Dr Eric Pohl. Eddie was starting to feel decidedly uncomfortable.

# CHAPTER FOURTEEN

Some of Australia's most expensive real estate was in Brighton Bay. As Bill drove along the Old Point Road, he looked up at the million-dollar luxury low-rise apartments overlooking Shaggy Bay and tried to visualise what had been there when he'd last seen it. He couldn't. He hadn't been to Brighton Bay in nearly thirty years.

The dirt road down to the point at Shaggy Head had long since disappeared, making way for a neat, well-paved and guttered street that ran down to a broad car park, bordered by a surf shop, snack bar and coffee lounge. Bill had wandered down there, drawn by some vague memory, hoping to stop and look out over the waters of the bay to the far horizon. He drove his car slowly in and once around the car park, dodging young men with their surfboards under their arms and families of tourists struggling with their loads of beach accoutrements. The car park was full. He did another circuit. Same result. As people streamed back and forth to the sandy beach along the point, Bill stopped the car and waited while a young man fiddled with his car keys and traded jibes with his mates outside the snack bar. He unlocked the car door and stood beside it as Bill sat in the hot sun waiting. A car horn beeped behind him. He looked into his rear-view mirror. There were other cars backed up. Bill swung the steering wheel and pushed his foot down to the floor.

The road around the point was adorned with huge houses, all wildly different in design but each a stunning architectural achievement. He couldn't help but marvel at them as he swept around the giant headland on the Point Road, remembering an isolated cow paddock with cattle picking their way between the rocky outcrops searching for patches of the windswept grass. As he swung right off the Point Road down towards the old town, he looked down to where the village stretched below back to the old main drag. Cruising gently down the hill, he felt as though he'd stepped through a door into a warm, familiar, family home. The broad street was still flanked by the stately old bay houses, red brick and wide verandahs welcoming the fresh sea breezes that swirled from north and south around the headland.

Brighton Bay had been 'discovered' in the early 1970s, first by the wandering Californian surfers who were captivated by the perfect waves that peeled along the headland and brought the surfing culture to the Bay; and then by the hippies and alternative-lifestylists who settled in the town and gave a new artistic feel to the sleepy fishing village. The real-estate explosion of the eighties had seen huge money pumped in, and by the early nineties it had become a retreat for Melbourne and Sydney's rich and famous.

But Brighton Bay had retained its heart – the expansive streets lined with broad grassy footpaths and leafy trees, the old wooden town hall with its wide verandahs, the stone courthouse, solid, permanent. Bill pulled up beside the little two-room building that had been the Brighton Bay police station, now the tourist information centre. It still had the same wooden boards on the verandah where the young constable had stood alongside Vince Donnelly, all those years ago.

*We'll find whoever done this ... If we keep our minds on the job and we stick to it, we'll get the bastard. I don't care if it's the Archbishop of bloody Canterbury, son, we'll get 'im!*

The Precious Pennies childcare centre was located on the river side of Halls Road not far from Barrons Landing, on what used to be the Astors' spelling paddock. It was a neat, modern little building surrounded by brightly coloured playgrounds and adorned with cartoon faces that all seemed to say 'come in'. Bill wrestled briefly with the childproof gate and dodged the toys and toddlers through to the office, where a young woman with wild hair and earrings everywhere was making jolly with a couple of trendy mums depositing their kids. He avoided them, stepping aside to study the busy noticeboard, waiting for the customers to leave. His face was all too public at the moment, and Bill knew well enough how quickly scandal spread in towns like Brighton Bay.

Pinned open at the top of the noticeboard was an information brochure on the Precious Pennies childcare group, showing their several locations throughout the Northern Rivers, with a pleasant photograph of their founder and the proprietor of the Brighton Bay centre, Councillor Faye McCabe. As he looked at Faye's smiling face, Bill felt warm and contented for the first time in many months, and he couldn't help but smile back at her.

"Can I help you?"

The untidy-looking young woman had seen off the customers and was now scouring around picking up teddy bears and other fluffy toys, which she collected in a bundle in her arms.

"Yeah, I was looking for Councillor McCabe."

She didn't look the type to watch the evening news. If she recognised his face, she wasn't letting on.

"Oh wow, really? You've just missed her, mate. She's gone up to do her morning laps at Loxton Park."

Bill hardly heard the answer. He was looking at the framed photo on the office wall. The famous picture of the lost McCabe children, sitting on the back steps of the old house in Bentley Street, wrapped up in their towels and dipping biscuits in their milk. He felt that hollowness in his chest, remembered his guilt and the awful burden, remembered why he'd come. Below the photograph was another frame, bordering a set of mounted coins of the imperial currency, old and worn, but still polished and well cared for. Like the photograph above, they were familiar faces, fondly remembered; old friends from another lifetime. A florin, two shillings, two sixpences, two threepences, a halfpenny, and two brown pennies.

"She'll be on her way back soon though. She walks up, so you might even catch her coming back along the Bay Road."

As he drove back through the town towards the Bay Road, Bill Keliher asked himself what he would say to Faye McCabe, his ex-lover, the mother of the McCabe children, the most celebrated tragic figure in Australia, an old friend whose sweet fragrance still disturbed his sleep. How could he explain? How could she possibly forgive?

From the intersection of Halls Road, the Old Bay Road rose up onto the headland, where it stretched out for the best part of a kilometre up to Shaggy Head. As Bill drove up the rise he asked himself why he was there. What did he really hope to achieve? What he had to say couldn't bring the kids back, it couldn't answer the important questions. It could only open old wounds that had destroyed his life, and theirs, that had kept them apart, and maybe always would.

As he reached the crest Bill touched the brake, flicked the indicator on, and pulled into the kerb. He should not have come back. As usual he had no good news for this woman, only reminders of the pain she was still struggling to escape. He looked across his shoulder, preparing to swing back down towards Halls Road, through the town and away from Brighton Bay for ever. He turned the wheel to pull out from the kerb and looked up the Bay Road to the point.

There she was. Off in the distance, an athletic little figure striding down the sealed footpath, wearing white shorts and a blue singlet top, her swimming bag slung loosely over her left shoulder. She still walked the same way. Head always upright, her arms swinging freely at her sides, as though she had somewhere to get to in a hurry. He remembered jogging up the hill in bright sunlight, his third lap past Bentley Street, hoping he would see her; and there she was, off in the distance up along the Bay Road, a bag of groceries in one arm, the other swinging forthrightly in that strange, determined way she walked. He quickened to almost three-quarter pace, and he noticed she had slowed considerably when she saw him coming, so they met up a long way from Bentley Street. He offered to carry her groceries for her, as any gentleman would, and she graciously accepted as a lady would, married or not. And they walked back together, chatting, laughing.

Bill Keliher had no idea where life was headed. He knew where he had been. He knew about the cataclysmic things that could happen – some big, but some so small they were noticed only by those whose lives they changed so drastically. They had changed his life, a random, disconnected series of accidents that had kept him and Faye McCabe apart. He knew there was still so much between them, so much that had to be settled. His future had become more threatening, less knowable than he had ever imagined it might be. But now, more than ever, the past had to be settled.

Faye McCabe could see a big man in long shorts and

a tennis shirt plodding up along the Bay Road towards her. For a moment she had a flash of memory, of a broad, handsome, younger man walking towards her in the bright early-summer sunlight. As they drew closer she slowed with growing recognition. She had last seen Bill Keliher as a sad and lonely figure being bullied and buffeted before the television cameras. She stopped and laid her fingers on her lips, struck by emotion.

"Hello, Bill."

Her beautiful eyes were filled with tears, and with such sadness that he took her in his arms and hugged her. He hadn't planned it. It happened naturally, spontaneously, like their first embrace all those years ago, on the grassy headland looking down across the moonlit bay. She held him tightly, wanting to give strength, and taking it, content to ask nothing and say nothing, simply to cherish and believe.

"Can we go somewhere and talk?"

She almost blushed as she looked up at the signpost beside them. It read 'Lookout', with an arrow pointing down towards the bay.

"You remember the lookout, I hope."

The carpet of soft grass that they had once shared in youthful passion was long gone, replaced by neat cement pavers and a wooden bench bordered by iron balustrading. They walked arm in arm and settled on the bench together.

Bill told her what he could about the charges. She had a right to know, and he had been over it a dozen times in his head so he could get it right, leave nothing out. He tried to relate clinically and accurately the details of what he understood to be the allegations against him, not mitigating anything or leaving anything out, determined to give it all as he understood it to be. But as he articulated the particulars of each successive case, the shame of his circumstances became heavier, each word like a tonne weight on his straining consciousness, until eventually it overwhelmed him. He stopped, the story incomplete. He could no longer look at her. He sat hunched forward on the bench staring at his two big hands clasped in front of him.

"It's all lies. All of it." His voice was desperate, pathetic. "You've got to believe me."

Faye took his hand in hers and held it tightly. She looked into his eyes and spoke with a sincerity that could leave him in no doubt.

"Never for one second did I believe any of it. Never. No matter what anybody ever says, Bill Keliher, I know you're a good man. I've always known that."

He loved her. He knew that more clearly now than he ever had. He had loved her since they first met, he had never stopped – not through her rejection of him or the tragedy that had torn their lives apart; not through all those painful, confused years when he had tried to drink her memory away and then work her memory away; not through the wild days with Joan or ever once throughout their marriage, their life together, their divorce. And not since. He had to tell her now, tell her what he'd come to say, settle what still stood between them.

"I lied to you about that day, Faye! I lied, God forgive me, I lied!" He had her in his arms again, holding her tightly, his mouth pressed against her ear, whispering his confession. "I'm so sorry, Faye." He squeezed his eyes shut. "I saw the kids that day, Faye, I saw them just up here on the Bay Road. They said they were going to the beach. I didn't know, I thought you must have said that they could go. I gave them a lift. It was me who took them to the beach. God, it was me!"

He could feel the breath frozen in her body, her arms rigid as he spoke. His mouth was dry and his heart was pounding in his chest, but he went on unburdening his guilt in a hoarse, whispered confidence. He had kept the secret bottled up so long that it gushed out with its own momentum, unplanned and unexpected. His head was spinning but the words seemed to flow unconstrained.

"I never told anyone I'd seen them. I don't know why. I've asked myself a thousand times. I guess it was just the whole thing that was happening between you and me back then. Maybe I thought people would start asking questions about us, I don't know. I don't know. I'm so sorry. I thought they would turn up. I just ... I thought they would come home. I thought they must be lost somewhere, and they'd come home." Bitter tears welled into his eyes. He released his grasp on Faye and looked her in the face. "By the time I realised, it was too late." A tear broke loose and rolled down his face. He dropped his head in shame. "Please forgive me, Faye. I'm so sorry."

Faye reached one hand up and touched the big man's cheek. He couldn't look at her. She leaned forward until her forehead rested gently on his shoulder and whispered softly into his chest.

"For ten years I hated myself for what happened to the kids. I attempted suicide once, and I thought about it a hundred times." Bill felt one of her warm tears drop onto his shirt. "I blamed myself for letting them go out alone. I asked myself a million times, how could I have let them go out alone? A nine-year-old boy and his baby sister. How could I have done that? I decided it was all my fault." She sniffled, slipped a tissue from her pocket, and wiped her eyes. "But you know something, Bill? I was wrong. It wasn't my fault, and it wasn't your fault either. It happened to us in our lives, and we've got to cope with it."

Bill put both arms around her. "I should have told you."

"I already knew. Vince Donnelly told me years ago. He said the girl from McKay's shop down at Shaggy Head saw you drop them at the beach. Vince kept it under his hat for years before he told me. He said you were one of his prime suspects for a while, until he worked out you were back in the station all that morning. Then he fleshed out what was going on between us and he put two and two together. I guess he never raised it with you."

Bill Keliher smiled sadly to himself. He should've been angry at the thought that old Vince could ever have suspected him, but he couldn't. Vince suspected everybody, even the Archbishop of bloody Canterbury.

"No, he never did."

They sat together at the lookout for a long time, wrapped in each other's arms like two young lovers, peering out across the glistening waters of the bay, speaking softly, healing, taking strength. He had almost forgotten the sweet comfort of her touch, and the depth of her courage, and now they soothed him, and steeled him for the fight ahead.

As he dropped her at the gate of the Precious Pennies childcare centre Bill took Faye McCabe gently by the hand.

"It's still a beautiful town you've got here, Councillor."

"I hope you'll be back soon."

"As soon I can hold my head up."

She smiled and, stepping forward, reached up and touched him on the cheek.

"That'll be soon." She leaned forward and kissed him softly on the lips, then turned and walked inside.

As Bill swung the car back out onto the Pacific Highway and headed north, he punched Frank Vagianni's mobile telephone number into the car phone.

"Okay, Frank, I'm ready to talk now."

# CHAPTER FIFTEEN

Bill Keliher drove straight through to Surfers Paradise, where Frank had teed up a conference with the lawyer. With Frank chiming in from time to time with questions, he told the whole story, starting with his brief affair with Faye, and her rejection of him, and his heartbreak as a young man in love. He spoke about the day itself, how he had picked up the children on the Old Point Road, how just being close to them had made him feel somehow close to her. He had dropped them off at the beach, and when the alarm was raised that evening he felt too foolish and ashamed to mention it. He thought they would turn up, but they didn't. By the time he realised what was happening it was too late to speak up. Everyone had assumed that because the children were seen down at Shaggy Head, too far for them to have walked, they had been abducted from the Old Bay Road. Hundreds of man hours were spent scouring the area for clues that weren't there to be found. Because of him, precious days were wasted.

Over the years, he had tried to make up for his deception. He'd done everything he could to find the children. His last real goal in life was to give Faye McCabe a resting place to lay those kids. Then, on the thirtieth anniversary of their disappearance, the calls had started. It was a young girl's voice, using Catherine's name. He related verbatim what he could remember of the calls. There had been six in all, he thought, spread over about two weeks. Then they had stopped, abruptly, the last one on the eleventh of January.

The message was always the same. She knew he had picked up the children. She wanted to go home. It was some kind of blackmail approach, or at least a threat of some kind. She never really said. But it was clear to Bill that she and whoever put her up to it knew that he'd concealed crucial information in the McCabe investigation and they would expose him if he didn't do what they required. He had asked if they could meet and she had said they would. She was going to ring him with a time and place. But then the calls stopped.

He didn't know Radovic and he had no idea why he would want to blackmail him. Until Morrie Fleet told him about Radovic's phone records he had no idea who or where the calls were coming from. But he went to see Lenny Fiske and Lenny told him his story. And he told him there was a little girl at the unit, and that seemed to tie in with the calls Bill had received. And yes, he did write Lenny out of the murder, because he believed what Lenny had told him, and he hoped that if Lenny walked he would be the key that would help Bill unlock the mystery. But it looked like someone else had thought the same thing, because they got Lenny.

He had concealed crucial information. He had lied, to everyone. And he had conspired with Lenny to pervert the course of justice. But he hadn't harmed the McCabe kids, and all he'd done for the past thirty years was try to find them. And he hadn't kidnapped any of those others. He hadn't raped or kidnapped anybody. He didn't know anything about those charges and he had no idea why anyone would want to say he did.

It was a humiliating exercise for Bill Keliher, pleading his own innocence and confessing a lifetime of mistakes and foolish deception to a man he hardly knew and didn't like, and an old friend who had himself been a victim of that deception. It was an exercise made immeasurably more stressful by Moran's refusal to sit still and listen: he spent the whole time walking around the room, putting golf balls into a paper cup, or twanging absent-mindedly on a guitar he produced from underneath his desk. He looked totally uninterested in anything Bill was saying, except when he heard something he didn't like or didn't seem to think was the whole truth, at which point he would fly headlong into the conversation, making his point in the most abrasive and obnoxious way he could. But Bill felt strangely purged by the experience, grateful for the lawyer's brutal and uncompromising rigour which denied him the luxury of any self-deception. By the end the truth was out in its entirety, told to an old friend who cared deeply, at the insistence of a man who didn't seem to care at all.

When Bill had finally finished, Moran dropped his feet down off his desk and put the guitar back on the floor. Listening to confessions made him feel uneasy.

"Is that it?"

Bill nodded.

"What are we trying to sell here, Bill?" His client looked up at him and they held each other's gaze. "You've been framed maybe? Is that it?"

"I'm not trying to sell anything."

"Bullshit!" Moran was back up on his feet parading around the room. "That's hogshit, pal! You've got to have a story to sell. They've sure as shit got one. And if you can't come up with a better story than the one they're selling, then you're up shitter's ditch! So you better start thinking fast, Billy-boy. What's your story? You been set up, buddy? By whom? For what?"

Bill Keliher looked like he'd asked himself the same questions more than once.

"I don't know."

"Fair enough. Too hard." Moran was pacing around the room, listening to the sound of his own voice. "Let's start with an easier one then. How the fuck did your blood get all over Melissa Smith?"

"I don't know."

"Really?" He stopped and looked at Keliher in feigned surprise. "You don't know? Gee, that's too bad. Okay, here's another one: how come Elizabeth Nichols positively identifies you as the one who jumped her?"

"I don't know."

"You don't know that either." Moran was quieter now, more solemn. "What about Ron Morris? Why is it he immediately picked you out of a line-up as the one who raped Sandra Hershey?"

Keliher bowed his head and they waited out the lengthy silence.

"I don't know."

Moran boomed out his next question with all the derision he could muster.

"You got yourself an identical twin somewhere out there that you haven't told us about yet, Billy?"

Bill Keliher had no answers. He stood up slowly and walked towards the door. Eddie was still questioning.

"One that shares your DNA maybe?"

Bill Keliher stopped in the doorway and looked at them both, the lawyer staring back at him with an accusing look spread across his face, and Frank, his head bowed sheepishly, ashamed to look his old friend in the eye. The big man steadfastly held Moran's gaze. There was something different in his eyes, something that Eddie couldn't quite fathom. They stood looking at each other until the lawyer turned away, shaking his head.

"You listen to me, both of you." There was a new strength in Bill's voice that made Frank look despite himself. "I'm innocent of these charges. All of them. That's *innocent*! You understand that, Moran? As in, didn't do it, don't know anything about it! Not as in, the coppers can't quite prove it, or by some shifty bloody bullshit you can get me out of it. Not as in hoodwinking the jury into believing a lie, Frank!"

Frank's eyes fell away. "As in I didn't do it!" He was breathing hard, his eyes burning intensely. "And I don't know why these people have identified me, and I don't know how they've come up with this DNA shit. I just know I'm innocent. Think you can get your mind around that concept, Moran?" Eddie watched him, silently assessing, intrigued and apprehensive. "You want to know if I've been set up, too bloody right I have! I don't know how and I don't really know why either. But I know it's got something to do with Catherine McCabe and I'm going to find out what it is. Because I've been looking for those kids for thirty years and someone doesn't want me to find them, but I will! I will! Sooner or later I'll find them, and none of this shit or anything else is going to stop me!"

He pushed out the door and was gone. Eddie stood there in the silence of the room, looking across to where Frank was sitting on the couch in the corner, leaning forward with his elbows on his knees and a stupid look on his face. Eddie knew what was on his mind, but he wasn't interested. Keliher had just given them a story that involved covering up evidence in the McCabe case, getting phone calls from some kid who had disappeared thirty years ago, and fabricating evidence for a double murderer whose file was now in the hands of the weirdo bum buddy of the man charged with kidnapping the McCabe kids in the first place. And the only answer that he had to a rock-solid Crown case complete with DNA and positive ID was 'Hey, I'm innocent'. That, and that damned look in his eyes that Eddie couldn't fathom.

"You know what, Frank? Deal's off. I'm not interested in Eric Pohl any more. Slick's out of hospital now, she'll be back at work next week. Pohl can have Fiske's file if he wants it that bad. And I'm not interested in your mate either. Whatever weird shit's going on with him and Pohl, that's their business. I don't want to know."

Eddie lit himself a smoke and sat with his back to Frank, sucking on his cigarette and staring out through the expansive window to the beach below. Eddie was a logical, clear-thinking guy who liked to think he had everything worked out. As Frank watched him sitting, smoking, thinking, he could tell he wasn't happy.

"If you asked a hundred people to pick a number between one and ten, you know what seventy-five of them would pick?"

Moran glanced back at him, the venom gone.

"What?"

"Seven."

"Is that right?"

"That's what they taught us in the police force."

Eddie sat patiently, waiting for the punchline. Frank had another question.

"If you arrange three lines of four photographs on a board, do you know which ones are right smack bang in the middle?"

"Six and seven. They're the first ones that you'd look at."

"Exactly. And they're the ones your eyes naturally come back to every time. Most people pick seven. That's what the coppers always taught us anyway."

"You're saying they could be mistaken."

Frank wasn't answering questions. He was asking them.

"When I was a copper, if we got a complaint against another copper, where do you reckon we'd put his photo on the board?" Eddie thought he probably knew the answer, but Frank didn't wait for a reply. "Number one, number four, number nine or number twelve. Nowhere near the middle. Whoever put together Bill's photo board wasn't leaving anything to chance."

Eddie shrugged. Maybe it meant something, maybe not.

"One last question, Eddie. You've seen coppers charged before. Usually it's all hush-hush and the lid's kept on it till it gets to court, right? You ever seen a copper dragged before the press like Bill Keliher was? If someone really was trying to discredit him, do you reckon they could have done a better job of it than what they done to Bill?"

"You think someone's trying to do a number on him?"

"I don't know. But it's possible, isn't it?"

It was possible and Eddie knew it. While Frank was in the mood to answer questions, Eddie thought he might just pop the big one.

"What about the DNA?"

"Give me a break, Eddie. I don't even know what DNA is. You're the lawyer."

Eddie sat back and looked at his erstwhile client, guilty as sin and free as a bird, an inquiry licence in one pocket and a gun in the other. It was true. He was the lawyer, and he could always find an answer, or at least an argument. The case against Bill Keliher looked hopeless, but that wasn't what scared Eddie. He was used to hopeless cases. When you had a guilty client you had nothing to lose. And nothing to fear. He remembered the photographs of Elizabeth Nichols, a young girl with an ugly hole in her left breast and a devastated look stamped on her face. And he remembered Slick, a tough chick who was all attitude, lying in a hospital bed, her body bruised and broken, her spirit all but crushed. Somehow this case was different. Weird. Complex. Maybe a bit sick. Eddie Moran wasn't scared of hopeless cases, but there were some things you were best to stay away from. Like the truth. Sometimes the truth was the scariest thing of all.

\*　　\*　　\*

Bill Keliher went out through the back door of the unit and skipped over the rear boundary fence. The house behind was in total darkness; he had been watching it on and off for hours and had deduced it was unoccupied. He moved quickly through the yard out towards the footpath. He stopped inside the fence-line, sheltering in the shadows, peering out into the street for signs of life. He had to be sure he wasn't being followed.

As he slid through the front gate onto the footpath, he kept one eye fixed on the parked car down the street. No sign of movement. No one was waiting for him. No one was watching. He had to be sure. Everything was uncertain now. He couldn't afford to make any mistakes.

Staying in the shadows of the foliage when he could, he scampered down towards the beach, over the embankment and down onto the sand. As he arrived there the darkness enveloped him completely. He felt comfortable now, down on the ocean front hurrying north under cover of the night, protected from spying eyes and yet still able to see ahead of him and back behind him, where there was no one.

He walked north for some time, counting off the street fronts by the lights. He knew how many streets he had to go. He had counted them in daylight, careful not to demonstrate his plan, knowing that he may be under surveillance.

He saw the yellow light where the street ended at the beach front and he headed up into the soft sand, up the incline onto the grassy verge and then onto the street. He moved within the shadows as the odd car passed slowly on the esplanade, then crossed the beach road and continued quickly along the footpath towards the lights of the Gold Coast Highway. As he arrived he slipped quickly into the telephone booth and punched in the number. Listening to the dial tone, he cast his eyes around the area, searching for any sign of covert observation. The traffic was moving normally, no parked cars or vans in the immediate vicinity, no pedestrians.

"Hello."

He recognised the voice immediately.

"Dr Pohl, it's Bill Keliher. I've just been released on bail. When can we meet?"

# CHAPTER SIXTEEN

Eddie touched one finger on the B-string and slid it all the way up to the fifteenth fret. Then he closed his eyes and squeezed it up till it sang the sweetest song. He could feel the notes mixing with the bourbon in his brain as his fingers danced a little on the strings, then jiggled it and squeezed it up again. Eddie loved to play the blues.

The Attic was a little place above the laundromat on Chevron Island. Boris Levsky owned the building and did a roaring trade with the laundry, which almost made up for the hiding he was copping on the restaurant. The trouble was that Boris liked to entertain his putty-nosed friends from the fight game, most of whom rarely paid and whose presence tended to put off the tourists and the decent folk that would occasionally venture in. Still, no one caused trouble in the Attic, or if they did they only did it once. You could always get a drink there after trading hours, and every Monday night some of the local musos got together to play a little blues. Eddie had an open invitation, and he came whenever he felt the need.

The kitchen was long closed, and the only table in the restaurant that was occupied was the big one over by the stairs, where Boris and a nest of his mates were drinking beer and coffee, smoking cigarettes and talking in whispers and riddles. The bar was relatively full with divorcees and desperates trying out their best lines on each other, and an hour earlier one of the Maori doormen had ventured over to quietly warn the band that a group of coppers had come in for a drink. Eddie wasn't sure why they needed to be warned but he could guess.

"Hello, Mr Moran!"

Eddie had just settled on a bar stool at the near end of the bar and was about to have a quiet smoke. The thought of being recognised by someone didn't instantly appeal to him, but when he turned around he was pleasantly surprised.

"Detective Kelly. What's a nice girl like you doing in a low-brow joint like this?"

"Listening to some pretty cool music actually."

She had a coy smirk on her face and that look that women in bars like this tended to get around closing time. The buttons on her tight-arse blouse seemed to have worked themselves undone right down to the cleavage and the normally pulled-back hair was falling softly on her shoulders. By the sound of the way she got the sentence out she'd been drinking for a while. As she talked about how wonderful his guitar-playing was,

Eddie glanced towards the other end of the bar and caught the eye of one of the circle of burly young detectives who shot back a look of cool resentment.

"You know, you are such a bastard!"

As she spoke she swayed a little eastward and slopped a swallow of her drink onto the bar.

"Thanks. I try."

Kelly responded with more hilarity than the line deserved. She was trying to flirt with him. Eddie could tell these things – he had a well-trained eye.

"You were so mean in that Radovic trial! How could you be so mean to me?"

It was Monday. Eddie had played enough guitar for one night. He had no one to go home to. Maybe this was a game that he should play with Sasha Kelly. He put on his most charming smile.

"Was I that mean to you?"

"No, I don't care. I don't care about Radovic. Lenny Fiske got him. They got Lenny Fiske. Who cares? They're all bastards."

She took another swig of her drink as the question flashed into Eddie's mind what evidence there was that Lenny Fiske 'got' anybody. He could see the edge of her white-laced bra just inside her open blouse and he could smell the fragrance of her perfume. The question flashed out again. No sense in taking minor points. Eddie shrugged and gave her the line all coppers liked to hear.

"It's just a game really, isn't it?"

"That's all it is. Just a game. Who cares about Radovic? He was an old paedophile anyway."

Paedophile? Where did this come from? The word hit him like a left hook. There had been plenty said about Radovic's shady past, and following his murder the press had lumbered him with everything but the Great Train Robbery, but no one had ever mentioned kiddie-fiddling. Eddie drew back on his cigarette as Kelly drained the last of her drink. He remembered Bill Keliher's claims about the phone call from the little girl and what he said Lenny Fiske claimed to have heard at the unit.

"Can I get you another drink, Sasha?"

"Yes, Eddie, you can."

*　　*　　*

The following morning Eddie found Frank down at Levsky's gym watching Aussie Joe going through his paces with some big bull-headed Islander. He pulled Frank aside and tried to fill him in on what Kelly had told him about Radovic, but Frank couldn't seem to get past the proposition that Sasha Kelly had tried to chat him up.

"So did you pork her, Eddie, or what?"

"Never mind that, Frank, listen to what I'm telling you."

"Mate, I don't know how you could do it! She's a bitch."

"Frank, did you hear what I just said?"

"Mind you, she's a good sort. I bet she was a top root."

"Frank!"

"Was she a good root, Eddie?"

Eddie sighed in sheer frustration. There was work to be done and he needed Frank to do it.

"Yeah, pal, she was unbelievable."

Frank looked disappointed. "You didn't root her, did you, Eddie?"

"No, mate."

"Fair enough."

Now that Frank could concentrate, Eddie took him through the conversation he'd had with Kelly. She had told him that when the scene of crime investigators went into Radovic's penthouse, they had discovered sophisticated sound-monitoring equipment in several locations through the unit. Within hours Kelly's boss was contacted by the New South Wales Juvenile Crimes Commission, who laid claim to the bugs, saying they had been in place for some time. Radovic, it seems, was under JCC investigation for involvement in an Australia-wide child pornography and paedophilia ring the JCC were targeting. They told them the whole thing was confidential and had to remain strictly top secret. A huge bunfight had then developed between Kelly's boss and the JCC. Kelly wanted the surveillance tapes to prove exactly what had happened in the unit, but the JCC refused to give them up and ordered her to keep the whole thing hush-hush. She bucked about it but eventually the word came down from the Police Commissioner and she had to pull her head in. She had never even heard the tapes.

"If this business Keliher's telling us about the phone calls is true, they'll be on the tapes."

"And so will whatever conversation led up to them being made."

"Exactly. And my guess is that if there was a little kid taken from the unit that night, there's now an ongoing JCC investigation to get the kid back, and that's why they're so sensitive about giving up the tapes."

"So sensitive that they even let Lenny Fiske get away with murder."

"And Bill Keliher get away with perjury."

The tapes didn't hold an answer to Bill Keliher's problems, far from it. But they might have an answer to a couple of questions that had been rolling around in Eddie's head, in particular whether what Keliher had told them was the truth and, if it was, why someone might be trying to set him up.

The problem was, how would they get to listen to those tapes if the JCC wouldn't even show them to the coppers? Eddie drummed his fingers on his chin as he mulled it over. The JCC's main focus had to be to get the kid back.

"We've got to offer them an exchange of prisoners," he said eventually. "Our information for theirs."

"We haven't got any information."

"Then we'll make some up." Frank could almost hear the cogs whirring in Eddie's brain. "But first we need to know as much as we can find out about the late Bernie Radovic."

\*      \*      \*

Sasha Kelly had just heard something that she wasn't very pleased about. She stepped out of the lift and came round the corner like a runaway train. As she passed Des Clarkson, the officer in charge of the exhibit room, he put his head down as though he hoped the bullets might pass safely overhead. There was nothing he could do. The way she was moving he didn't even have a chance to warn the Box.

When Kelly strode into the exhibit room, Frank was sitting on the floor surrounded by the Fiske exhibits. She stopped dead with her hands on her hips and stared at him. Frank knew from the flat feet who it was. The one person he had hoped he wouldn't see. Trying to keep a secret in a cop shop was like herding cats.

"Well, well, well. If it isn't Exhibit A for arsehole."

"You know, Kelly, you're as funny as a circus."

"Only when there's clowns around, Frank."

Frank looked up. She had her hair tied back tightly in a pony tail and she was all dressed up like a bundle of business. Her skirt was wrapped around her hips like it was painted on, and her blouse was stretched so taut across her chest you could almost feel the buttons straining, threatening, promising. Eddie had assured him that the young coppers had repatriated her before he got the chance to lay a tread on her, and Frank figured it was true, but couldn't help but fantasise that maybe it was all a lie. He had to admit it, she looked good. Too bad she was a complete bitch.

"What do you think you're doing on police property?"

"I'm a private investigator, remember? I'm investigating. Want to see my licence?"

"Who said you could see the Fiske exhibits?"

"I'm retained by Fiske's lawyer."

"Who?"

"Eddie Moran."

The answer stopped her in her tracks. Frank detected a slight blush. Was that bastard Eddie holding out on him?

"What for?" Kelly was in Gestapo mode again.

"To finish the Radovic investigation."

"It's closed."

Frank didn't like being treated like a probationary constable by some sheila half his age. Especially not this sheila.

"For you maybe it's closed. Only problem is you never got the murderer."

Sasha didn't like the idea of Frank Vagianni being in the Surfers Paradise police headquarters. He had caused her a lot of grief and heartache just a few years back and his very presence made her feel uneasy. She had been vilified over the Waterworld affair. It had been the hardest time of her career. If the Fitzgerald Inquiry hadn't got her out she never would have lasted in the force. She had breached the unwritten code, breaking ranks, speaking out against her workmates. She had been ostracised. And although Vagianni had never once confronted her, he was the one she blamed. She maintained her tough exterior.

"What would you know about the Radovic case, Frank?"

"More than you by the looks of things."

"What's that supposed to mean?"

Who did she think she was talking to? If Sasha Kelly hadn't spilled the beans over the Waterworld loot, he'd still be her boss, he'd still be a copper, and he'd still have a tin full of folders buried underneath the Hills hoist in his backyard. This sheila needed to be educated.

"Well, for a start it means I know that whoever knocked Radovic didn't go there for him. They came there for his girlfriend, and maybe something else."

He could see straight away that she was interested.

"Why?"

"Because Radovic took one bullet, clean, in the lounge room. And whoever popped him then went to all the trouble of forcing a locked bedroom door just to get the girlfriend. That's not easy to do. It hurts your shoulder. Ever tried to force a locked door, Sasha?"

"Maybe he was just getting rid of witnesses."

"They were wearing balaclavas. You know that – one of them was still on the lounge room floor. She couldn't identify them. No, they went there specifically for her. And maybe someone else."

"Like who?"

Kelly really wanted to know. The way she asked the question told Frank that there was something troubling her about the story so far. He remembered what Eddie had said about exchanging prisoners. If Kelly wanted to she could have him turfed out on his ear. On the other hand she could give him information, maybe even help.

They'd both be a lot easier to get if he got her interest first. He decided he would take a punt.

"The kid."

"What kid?"

She was bullshitting. Frank could see it in her eyes. He could hear it in her voice. It was time to call her bluff.

"The young girl they had at the unit."

Sasha Kelly stood in the doorway sizing him up. "Did Fiske tell you about the child?"

One of Frank Vagianni's strengths was his ability to think on his feet. He made up the story on the spot, keeping it sufficiently vague to ensure that Kelly couldn't pin him. Fiske had told a family member certain things about the incident and they'd been passed on down the line to another distant family member who had a big quid. When all the press hoo-ha blew up about Lenny being right for it after all, this well-heeled distant relative had retained Fiske's lawyer to look into it, and in particular to find out if there was any truth to a rumour going round that there may have been a little kid at the scene who might have been kidnapped or hurt, because this particular bloke was a philanthropist and didn't want to think that any relative of his, distant or otherwise, had hurt no little kids. It all sounded like bullshit to Frank, which of course it was, but Kelly seemed happy to swallow it, at least for the time being.

Frank soon found out why. Kelly seemed almost keen to tell him. They had found a child's doll at the premises, pushed under the bed in the second bedroom.

The more experienced detectives had dismissed it as a memento kept by the bookie's girlfriend Emma Ronson; there were no children's clothes in the unit and no other sign of any kid. But Kelly had convinced herself there was something significant about the doll. You don't shove a cherished childhood memento underneath the bed. Frank could see she had a bee in her bonnet, probably aggravated by the JCC putting a lid on the tapes. That's why she'd spilt the beans to Eddie on the piss. She couldn't put it down. Frank knew as well as anyone how obstinate she could be, and he pitied the poor slobs at the JCC who'd had to try and hose her down. But maybe this time she was right. If Lenny Fiske was to be believed, there had been a kid in there that night. And if that was right, where was she now?

Before long, Kelly was wading through the Fiske exhibits, explaining where each had been found and what, if any, significance had been attached to them. Most were the standard crap that got washed up at murder scenes, the sum collection of years of hoarding by the deceased. In this case it wasn't too bad; the penthouse was just a holiday apartment so it hadn't managed to collect the kind of baggage most joints do. But there was enough. The usual boxes full of meaningless and seemingly irrelevant paperwork. Except of course it wasn't really meaningless. Experience had taught Frank that everything meant something to someone; the trick was to work out what, because it was only then that you could decide whether it really was irrelevant.

He leafed his way through a pile of bank statements from half a dozen separate cheque accounts, three in Radovic's name and another three in names that Kelly could confirm were aliases he had used – Bernie Radley, Bernard Raddock, and Stephen Rudd. Frank made a note of them. There were handwritten notes of what looked like horses' names and figures, scribbled telephone messages, a wad of accounts from a Sydney horse trainer. A couple of used chequebooks in the bottom of the box; Frank flicked through them. Nothing startling. Payments for electricity and telephone, lease payments, doctor's bills, accountants, and solicitors.

He flicked back a couple of butts. 'Dr Forrester – $285 – medical.' He had read the name somewhere else. He rummaged back through the pile of scribbled handwriting. Eventually he saw it on a strip of blue-lined paper that had been torn off a full sheet. 'M. Forrester.' No telephone number. No address. Only one other word on the paper, in the top left corner. 'Eric.'

"Here it is."

Kelly pulled a single photograph from a bundle in her hands. She handed it to Frank and he took a close look. It was a colour photo of a small rag doll lying on a desk somewhere in some police station. It was a kid's doll without doubt, not an adult's decoration of the kind some women liked to splay across their beds for some reason that eluded Frank. No, this was a working doll, the grimy, well-worn type that put in the hard yards every day with some snot-nosed kid, and got dragged around and cuddled and played with till it had skin and bark off everywhere. This one looked like it had been around more than most, and while it was no ornament it might well have been an adult's heirloom. It was hard to say how old it was but it looked to Frank to have a good few miles on it.

"Was it tested?"

"Not that I know of."

Frank wasn't sure what you would test it for, but Kelly was right, there was something about the doll that didn't fit in with anything but Lenny's story. So if there was a kid in that unit, who was she and where did she end up? Frank didn't know the answers yet, but he figured the word 'Eric' on that piece of paper might have a lot to do with why Dr Eric Pohl was interested enough in Fiske's file to break legs.

"Where's the doll now?"

"Can't say."

"Can't say or won't say?"

"That's it, Frank. Time's up. Show's over."

That must mean the JCC had got the doll and they weren't giving it back. The beautiful Sasha was annoyed and maybe a little bit embarrassed. She probably figured Eddie had told Frank about the JCC.

"Can I get copies of some of this stuff?"

"No you can't. See you later, Frank."

Maybe Kelly was smarter than he'd given credit for. She'd given Frank just enough to get him interested and maybe get him stirring up the kind of trouble she was looking for. But she wasn't handing anything over to him. She wasn't going to cross the JCC and she wasn't going to risk a black mark with the Police Commissioner.

"Come on, Kelly, you owe me!"

Frank had no sooner said it than he realised he shouldn't have. Resurrecting the Waterworld debacle was never going to win him any points.

"Bullshit, Frank! You pocketed that money and you know it!"

"Not according to the jury I didn't."

"You're nothing but a crook, Frank."

"Why don't you get a dick in your ear, Kelly."

Things degenerated pretty quickly from there, and Frank soon found himself back on the footpath, cursing Kelly under his breath and tossing everything over in his mind as he headed for the car park. Being thrown off his own turf by Sasha Kelly twice in one lifetime was almost too much to cop. But still, it hadn't been for nothing.

Frank slipped the chequebook from his pocket and leafed back through the butts. Some details can stick in your mind like a pebble in the bottom of your shoe and annoy the hell out of you. 'Dr Forrester – $285 – medical.' Once, twice, three times. There weren't too many doctors Frank knew of who charged over two hundred for a consultation, even on the Gold Coast. Certainly not GPs. This Dr Forrester showed up regularly in Radovic's cheque butts, always collecting in the hundreds.

As it turned out there were no fewer than sixty-three medical Doctors Forrester Australia-wide. But of them only fourteen were specialists, so Frank did the ring-around posing as a clerk from the Public Trust Office. "We've got a bequest here to a Dr Forrester on one of our deceased estates in the name of Radovic. Did you have a patient by the name of Bernard Radovic? No? What about Bernie Radley? Bernard Raddock? Would you believe Stephen Rudd?" The nice thing about self-interest is that you always know it's trying: if a medico couldn't find the name in his patient list to pick up a free nest egg, then it wasn't there.

By the time Frank came to the bottom of his list he was convinced. Dr Forrester was a myth. Radovic had been making payments to someone he didn't want to talk about. But who? With a guy like Radovic it could be anybody.

# CHAPTER SEVENTEEN

Edwin C. Moran stepped through the automatic doors of League Headquarters to meet the waiting throng of media representatives. His client, Rocky Sellic, the huge square-jawed Queensland front-rower, had a vacant smile across his face and for the first time in days looked as though he might be understanding something of what was going on. He no longer had to look dumbfounded and confused; he had been acquitted of all charges.

"The judiciary came to the only conclusion available to them on the facts."

Eddie loved this part of the job. There was nothing better than doing doorstep interviews and sticking it up everybody's nose, and on this one the client had demanded that he do it. The interstate series was deadlocked at one-all with the decider to be played in Brisbane in two weeks. Sellic, Queensland's form front-rower, had been cited for eye-gouging and the Sydney press had been parading footage of one of their glamour-boy back-rowers with blood streaming from a badly mauled eye to prove it. It wasn't the first time Rocky had been accused of conduct unbecoming, and in the powder-keg atmosphere of a looming interstate decider the New South Wales media and public were baying for his blood. The Sydney press were calling it 'The Rocky Horror Show' while all of Queensland claimed victimisation. It was a promoter's dream. Anything Eddie Moran could say to inflame the situation would be more than welcome. He was the right man for the job.

"Up in Queensland we're starting to think some of these Blues are just big sissies."

The media scrum erupted with a frantic barrage of questions but Eddie didn't wait around to answer them. Normally he would have loved to feed them more inflammatory one-liners than they could possibly fit into a half-hour show, but today he had more pressing matters on his mind. He strode off along the footpath, shadowed by the hulking Rocky who dutifully delivered the line Eddie had made him practise so many times that even Rocky couldn't stuff it up: "I'll give my answers out on the paddock next Wednesday night!" They walked along the street far enough to let the television crews get some good footage for the news before Eddie turned and waved team management to pick them up.

The car pulled into the kerb and Rocky clambered in.

"It went well," Eddie reported through the open door to the manager; it was nice talking to someone who looked like he spoke English. "I've got someone to see in town. I'll catch you later at the airport."

Eddie was in Sydney only for the morning, but he wanted to make sure he spoke to Peter Rosenthal. They hadn't learned much more about Radovic from the exhibits but they had answered at least one question: there had been a kid in that unit, and Bill Keliher was telling the truth about getting calls from her. Beyond that they hadn't moved far forward, but it would be a big help to listen to those tapes. Now was the time to take direct action.

The Juvenile Crimes Commission was like all the other lawyer-staffed bureaucracies that had sprung up in recent years to rid the world of its ills: it was staffed by clear-visioned and cold-hearted equity lawyers who couldn't decide whether they wanted to be spooks or pen-pushers. The one thing they knew was what the legislation said, and if it wasn't right there in black and white then you didn't get the time of day. It would be useless trying to talk any of them into giving up the tapes. They were just pissants and shiny-bums who would refer you to the secrecy provisions of the Act. But Rosenthal was different. He'd been a barrister and then a judge for a long time. He had a reputation as a good lawyer and an intelligent man. He talked a lot of rhetoric about balance in the investigative process, and he was committed to the rights of the individual. Eddie might just be able to snow him.

The first job was to convince Rosenthal that there was a good reason why he should share the information with them. The best reason was always self-interest, and that meant convincing Rosenthal that Eddie had information he could trade. This was going to take a bit of 'show me yours and I'll show you mine'. And Eddie would have to be the first to drop his dacks. So he had to come up with something that sounded at least half-convincing.

So far they didn't have much. They knew there was a kid involved and that someone had got her to ring Keliher. Plus they knew that the JCC suspected Radovic to be a paedophile, and he'd been paying money to someone who might have some connection with Eric Pohl. And they knew that Pohl was vitally interested in the Radovic murder. It wasn't much at all. All Eddie had to do was make it sound like something.

"The information we have is that Radovic and his girlfriend Ronson were involved in a child-porno scam along with others here and in Victoria."

Peter Rosenthal's face was completely blank; it was hard for Eddie to gauge how he was doing. At least he knew the Commissioner was interested in what he had to say. He hadn't hesitated in agreeing to see him and he now listened attentively, albeit blankly, as Eddie spun his story.

"Our informant tells us there was actually a kid in the unit when Radovic and Ronson were shot."

Eddie was watching for any sort of reaction as he said it. There'd been no mention in the Radovic case of a child being at the unit, and this had to tell Rosenthal that Eddie had some pretty good inside mail. But if he was impressed he wasn't showing it.

"There were two gunmen. One of them took the kid with him."

It was a powerful line. Still no reaction.

"Depending on what's on the tapes, we may be able to convince our informant to give us names of others in this porno scam."

Rosenthal had his hands clasped neatly in front of him, two extended fingers touching his chin. He continued to stare blankly at Eddie for a long moment, as if waiting to hear more, and then finally responded.

"What tapes?"

"The tapes you got from the bugs you had hidden in the unit." Eddie came straight back at him with it. This was no time to hesitate or be defensive; Rosenthal had to believe that Eddie had the goods. "This place leaks like a sieve – you should know that."

Rosenthal smiled dryly, either at Eddie's bald-faced impertinence, or because he knew it was true, or both.

"Any information this Commission gathers is strictly protected by the secrecy provisions of the Act. It is not compellable in any way. It can't even be subpoenaed by the courts."

Eddie didn't like the sound of this. Rosenthal was making noises like any other bureaucrat. He was going to have to make his point loud and clear, even if that called for some embellishment.

"We've got information that might help to find that kid."

"If you've got information then it's your duty to disclose it." His voice was measured and dispassionate. "The Commission will gratefully accept whatever assistance you can give. If you withhold relevant information you may be in breach yourself."

There was something about the tone of his voice that was making Eddie feel a little desperate. If Rosenthal really thought he might get the information without coughing up, Eddie had to disabuse him of that notion straight away.

"It's confidential information obtained from a prospective witness on behalf of a client. It's subject to legal professional privilege and you know it. I can't reveal it, and you can't force my client to reveal it. But I can get him to agree that if you let us hear the tapes we'll hand over all the information we've got."

Rosenthal spoke quietly again, as though he were reciting sections of legislation.

"Secrecy provisions apply under the Act. It would be an offence for me even to tell you whether any tapes exist."

If Eddie didn't start to make some sort of an impression he'd be out in the street in another five minutes. It was time to play the wild card. He slammed one hand palm-down on the Commissioner's leather-inlaid desk.

"Bullshit! Don't feed me your fucking jurisprudential horseshit!" Rosenthal was startled but had enough poise not to react beyond the distasteful look that washed across his face. "You had a bug in that unit and you know what happened that night. Now I'm offering you information that could lead you to that kid. But I want to hear the tapes!"

Judge Peter Rosenthal was a man unused to being barked at. The disapproving look remained as he lifted the receiver from his phone and spoke sedately into it.

"David, Mr Moran is leaving now. Could you please come in and show him back downstairs."

Eddie wasn't waiting. He stood up and headed for the door.

"Mr Moran." When Eddie turned back the judge looked somewhat more forgiving. "Do you have any idea how many children disappear around this country every year? Some of them you never even hear about." He sighed as though he knew every one of them personally. "We have a very big job to do. There are some very sinister, very dangerous people involved. We're working hard and we know what we're doing. You'll just have to leave it to us."

As David the man-mountain politely ushered him out of the building, Eddie tossed over in his mind what had just happened. He hadn't even come close to hooking Rosenthal. The rabid outburst would have drawn some sort of reaction from most people, but Rosenthal wasn't going anywhere near it. Either the scenario that Eddie had put up wasn't even in the ball park and Rosenthal knew he was just fishing, or it was at least close to the mark – maybe spot-on – but they already had the information he was peddling.

Or maybe, of course, they couldn't bring Eddie into the loop because one of Eddie's clients was the target. Maybe there was something on the tapes that they didn't want to share with the enemy.

# CHAPTER EIGHTEEN

Eric Pohl flicked on the switch and squinted against the harsh light reflecting on the white tiles. As he limped gingerly through the *en suite* bathroom to the toilet bowl, he tried not to look at the expansive mirror bordering the lacquered vanity. Pohl was a vain man by nature and he found it difficult to resist the temptation to lay his eyes on his own image, but he knew better than to look at this hour of the morning. His ageing body sagged and drooped at the best of times, but now he could feel his face and neck, stretched by lack of sleep and dehydrated by the alcohol, following suit, the sallow skin hanging from his eyes like a lifetime's dirty washing.

As he drained his bladder into the bowl he wondered what time it was. The dry bitter taste in his mouth told him he had been asleep long enough for the intoxication to have soured into that dull, exhausting ache that always seemed to follow it these days, and he could no longer hear the sound of music being played downstairs.

Even the grunts and cries that had filtered through from the billiard room and the other bedrooms had stopped altogether. They had thrilled him to sleep the night before; in his drunken state he had tried to masturbate, imagining himself a young man again, remembering the parties and the glorious young men. But it was no use.

Parties at the home of Dr Eric Pohl had always been a seductive mixture of affluence, beauty and power. Subtle, artistic, intelligent and tasteful, they were to Eric's guests whatever Eric's guests imagined they should be. Some of the nation's leading businessmen mixed with artists, lawyers, politicians and academics at Eric's parties, and all of them felt privileged to be invited to his magnificent award-winning multi-storeyed home on the banks of the Yarra River overlooking the city. Liberace had tinkled on the keys of the magnificent grand piano, and famous authors and unknown poets had recited on the patio against the backdrop of the city lights of Melbourne. They were served the finest delicacies by fresh-faced youths with perfect bodies and glistening white teeth; some occasionally asked themselves the question but no one ever thought to assert the answer. After all, Eric Pohl's private life was his own, more so in this day and age than ever. His hospitality was unquestionable, his parties entertaining, sumptuous, and tasteful. What happened when the guests had departed was for Eric, and perhaps for those close friends of his who always seemed to be the last to leave.

It was after all the guests were gone that Eric's real talent as a host came to the fore, when the handsome young waiters put down their trays and mingled with his special friends, drinking expensive alcohol and handing around tablets and white powder. Then Eric's hospitality was unbounding, no indulgence unattainable, no predilection taboo. As the lights went out and erotic images danced across the ice-white walls, the inner circle drank and sniffed and laughed in the sunken lounge room, while others caressed in the darkness or wandered off hand-in-hand to the bedrooms upstairs.

As Eric Pohl walked back past the vanity, he was compelled to glance at his reflection. He wished he hadn't. Instead of the sensual, well-toned body he had dreamed of, there was an old man, shrivelled and sagging like rotting, unpicked fruit. Groaning in agony he reached out and flicked the light off, killing the ugly image instantly. He groped out through the darkness of the bedroom and fell onto the cool satin of the sheets.

"Hello, Eric."

"Shit!" The sound of a voice in the bedroom shocked him, and he clutched at his chest where his weak heart was beating violently. "Shit! Who's there?"

He grappled with the bedroom lamp and clicked it on. In the shadows of one distant corner of the room he could see the burly outline of a lone, familiar shape. The face was back against the wall beyond the light, the features still shrouded in darkness, but he could see the thick strong forearms with the familiar faded blue tattoo – a Christian cross with a capital B framed into the lower right-hand corner. Eric Pohl knew whose insignia it was.

"What's the matter, Eric? Don't you recognise your old lovers any more?"

"Stephen. What are you doing here?"

The dark figure rattled off a cold humourless chuckle. "Thought I'd come to your little party, even though I didn't get an invitation."

"I didn't see you." Pohl's body was rigid with fear, his voice breathless and shallow.

"No. But I saw you, Eric." The voice was sombre, deathly serious. The figure stood up slowly in the shadowy corner of the room, his face still hidden in the dim light. "We've been keeping a close eye on you."

As the man stepped out of the darkness, Pohl gasped a thin breath. He could see the surgical gloves stretched over both hands and the dressing-gown cord trailing on the carpet.

"Don't, Stephen. Please don't."

His whole body had begun to shake and his voice trembled as he drew his hands and feet in close to him.

"You've been talking to people, Eric."

"No, Stephen, no. I don't know anything."

"Oh yes you do, Eric. You're a very well-read man."

Tears welled in the old man's eyes and his voice was no more than a whisper.

"Please, Stephen."

"What's the matter, Eric?" The voice was soft and soothing as he stepped towards the bed. "You're not frightened, are you?" He sat gently on the bed and shaped a smile on his lips. "This is just like old times. All I want is one small kiss."

As he leaned forward and put his hands on Eric's cheeks, the old man closed his tearful eyes and surrendered to the fate he had created. He felt the cord coil silently around his throat and close around him warmly, quickly, tightly. As breath, then life, ran out of him, the old man shook and shuddered. His eyes and mouth jerked open in a surprised expression.

Stephen Rolfe stood up beside the bed dragging with him the withered body of Dr Eric Pohl. He pulled the cord, squeezing the throat until his arms were aching, holding the old man's face close to his, looking into those blank, shocked eyes. He held the body there, his teeth clenched, his eyes bulging in his head, the muscles in his arms and shoulders quivering violently until they finally collapsed and the corpse dropped to the floor. It felt good.

# CHAPTER NINETEEN

Stan Rosleigh was one of Sydney's most experienced magistrates. He had been on the Local Court bench as long as anyone could remember and in that time he'd presided over plenty of controversial cases. But the Bill Keliher case seemed to be attracting more than its fair share of interest from all over the shop. The press was full of it, the police were all pumped up about security, and the department seemed unusually on edge. So far Stan had received no fewer than four calls from those on high to say what an important case it was and how outraged the public were about the whole thing and enquiring whether Stan could use some special facilities or assistance in keeping order in the courtroom. Stan was from the old school. He had a nice short fuse and he knew how to speak up if he wanted to be heard. He'd never had any problem keeping order in his court before and he couldn't see why he would start now. The only one Stan Rosleigh expected any trouble with was Edwin C. Moran. And he'd soon attend to that.

The committal proceedings in relation to the charges against Inspector William Keliher had been listed for a five-day hearing in the Local Court at Sydney. The statements of all Crown witnesses had been furnished to the defence and would be tendered at the hearing subject to the right of cross-examination by Eddie Moran on behalf of the defendant. All Stan Rosleigh had to decide was whether there was a case to go to a jury. He wasn't going to be looking for any fine points of law, and he wasn't too interested in what a jury was likely to do at trial; if there was anything there at all, Stan would shoot this one straight through to the District Court and let them sort it all out. And he'd been assured there was plenty there. The Crown had a rock-solid case, so all Stan had to do was sit back and make sure everyone behaved themselves, and then commit Bill Keliher for trial at the next sittings of the District Court. But he wasn't going to stand for any of Moran's shenanigans in the process.

As Eddie strode up to the front doors of the court building the small crowd parted, allowing him to sweep through unimpeded. It was obvious he had things on his mind. He was already chewing viciously on a stick of gum and scowling in anticipation of the job ahead. He didn't like this case. It had snakes and vipers all over it and he wouldn't know how dangerous they were until he'd put his hand down all the holes and pulled them out one by one. This was the preliminary hearing, and this was when he had to go exploring, round every blind bend and down every dry gully, looking for the good bits and finding out just how bad the bad bits really were, testing the real strength of this Crown case. There was no jury here, only the magistrate, so if there was any nasty news now was the time for him to hear it, for him to lead with his chin, ask all the questions that he needed to and hear the embarrassing answers. But this one was going to be harder than most. There were no neat issues here. This wasn't a case of 'Sure I did it, but I didn't know the gun was loaded', or 'Yeah, but he threw the first punch', or 'I was insane at the time.' This was 'I didn't do it, you've got the wrong guy altogether.' And there was evidence everywhere to sink him, seemingly strong evidence, even independent forensic proof that he wasn't the wrong guy, that he did do it.

Eddie's stomach was churning as he walked into the main foyer. He had pored over the police briefs late into the night and the statements of the witnesses had intruded into his fitful sleep, leaving him drained and irritable. There were five witnesses who, to varying extents, purported to identify Keliher as the culprit. Eddie had to defuse each one of them. If he was going to stop their evidence from going to the jury at the trial, he had to undermine each witness here at the committal hearing. If he could convince a trial judge that their identification was faulty or unreliable, the witnesses would still give evidence of how the offence had been committed, but they would not be allowed to say that Keliher was the one who had committed it.

Identification evidence was notoriously unreliable. Lawyers understood that implicitly, and stringent rules had grown up to prevent the enormous potential for injustice that arose when the human mind played tricks with memory and perception. It could all work in the favour of a guilty man, but in this case it helped to churn up Eddie's stomach even more.

He was running late for his appointment with Bill Keliher and when he got to the agreed interview room he burst straight in. The look on his client's face suggested that he barely tolerated yet another brash entry by his abrasive lawyer, but he restrained himself.

"Good morning."

Sitting alongside him was a well-groomed, pleasant-looking woman with short-cropped auburn hair. He was about to introduce her, but the younger man rolled his eyes and turned on his heels.

"Outside," he grunted as he pushed the door back. "I want to speak to you alone."

Faye McCabe looked embarrassed, and Bill Keliher was furious as he got up and followed the lawyer out.

"Are you kidding?" Eddie snapped at him in a coarse whisper as the door clicked shut. "Are you fucking insane, or what?"

Bill Keliher clenched his teeth and seemed about to take the scrawny lawyer by the throat and shake him, but he didn't get the chance. Eddie wasn't waiting for an answer.

"Do you know what the press will do to you, and to her, if they see the two of you together here? Can you work that out? You're on abduction charges here, pal! Rape and abduction! And as far as they're concerned you're as guilty as sin! You're guilty until proven innocent, pal, don't you know that? If they see you here with the mother of the McCabe kids it's all over for you. And for her! They'll have her pegged for all the kinky shit under the sun! She'll be another Lindy Chamberlain! And you'll be the Yorkshire fucking Ripper!"

He was right. Bill's heart sank as he realised what he had done. Faye had telephoned to say she wanted to be there to stand by his side, to help him through it. Bill had agreed, partly because he had felt utterly without support and her faithful hand was like a life raft to a drowning man, but mainly because he had simply longed to see her again and speak to her. But Moran was right: if anyone from the press recognised her with him they would crucify them both. Bill cursed himself for having been so stupid.

"I'll ask her to go."

"Do it!"

* * *

Eddie was sitting at the bar table bouncing one foot on the floor and still chewing on his gum as Elizabeth Nichols approached the witness box. He had insisted that Parforth call full evidence in chief from her, rather than just tendering her statement. Her evidence was crucial, and Eddie had to be sure she'd actually say what was in her statement.

Parforth had called her as his first witness. Bruce was no Einstein, but he'd been around the criminal courts long enough to know that you lead out with your best punch, and it was a fair bet Nichols was going to be a good one. She'd tell her sad, pathetic story and everyone would feel extremely sorry for her, and then she'd identify Bill Keliher as the culprit and everyone would hate him with a vengeance. The papers would carry her story as the lead tomorrow and reinforce the notion that Keliher was a cruel beast who deserved no fair consideration whatsoever. And Rosleigh SM would do his best to make sure Eddie didn't get a chance to savage her. It could all be side-stepped by letting Parforth tender the statement, but then Eddie wouldn't have it from the horse's mouth.

So Elizabeth Nichols told her story. She was a good witness, and everyone felt sorry for her, even Eddie. But Eddie didn't show it; he sat watching her intently, assessing every move and gesture, every change of expression, every word, every intonation. He had to know where she was coming from before he could work out where he should go. He had to understand why and how what was unfolding here in front of him was consistent with the innocence of his client. He had to know what was true and what was false, what was accurate and what mistaken.

"Finally, Ms Nichols," Parforth said eventually, to the relief of many in the public gallery, "are you able to identify the man who attacked you that night?"

"Yes."

"Is he present in this courtroom today?"

"Yes." The answer came as no more than a timid whisper.

"Could you indicate that man for the court please, Ms Nichols?"

As Elizabeth Nichols raised a faltering finger in the direction of Bill Keliher the eyes of everyone in the courtroom followed it to the big man slumped forward at the bar table. Bill looked up at her, feeling her pain and her fear, searching for an explanation.

"Witness indicates the defendant," concluded Stan Rosleigh triumphantly, as though he personally had the job to prosecute.

"I have no further questions for this witness, thank you, Your Worship." Parforth glanced to the press gallery where the scribes were completing details for tomorrow's lead story, and then sedately resumed his seat.

Eddie bounced to his feet.

"You just pointed at my client, witness. Do you know what his name is?"

"Mr Moran!"

Stan Rosleigh SM was a big man and when he raised his voice in anger he could find some volume. As he bellowed Eddie's name the whole court resounded and everybody started. Everyone except Eddie. He stayed slumped forward on the lectern and waited several seconds before turning to Rosleigh with a slightly irritated air.

"Yes, Your Worship?"

"Is that gum you're chewing, Mr Moran?"

Eddie stared back at him, chewing vigorously.

"Would Your Worship like some?"

A light snicker rustled through the press gallery as Rosleigh set his teeth.

"Get rid of that gum immediately," he growled with palpable malevolence, "or I'll have you thrown out of this court!"

Stan and Eddie faced each other in the silence of the court, the lawyer still chewing casually. As seconds passed, the gallery looked on, waiting for the explosion.

Eddie turned, still chewing, and faced the witness. Then he swallowed loudly. *Gulp*! The offending gum was gone.

"What's his name, witness?"

The sound of snickering and muffled laughter in the gallery had Rosleigh glaring about the court. Eddie was waiting for an answer from the witness.

"Well?"

"William Keliher."

"Right. What does he do for a living?"

"He's a policeman."

"Yeah? What's his rank?"

"He's an inspector."

"That's right. That's exactly right. How'd you know all that, witness?"

"I read about it, and I saw him on the television."

"Read about it in the newspapers?"

"Yes."

"Did they have a photo of him with that story?"

"Yes, outside the police station."

"That's right, the same one as was shown on the TV, wasn't it?"

"Yes, that's right."

"That was the night of his arrest?"

"Yes."

"And you saw the papers the next morning?"

"Yes."

"And you knew then that he was charged with attacking you, didn't you?"

"Yes."

"And you believed he was the one who did it?"

"I didn't recognise him at first from the TV but then when I saw him in the papers I remembered him."

"Is that right?" It was a perfect answer for Eddie and one he could easily drive home. But he didn't need to, and Elizabeth Nichols didn't deserve to be savaged. "Anyway, you were first asked to look at a photo-board display about a week later, weren't you?"

"Yes."

"And you believed that there would be a photo of the culprit on that board, didn't you?"

"Yes."

"And you wanted to identify the culprit, didn't you?"

"Of course I did."

"And when you saw the photo board you recognised in photo number seven the same face you'd seen a week earlier on the television."

"Yes."

"And so you picked him out."

For a split second Eddie held his breath, hoping for the right answer.

"Of course."

"Thank you."

Mr Rosleigh SM grunted impatiently as if to say, 'There, see – I knew you didn't have anything relevant to ask', and excused the witness as Eddie scribbled in his notes. It was as good a start as they could have hoped to have. Nichols' identification evidence was irreparably tainted by the photographs she had seen in the press; there would always be a risk that subconsciously or otherwise she had picked out not the man who had attacked her but the man depicted in the press reports. No District Court judge could ever allow her to give evidence identifying Bill. And that meant one of the identifications was already gone.

Things didn't go so smoothly with the second witness. Ron Morris was a tall, handsome, athletic-looking man in his mid forties. He gave his evidence in a clear, concise and factual fashion, respectfully and unemotively. He was a most impressive witness, and when Parforth finally asked the question whether he saw the man in court today, Morris confidently and convincingly indicated Keliher. Eddie probed as best he could for weaknesses, and Morris conceded that all this had happened over twenty years ago, and on the night the light had certainly been less than perfect, but he felt he'd got a clear view of the attacker just the same. The photo-board procedure had taken place before any charges had been laid, and although Morris agreed that he had subsequently seen the press reports with photographs of Keliher, he had never seen the man before identifying him for police, except on the night of the offence. His identification from the photo board had been recorded and the video left no doubt: Morris was convinced that number seven was the culprit. That meant that either his attention had been drawn to number seven because of something he'd been told, or Bill Keliher showed a remarkable resemblance to the rapist. There was a third possibility, but Eddie didn't want to think about it.

Parforth filled in the balance of the morning by tendering exhibits through the main investigating officer, Detective Wally Messner. By the time Rosleigh adjourned for morning tea, Eddie was in need of strong black coffee.

"Oh, before you go, there's something I should mention." Parforth had a sheepish look about him as if he was up to something. "Actually, I may have an application to revoke your client's bail."

"What?"

Eddie was sneering uncomprehendingly. Keliher had attended the court as and when required. There had been no complaint by anyone that he had breached any of the conditions of his bail. What could be driving the suggestion that the Crown might ask the magistrate to pull his bail? Whatever it was, Eddie was going to have to kill it off right now, because at the moment Mr Rosleigh SM wasn't all that kindly disposed towards him, and he was a living certainty to grant any application Eddie was opposing.

"We think he may have breached a condition of his bail."

"What?" This was sounding uglier every second, and a little flock of butterflies took off in Eddie's stomach. There was a hint of hesitation in Parforth's voice as though he wasn't entirely sure of his ground, and Eddie was determined not to give him any chance to find his feet. "What condition of his bail?"

"Apparently he was picked up recently on a speed camera in Victoria."

In Victoria? What was this all about? It was the first Eddie had heard of Keliher being in Victoria. So what should he do? Should he deny it? Eddie had a bad feeling about denying anything, particularly given Parforth was talking photographic evidence.

"Yeah, so?"

"Well," Parforth commenced a little shakily, "that's a breach of his bail conditions."

"What?" He had a damned good point, but Eddie wasn't about to concede it. He needed time to think about a counter, and the best he could do was try to sound as outraged as he could. "What the hell are you talking about, Bruce?"

"He's not allowed to leave the state."

"Yeah!" Eddie was thinking on the run. "Except for reasons related to the preparation of his defence! Remember?" He shook his head in frustration. "Jesus, Bruce! Try and stay up with the game here, will you."

Parforth pouted with a look that fell somewhere between insulted and embarrassed.

"Well, are you saying he was in Victoria to prepare his defence?"

Eddie liked the sound of it, but so far he didn't know enough to commit himself one way or the other; he was going to have to bluff his way straight through it.

"What?"

"Well, I mean, he was in Victoria. What was he doing down there for this case?"

"Are you serious?"

"Yes."

"You can't be!"

"Well ... "

"You don't seriously think I would divulge privileged information to you?"

"Privileged?" Parforth looked mildly horrified. It hadn't occurred to him he might be encroaching on lawyer–client privilege.

"I hope this isn't some sort of threat designed to try and prise privileged information out of us, Bruce. I'd be very disappointed if it was."

"No, no, certainly not!"

"All right." Eddie nodded trustingly. "I'll accept your ethical assurance on that." Parforth nodded gratefully. "We'll say no more about it then."

It didn't take Eddie long to find Bill Keliher and shuffle him into a witness room.

"What the fuck is going on?"

Eddie didn't want the message to be lost in understatement. They had the world's strongest Crown case against them, they'd got bail in the first place more by good luck than any merit, they had a magistrate who probably spent his weekends wearing a white hood and burning crosses and was about as fond of Eddie as he was of sandy sandwiches, and after Nichols' evidence all of Australia would like nothing better than to see William Keliher thrown straight back in the slammer. All Parforth had to do was make the application and Bill would be gone faster than free beer. So what in God's name had possessed him to take off to Victoria without telling anyone?

Bill Keliher set his jaw and looked the lawyer in the eye with a mixture of defiance and resentment. He knew the man had talent, he could see he was in there working for him, he even had a faint impression now that he might somehow achieve something for him, but he didn't like him, and he couldn't trust him. To Moran the truth was expedient, irrelevant. All this was no more than a hollow performance for which the loudest applause would go to he who danced the fastest jig and told the biggest lies.

"This is just a game to you isn't it, Moran?"

"Too right, pal! A game I want to win! Now what were you doing interstate?"

"I don't know what you're talking about."

"Bullshit!" Eddie slapped the table and jumped up to his feet. "Absolute fucking hogshit, pal! You're lying and you know it! It's written all over your big boof head!"

Bill Keliher's eyebrows lowered and the corners of his mouth dropped into an angry scowl.

"Listen, you little shithead." His voice was deep, and hard, and deadly serious. "You might get away with that sort of bullshit with your grubby clients and your fancy lawyer mates, but you speak to me like that again and I'll put one on your chin. And if I do, you better put a jumper on because it'll be pretty bloody cold and dark when you wake up again."

Eddie looked him in the eye. He'd been arrested, pilloried, imprisoned, humiliated and abused, but he still had enough in him to mean every word he said. There was something different about Bill Keliher. He still felt insulted, still wouldn't let his lawyer treat him like a piece of shit.

Eddie slumped back against the wall, defeated. He shook his head and slid down the wall until he was sitting on the floor, his trousers halfway up his skinny calves.

"You're not used to trusting lawyers are you, Bill?" Keliher was staring at him. The scowl said it all. "Fair enough."

Eddie pulled a cigarette from his pocket and lit up, ignoring the 'no smoking' sign.

"You know what I'm not used to, Bill? I'm not used to clients telling me they're innocent. Like you did in my office a couple of weeks back." Eddie took a deep drag on his cigarette and looked Bill in the eye. "And I'm particularly not used to believing them if they do."

Bill Keliher held his gaze with that same unfaltering certainty.

"So we're both on kind of a steep learning curve here, pal. We're breaking new ground. You understand what I'm saying to you?"

Bill Keliher said nothing. He was listening, assessing, evaluating.

"And if we're going to make it work we're going to have to learn very bloody fast. You with me, pal? Because these are serious charges and this is a very strong Crown case. And if it's true that you're innocent then this one isn't just a game. This one's the real thing. That raises the stakes. So if I sound a little touchy it's because I figure if I don't get this one right then I fail the big test. And I don't want to do that. You with me, Bill?"

Bill Keliher wasn't sure, but that sounded vaguely like the closest Eddie Moran would ever come to an apology. And, for the first time, Moran looked almost as desperate as Bill felt.

"I went to see Dr Eric Pohl."

# CHAPTER TWENTY

Dr Eric Pohl had first contacted Bill by telephone two days before he was arrested.

"I'd like to meet with you, Inspector Keliher. We had a mutual acquaintance."

"Who?"

"Robert Allen."

Bill Keliher had kept a close eye on the man he'd once charged with the McCabe kidnapping. Following his acquittal Robert Allen had wisely fled the state, relocating to Tasmania where he was soon charged with several minor drug offences. He then left the country for New Zealand, where he lived for more than a decade. The police there seemed to lose track of him, and Bill next traced him to a hospital in Sydney where he was being treated for an AIDS-related illness. By then he was considered ancient history, and no one was interested in paying close attention to a dying man. But Bill did what he could, discreetly. He still believed that Allen was the one real lead they had, the one person who could tell them what had happened to the children. He spoke to informants, people who knew him. He tried to get someone to get close to him, but nothing seemed to work.

When Allen finally died in ninety-five, Bill felt an emptiness that stayed with him for weeks. It seemed as though the last hope was gone. He cursed himself for not fronting Allen, pleading with him to make a clean breast of it before he moved on to meet his maker. But how could Bill have done that? He was the one who had been accused of framing Allen, bashing him and fabricating evidence against him. Why would Allen speak to him? Wouldn't he be more likely to complain of police harassment? But Bill knew that, whatever the likely consequences, he should have tried. Now Allen was dead, and the secret of the children had died with him.

With the help of Wally Messner, Bill had canvassed some of Allen's closest friends and associates. Through them he had learnt of Allen's friendship with the university professor Dr Eric Pohl. He had intended to get to Pohl eventually, but so far he hadn't done so. And then, out of the blue, Dr Pohl had rung him, wanting to meet with him regarding Robert Allen.

"Why didn't you tell me about this earlier?"

Eddie Moran was remembering a long conference in his office when Keliher had poured his heart out to him and Frank Vagianni. If this was true, why hadn't it come out in the conference? Keliher had known they suspected Pohl had lifted the file on Lenny Fiske – why didn't he say then that Pohl had contacted him?

"Because Pohl wanted to talk to me about your ex-client Robert Allen. And I knew you wanted to pin Pohl for your own reasons."

"And you didn't trust your own lawyer."

"Not really, no." It was a good call, and Eddie took it on the chin. "Listen, you talked about that test you don't want to fail. Well I've got a test to pass too. I've been at it for a long time and I don't intend to fail either. I don't need anyone's private agendas getting in my way."

"So who did Pohl get to break into my office?"

"I don't think he had anything to do with it."

When Bill Keliher received the call from Eric Pohl, they arranged to meet several days later at a Sydney hotel. But Bill never made the meeting. Within two days of their conversation he was arrested on the sex charges and remanded in custody at Silverwater. It wasn't until Moran managed to get him bail in the local court that Bill was able to make further contact with Pohl. But by then the professor was jumpy, for reasons that were not clear to Bill. He gave various clandestine instructions as to how Bill might contact him, and after a few false starts Bill had persuaded him to meet with him in Melbourne about two weeks ago. They'd met on the beach at St Kilda down in front of the Stokehouse Restaurant, where Pohl had nervously explained to him all about his relationship with Robert Allen.

He had met Allen in Sydney in the late seventies at the home of a mutual acquaintance "who had too much money and an insatiable appetite for French champagne and young boys." He and Robert "fell hopelessly in lust with one another and spent a glorious week together" in Sydney before Pohl returned to Melbourne. After that they stayed in touch and saw each other irregularly until, several years later, Allen contacted him from prison saying he had been wrongly accused of the McCabe kidnapping and seeking his assistance. Convinced of Allen's innocence Pohl had given him support and got him a lawyer. When he was acquitted Pohl felt vindicated.

But years later, when Robert Allen became seriously ill, he said things that had begun to worry Pohl. In bouts of dark depression he had wept bitterly and sobbed of unthinkable atrocities perpetrated on young children. He talked of a secret group that practised witchcraft and Satanic rituals including mutilation and human sacrifice. At first Pohl hoped these were just horrific delusions sparked by his illness, but as they continued to haunt him Pohl increasingly feared otherwise. Then, shortly before his death, Allen had intimated that he knew more about the McCabe case than he had told.

"I do not subscribe or adhere to the taboos imposed by modern Western culture on our sexual behaviour, Mr Keliher," Pohl had defiantly asserted. "I believe that sexual love can be shared with children as with men or women. But I don't condone the abduction or enslavement of anyone!"

According to Pohl, Allen had never told him what had happened to the McCabe children, only that he knew they'd been taken by someone who had been connected with the Brethren. Eric Pohl knew the group that had called themselves the Brethren: he had been one of their members. It started out as a kind of closeted society of Melbourne university academics who got together in the sixties to advocate and experiment with freedom of sexual expression. It had thrived for a time, recruiting students from the universities. But as its gatherings began to boast younger and younger boys, more explicit and more violent pornographic literature, and an ever-widening array of illicit drugs, even the more reckless members began to sense the danger of continued association. The group splintered and eventually disbanded altogether in the early seventies. But liaisons continued.

"There is a great comfort in sharing the company and confidences of enlightened, like-thinking confreres, Mr Keliher. But unfortunately the Brethren produced some who were far from enlightened."

Shortly before his death Allen had received a visit from a man called Stephen Rolfe.

"Robert was discharged from hospital and I went to his home in Sydney for a week to care for him. While I was there Stephen Rolfe came to his house."

Pohl had known Rolfe for many years, ever since, as a tough, streetwise thirteen-year-old, Stephen Rolfe had been lured by the affluence and generosity of the Brethren to their lavish parties in palatial yet discreet off-campus residences in Melbourne. Abandoned by a broken, alcoholic family, the handsome young Master Rolfe had embraced and quickly immersed himself in the largesse of the group, experimenting liberally with all it had to offer.

"He was a beautiful boy. Unfortunately he grew into a very violent adult. We saw indications of that even in the early days."

When Stephen Rolfe burst into Robert Allen's house he obviously meant business. He ordered Pohl gruffly from the room, but even from downstairs the professor could hear the raised bullying grunts of his former protégé, followed by several loud bangs that sounded like Rolfe had emphasised his point the best way he knew how. When Pohl saw Robert Allen his appearance instantly confirmed it.

"Poor Robert had blood all over his face. He was terrified. He said Rolfe was looking for someone, a woman that he knew. He said it all had something to do with the disappearance of the McCabe children."

Allen refused to say who the woman was or how he was connected with her, but he claimed that if Rolfe found her he would kill her. He had remained distressed for several days and during that time he insisted, despite his poor physical state, that Pohl take him to various public telephone booths at the local shops and further afield, where he made calls to someone whose identity he refused to reveal to Pohl.

"He was quite paranoid. He said Stephen Rolfe was connected with some extremely powerful people and he couldn't tell me what it was all about because if he did I would be in danger too. It was all very clandestine. I would wait while he made his calls. But I was told nothing and heard nothing of these conversations. Except once. Only once."

It was the day before Pohl had left to return home to Melbourne. He had taken Allen, by a circuitous route at his insistence, to a telephone booth some distance from his house, and as usual waited while he made the call. To his surprise, this time midway through his conversation Allen called him to the phone booth.

"He put me on to a man who he said needed my help. When I took the phone the man told me that he needed to get urgent psychiatric help for a friend of his in Queensland. But it had to be kept absolutely secret. Robert had told him that I might know someone. I gave him the name of a close friend who practised up that way, but I said I'd need to give my friend a name. He said the person who required the help was a woman called Emma Ronson."

The name of Bernie Radovic's girlfriend Emma Ronson had meant nothing to Pohl at the time, but as requested he spoke to his psychiatrist friend, who assured absolute discretion. A week later Robert Allen died peacefully at home. Less than a month after that, Pohl heard the name of Emma Ronson again. She too had died, but not so peacefully.

It was a long, involved story, one that Eric Pohl had recounted, nervously at first, then with increasing ease and relief, to Bill Keliher on a blustery St Kilda beach, and one that Bill Keliher recounted now to his lawyer Eddie Moran. As they sat opposite each other in the fading light of Moran's hotel room, the lawyer sipping

Scotch and smoking cigarettes as his client faithfully related the whole story, answering questions, providing further detail when requested, a new comfort began to grow between them. Bill Keliher, against whom the evidence seemed so compelling, was sensible, rational, believable. Eddie did believe him; he still didn't really know why he did, but he knew he did. And, in a case where the evidence was apparently so strong and the stakes so high, it worried him. Across the coffee table, his client had begun to understand that now the stakes were high for both of them. For the first time, it seemed, Bill Keliher's lawyer was really listening.

"When Ronson was murdered, Pohl figured she was the one this Rolfe character was looking for. Then when Lenny Fiske was charged, it seems curiosity got the better of him. That's why he came to you to try to buy Lenny's file."

"You're saying he didn't send the goon who broke into my office?"

"No, but he did say something that might help you work out who it was. Remember the tattoo your receptionist saw on her attacker's forearm? Pohl says Stephen Rolfe had one just like it."

Eddie sucked hard on his cigarette and repeated Stephen Rolfe's name in his head. This was one animal he wanted to meet sometime soon.

"Have you checked out Rolfe?"

"Apparently his name came up on some old offenders indexes. But there's no other records on him. I'd say someone's lifted his files."

"Sounds like he does have some powerful friends."

Bill Keliher nodded thoughtfully. As they sat in the semi-darkness both men tried to make some sense of where they were. They had learned from Sasha Kelly that Bernie Radovic was suspected of involvement in child pornography and paedophilia. Now it looked likely that Emma Ronson, and probably Radovic as well, knew more than they should about the McCabe kids. Enough to think they could blackmail Bill Keliher. And enough to make someone, probably Stephen Rolfe, mad enough or scared enough to want to kill them both. But that still didn't explain why anyone would want to set up Bill Keliher on phoney sex charges.

"There could only be one motive for setting you up – they needed to discredit you. For some reason they believed Radovic or Ronson had told you the secret."

"Yeah, well, they hadn't." The words fell bitterly from Bill's lips. It had been a long day, spent listening to people accusing him of shameful acts, feeling the reproach and hatred in the eyes that stared at him from every angle, the weight of a mystery that he couldn't fathom. Stephen Rolfe, and whoever he was working for, seemed to have thought that the bookie and his girlfriend were willing to give Bill the answer he'd been searching for for over thirty years. If they were right, he'd come within a phone call of the truth.

Bill wrapped one big hand around his forehead and rubbed his tired eyes. Eddie clicked on a lamp and pushed an empty glass towards him.

"Scotch?"

Bill nodded silently and watched as the alcohol tocked quietly into the glass.

"It seems to me we're running out of people who can tell us what this secret is." Bill picked up the glass and stared blankly into it. "Allen's dead, Ronson and Radovic have been murdered, the kid – if there was a kid – seems to have vanished into thin air. And now they reckon Pohl's necked himself. Even if we find this grub Rolfe, he's not going to tell us diddleyshit. Who's left?"

"The psych."

Bill Keliher gulped down a swig of Scotch as if to fortify himself to speak.

"I don't know who he is, Eddie. Pohl wouldn't tell me."

Eddie Moran sipped lightly on his drink and sat back looking smug.

"I think I do."

\*   \*   \*

Frank Vagianni had drawn a blank with his ring-around to all the specialist Doctors Forrester that he could find a listing for. But he'd been asking the wrong question. It wasn't surprising the receptionists hadn't recognised the name Bernie Radovic: he wasn't the patient. Emma Ronson was. Given that the whole thing was supposedly so hush-hush, the good doctor might not have even opened a file or sent an account through normal channels. But God bless him, like any doctor worth his salt he had still insisted on his fee, and because it wasn't anything illegal Bernie Radovic had paid him out of his cheque account. He probably claimed it back on Medibank. That wasn't too bright under the circumstances, but then you didn't get to be an SP bookmaker because you were a Rhodes scholar. Eddie got Frank to fax him down the list of Doctors Forrester overnight. There were three psychiatrists on it, but the only one who was anywhere near Queensland was a Dr Milo Forrester, clinical psychiatrist, of Murwillumbah in northern New South Wales, about a half-hour south of the Queensland border. Eddie punched in the number.

"Good morning. Dr Forrester's rooms."

"Yes, it's Eric Pohl, could I speak to Dr Forrester please?"

"I'm sorry?" The shock in her voice was unmistakable. "Who did you say it was?"

"Eric Pohl."

"Dr Eric Pohl?"

"Sorry, wrong number. Bye."

*Click.* Eddie knew all he needed to. The receptionist knew exactly who Eric Pohl was and she knew he was in no condition to be making telephone calls. That meant Eric Pohl and Milo Forrester had been 'confreres'. It also meant that Milo Forrester was Emma Ronson's psych.

Eddie punched in another number.

"Hello. Edwin C. Moran, solicitor." Slick didn't sound too interested on the other end of the line, but at least she was back at work.

"Jesus, Slick, I told you, it's just 'Moran Lawyers', plural. Okay?"

"How about just 'Moron Lawyer'?"

"Yeah, you're very funny." She was obviously feeling better. It was good to hear her giving cheek again. "You know there's a downturn out there, don't you? Most secretaries are giving it regular to their bosses just to keep their jobs. You don't even give good phone."

"You got to do something about that hormone problem of yours, Eddie."

"Yeah, sure. Listen, I need you to do something. Get hold of Frank and tell him to get me whatever he can on a bloke by the name of Stephen Rolfe. He's from Melbourne but he should have some form in New South Wales."

"You think you might be on to something?"

"I don't know. All I know is, I smell a dirty great big rat."

\*　　\*　　\*

It was a professional gentlemen's club and they were all, without doubt, professional gentlemen. Older now, but all still recognised and well respected in their own circles. The sumptuously appointed decor of the club recognised and somehow complemented the extent of their achievement. They were all civilised men, successful and distinguished.

"She talked to Milo Forrester."

Their drawn, grey faces said it all. As he looked across the table at the other two he could see the mild panic in their eyes. How had it come to this? Where would it end? When did you stop paying for the follies of your youth? He only wished he knew.

"What did she tell him?"

"God only knows. She was completely mad."

Emma Ronson had the power to destroy them all. Even now. From the day she'd started talking about the McCabe children they were all at risk. The mystery of the McCabe case was the one thing that could destroy them all. They had understood that perfectly and they had done what needed to be done. They had hoped it would never come to this. They were all civilised men. No one wanted Emma to be hurt. But it became inevitable, for the sake of everyone. And it should have ended there. Why hadn't it? Why was all this still going on? Why had they all been summoned here to Sydney yet again to conspire in whispers like a pack of common criminals? Where would it all end?

"That halfwit Radovic! If he'd had more sense they'd both still be alive today."

Maybe it was true, but what could Radovic have done? By all accounts he had loved the child, so he was helpless. The human heart was always difficult to read and impossible to govern. Once love had intervened, the whole tragic mess was potentially disastrous. Love was such a dangerous emotion. Volatile, impetuous, unpredictable. Not dependable like lust. Lust was totally self-centred and therefore always manageable, but love was something else.

"Has anyone spoken to Milo?"

It was a good question, and he was pleased it had been asked. The answer wouldn't comfort them, but that was the point: they had to know where they stood, and where he had to lead them.

"I rang Milo and he denied ever speaking to her."

"Shit. That doesn't sound good."

"Surely Milo Forrester wouldn't say anything to anyone?"

"How can we be sure of that?"

It was true and they all knew it. Milo Forrester had been living in the north for more than a decade. Most of them hadn't even seen or spoken to him in nearly twenty years. He had married his young secretary and left Melbourne and his old life behind. How could they possibly know how Milo Forrester would react now, if he had learnt the truth about the disappearance of the McCabe children? The solution hung in the silence of the group and as he looked around the table he could see the answer written in their anxious eyes.

"Someone should get Rolfe to speak to him."

"Rolfe? Are you mad? Rolfe's completely out of control. Look what happened when we asked him to speak to Eric Pohl, for God's sake!"

"We don't have any choice!" He was beginning to grow impatient. He had played this game before. They all knew what the answer was, but each of them wanted to enjoy the luxury of pretending to try to avoid it. "We know she spoke to Milo, and at the moment we've got no idea how much she told him."

"We don't even know whether she knew anything."

"No we don't!" His voice was loud enough to break into the genteel calm of the Long Bar, causing the young barman to look up briefly, before he settled back to his task of stacking glasses. It was firm enough to demand the immediate and undivided attention of each of them sitting around the little table, to take their minds off their own sensibilities and focus on the issue. "But we've got to find out. Because if the story ever did get out, I don't have to tell you we'd all be finished. Totally and utterly." The words sounded like a death knell in the hush of their demure surroundings. "And the witch hunt wouldn't finish with us. They'd crucify every liberalist and free thinker in this country for generations to come."

They were civilised men. None of them liked violence. But the thought that they were doing this for someone other than themselves, for future generations of enlightened, like-minded confreres, somehow made it seem more palatable, a duty thrust upon them as professional gentlemen.

# CHAPTER TWENTY-ONE

As Eddie hurried down towards the courts that morning, he was trying to focus on the job at hand. Stephen Rolfe and whoever he was tied up with had a secret they wanted to hide; they thought Bill Keliher knew that secret and that's why they wanted him discredited. So what? Where did that take Eddie? Now he had a reason why someone might want to trump up the evidence, but if Keliher was going to beat these charges Eddie was still going to have to demonstrate that the evidence was in fact trumped up. Before he could do that he was going to have to work out who it was pulling all the strings. Stephen Rolfe might be doing the leg-breaking for these clowns, but it wasn't Rolfe who'd managed to get witnesses to identify Keliher, and it wasn't Rolfe who'd arranged to parade Keliher in front of the world's press. If the DNA evidence was bogus, whoever organised it had to be someone close to the prosecution process. Stephen Rolfe must have some very powerful friends indeed.

Wally Messner sat bolt upright in the witness box, staring resolutely out in front of him, begrudgingly answering defence counsel's questions but otherwise ignoring him, and doing his best to avoid eye contact with the defendant, the man he'd known for nearly twenty years, the man he'd worked with side by side, the one who'd trusted and relied on him, the one he had arrested and charged with sixteen sex offences. Bill Keliher never took his eyes off the witness: he was searching for answers that he knew must be there somewhere. Wally Messner was no fool. Surely he didn't believe that Bill had done these things.

Eddie spent the morning dredging through the routine stuff, trying to get whatever information he could that might lead to anything, as Mr Rosleigh SM sat back in his chair, eyes closed, pretending to be concentrating but in fact dozing lightly while Eddie examined Messner on the background of the investigation. Messner confirmed that the JCC had been involved in the Ether Man investigations almost from the time of the Commission's inception in 1992 as part of its general charter to oversee police investigation of serial crimes against children. Although most of the victims were young adults, there had been enough juveniles amongst them to enable the JCC to play a helpful role as part of a joint investigation, and the Commission's extensive resources had brought a welcome boost to the police probe. They had taken possession of all the original files and exhibits, and subjected them to renewed and intense scrutiny. Wally

Messner had been recruited almost immediately as part of a select eight-man police team who were to work closely with lawyers from the JCC, employing the latest and most sophisticated forensic techniques. Like all the others, he had been specifically instructed to keep his role in the investigation absolutely confidential, largely because the Commissioner, Judge Peter Rosenthal, had not entirely ruled out the possibility of police involvement in the crimes.

Police involvement. According to Messner the JCC suspected a police link as early as 1992, before anyone had purported to identify Bill Keliher, and before there was any DNA. What police had they suspected, and why? Eddie Moran needed to find out. The answers might just dredge up another suspect. But it was dangerous ground.

"Who did they think might be involved?"

"The defendant."

Bad answer, but Eddie had to keep on going.

"Anyone else?"

"No."

It wasn't getting any better but, like Macbeth, Eddie was now so steeped in blood there was no going back.

"On what basis did they suspect him?"

Wally Messner looked uncomfortable. He didn't want to answer the question, but he did.

"At one time he was a suspect in the McCabe kidnapping case." An audible gasp washed around the courtroom, loud enough to cause Stan Rosleigh to raise his eyebrows, though his eyes didn't quite come open.

As he spoke, Wally Messner looked for the first time directly at his old workmate Bill Keliher with hard, callous eyes. Bill held his gaze. How could someone like Wally Messner, who he'd worked with for so long, who knew him, actually believe that he was capable of all he'd been accused of? Messner's stare remained unflinching, and Bill returned it, probing for the answers. "Later he went to Manly, and it was during his time there that the first series of attacks occurred."

The journalists were all scribbling frantically now and several were already on their feet. They would wait just long enough to see what more might be said about the McCabe kidnapping; if nothing, they would dash to the door and their story would remain as it stood – TOP COP CHARGED WITH RAPE AND ABDUCTION CHARGES IS ALSO SUSPECTED OF BEING MCCABE KIDNAPPER! It was a great story. The damage was already done; it wouldn't help Eddie's client to stop now, and to get the job done he had to keep going.

"Why was he a suspect in the McCabe kidnapping?"

"He was briefly in their company the day they disappeared, that's all. A lot of people were suspects at one time or another."

Bill Keliher wondered if Wally Messner's answer was intended to defuse the bombshell he'd just dropped. To Bill it sounded almost as though it was, but why would Wally want to defuse it? Any cop who believed in his case wouldn't, certainly not if he had the years of experience Wally did. Anything you could do to prejudice the bad guy in the public's mind was a bonus you didn't refuse. The question had been asked and Wally was entitled to answer it. Obviously he knew Bill had given a false statement, and he could have added that to his answer and it wouldn't have looked good for Bill. But Wally hadn't mentioned it. He didn't want to talk about the McCabe case at all. And the more Bill looked at him the more he wondered: Was Wally Messner convinced that Bill was guilty?

"You arrested my client at about three in the afternoon, didn't you, Detective?" Eddie Moran was angry. He wasn't sure why; it was probably because he blamed himself for giving Messner an opportunity to feed the press that poison. It wasn't Messner's fault of course: Eddie led with his chin and he had asked for it, but he was going to get square just the same.

"Yes."

"But you and others from the joint task force first spoke to him about these matters at about nine that morning."

"Yes."

"And you asked him to supply samples of blood and hair, didn't you?"

"Yes."

The Smith complaint talked of the presence of blood and that explained why the police had taken blood from Keliher, to compare it with the blood found at the scene. But there was no mention of any hair found at the scene of any of the crimes, and yet the investigating police had specifically requested head and pubic hair samples from Keliher. Eddie knew that unless someone was starting his own private hair collection, there could only be one explanation.

"Why did you take hair specimens?"

"In several of the cases there were foreign head and pubic hairs found on the victim."

"How many cases?"

"Four."

"Four out of eight?"

"Yes."

"That's fifty per cent."

"Yes."

If any of these so-called foreign hairs belonged to Bill Keliher, Eddie would have heard about them a long time before this. Until now there'd been no mention of any foreign hairs, and that could only mean they didn't match Keliher's specimen.

"Did the foreign hair or hairs in each case match the foreign hair in each other case?"

"Yes, roughly."

"What do you mean roughly?"

"It wasn't conclusive."

"But they were all consistent with one another."

"Not inconsistent."

"But they were all inconsistent with the defendant's hair samples, weren't they?"

"Yes, they were."

As a stunned murmur rolled around the courtroom, Eddie did his best to look as though he had known all along this evidence was coming.

"None of these victims knew each other?"

"I don't believe so, no."

"So the only thing they had in common was the same attacker, according to the Crown case. Is that right?"

"Yes."

"Well, that makes the presence of a common set of foreign hairs pretty relevant, doesn't it?"

"We can't say they were common. They had similarities."

Wally Messner looked uncomfortable. Now was the time to square him up. Eddie put one hand on his hip and the other on the bar table, and leaned forward with a derisive sneer spread across his face.

"Why weren't they mentioned in the brief, witness?"

"We weren't relying on them."

"What?" Eddie was warming up and Messner looked at him with a stone face. Wally was a hard, dour, humourless man, and he had no tolerance for histrionics. "Is that your answer, witness?"

"Yes."

"You weren't relying on them?"

"That's right."

"You're not serious, are you?" Messner gave no answer; he just stared back impassively. "You mean you weren't relying on them to try to stitch up this accused!"

"I object!" Parforth called the words out so loudly that they momentarily roused Stan Rosleigh SM from his slumber. He stirred long enough to wonder who had raised the objection and why, before Eddie moved on without losing his momentum.

"I withdraw that. Why didn't you alert the defence

that hairs belonging to a potential alternative suspect were found in four of the eight cases?"

"I couldn't say they belonged to one suspect."

"Suspect or suspects!"

It was a good point, perhaps not quite as good as Eddie tried to make it, but good nonetheless. It was highly significant information, and the fact that it had been withheld from the defence raised some serious questions about the whole investigation. Eddie milked it for all it was worth, interrogating Messner on and on in a robust manner that in Eddie's own inimitable fashion finely balanced legitimate inquiry with what was little more than outright abuse.

Bill struggled to understand what Wally Messner was up to. He was playing a straight bat to Moran's questions, purporting to justify the decision not to reveal the evidence about the hairs on the basis that the police were not relying on it to prove anything. But he must have known from the outset that it would never be an acceptable response, and he must have known what Moran would seek to make of it. And yet Wally had revealed the fact that the foreign hairs were found. He didn't have to. He had not taken custody of the exhibits at any stage, he had not prepared the exhibit lists or the forensic statements, he could know about the hairs only from what others had told him. He was part of a major task force in which a lot of cooks had dipped into the same broth. He'd have had no trouble whatsoever sidestepping Moran's question about the blood and hair samples simply by responding that he'd obtained the specimens he was requested to.

A copper with Wally Messner's experience could do that in his sleep. Instead he gave an answer that opened up a subject that was sure to get him into trouble.

"You first got blood from Bill Keliher at about nine thirty on the morning of his arrest."

"Yes."

"What did you do with the specimen?"

"I delivered it to Senior Sergeant Dickson of the JCC."

"Why?"

"He had the Smith blood swabs and he was to deliver the swabs plus the defendant's blood sample to the forensic laboratory for comparison purposes."

"What time did you deliver the sample to Dickson?"

"About eleven."

"You didn't get a report back from the lab for about a week, did you?"

"Yeah, that'd be right."

Eddie pulled a page of a newspaper from the bottom of the untidy pile of papers stacked in front of him on the bar table and read aloud from an article about Keliher's arrest. In it the author quoted Messner as asserting that forensic tests had identified Bill Keliher's DNA in blood found at the scene of one of the attacks.

"That appeared the morning after Keliher's arrest. You told the newspapers on the day Keliher was charged that there was a DNA match, didn't you?"

Wally Messner hesitated for only an instant, but Bill noticed it. He was watching his ex-partner so closely he could hear every breath he took and see every twitch.

"Did I?"

There was a subtle wariness in Messner's voice as though he knew what was coming. Eddie didn't notice it, he was too fired up now, leaning forward glaring at the witness.

"Looks like it, doesn't it?"

"Maybe."

"But on the day Keliher was charged, there was no DNA match. How is it, witness, that you knew the results of the tests a week before the tests were done?"

"Well, I don't know for certain that I did."

"You did!" Moran was wildly waving the newspaper in front of him. "It's there in black and white!"

"You can't believe everything you read, Mr Moran."

"I'm swiftly learning that, witness! So what are you telling me, you didn't say anything to the press about DNA results?"

Bill could see the snide, derisive tone of Eddie's manner was grating on Wally Messner. He didn't like being the subject of ridicule.

"If I didn't have them, I couldn't have."

"What would you say if I told you the journalist had taped the comments?"

The anger evaporated instantly, replaced by what looked more like panic. Messner didn't stop to ask himself if Eddie was bluffing. He didn't play it smart, he jumped at the first out he could think of.

"Actually I think we had a preliminary finding late that afternoon."

"Who told you that?"

"Someone from the JCC, I think."

"That's not true, is it, witness?"

Eddie's voice had a tinge of genuine resentment to it.

"Yes it is!"

"Are you saying you positively remember being told that on the afternoon of Keliher's arrest?"

Suddenly the hesitation was back again. "I think so, yeah."

"By whom?"

Bill watched him and waited. Messner was hiding something.

"I can't remember."

Eddie slammed one hand flat down on the bar table causing Mr Rosleigh SM to unbalance slightly on his chair. He quickly regained his equilibrium.

"Witness, according to the forensic scientist's statement, Dickson didn't even deliver the samples to the lab until the afternoon of the day after Keliher's arrest! Now I ask you again: how could you accurately predict to the press that evening what the scientists didn't find until a week later?"

Messner looked like an errant schoolboy who'd been caught with one hand in the biscuit tin. The stone face and the anger were gone. He looked a weak and bumbling incompetent.

"Someone must have got their wires crossed and told me we had a match-up even though it hadn't been done yet."

"What!"

Eddie was off again, firing questions from all directions. As Wally absorbed them, Bill watched him closely, still trying to put his finger on what was colouring his replies.

When you've spent your lifetime around coppers you get to know what to expect. You know when someone's dodging, or off on a crusade, or chasing a private vendetta, or running dead, maybe trying to do someone a favour, or looking to get square. All sorts of games were played out in that witness box. But this was something different. Something Bill had never seen in Wally Messner. Was it just that Wally was uncomfortable giving evidence against a fellow cop? If it was, his reaction wasn't typical. No, it was more than that. A lot more.

Wally Messner was sitting on something that was causing him a distinct pain in the arse. He obviously wasn't enjoying sitting there, but at the same time he didn't seem to be too keen to stand up either.

# CHAPTER TWENTY-TWO

"Hi. I want to make an appointment to see Dr Forrester."

The matronly receptionist smiled patiently and peered over her glasses.

"Yes, did you have a referral at all?"

"Yeah, my sister recommended him to me."

"No, I mean do you have a referral to Dr Forrester from your general practitioner?"

"No, my sister was a patient of his. Emma Ronson. You remember Emma Ronson?"

Frank Vagianni was watching the woman's eyes as he asked the question. Nothing. No hint of recognition, nothing whatsoever.

"No. I'm sorry, sir, but doctor will need a referral from your general practitioner before I can book you in for an appointment."

The only photograph of Emma Ronson anyone seemed to have was one taken from a snapshot found in Bernie Radovic's unit. The media had extracted a head and shoulders shot which they had reproduced in various stories on the murder. Frank had cut one out, enlarged it and had it copied, so it now looked a fair facsimile of a standard family photograph. He pushed the photograph in front of the receptionist, keeping his eyes trained on her, waiting for any slight reaction.

"That's my sister there, see? Emma Ronson. Maybe you know her by a different name?"

The receptionist glanced briefly at the photograph and then looked back politely.

"No, I don't, I'm sorry."

She was about to go into her spiel again about the GP referral but Frank wasn't interested. Even if he could afford one, it would take a lot more than a psychiatrist to fix Frank's problems.

"No worries. Thanks, love. Good on you."

The little town of Murwillumbah was one of Frank's favourites. Nestled in behind the coast on the banks of the Tweed River it was typical of the leafy country towns that were dotted through the Northern Rivers district. It had the old nineteenth-century courthouse that was all red brick and cedar, and a good solid set of watch-house cells that told a crook he wasn't in there to watch videos. The main street was broad and busy and had at least one milk bar where you could still get meat pie and vegies on a plate and a milkshake in a metal cup to wash it down. Even at four thirty in the afternoon. And from the bench seats in the milk bar you could see the back door and the car park to the chambers of the good Dr Milo Forrester.

By five thirty Frank had read the *Northern Star* from back page through to front; he knew who was winning in the local Group 18 football competition, when the shire eisteddfod would be held, and what poor hippies' crops the cops had busted in the past week. He was halfway through his second milkshake and had just ordered a vanilla slice when the back door opened and out stepped a distinguished grey-haired gentleman who couldn't be anyone but Milo Forrester.

"Dr Forrester?"

"Yes."

"Frank Vagianni." He flipped his ID open and quickly flipped it closed again. "We're investigating the murder of Emma Ronson."

There was no mistaking this reaction. Milo Forrester had heard the name before and he felt none too comfortable with the mention of it. He hesitated, blinked and squinted before regaining his composure.

"Who?"

"Your ex-patient. Emma Ronson."

Forrester blinked again and squinted through his thick glasses.

"I don't believe I know her, Mr ... Sorry, what did you say your name was?"

"Vagianni."

"From?"

"I'm investigating her murder. We're aware that Ms Ronson was consulting you in your professional capacity for several weeks immediately prior to her death."

Forrester's pallor betrayed him immediately. Frank Vagianni had just enunciated a secret he had hoped would remain hidden, and Frank could see the good doctor's mind was now scurrying around, frantically looking for a way to get out from under. Eventually he found it.

"Are you a policeman?"

It was obviously a good mind, because even in its panic it had come up with exactly the right question. Frank was tempted to come straight back with exactly the right lie. But he didn't.

"No, I'm a private investigator."

Forrester breathed out slowly, and the colour seeped back into his face.

"I'm sorry, I don't know this woman you're talking about. Good day."

As far as he was concerned the conversation was over. He was already reaching for the door handle of his car.

"What about her boyfriend, Bernie Radovic? You sure as shit knew him. He paid your accounts, remember? He paid them by cheque. And the cheques all went through your account, doctor."

Forrester knew exactly what Frank was talking about. He looked a worried man. But any indecision that had earlier shown in his face was now gone.

"I'm a betting man, Mr Vagianni. I have an occasional flutter. I laid a couple of small bets with Mr Radovic, that's all."

Milo Forrester had been expecting, or at least fearing, that some day someone would ask the question. He had his answer ready.

"I don't think so, doc."

"Think what you like, Mr Vagianni. Good day."

\*    \*    \*

On the afternoon of the fifth day of the committal proceedings in relation to the charges against Police Inspector William James Keliher, the Crown closed its case. The defence made no submission and the presiding magistrate, Mr Stan Rosleigh SM, committed the defendant to stand trial on all sixteen charges before a judge and jury of his peers at the next sittings of the District Court.

As he walked out through the main doors of the courts building that day, Bill Keliher didn't feel the heat of the television arc lights or the squeeze of the crowd bustling around them. He heard nothing of the cacophony of shouted questions and angry insults that whirled around them. He could hear only the magistrate's words, still ringing in his ears: *I find that there is sufficient evidence to put the defendant upon his trial on each of the charges now before this court …*

It was a familiar formula that he'd heard a thousand times before. There was no malice in it, no sting, no final effect. It was merely a finding that there was a case to answer. If the Crown evidence was to be believed, and if nothing more was heard on the subject from the defence, then a jury not necessarily would, but could, return a guilty verdict. It was merely a threshold assessment of the prosecution case, a preliminary finding based only on the evidence of the Crown witnesses and without having heard anything of the defence. It had always seemed so bland and ineffectual, almost benign. Until that day, when it was said to him, about him. It had crushed him. He had known it was coming, waited for it, recited it in his mind. But when it finally came it had struck him to his heart, and for a long time afterwards it hung over him like the shadow of a hangman's noose, darkening his thoughts and deepening his shame.

Eddie Moran remained up-beat. Nichols' evidence had been tainted by her having seen the press coverage and the rest of the witnesses had ultimately agreed they couldn't make a confident identification. Except for Ron Morris; they would simply have to argue he was mistaken, probably misled by the way the photo board had been prepared. That left the DNA material. The forensic scientist who did the DNA comparisons had been unavailable to give evidence at the committal hearing, but Eddie would make contact with him in the next few weeks.

"He'll be some boffin that they've shonked somehow. I don't know how, but Messner knew the DNA was going to come in positive before he even had the results. He's pulled some stunt and we're going to nail him. Trust me, things are going fine."

Bill did trust Eddie Moran, and that was a big step forward from where they'd started out. But he couldn't agree with Eddie's assessment that things were going fine. Bill Keliher had been committed to stand trial on sixteen sex offences, his career was in tatters, and everybody, even his old workmates, seemed convinced that he was guilty. He had returned home after the hearing to find that someone had broken his front window and the word 'Sicko' had been painted on the front gate to the unit complex. The agent had asked him to find somewhere else 'in everyone's best interests' and he'd spent three nights in a motel before moving in with his brother's family out at Penrith. He had already been convicted in the press and in the minds of the public; any jury was going to treat him as guilty until proven innocent. Any little piece of evidence linking him to any of the attacks would be enough. The jury weren't going to buy some theory that Ron Morris was somehow misled by the positioning of the photographs, or that the cops had somehow trumped up the DNA. A reasonable doubt wasn't going to save Bill Keliher. He was going to have to come up with some proof – proof that this was all a set-up that had something to do with his search for the McCabe kids and a sick call that he'd received in the middle of the night.

*Is that you, Constable Keliher?... It's Catherine McCabe. Don't you remember?... You drove us to the beach in your police car ... I want to go home, Constable. Please take me home.*

Bill kicked the engine over and flicked on the headlights. He had told his brother and sister-in-law he had a friend to see and would be out for a few hours. They didn't ask questions; they were happy to have a little space without him.

The few days that followed the committal order had

been the worst. Every newspaper, every television bulletin was full of the story, each leading with the link to the McCabe case, the news that Bill had been a suspect for that crime too. He was horrified by each successive article and announcement, wondering what Faye McCabe made of it all. What could she think? How could he reassure her? Every minute of every day he wanted to ring her, tell her that it wasn't true, explain to her what was going on and why all these lies were being told about him. But how could he? What could he tell her?

Eventually she telephoned him. The message that she had was simple.

"Please don't forget that I believe in you, Bill. Whatever anybody thinks, I know you're a good man."

The dark thoughts and deep shame had evaporated with that call. They were replaced with the determination that had temporarily abandoned him, a determination to clear his name and complete the job he'd started with Vince Donnelly a long time ago.

*We'll find whoever done this ... If we keep our minds on the job and we stick to it, we'll get the bastard.*

Bill Keliher felt sure that he was closer to the answer now than he had ever been. This whole nightmare was happening because he had got too close, and he knew that when he found the proof to beat these charges the answer would be there, right in front of him.

Frank Vagianni had hit a brick wall with the doctor. If Milo Forrester knew anything about Emma Ronson then he wasn't letting on. And so far nothing had come up on Stephen Rolfe. Frank still had enough mates in the Queensland force to get into the police computer, despite Sasha Kelly's regular directives regarding the strict embargo on access for unauthorised purposes. But there was nothing on Rolfe in the computer for Queensland or any other state. The only trace of him was the mention Bill had found in the old offenders lists in New South Wales. Whoever had cleaned him up had done a first-class job.

That brought the spotlight back onto the coppers – why they had set up those photo boards the way they had, why they had lined Bill up to take the long walk in front of the TV cameras, why the evidence about the foreign hairs had been buried, and how Wally Messner had known Bill's blood sample was going to match up with the blood of the offender before the tests were done. To Eddie Moran the answer was simple: Wally Messner was trying to stitch up his old boss. But Bill knew that if that was the answer, then it was far from simple.

Sometimes there's only one way to get an answer. Sometimes you've just got to ask the question.

"G'day, Wally."

"What are you doing here, Bill?"

"I came to talk to you, Wal. I want to know what's going on."

Bill could barely make out Wally Messner's face silhouetted by the porch light. There was a long, tense silence. Then Wally turned and called something to his wife, took the dog's leash from a verandah post and whistled up an overweight black labrador.

"Come on, we'll go for a walk."

They walked side by side along the dark suburban footpath, trailing behind a fat black waddling dog in the blue shadows of the street lights, until eventually Wally stopped in his tracks.

"Look, Bill, I don't know whether you done it or not. Right?" He was breathing short and shallow, more emotional than Bill had ever seen him. "I'm just a fuckin' dumb cop, right? I don't know what the fuck's going on and I don't want to. I just do what they tell me." He turned and faced Bill front-on, and even in the darkness Bill could see the intensity in his eyes. "But you're right. They're dealing from the bottom of the deck. And you don't do that to a copper. I don't care what he's done. You don't do that."

Bill's breath was frozen in his chest. He was stunned and terrified by what had just been said, and what might be yet to come.

"I haven't done anything, Wal. Nothing."

"These bloody JCC lawyers, mate. They'd like nothing better than to put a copper down for this shit. "

He had something to say, but he still wasn't saying it.

"Why me, Wally? What the hell's going on?"

"Listen, when the JCC was first set up they got hold of all the old files, including some of the internal memos on the McCabe file, stuff we'd never even seen. Years ago that Vince Donnelly had put through some memo about you being a suspect at some stage, and some clown in the

Commission got hold of it and married it up with the attacks while you were at Manly. That was it. From that point they were convinced. You were the pea. It didn't matter whether you done any of it or not, they were always going to do their best to fit you with it."

That explained why they had got interested in Bill as a suspect, but you don't pull evidence from thin air. He was still struggling to understand what Messner meant by 'dealing from the bottom of the deck'.

"Mate, no matter how red hot they were, I didn't do any of it!"

"Listen, it's a bullshit investigation, all right." Wally glanced nervously across his shoulder as he spoke. "The JCC lawyers are calling all the shots; us coppers are just there to join the dots. You've seen the ID boards – you can see they're doing their best to help you along. And they've buried shit everywhere. Everywhere! Like the hairs they found at the crime scenes. They didn't match your samples so they buried them. They're just gone! And a couple of the earlier descriptions. Same thing. They didn't match up with the IDs so they kept them under wraps."

"What earlier descriptions?"

"One of the recent victims initially told the uniformed blokes she thought her attacker had a bald head. That doesn't sound much like you, does it."

Bill Keliher always had been known for his big hair. The complainant hadn't seen the face of her attacker, who had grabbed her from behind, but in the struggle she believed she had touched his bald head. She could have been mistaken, but nonetheless it was a substantial discrepancy, and it should have been revealed to the defence.

"Another one of the victims described her assailant as having a tattoo on his forearm. They knew you had no tats, so that got buried too."

Bill felt his stomach muscles tighten.

"What sort of a tattoo?"

"A cross, or a crucifix of some sort."

Bill was suddenly conscious that they were standing together on the footpath of a quiet suburban street, whispering at each other like two grubby conspirators in a cheap spy movie. But it was time to fill in a bit of background for Wally, give him enough information to help him recognise what might be of significance. As the fat lab led the way down towards the soccer fields Bill launched into the story – not the whole story, but as much as Wally had to know. He told him how he'd received calls from what sounded like a young girl using the name Catherine McCabe, and that the purpose of the calls still wasn't clear to him. He later discovered that the calls had come from the unit of the murdered bookie Bernie Radovic, so he went to see Lenny Fiske, who gave him the story about being recruited by Steve with the tattooed forearm, and having heard a child screaming in the unit when Radovic and his girlfriend copped it. He told Wally what they'd heard about the JCC investigation of Radovic for paedophilia and child pornography, and the fact that police had found the child's doll in the unit, the involvement of Eric Pohl and

Robert Allen, and the mysterious appearances by Stephen Rolfe, the man with a cross tattooed on his forearm. And he told him that they'd been to Peter Rosenthal for help, but he'd refused to give them any information, merely saying that there were dangerous people involved and to leave the job to the JCC.

As he spoke Bill could sense that his confidant was becoming even more agitated than he had been on the street corner, his shallow breath now grunting audibly with each step. When the name of Peter Rosenthal was mentioned he finally jumped in.

"Bill, that DNA business in court today," he rasped breathlessly. "I didn't make it up. I was told the day you were arrested there was a match-up."

"What are you saying, Wally?"

"That didn't come from the troops, Bill, it came from the top!"

Bill Keliher stopped in his tracks. "Rosenthal?"

Messner was facing him now, his eyes wide open with alarm. For a moment he looked incapable of speech but then he suddenly blurted out a warning.

"You bloody watch your back with him, Bill!"

Wally Messner's eyes were glistening with the intensity of a secret that he'd held in for too long. Bill had seen that look in enough eyes to know that now was the time for true confessions.

"Wally, I want to know what the fuck's going on here. What are you doing in the middle of all this?"

"Rosenthal's a closet queen, all right? He's a fucking rock-spider! Likes the young hairless boys!" He held Bill's gaze for a moment, but then the intensity drained from his eyes and he looked away self-consciously. "He got himself in a heap of shit years ago when he was still a judge, dick-fiddling with some young bloke down the local dunnies. Would have rooted his career, but it got swept under the carpet." Messner rubbed his thumb against two fingers signalling that money had changed hands. "A couple of blokes have been looking after him for years."

There had long been rumours that Wally fed his gambling debts by topping up his pay cheque the easiest way a copper can. But even by the standards of a crooked cop, protecting paedophiles was about as low as you could go. The anger welled in Bill's chest and throat and suddenly erupted without warning. Before he knew it he had Wally Messner by the throat.

"I get it, Wal! You and your grubby mates are copping a sling from Rosenthal to disappear his sexual indiscretions, so as a pay-off he puts you into the McCabe investigation to spy on me!"

They were nose to nose now, Keliher snarling and breathing venomously into his ex-partner's face. The thought that Wally Messner had stood beside him all those years, spying, taking mental notes as to whether he might be the one who had carried off two children, burned in Bill's brain, clouding any rational thought.

"Get your fucking hands off me!" As Messner growled the words Bill could feel the unmistakable hard edge of a revolver pushed up under his rib cage. He slowly released his hold but Messner clung tight to his shirt, holding them together in intimate collusion.

"Fucking pay-off!" he seethed through his clenched teeth. "You've got to be kidding! I put my hand up for the McCabe case when no one else wanted to know about it. I did it because I had two little kids of my own and I felt sick that some bastard had done that. And because I had more respect for you than any other copper in the job. I worked my arse off on that case and you know it!" It was true, and as Bill stared into the tearful eyes of his old partner the anger drained away. Now all he felt was pity and disgust. "Rosenthal didn't come along until years later. He offered me cash payments under their paid-informant provisions to keep the Commission advised of our investigation, that's all. Next thing I know I'm recruited to be part of this Ether Man investigation."

He stepped back, quickly tucked the gun back into his ankle holster, and turned to walk away.

"Wait." The word crackled painfully from Bill's throat, but he was running out of options, and pride was a luxury he could no longer afford. "I need your help, Wally."

"Well you can't have it, Bill." Wally Messner was standing below a yellow street light with a sad look on his face. "Look, I don't know what the fuck's going on here and I don't want to know. As far as I can tell, you could be as round as a bloody hoop for these charges. I hope to buggery you're not because I always thought you were a better man and a better cop than I could ever be. And if you're guilty then the rest of us are fucking doomed. All I know is Rosenthal isn't playing with a straight bat, and him and his boys have been cutting a lot of corners to put you away. So now I've told you and now you know. And I've said all I'm going to say. And if you ask me anything about any of this ever again I'll fucking deny every word of it! "

With that Bill Keliher's ex-partner turned and headed off along the footpath, following his waddling black lab.

# CHAPTER TWENTY-THREE

"KISS, pal. That's the golden rule." Eddie had stopped roaming around the room and was now standing over them. "K-I-S-S. Keep It Simple Stupid. That shouldn't be too hard to understand, even for two blockhead coppers!"

Frankie Box looked across at Boof Keliher. They'd been arguing the toss for what seemed like hours, and everybody was showing the strain. Moran wasn't trying to be obnoxious, it came naturally to him.

"He's right, Bill."

"Yeah he is," Slick chimed in. "He's a pain in the arse, but he's still right."

In the six weeks since Bill had seen Wally Messner, they hadn't been able to get anything on Rosenthal. Even if it was true that he was a paedophile and had been getting police protection, that didn't give him a motive to frame Bill Keliher on false charges; or if it did, they hadn't been able to work out what it was.

And if Dr Milo Forrester knew the answer, he wasn't sharing it. He'd given Frank Vagianni short shrift, and now no one seemed to know where he was. A week after Frank had been to see him at his surgery in Murwillumbah, the whole building had gone up in flames. The good doctor had put in a hefty insurance claim and then gone to ground. There were rumours around that the Murwillumbah police were investigating Forrester for arson, which probably explained why he was proving hard to find, but the bottom line was that whatever Milo Forrester could say about Emma Ronson he was keeping to himself.

"We don't need it any more, buddy. We don't have to go that way."

Eddie Moran wanted them to keep it nice and simple. The hairs found at the crime scenes had been lost, as had some of the original statements on the earlier offences. He had subpoenaed all the files and although he hadn't turned up anything about the offender with the tattooed forearm, the police notes of the bald-head account were there. Eddie had a classic case of police incompetence and overexuberance to put to the jury. The police had started with a suspicion of Bill arising from the McCabe case, one that had been subsequently proved to be unwarranted. They then noticed that the first series of offences happened while he was stationed at Manly, and they put two and two together and came up with five. From there they disregarded anything that tended to exonerate him and concentrated on what seemed to implicate him. They thereby misled themselves to such an extent that they were convinced they had the right man and decided to announce it to the world, making his arrest a media event to celebrate their brilliance. So convinced in fact that they confidently told the press that they had fingerprint and DNA evidence even before the tests had been done. As it turned out, the samples didn't match, and they had a major embarrassment on their hands. So they doctored up the DNA evidence to hide their own incompetence.

"I can sell that to them, pal, I'm telling you."

"But it's not the truth."

"Give me a break! What's the truth? That the Juvenile Crimes Commissioner is a child-molester and he's trying to set you up for God knows why? What the fuck am I supposed to do with that?"

Eddie Moran took off again, striding around his office and waving his arms about as he spoke.

"We've got a bloody good judge in Michael Fraser. He's young, he's intelligent and he's intellectually bloody honest. He's not going to get swept up in any of the media hype, he's going to apply the law. And that means he'll rule out Nichols' evidence. Trust me, he will toss it! And with this bullshit press announcement about fingerprints, I'll blow enough smoke over the DNA to ensure they have a doubt."

"What about Ron Morris?"

Eddie Moran grimaced slightly at the mention of the name.

"Morris is an intelligent witness." He had stopped pacing and was more contemplative. "He won't shy away from propositions that are reasonable. Leave him to me."

The tone of Eddie's voice was less than reassuring. An anxious silence settled on the meeting before Slick spoke up confidently.

"Don't worry. Eddie'll get him."

Bill had to hope he would. The truth was he had no alternative. Even though Bill believed what Wally Messner had told him, that Rosenthal was a corrupt paedophile, he had no proof other than Wally's say-so, and he knew well enough that Wally would deny it all. And even if he could prove it, where did that take him? It still didn't prove that Rosenthal and perhaps others had conspired to set him up. And most importantly it didn't answer the question that was still burning in his brain: why? Why did Rosenthal want to discredit him?

A week later the trial commenced in Sydney before His Honour Judge Michael Fraser QC, a relatively recent appointee to the New South Wales judiciary. Fraser was broadly well regarded, a university medallist who went straight to the bar from law school and had enjoyed an excellent reputation and a lucrative practice mostly in insurance law before accepting his appointment. Erudite and urbane, his politics obscure, he was generally considered one of the current government's best appointments, and Eddie Moran was pleased to have him. Few of the cases in his long career at the Sydney bar had been criminal, but nonetheless he seemed to have some empathy for people and his natural intelligence ensured that he would understand that occasionally people got it wrong – sometimes honestly and often for the very best of motives, but wrong just the same. He wouldn't discount out of hand Eddie's central premise, that errors might have flowed from incompetence, or overzealousness, or perhaps even a selfish need to save face. For a short while Fraser had been a contemporary of Peter Rosenthal at the bar and also on the bench. Eddie figured he probably had some degree of respect for Rosenthal; that wouldn't affect his judgement on anything that Eddie wanted to run before him, but it would be disastrous if they started making any outrageous and unproven allegations about the Juvenile Crimes Commissioner, no matter how true they were.

The first few days of the trial went as well as Eddie could have hoped. He ran a voir dire on the identification evidence; the jury were led out to wait while legal issues that were said not to concern them were decided in their absence. Each of the complainants who made any assertion, however half-hearted, regarding identification of the accused's photo was called to give evidence and was cross-examined by defence counsel. The only exception was Ron Morris: his identification was so clear and unequivocal, made in video-taped circumstances that could not be attacked, and Eddie had no basis to argue against it being led before the jury. They would hear his identification, and Eddie would have to do his best to convince them he was wrong. But with the others it was different. Most of their identifications were weak and equivocal at best, and Elizabeth Nichols' had been given in contravention of all the rules and contrary to strong judicial warnings about the danger of identification witnesses supplanting subsequently sighted images for their memory of the actual offender. None of them should be permitted to identify Bill Keliher in the highly suggestive circumstances of his sitting in the dock, since none of them had been able to identify him in the photographic line-up, except for Elizabeth Nichols, and her identification had been irreparably compromised by her sightings of Bill Keliher on the television and in the newspapers.

His Honour Judge Michael Fraser QC unhesitatingly agreed. He ruled that none of the witnesses cross-examined on the voir dire was permitted to give any purported identification evidence. They would give evidence of their recollections of the incident and the offender, but they would not be asked and would not be permitted to say if the accused was or looked like or was in any way similar to the man who had attacked them. It was a major victory for the defence. The DNA match-up and the evidence of Morris were now the glue that held the Crown case together. If they could prove that Bill Keliher had attacked either Melissa Smith or Sandra Hershey, the similar facts rule would allow the jury to convict him of all sixteen offences.

Eddie was nibbling at a fingernail as Martin Benfield BSc was led to the witness stand. Benfield was a small man with big glasses, and as he settled unassumingly in the witness box, Eddie snarled at him angrily just for the sport. He didn't have to discredit the scientist from the forensic biology laboratory, although of course it wouldn't hurt. All he had to do was kick up a little dust, create a little doubt. If he could cast a shadow over the integrity of the DNA testing methodology, that would be great. But Benfield had merely compared two samples sent to him, one taken from Bill Keliher and the other marked as being a scraping taken from the scene of one of the attacks. His findings would have no significance at all if Eddie could convince the jury that the police had switched samples before they had even got to the laboratory.

Benfield's evidence was tidy and efficient. All i's were dotted and t's crossed. Eddie exuded confidence as he rose to cross-examine but he knew he had to get in quickly and not hang around.

"Witness, did you perform any sex-typing as part of your examination?"

"Er, yes." Benfield shifted in his chair and squinted through his glasses. "Profiler Plus STR and sex-typing were performed using PCR-DNA technology and automated fluorescence-based detection. An ABI Prism three-seven-seven DNA Sequencer was employed, together with ABI Prism Genescan Analysis and Genotyper Software."

Bad start. Eddie wished someone would teach these blokes how to speak English. It was time to run for the comfort of a motherhood statement that he could park and perhaps pull out later if he needed it. All scientific examination and comparison had some element of subjectivity – there was always the possibility of human error. That's all Eddie needed from this witness. He exhausted his rudimentary knowledge of DNA testing procedures in a few lead-up questions and then rounded off with a nice, safe proposition for the witness.

"Scientists are mostly dedicated people, aren't they?"

"Er, as a general rule I would say so, yes."

"Of necessity they tend to get close to their casework?"

"Yes, that can be true."

"And of course, like all of us they can be influenced by all sorts of things that they see or hear outside the scientific process."

"Yes, of course."

"Like all of us, they are susceptible to bias of one kind or another, whether it be conscious or subconscious."

"True."

"And that bias can affect the subjective judgements and assessments that are an inevitable part of the process of scientific examination."

Benfield licked his lips and squinted through his glasses at Eddie. Then he pulled a crumpled handkerchief from his top pocket and cleaned his spectacles.

"Well, that's true," he commenced, in a fashion that suggested he was very glad he had been asked. "That's why we've put in place procedures to eliminate the risk of individual bias. What happens is our scientists decide what tests are to be carried out and then laboratory technicians perform the tests under strict supervision. The results are then read independently by two separate scientists. Neither the origin of the test sample nor the results recorded by the other reader is known to either of them when they do their readings. The case scientist then rereads the tests before compiling a report. Of course, all such case reports are also routinely peer-reviewed, which involves another forensic biologist checking the scientific and technical correctness of the casework. That system ensures that the risks of bias and human error are eliminated."

Eddie held his head high and tried to look as though it was the answer he'd been hoping for.

"Thank you, witness."

Parforth was quickly on his feet in re-examination.

"So what does that mean, Mr Benfield? How confident can you be about the accuracy of these results?"

Benfield looked up through his big glasses, as if surprised to be asked the question.

"Oh, absolutely confident. There can be no doubt that these samples came from the same source."

Eddie Moran kept his head down, trying to give the impression to the jury that he wasn't the least bit perturbed by the evidence. Behind him Bill sat in the dock, alone with his thoughts. He had no doubt that the scientific testing had been done correctly and the samples were both his blood. Someone had deliberately switched the crime-scene scraping for his sample. That was a very big step to take. There were plenty of coppers around who wouldn't be averse to giving some grub a little help along if they were convinced he was guilty and didn't quite have the goods on him. But switching blood samples was going way out on a limb. There weren't many coppers Bill knew who would risk it, particularly on a high-profile case like this, and never to sink another cop. There would have to be a lot more than a bit of face to save. Eddie might convince the jury that this was a case of police incompetence or overzealousness, but it was an explanation that didn't wash with the defendant.

Benfield's evidence was the first major blow the Crown had struck, but already Bill could feel a change of atmosphere within the courtroom. The jurors were looking over at him accusingly, as though trying to understand how someone like him – someone who looked just like them, someone who appeared normal, rational, responsible – could have committed all the crimes the prosecutor had described in detail in his opening. At first Bill tried to return their stares, hoping to show he had nothing to be ashamed of, but as he did each individual looked away as if they feared even eye contact with the demented beast who had perpetrated all these crimes. He soon gave up and sat gazing blankly into the space in front of him, hiding in the sanctuary of his own thoughts.

*Please don't forget that I believe in you, Bill. Whatever anybody thinks, I know you're a good man.*

Her words soothed him. On his way back down to Sydney he had called in to see her. They had said their goodbyes for now; there was no doubt that the outcome remained at best uncertain, but come what may he would do what he could to continue the search. And now, as he closed his eyes to hide from the stare of the uncomprehending jury, he saw Faye's face, at once the mature woman that she was now and the young lovely vibrant woman she had been. They were one to him, they always had been.

The evidence of the complainants filled most of the remainder of the week. It was sad, brutal, at times shocking. It told of bodies that had been defiled, abused and scarred, lives that had been destroyed. Eddie cross-examined sparingly and gently: he had no need to challenge any of it, only to make the odd point here and there that he might use in his address. He drew out the evidence of the bald head, and underscored and emphasised it as best he could. He even found the woman who had a vague recollection of a cross tattooed on the forearm of her attacker. They were little points, well handled and valuable to the defence.

The big test came on Thursday afternoon when Ron Morris took the stand. The only way Eddie was going to have a chance of convincing the jury that the DNA evidence might have been doctored was if it stood alone. Forensic evidence could be the strongest evidence of all, but juries still felt uneasy about convicting solely on the say-so of a scientist. They would be particularly likely to feel that way in this case, given that so much evidence had been passed over by the investigators, and that the DNA match had been announced before the tests were even done. But first Eddie had to negative Ron Morris.

It wasn't going to be an easy ask. Morris looked like a good witness even as he walked to the stand. He was wearing a conservative blue suit and a tasteful tie that was neither trendy nor old fashioned. He walked confidently and purposefully, but with no hint of strut or swagger. And as he took the oath to tell the truth, the whole truth and nothing but the truth, he spoke with a clear firm voice, unrushed and free of any nervousness or hesitation.

He gave his evidence clearly, candidly and unemotively. It was a poignant tale, one that touched on events in his life that apparently had deeply affected him, but he spoke with controlled rationality, evidently intent on not straying from the facts. He told how he and Sandra Hershey had been friends, she three years his junior and still a pretty, vivacious young schoolgirl. They often walked home together from the bus stop but that afternoon he had not seen her. At about eight thirty that night he was walking down towards the oval on his way to a friend's place when he saw what looked like a tall man coming from the trees beyond the oval, carrying something on his shoulder. As Ron continued on his way, the man appeared to squat down, as if he was hiding. When Ron was within about thirty metres of the park, the man climbed out of the storm drain and crossed the road, heading east. As he got to the corner, under the street light, he looked directly at the witness and then broke into a sprint and disappeared into the darkness. Within moments Ron heard the faint moan of a woman coming from the drain, and it was there that he found Sandra Hershey, her naked body bruised and bloody, reeking with the pungent smell of chloroform.

It was a terrifying story, and the strain of his recollection reflected in his manly face. When he had finished, Parforth paused for effect, aware of the power of the evidence and keen to let the jury soak it up before he finished with the cruncher.

"Mr Morris, you say you got a very clear view of the man as he stood below that street light and looked directly at you. Is that man in this courtroom here today?"

The witness looked at the same time both sad and disgusted.

"Yes, he is."

"Would you point him out for the jury, please."

Morris lifted one arm confidently and pointed straight at Bill Keliher, his eyes cold and unfaltering.

"That's him right there."

Bill returned his gaze, holding it for a long moment. There was no hint of hesitation in the eyes of the witness. His accusation was certain and uncompromising. As Bill looked at him he wondered what it was that had so convinced him.

"Cross-examination, Mr Moran?"

"Thank you, Your Honour."

Eddie rose to his feet still planning his approach. It had to be careful. It had to be rational. Morris was an intelligent witness and he was trying to be detached and moderate. Provided Eddie stuck to propositions that were sensible and plausible, Morris would cooperate.

"Mr Morris, these events happened in 1974, correct?"

"Yes."

"You were about, what, nineteen years old?"

"Yeah, I'd say so, yeah."

"And I think you're forty-one now, aren't you?"

"Forty-one, yeah. Nearly forty-two."

"Nearly forty-two. Nineteen's a long, long time ago, isn't it?"

"It sure is."

"You've seen and done a lot of things since 1974, haven't you?"

"Yeah, I guess I have."

"Met a lot of people?"

"Yeah."

"How many people do you suppose you've met since 1974?"

"How many have I met? Geez, I don't know."

"It'd be thousands wouldn't it?"

"Oh, I suppose so. I don't know."

Eddie paused for a moment and nodded thoughtfully. He wanted to give the jury a few seconds to reflect on that. Morris must have met thousands of people since 1974.

"How many people do you think you've actually seen since 1974?"

The witness raised his eyebrows. It was an odd question to be asked.

"Seen?"

"Yeah, seen. Actually physically seen, laid your eyes on them. You know, not necessarily in the flesh, just anywhere. On TV, in movies, in the newspapers, in magazines, on the street, at football games, whatever. Anywhere. How many people do you reckon you've seen in the past twenty-two years?"

"I've got no idea."

"A million maybe?"

"Maybe."

"Maybe more?"

"Maybe. I don't know."

Eddie paused again to let them think about it.

"In twenty-two years you'd have seen faces that didn't even register in your consciousness, wouldn't you? I mean people that you pass in the street or you see in the crowd at a football game, or on the news. Maybe a face in the stadium at the Olympics, I don't know, anywhere. People you don't know, they don't mean anything to you. You see them all the time, don't you?"

Ron Morris was obviously considering the proposition carefully.

"Yeah, I guess you do."

"And half the time their faces don't even register do they?"

"That's true."

"Out of that million – maybe more – people that you've seen since 1974, how many do you think would be like that, people whose faces you saw but you were hardly even aware that you'd seen them. They didn't register in your consciousness, you just saw them and thought no more about them. How many do you think?"

"Oh, plenty, I'd say."

"They'd number in the hundreds of thousands wouldn't they?"

"They might, yeah, I guess."

Eddie took another break, again nodding as though he were still processing the information. He had the jury interested.

"But you understand, don't you, that although your conscious mind doesn't necessarily record details of all those hundreds of thousands of nameless faces that you see in the crowd over the period of a lifetime, your subconscious takes it all in and stores it back there somewhere in the back of your brain."

"Sure. The human mind's an amazing thing."

"That's right." Eddie announced it, and let it sit for a moment in the silence of the courtroom before he followed up in a quiet, almost conspiratorial tone. "The human mind's an amazing thing. And it can play tricks on us, can't it?"

"I suppose it can."

"Tricks like supplanting one image for another in our memories. Making me remember my old mate Fred driving around in a green FJ when in fact it was a blue FB and it was my other mate Jack who had the green FJ. That sort of thing. That happens, doesn't it?"

Eddie held his breath waiting for the answer. If he could get Morris to agree to this he was halfway home.

"Sure. Yeah, I'm sure it does."

Beautiful response. He needed only one more answer to create a doubt. Eddie thought about the question, framed it carefully, and then delivered it in measured terms, the jury listening to every word.

"Wouldn't you agree that it's possible that your mind played one of those tricks on you in relation to this accused? That somewhere in the past twenty-two years you've seen the accused's face, in some television news report about some crime he was investigating, or in some newspaper article, or maybe just in the street somewhere, and your mind has confused that memory with your memory of the man you saw that night? Wouldn't you agree that that's quite possible?"

"I would ..."

*Bingo*! That was it. Even Ron Morris conceded that he could be mistaken about the identification. Eddie didn't need any more than that, and he wasn't likely to get a better answer than he already had. Now was the time to finish up and sit down quickly. Morris was sounding slightly hesitant about his answer and Eddie didn't want to let him have the chance to qualify it or retract it.

"Thank you. No further questions."

"I'd agree with that general proposition but—"

"Thank you, Mr Morris, that will be all."

Parforth leapt to his feet. "Well, I object, Your Honour."

The judge didn't need to hear his argument. He peered benignly over the top of his spectacles at defence counsel.

"Yes, the witness should be allowed to finish his answer."

"He had finished, Your Honour."

There was a hint of desperation in Eddie's quick

reply, but Michael Fraser QC was measured and polite as always.

"Well, I don't think he had, Mr Moran."

Ron Morris was eager to agree. "No, I hadn't."

"Yes you had!"

"Thank you, Mr Moran." The unflappable Judge Fraser was not about to let the disagreement descend into a bar-room brawl. "I don't need to hear you further on that point. Yes, Mr Morris, you may complete your answer."

"Well, I was going to say that I would agree with the general proposition, but in this case I've had that man's face very clear in my mind since the night it happened. In fact for a lot of years I had a real problem with that face. I couldn't get it out of my mind. I would see it in my dreams and even sometimes when I was awake. It took me a long time to stop having nightmares about the incident, and every time I had a nightmare I would see that face, clear as day. Time after time. There's no doubt in my mind that that was the face I saw that night. No doubt at all."

It was a strong statement, and there was no doubt that the jury was moved by it. Eddie wondered where to go from here. Morris had his bristles up. He was on guard now, determined to ensure that Eddie didn't get the chance to hoodwink or misinterpret him. To question him further was to risk providing him with the opportunity to clarify and perhaps retract some of his earlier answers, and maybe even slip in more self-serving anecdotes about how the incident was burnt into his consciousness.

"Any further questions for this witness, Mr Moran?"

Judge Fraser was once again peering down across his glasses.

"No, Your Honour."

Eddie sat down and resumed chewing on his fingernail. It had not been a good day.

# CHAPTER TWENTY-FOUR

The Masked Mauler sat in his little office on that Friday morning retracing the final moments of the previous night's bout when he had dropped the Claw to the canvas with a German suplex and then pinned him for a three count. He was having trouble savouring his victory.

Frank was depressed. Eddie Moran had sounded ominously downbeat when they'd spoken by telephone on Thursday afternoon, and the television reports that night had showed why. The lead story on every bulletin announced that an eyewitness had positively confirmed that a man spotted running from the scene of the 1974 abduction and rape of Sydney schoolgirl Sandra Hershey was Police Inspector William James Keliher. Newsreel footage showed the tall well-groomed Mr Ronald Morris endeavouring unsuccessfully to avoid the horde of journalists and shield his face from the cameras as he left the court building. It was followed by a still-shot of Bill Keliher in his inspector's uniform with Morris's words printed across the screen as the newsreader reported them:

*Every time I had a nightmare I would see that face, clear as day. Time after time.*

It sounded like Eddie hadn't laid a glove on Morris in cross-examination, and that meant Bill was in big trouble. This was one case where the jury was going to feel a lot more comfortable about convicting than acquitting. A conviction meant that the police had got the right man after all, and everyone could sleep soundly at night, confident in the knowledge that the Ether Man was behind bars. As smart as Eddie was, and notwithstanding all the questions he'd raised about the investigation, the jury couldn't help but be impressed by an eyewitness who claimed he'd actually seen Bill at the scene. Independent, first-hand identification wasn't like scientific mumbo jumbo or even a police statement; it was real evidence from real people who were there at the time and saw it happen, and unless you could knock some big chips off it the jury was going to believe it every time.

The rap on the outer office door was short, sharp, and confidential. It wasn't demanding like a debt-collector's knock, or attention-grabbing like a salesman's; it was one of those efficient, guarded, secretive little raps that come from a new client with a private problem. Frank didn't always answer knocks on his office door these days, but there was something about this one that made him feel he should.

"Can I help you?"

The man standing halfway down the corridor, a briefcase in one hand and a newspaper in the other, had a vaguely familiar face. He was pacing nervously up and down the hall as though he were planning an escape.

"I was hoping we might help each other, Mr Vagianni."

"Sure. Come on in."

Dr Milo Forrester looked very different from when Frank had seen him last. Either he was going for Weight Watchers' Slimmer of the Month or he had some kind of serious health problem. He also seemed to have lost his snappy dress sense in the past six weeks. The grey silk suit and navy bow-tie were gone, replaced by jeans and a dark crumpled shirt, which complemented perfectly his unkempt hair and grey-specked, unshaven chin. He had a shifty look about him, even for the kind of person who ordinarily graced Frank Vagianni's office, and Frank wasn't a bit surprised when Forrester asked if they could lock the outer office door while they were conferring. As soon as they were settled on either side of Frank's broad desk, Forrester came straight to the point.

"Shortly after you came to see me I received another visit from a man who wanted all my records on Emma Ronson. When I told him I had none he incinerated my chambers and threatened to kill me and my family."

Milo Forrester was speaking in measured and precise terms that were designed to release only such limited information as Frank Vagianni needed to know. He had rehearsed his story and he wasn't going to tell more than he had to.

"Did you know this bloke?"

Frank wasn't interested in letting him dictate the conversation. Forrester hadn't knocked on Frank's door in his crumpled shirt because he had a lot of options. So, for whatever reason, Frank had him over a barrel, and the sooner they both realised that the better. If he was here to tell a story, Frank wanted the whole story. So he asked the question up front, and he waited a long time for the answer.

"Yes."

Frank was an investigator, not a dentist. He wasn't going to sit there pulling teeth from Dr Forrester for the next few hours. The best way to get the conversation going was to let the doctor think that he was way ahead of him.

"His name wouldn't be Stephen Rolfe by any chance, would it?"

"Yes!" The strategy had worked. Forrester looked shocked, and then relieved that the detective knew as much as he apparently did. "Yes, it was Stephen Rolfe! How did you know?"

Frank had to maintain the initiative until he could get Forrester to start talking freely, so he dropped another name.

"I take it you knew Rolfe through your friendship with Eric Pohl."

It was clear that Milo Forrester hadn't expected to hear mention of that name. He suddenly had a hollow, defeated look in his eyes, as though he'd decided there was no longer any point in masquerading.

"You're obviously better informed than I had anticipated, Mr Vagianni." Forrester was fumbling nervously with his fingers. His eyes had drifted into space somewhere and there was a slight tremble in his chin. They sat in the silence for a long time as Forrester formed words with his lips but no sound came out. Eventually he dropped his head so low that Frank could see the shiny skin around his crown. "You must understand that much of what I have to talk about goes back to my youth," he began in a hoarse whisper. "It concerns matters that could be devastating to me, at both a professional and private level."

"Let's start at the beginning: you had a sexual relationship with Dr Eric Pohl."

Frank figured that was a good ice-breaker, a winner either way. If it was true it further served to demonstrate that Frank was an all-round genius and knew all there was to know about the skeletons in Milo's closet, and if it wasn't it was the kind of slur that the doctor would probably want to explain away in as much detail as he could. It had the desired effect. Forrester seemed to snap out of the melancholic trance he'd fallen into and looked Frank squarely in the eye.

"Yes, at one time. Briefly. Many many years ago." He paused again, as if remembering, and looked down at his hands cupped on the desk in front of him. "When I started at the university I was only seventeen. I was just a boy really. Still very much confused about a lot of things. Including my sexuality, I suppose. Eric Pohl was tutoring me in Modern Political Ideologies in my first year. He and a couple of other young members of the academic staff had a house just off campus. A lot of us went there, experimented in all sorts of things."

"Including child sex?" Frank had to be as hard as possible, keep it all up front, keep it moving. Forrester tried to look offended, but he recovered quickly.

"Including all sorts of sex, Mr Vagianni. Sex with everyone and everything. There were drugs of course to help us along, expand our minds, remove our inhibitions, blur the boundaries as it were. But before I knew it I became immersed in what I suppose could only be described as quite unseemly and unnatural behaviour."

"And illegal."

"Yes. Undoubtedly. But that was the sixties, Mr Vagianni. People were pushing the limits everywhere, questioning everything."

Frank had bought the Woodstock album too, but he couldn't remember anything on it about kiddie-fiddling.

"What do you know about the McCabe kidnapping?"

This time Forrester looked genuinely shocked, baffled as to how Frank had made the connection with what he'd come to talk about. He sat with a bewildered look on his face for several seconds, then blinked and stared blankly at the desk.

"There was a close-knit group of us, spread over various universities in several states. Mainly academics, some students like myself, and others. The inner circle called themselves the Brethren." Forrester looked up at Frank to gauge the recognition factor. Frank Vagianni had heard the name before. "At first the only rule was a kind of pure unbridled hedonism. 'If it feels good do it.' Even sometimes when it didn't feel good we did it anyway, just to experiment. But then it got more serious, more ideological, more secretive. People were starting to delve into the occult and there were a lot of other influences coming in. The whole thing went underground, and there were rumours."

"What kind of rumours?"

"Violent rituals. Human sacrifice."

"What?"

Frank hadn't intended the reaction. Forrester looked alarmed, and Frank hoped he wouldn't clam up on him. He didn't.

"I never saw any of this. But I heard things. And I guess by that time I already knew that we were all completely out of control. I backed away, tried to dissociate myself. Most of us did. But we still heard stories every now and then."

Frank could see that they were treading on some very touchy subjects. It was time to start dancing before Forrester got cold feet.

"I asked you before: what do you know about the McCabes?"

"I was still at the university. Child sex was the fashionable topic of the time, the big taboo that we all had under siege. When the McCabe children went missing there was talk that people from the Brethren had them, or at least knew where they were."

"What people?"

"I don't know." Forrester shook his head and looked genuinely sorry. "By then I'd extricated myself from the whole scene. And there was so much paranoia about the case that no one would talk to anyone about it."

"What did Emma Ronson have to do with the McCabes?"

The look of surprise leapt back onto the doctor's face.

"Why do you ask that?"

"Because you know bloody well that's why you're here! Emma Ronson knew what happened to those kids and that's why Stephen Rolfe killed her. And she told you what happened to them, and that's why Stephen Rolfe wants to kill you too. And unless you can convince me to save your miserable arse, I'd say he's going to do it very soon! So let's cut the bullshit and get on with it."

Dr Milo Forrester didn't seem to enjoy being spoken to so gruffly, but he'd run out of options. A look of mild resentment washed across his face before he spoke again.

"Emma Ronson was a deeply disturbed woman." He lifted his briefcase onto the desk and laid it flat. "Do you have a cassette player?"

While Frank rummaged through the rubbish on the shelves behind him searching for a hand-held dictaphone he knew he had somewhere, Forrester filled in the background.

"People like Eric Pohl rarely contact me these days. When he asked me to see Emma and he stressed the confidentiality of it all, I kept it absolutely secret. I saw her and her boyfriend Mr Radovic at my home. I had never met him before but it became apparent to me that he knew many of the people who had once formed the nucleus of the Brethren. He was a good deal older than Emma, but they were in a relationship together, and I must say he seemed genuinely fond of her. He said that Emma had been having what he referred to as 'weird turns' during which she had said things that were upsetting a lot of people." For the first time a wave of emotion seemed to flood into the doctor's face. His eyes glistened with moisture and his chin began to tremble. "He was clearly in fear for both their lives, Mr Vagianni."

With a final tug Frank dragged the dictaphone free of the paperwork and other rubbish on the shelves and slapped it on the desk next to Forrester's briefcase. The doctor took one of a number of cassettes lined up in the briefcase and handed it to Frank. Frank slipped the tape into his machine and pushed down the play button.

It wasn't the best tape recorder in existence and the quality of the sound was less than perfect, but it was good enough to make out clearly the recorded conversation between Dr Milo Forrester and a young girl.

"*Hello, Dr Forrester.*"

"*Hello. What's your name?*"

"*Catherine.*"

"*Hello, Catherine. How old are you, Catherine?*"

"*I'm six. No, I'm seven.*"

"*Seven years old. Gee. And what's your second name, Catherine?*"

*"Catherine McCabe."*

Frank Vagianni clicked the tape off.

"That's the kid! She's got to be the one they got to ring Bill! Who is she, doc? Who's the kid?"

"That's no child, Mr Vagianni. That's Emma Ronson."

# CHAPTER TWENTY-FIVE

Doctor Milo Forrester had conducted a total of four consultations with Emma Ronson over the period of one month immediately prior to her death. She had presented as a withdrawn and anxious individual who complained of recent blackouts in which she 'lost time' for up to several hours. Her partner Mr Radovic referred to 'weird turns' when she didn't seem herself and behaved erratically. Ms Ronson had grown increasingly distressed by these episodes. She spoke of an emptiness in her life, a feeling that she was utterly alone, unable to connect with anyone around her, observing life in a detached fashion, 'as though through a television screen'. She gave a history of being orphaned at about the age of six and raised by her father's brother and de facto wife on a rural property outside Gosford. She recalled that her adoptive parents were extremely strict, but beyond that she claimed to have absolutely no childhood memories whatsoever before the age of about fourteen. That was when she ran away from home and went to Sydney where she survived on prostitution and petty crime.

"She was a beautiful woman, and I think a most intelligent one." Faced with the steely gaze of Bill Keliher, Milo Forrester faltered slightly and lowered his eyes. Keliher's hostility was palpable, and the doctor was finding it increasingly uncomfortable to sit opposite him in the compact Sydney hotel room, recounting his contact with Emma Ronson. "My initial impression was that she was suffering mild schizophrenia, possibly combined with epileptic episodes. But on the third visit this other business just came out of nowhere."

On her third visit to Dr Forrester, Emma Ronson had appeared unusually nervous. The doctor suggested hypnosis to allow her to relax more fully, in the hope of increasing her receptiveness to therapy. She agreed and he began the process of hypnotic suggestion, to which she seemed to respond exceptionally well, quickly descending into a state of profound rest. Her anxiety apparently resolved, Dr Forrester eased his patient into therapy by gently posing his first question of the day to Emma Ronson. It was answered by someone he had never met before.

"I was suddenly talking to a child. Her voice, her manner, her demeanour, it was as though she was a little girl."

Bill Keliher's eyes were burning with an anger that suddenly erupted.

"What the bloody hell are you talking about?"

He was leaning forward in his chair as if about to leap across the coffee table and throttle Milo Forrester. Frank Vagianni took him firmly by the elbow and tried to calm him down.

"Hang on, Bill, hear him out."

Keliher looked at his old friend with an expression of bewilderment and anger. He had a head full of infuriating questions that he couldn't answer and a criminal trial that was going down the dunny fast. The court had adjourned for the weekend on a bad note for Bill and he was under pressure. Frank had flown Forrester straight down on the afternoon flight and they had grabbed Bill on his way back from the court. He was in the mood to rip somebody's head off, and unless things improved quickly, it looked like it might be Milo Forrester's.

"I had never struck a case of dissociative identity disorder before." Forrester was stuttering as if his life depended on his words.

"Of what?"

"Split personality, Mr Keliher. Multiple personality disorder."

The doctor fumbled with the tape player, bundled the tape in and pushed the button.

"*Hello, Dr Forrester.*"

The sound of the childlike voice on the tape stung Bill like an electric shock. He recognised it instantly, the voice of the little girl who had rung him repeatedly, pleading for his help.

*I want to go home, Constable. Please take me home.*

Bill listened in a kind of trance as the young girl told her story gradually but openly, prompted and encouraged by the placid questions of the doctor. She was lost and she wanted to go home. She missed her mummy and her daddy. She still remembered them and she wanted to go home.

*"They think I can't remember Mummy and Daddy but I can. I just didn't talk about them after Michael went away. But I remember them."*

Bill listened in amazement, with a growing sense of overwhelming sorrow, and at the same time elation, as though he were chatting with a long-dead friend. He listened as the fragile voice remembered that hazy morning in the early days of the summer of 1965.

*"The policeman took us to the beach. Constable Keliher, the one that always smiled at Mummy. He took us for a ride in his police car. He drove us to the beach. That's where we met Peewee. He was nice to us at first, but he was a bad man!"*

The story became more laboured and circuitous from that point as the doctor did his best to steer the conversation to and from a subject matter that was clearly distressing to his patient, but which she seemed to want to talk about nonetheless. He would gently guide her to it, allowing her to remain with it long enough to have her say, and then retreat when it threatened her too much, moving on to other things, happy memories of a distant childhood, and then walk back with her into the dark corners when she was ready. In bits and pieces they heard the story of a little child who with her brother

Michael met a man that she called Peewee at the beach at Shaggy Head. He bought them lunch and took them for a swim. Then they played chasie on the beach till it was nearly dark. He said they should come back to his house and he would ring their mother to come and get them because it was too dark for them to walk home now. And he bought ice cream and chips and soft drink and they went home to his house.

"Jesus! What does all this mean?" The rage was gone from Keliher's voice. Now he was just desperately seeking answers. "Does this mean Catherine McCabe survived all these years? Does this mean Emma Ronson was Catherine McCabe?"

Dr Forrester looked uneasy as if reluctant to respond.

"I'm sorry, Mr Keliher. I don't know what it means." He lifted one hand absently and smoothed the thinning hair behind his ear. It was an unsatisfactory answer and he knew he would have to do better. "You will hear as the tapes continue that she claimed to have been subjected to abuse, in her case mainly psychological abuse. Victims of such abuse, particularly children, because they find it altogether too difficult to deal with it, can sometimes simply erase the memory completely from their conscious mind. It remains, however, in the subconscious. And occasionally, in rare cases, the memory will re-emerge, suddenly and without warning. It's possible therefore that these are the repressed memories of Catherine McCabe. Equally, however, they may be episodes of pure fantasy invented by what was obviously a most disturbed mind."

The anger returned quickly to Bill's eyes. He lunged across the table and caught the doctor's throat in one big hand.

"This woman was murdered nearly twelve months ago, you little shit! When the bloody hell were you planning to tell someone about this?"

Forrester was gasping for breath, his chin bobbing up and down and his mouth forming words that wouldn't come. Bill's jaw was set like stone, the pain and frustration of a thirty-year odyssey burning wildly in his eyes. He had to blame someone, had to make someone pay. Frank could understand that, and maybe Milo had it coming. But if Bill killed him now, they'd never get the rest of the story. He waited until the doctor had turned slightly blue before he took his big friend by the arm again.

"Okay, Bill, come on, settle down."

Frank watched as the emotion passed, the muscles in Bill's jaw gradually relenting, his arm relaxing and his hand withdrawing from the doctor's neck. He sucked in a lungful of air and blew it out, looking down at the tape player and the little pile of tapes beside it. The doctor dropped back into his chair, gagging and spluttering as Keliher stared at the tape recorder. Bill knew with certainty what they were all suspecting. He had found Catherine McCabe.

He stood there motionless for minutes, the silence of the little room broken only by the wheeze of the doctor's gasping breath. After thirty years he had come within a telephone call of finding her alive. He felt numb, wondering what to do next. The answer was plain enough: he was looking at it. Bill stooped down and gathered up the tapes. An innocent child had died thirty years ago. But she'd come back, briefly, to tell her story. He pushed the next tape into the recorder.

The ice cream had tasted funny that night while they were waiting for their mum to come to Peewee's house, and Catherine felt very sleepy. When she woke up the next morning, Peewee was different. He was angry with her and he locked her in the wardrobe all that day. She heard them hurting Michael – Peewee and another man called Robert who came to Peewee's house. And when she saw Michael she could see he had been crying and he could hardly walk but he told her everything was all right, that Peewee had told him they could go home soon. Then Robert made them eat mashed potato that tasted funny and she woke up in a dark place and she started crying but Michael was there too and he said to stay quiet or Robert would get mad again. Then Robert and a different man took them to another house and put them in a dark place downstairs where there were mice and cockroaches. And at night they would take Michael somewhere and sometimes she could hear him crying.

It was a sick, harrowing story told with the disarming honesty of a child. It traced the children's journey through captivity and shameful abuse, from the house of 'Peewee' in Brighton Bay to another house, probably somewhere in Sydney, after a long journey in which the children travelled alternately on the back floor of a car covered with a blanket, or lying in the boot with a torch light to keep them comforted. How long they had remained locked in the basement of this house was hard to tell, but it sounded likely that Michael at least had been subjected to systematic sexual abuse there, before the children were moved again in similar fashion, this time to a location somewhere in dense bushland.

*"There were trees all around, and there were spiders in the house. Lots of spiders and crawly things. The scary man put us in the ground. It was dark. I was scared when he took Michael away."*

They had been hidden in some kind of basement by another man, whom she described only as 'the scary man'. He fed them in this basement area and kept them there together at all times, except when Michael was removed occasionally for short periods by the scary man and sometimes others who would sing strange songs.

*"They hurt Michael. He cried a lot. But he said we'd be going home to Mummy and Daddy soon. Then he got sick and I couldn't wake him up. And the scary man came and put him underneath the fire engine. Then Robert came and took me away. He said Mummy and Daddy came to get Michael, and they'd come for me soon. But they never came. I want to go home."*

As the last tape clicked off, Bill Keliher tipped the bottle into his glass then handed it across to Frank. He took a deep bitter swallow of the whisky and felt it burn a cruel track into his stomach and up into his brain. His heart was aching, his head spinning. He didn't want to be able to think any more. He wanted to forget. He wanted to be numb. He poured another mouthful in and gagged a little as he forced it down.

Frank Vagianni poured himself a drink and took a gentle sip. As they sat together in the silent room he wondered what was going through the big man's mind. No one had been closer to the McCabe case than Bill Keliher, no one had worked harder, no one had been more committed, not to this case or any other. Now, at last, he had an answer. So what was he thinking?

"Shit!"

Bill Keliher shot to his feet so suddenly that Milo Forrester cringed and wrapped both arms around his head. Bill had a stunned look on his face, as if he'd been zapped with a cattle prod.

"Shit!" he repeated. "I think I know who the scary man is! I think I know where Michael's buried!"

# CHAPTER TWENTY-SIX

Bill Keliher and Wally Messner sat beside each other in the front seat of the police car, looking out into the predawn light. It was nearly twelve months since they'd been to the old bush shack where Herbert Lancelot Montgomery had lived and died. The scrub had long since begun reclaiming it, and the house was now almost immersed in the thick lantana undergrowth. The grass in what was left of the clearing had grown much longer and they watched as a young constable, his camera gear slung over one shoulder, struggled to step his way towards the water tank.

"He's a good kid," Wally grunted at last. "Came up on his own time. I never told him nothing, just said it was to do with an old case we had together."

Bill Keliher said nothing. He needed to keep a lid on all this until he was sure he had it right, and he needed Wally Messner's help to do it. Messner had gone out on a limb. When Bill had telephoned him late the previous night, he didn't tell him much, just that he had a new lead on the McCabe case, and he thought one of the bodies might be buried up at Herbert Montgomery's bush shack after all. He needed a couple of coppers to check it out with him, but he didn't want the word getting out until they knew for sure. Wally didn't hesitate: he'd get it organised and they drive up there together at first light. Just like the old days, Wally solid and reliable as ever. But Bill didn't have it in him to feel grateful to Wally Messner.

"Get a photograph of everything before we start digging."

Bill was used to issuing instructions to police constables, but by the way the young man looked to Wally Messner it was clear he wasn't taking any orders from the disgraced inspector. Messner nodded his assent and the constable began to click away, photographing the ramshackle shanty, the outhouse and the water tank.

"And the old truck," Bill called to him, looking up towards the old pre-war jalopy propped up adjacent to the overgrown boundary fence. "Especially the old truck."

They started with the underground rations cellar behind Montgomery's hut. The constable photographed the trapdoor covered with lantana shoots before they pulled them clear and opened it up. It was just as Bill and Wally had left it twelve months ago, except with more cockroaches and spider webs, a bundle of empty rusting tins and rotting paper piled up in the corner. They flashed the torch lights around it thoroughly as they'd done last time, but they didn't step down into it; if Bill's hunch was right, the forensic people would need to take a close look at it later. As Bill bent over and looked into the shallow little cellar, the trap-door in one hand and his torch in the other, he remembered the words of Emma Ronson.

*The scary man put us in the ground.*

Bill had to lift his feet up high as he walked through the long grass towards the top boundary where the wreck of an old truck sat on a platform of two hardwood logs, partly obscured by the encroaching undergrowth. He had seen it there when they last came, dumped on the boundary line like all the wrecks that littered farms and yards and rural properties throughout the country. He had ignored it, thought nothing of it. But something had lodged in his brain, one tiny detail he had not forgotten. The red paint. The original paint job was long gone, obscured by rust and weather, but at some stage, long ago, someone had given it a facelift, splashing the few remaining body parts with red paint, slapping it on thickly with a house paintbrush. The colour was hardly recognisable now, cracked and faded and caked in decades of dust and dirt, discoloured by rust and marred by nesting insects; but it was still there. Faint and patchy, but still there.

*Then he got sick and I couldn't wake him up. And the scary man came and put him underneath the fire engine.*

Bill pushed the shovel into the long grass at the edge of the hardwood platform and began digging, grunting and huffing as he spooned the soil away and threw it back behind him. Wally Messner joined in, slowly and methodically at first, as he had twelve months ago when they had dutifully exhumed the old man's mangy dog. But as he worked shoulder to shoulder with his ex-partner he became infected by the big man's urgency and before long they were heaving and grunting in unison, and had cleared the grass and earth from all around the base of the old wreck. The constable stood back and watched, intrigued, as they started digging into the soft soil underneath the chassis. Something was happening here that he didn't fully understand. How could he? He wasn't even born when two children disappeared on a hazy morning in the early days of summer 1965. Bill Keliher had dropped his shovel and was now on all fours, reaching in under the wreck and dragging loose soil out with his hands. Wally Messner got down beside him and reached in beneath the wreck. The young constable dropped to his knees and joined in.

"Jesus, Bill! Jesus!"

Wally Messner was gasping breathlessly as the first remnants of decayed fabric and bone appeared in the shallow grave. He looked across at big Bill Keliher. Bill had stopped dead, as though shocked to find what he had been predicting all along, his hands frozen on the loose soil as Wally carefully dusted back the earth. There were fragments of what appeared to be grey blanket material and a light cotton garment wrapped lightly around dirty, almost-dry bones that exuded a distinctive musty odour. Bill Keliher's face was drawn and grey. When he finally looked up at Wally Messner his eyes were glazed with tears.

"You did it!" Messner whispered in amazement. "You finally found them!"

Bill Keliher pulled his hands away and dropped back onto the grass behind him. He squeezed his eyes shut and wrapped one hand across them shutting out the world around him. He had found them. At last, after all the pain, the frustration, and the disillusionment, after all the soul-destroying heartache of the past thirty years, he had found them. At last, he could bring them home.

"What's this?" The young constable had plucked a small brown metal object from the soil.

"It's a coin of some sort." Wally Messner brushed away the caked-on dirt. "Jesus! It's a farthing." He held it up in front of his face in the early-morning light. "A 1929 farthing!"

\* \* \*

Mrs Enid Beatty, the long-estranged sister of Herbert Lancelot Montgomery, lived alone in the family home at Liverpool. When Frank Vagianni telephoned her to say he was an investigator acting on behalf of William Keliher, she was surprisingly cooperative. She had been staggered to hear that Inspector Keliher had been accused of all those terrible crimes and she didn't believe for one moment that he had done any of it. Someone must have it in for him to be telling all those lies about him, and she would do whatever she could to help. Frank explained that he didn't need much, they were just looking at any cases Bill had been investigating at the time of his arrest, and her brother's name had come up. Mrs Beatty seemed a little embarrassed to begin with, having to acknowledge her wayward brother once again, but she recovered quickly and soon she was chatting openly about the papers she'd discovered when her brother died. Yes, she did still have them somewhere in storeroom and yes, Frank Vagianni was welcome to look through them. She had taken out his medal, and one or two bits and pieces that had some connection to their family, but the rest were just old papers that had no value or significance to her, and Frank was welcome to them if he'd like to take them away.

Frank Vagianni took Mrs Beatty up on her kind offer. By lunchtime he and Eddie had the contents of the little carton spread all over Eddie's hotel room, and were examining in minute detail the last known possessions of the late Herbert Lancelot Montgomery. Discharge papers, old letters written in faded ink on stained and yellowed stationery, old photographs, postcards, magazines and newspapers. They meticulously examined each one in turn, not really knowing what they were looking for, but noting down names, and dates, and places. They were still waiting to hear back from Bill as to what, if anything, he'd found up on the property, but in the meantime they wanted to know all they could find out about the old man who'd lived and died there. They weren't disappointed.

"Holy bloody fuck-a-duck!" It was an impressive combination of expletives, even for Frank. Obviously something pretty special had taken his attention. He held out a little, dog-eared, black and white snapshot. "Eddie, get a load of this!"

# CHAPTER TWENTY-SEVEN

On Monday morning the trial of William James Keliher was stood down until after lunch, to allow the prosecutor to make necessary arrangements to satisfy defence counsel's request for the re-call of Mr Ronald Morris. When Judge Michael Fraser QC resumed his seat on the bench at precisely two o'clock, Mr Morris was standing in the witness box.

"Witness, you remain bound by your former oath. Do you understand that?"

"Yes, Your Honour."

"Very well, take a seat. Mr Moran has some further questions to ask you."

Morris settled comfortably in the witness box while Eddie Moran was still loading folders from his briefcase onto the bar table.

"Mr Morris," he commenced forcefully, "when you gave evidence last week you told us that you suffered nightmares following the attack on Sandra Hershey." He dropped the last folder onto the table in front of him and stopped, looking directly at the witness. "What was it that upset you so much about that incident?"

Morris raised his eyebrows, looking somewhat puzzled by the question.

"Well, the whole thing. The violence of it. It was disgusting."

Eddie Moran leaned forward on the bar table, glaring brazenly at the witness.

"Had you ever experienced violence of that kind before?"

"Never."

"Were you revolted by the violence, Mr Morris?"

Moran's tone was cruel now, almost mocking. The witness's distaste showed in his eyes but he answered politely and dispassionately.

"Of course. Sandra was a friend of mine."

"You were friends, were you?"

"Yes."

"Just friends?"

The witness looked surprised. "What do you mean?"

"Well, you know, Mr Morris, you were nineteen years of age, full of adolescent hormones; she was nearly sixteen, a pretty young thing." Eddie Moran was back at his obnoxious best, waving his hands about provocatively and casting about the courtroom with a snide, discourteous air. "I think you described her as 'vivacious', didn't you?"

"Yes."

Parforth was enjoying this. He could see the jury weren't impressed with Eddie's irreverent line of questioning. It was already getting a bit tacky, but Eddie was about to go one better.

"She had nice big breasts, didn't she?"

"I object!"

Parforth was quickly to his feet but he didn't have to speak. The judge was already grimacing.

"Mr Moran! Is this really necessary?"

Eddie Moran looked up at the judge with such confounded innocence as he could feign.

"I'm just trying to establish the relationship between the witness and Ms Hershey, Your Honour."

He had the attention of everyone in the courtroom. The jury knew exactly what he was insinuating. If it had no substance, it was unforgivable of him to raise the implication; but if it were even half true, they were already interested. On the reckoning of Judge Michael Fraser, it was nothing but a cheap shot.

"Then I suggest you do it in a less objectionable fashion."

"Yes, Your Honour." Moran looked unchastened as he leaned contemptuously on one hand, glaring at the witness. "You a single man, Mr Morris?"

"Yes."

"Ever been married?"

"No."

"Really? You're forty-one years old and you've never been married." He curled his lip and looked disapprovingly around the courtroom. It was the Eddie Show in full flight. "What, are you gay, or what?"

"I object!"

A loud murmur of amusement and outrage flooded through the courtroom. Eddie had both palms up in front of him as if physically to defend himself.

"Still just trying to work out this relationship, Your Honour!"

For the first time since the trial had begun, Judge Fraser looked at risk of losing his decorum. He was peering angrily over his glasses when the witness intervened. Ron Morris spoke up warmly and with good humour.

"That's all right. I'm happy to answer. No, I'm not gay."

Eddie picked up the answer and swept along brightly, as if the controversy had never happened.

"Okay, well there you go! So you're a nineteen-year-old, good red-blooded Australian boy who meets every afternoon with this pretty, vivacious sixteen-year-old girl who may or may not be considered to have big breasts, and walks her home to her place." The judge winced and glared at Eddie, but said nothing. "Were you sexually attracted to this girl at all, Mr Morris?"

The witness's handsome features softened in a knowing smirk.

"When I was nineteen I was sexually attracted to all girls with big breasts."

It was Ron Morris's attempt to be flippant, to match Moran's irreverence with his own wit, but it backfired. The callously impersonal references to the victim of this shocking crime were shameful enough coming from the profane mouth of the defence lawyer, but to hear them repeated by Sandra Hershey's childhood friend, the man who had seen her in her ravaged state, came as a shock to the jury. Eddie sensed it straight away, and drove it home.

"Well there you go!" he announced obnoxiously throughout the courtroom. "So she did have big breasts after all!" The sarcastic grin faded on his lips as he ran his eye along the faces of the jurors one by one, silently inviting them to understand that Ron Morris perhaps wasn't what he seemed, perhaps wasn't just the caring benefactor, the old friend that he claimed to be. "And I take from that answer that you mean you were attracted to her."

"Yes."

"Ever ask her out?"

"I might have." For the first time there was a hint of indecision in Ron Morris's manner, as if he was wondering what Hershey may have told them about that. "Yes," he said weakly, "I think I did." And then he added, "Once or twice."

It was a jittery reply and Eddie knew the jury were surprised by it, and intrigued, not only by the words themselves but by the awkward way that they had stumbled out. He sneered before he posed the next question.

"How'd you go?"

"No." Morris shook his head uncomfortably. "No, we didn't go out together."

"I guess you weren't her type."

"I guess not."

He looked a different man now, not the confident relaxed witness who a few short days ago had seemed so certain in his recollections, but a nervous suitor craving whatever audience he could get.

"At that time you were working on a building site just a few miles down the road from there, weren't you?"

"Yes."

"So you knocked off at about what, three o'clock, I suppose."

"That's right."

"You'd have made the bus stop by about three thirty at the latest."

"Yes, I'd say so."

"Sandra Hershey's school was way over at Mosman. She would have had to take a bus to Manly Wharf and then connect through to Harbord. And that school didn't get out till three thirty. Must have been close to half past four, maybe later, by the time she got to that stop."

"That could be right."

"So, what, you'd wait maybe an hour, an hour and a half for her to get there?"

"Sometimes."

"Really? You waited for her all that time?"

"Sometimes."

The answer was hesitant, reluctant, and Eddie paused to let the jury properly digest it. He could see they hadn't missed the point. They were looking suspiciously at Morris, visualising him as a rejected young man, waiting alone and lonely at the bus stop for an attractive, vital young girl, the object of his spurned affections.

"Well, you told the prosecutor last week that this day you didn't see her. You expected her to be on the bus but she wasn't there, so you walked home without her."

"Yes."

"But you knew she wouldn't be on the bus that day, didn't you?"

"No."

"Yes you did!" Eddie boomed the words into every corner of the courtroom so loudly that several jurors gave a start. He fell silent and remained so for several long seconds. He knew then he had the jury interested. They were watching, waiting for him to catch this witness out. He would try not to disappoint them. "It was a Thursday. Every Thursday she had netball training. You knew that, didn't you?"

"Yes, I probably did."

"You knew that every Thursday night she came home on the late bus just after six, just as it was getting dark."

"Yes."

"In her little short netball skirt and her tight blouse."

"I object!"

"Just trying to paint a picture for the jury." Eddie didn't look up at the judge, he didn't miss a beat. "You knew she'd be late that Thursday, didn't you, like she was every Thursday evening."

"Yes."

He stopped. Before he asked the next question, Eddie waited for utter silence in the courtroom. When finally he spoke, he did so with the quiet intimacy of a confessor.

"Did you wait for her that night?"

"No."

"You sure, Mr Morris?"

"Yes."

Eddie held his gaze as the jury pondered the possibility of the spurned young Ronald Morris lurking alone in the night-time shadows, waiting for a pretty teenage schoolgirl to arrive. The scowl that had crept onto Morris's face complemented the growing impression of a dangerous man with much to hide.

"Mr Morris," Eddie resumed more robustly, "you say the first you knew of this attack was when you left your house that evening at about eight o'clock and walked down the hill towards the oval. Where were you going to at that hour of the night?"

"I'm not sure, most likely to the shop for cigarettes."

"At that time the only corner shop was the one back up the hill, wasn't it? In the opposite direction to the oval."

"Yes." There was a note of agitation in his voice. "Actually I think I must have been going out to visit a mate."

"A mate. What mate?"

"Pardon?"

"What mate?" Eddie almost shouted it. "What's his name, this mate of yours that lived within walking distance of your house? He must have had a name! What was his name?"

"Well, I can't recall at this very minute."

Morris was sounding unconvincing, just when he needed to come up with some strong answers.

"Can't recall? He must have been a pretty good mate for you to be dropping in on him on spec at eight o'clock at night! Surely you can remember this good mate's name!"

A look of wild anger flashed into Morris's eyes. He glared at the skinny lawyer as if he'd like to throttle him, but when all he got was Eddie's trademark cocked head and curled lip he spoke plaintively to the judge.

"Look, I didn't know I was on trial here!"

Eddie wasn't about to slow down. It was time to move in for the kill, and unless and until the judge stepped in to pull him up, Eddie was going to keep on going.

"You ever been on trial, Mr Morris?"

"What?"

"Have you ever been on trial? Ever been charged with a criminal offence?"

"No."

"Sure?"

"Yes, of course I'm sure!"

"Ever heard of Stephen Arnold Rolfe?"

Morris jumped to his feet.

"Look, I object to this!" He bellowed it so angrily that everyone in the courtroom was startled, including Eddie. At the back of the courtroom Wally Messner whispered instructions to two associates and they moved quietly and unobtrusively closer to the witness box. Judge Fraser looked silently over the top of his glasses at the witness for several seconds before he finally spoke.

"Well," he commenced thoughtfully, "on what basis, Mr Morris?"

"I'm not on trial here!" His voice had an agitated shrill to it, and when he heard it Morris cleared his throat, which seemed to settle him somewhat. "I seem to be being accused of something here, Your Honour. Surely I don't have to sit here and cop this sort of treatment."

Judge Fraser was a tad bewildered, struggling to understand what Morris had become so sensitive about. He spoke in a measured, soothing voice intended to reassure the witness, although it seemed to have the opposite effect on Mr Morris.

"Mr Moran is entitled to cross-examine you on behalf of his client, and you are obliged to answer his legitimate questions. If he oversteps the boundaries of what is permissible, Mr Parforth will ask me to intervene on your behalf. In the meantime you must answer the questions."

Ron Morris was in just the sort of mood Eddie wanted him in, and he didn't intend to allow him any time to simmer down.

"You ever heard of Stephen Arnold Rolfe, Mr Morris?"

"No I haven't!"

"You ever go by that name?"

"No!"

"That's not true, is it?"

"Yes it is!"

"It's not!"

"It is!"

"You're lying, witness! You've been lying since the moment you climbed into that witness box!"

"What the hell are you talking about?"

Eddie Moran was leaning forward, snarling at the witness like a cheeky schoolboy hurling insults across the back fence. "When you were leaving the court last week, you did your best to hide your face from the waiting media, didn't you? Why'd you do that, Mr Morris? Why were you so keen to obscure your identity."

"I can do without having my face on national television, that's why!"

"You sure can, witness! You sure can!" Eddie was now rifling through the folders he had stacked up beside him on the bar table. "Because when you get your face on television, a lot of people from your past might just recognise you." He hastily selected one of the folders, slapped it open, and commenced leafing roughly through the pages. "People who know you by another name!" When he found his place Eddie dropped a pointer finger on the page and read aloud. "In 1971 at the age of fifteen you were convicted under the name Stephen Arnold Rolfe in the Children's Court at Melbourne of the rape and sodomy of a seventy-three-year-old woman."

"What!"

"You were committed indefinitely to a criminal reformatory."

"I told you before, I've never even been charged with a criminal offence!"

"In 1974 when you turned eighteen you were released to a halfway house under strict supervision. You walked out of there three weeks later – that's five months before Sandra Hershey was attacked – and you never returned."

"That's not true! My record's completely clear!"

"Which record? Your record in the name of Ronald Morris? Yeah sure, that's clear. Or are you talking about your record in the name of Stephen Rolfe?" Eddie shoved aside the folder he had been reading from and commenced paging frantically through a second until again he found his place and pinned the page down with his finger. "Or maybe you mean your record in the name of Troy Peter Mansell, the name you were convicted under in 1981, when you served five years for rape and grievous bodily harm?"

Morris eyed the lawyer with a murderous venom that betrayed him instantly. No one believed the answer that he eventually growled.

"I've never heard of Troy Mansell."

"Not many people have any more! His records are all gone!" Moran was leaning forward, taunting him, daring him to respond the way he wanted to, violently, lethally. "Or at least his police records are gone, anyway. Seems someone got rid of them. But whoever it was forgot to go back to the old New South Wales Prisons Department files, Mr Morris. If you've got the right name you can still find Troy Mansell's prison records in the department archives, just as you can still turn up Stephen Rolfe's juvenile detention records in Victoria, so long as you don't try to get to them through police criminal history details, because there are none. They're long gone!" Eddie pulled one document from the prison files. "But your prison records have a photograph of you in them, don't they, Mr Morris? They always put a little mugshot of you on the file!" Eddie held the document up and jammed his finger onto the small head shot in the top right hand corner. "Right there on your Reception Details form, isn't that so?"

Eddie slapped the document back down onto the bar table and snarled at the witness.

"It is, isn't it!"

Morris's eyes narrowed. He was like a cornered beast, fighting for survival, looking for the opportunity for flight. He thought the records had been lifted, every trace removed. But somehow, something had been overlooked.

"Well, witness? Yes or no?"

"Yes."

"And you were convicted and gaoled in 1981 under the name Troy Mansell, weren't you, witness!"

"Yes."

Eddie had what he needed, what he knew he'd get. Stephen Rolfe had threatened too many people, made too many enemies. When you play that game eventually it catches up with you, and it had just caught up with Stephen Arnold Rolfe. His time was up, the game was over. The moment Dr Milo Forrester had seen him on the Thursday evening television news, trying hard to hide his face from the cameras as he walked out of the trial of William Keliher, he recognised him as the vicious young boy he had first met at the house of Eric Pohl in the late sixties, the handsome, athletic youth who had found himself a place in the home of the Brethren, immersed himself in their largesse, learned from their poisonous example, and graduated to become their henchman, dealing out threats, bashings and sometimes worse to the wayward and recalcitrant, like Milo Forrester himself. Now Milo was on the run, and to survive he had to stay a step ahead of Stephen Rolfe, the man who had officially disappeared long ago with his police records. Unfortunately for Stephen Rolfe, he could change his name, he could change his records, he could even change his passport and his birth certificate, but he couldn't change his face. Milo Forrester recognised it immediately. He couldn't forget it. And he remembered lots of other things about Stephen Rolfe. Important things, such as when he had got into trouble, and where, and why, and what had happened to him when he did. They were useful details, because no matter how many good friends you have out there, it's hard to bury something down so deep no one will ever find it, to lose something so completely that it doesn't leave some trace somewhere – waiting to come back to haunt you, waiting to pop up one day and bring it all undone.

"Then why did you lie about that when I asked you earlier?"

Morris sat silent in the witness box. He was still trapped, still looking for the way out.

"It's a part of my past I'm ashamed of. I've tried hard to forget it."

"Garbage! That's a complete lie, isn't it!"

Eddie was trying to drag him back into a stoush, put him off his game again, but Morris was in survival mode now, tentative, guarded, listening carefully and answering with caution.

"No."

"Yes it is! Isn't it?"

"No."

"Well this rape you committed when you were Troy Mansell, it was a violent rape, wasn't it?"

"Yes."

"So when you told us earlier that you were disgusted by the violence done to Sandra Hershey, that it gave you nightmares, that you'd never experienced that kind of violence before, that was a lie too, wasn't it?"

Morris's eyes narrowed again. It was obvious for all to see that the witness didn't like the sound of where this line of questioning was leading. As he sat in silence considering his answer, every eye in the courtroom was on him and each silent second added to the guilt reflected in his face.

"It was a lie, wasn't it?" Eddie repeated quietly.

"Yes."

"You didn't see Bill Keliher leaving that park that night, did you?"

"Yes, I did."

"You didn't see anybody, did you?"

"Yes I did."

"That's not true. You're lying, aren't you?"

"No."

"Yes you are. You're lying."

"No I'm not."

"You did it! You attacked and raped Sandra Hershey, didn't you!"

"No!"

Morris had the panicked look of a man who'd suddenly realised that he'd started a fight he was going to lose, and lose badly.

"One of the complainants in this case recalls a distinctive tattoo on the right forearm of her attacker. Troy Mansell's records show that he also had a tattoo on his right forearm, don't they?"

"Yes."

"Mind if we see that tattoo, Mr Morris?"

Morris glanced vacantly about the courtroom as though casting for help. Then he turned back to Moran, his mouth shaped oddly as though he were about to speak, but as the seconds drew on and on he said nothing. Eddie glared at him, his loathing mounting with each second. He was thinking about Slick lying bruised and battered in a hospital bed, about photographs of young girls and women, ravaged, twisted obscenely, lying naked in the dirt where they'd been dumped, the ugly gaping hole bitten into the soft white breast of a pretty adolescent girl, hardly out of high school. And a proud, brave man who'd been pilloried, imprisoned, humiliated, insulted and abused, but still had enough in him to believe in himself. And to make his half-smart arsehole lawyer believe in him too. And to keep going, when everyone else had given up, to keep going until he found two lost kids he'd always said he'd find.

Morris was squirming in the witness box, and as he grew more and more pathetic in his indecision, Eddie's hatred for him gathered until it finally exploded in a torrid barrage.

"You've got a tattoo of a cross on your forearm, haven't you? Haven't you, Mr Morris! Or sorry, is it Mr Mansell now, or maybe Mr Rolfe? Whatever it is, you've got that telltale tattoo right there on your forearm, haven't you?"

The judge had a new authority in his voice now as he demanded a response.

"Answer the question, witness."

Stephen Rolfe wasn't answering any more questions. His mind was racing without direction from one proposition to another, lurching erratically here and there, searching for escape but finding only danger at each turn. The one thing he knew and knew for certain was that anything he said now was going to do him damage. He settled, hardened, and stared back blankly at the judge.

"I direct you to answer the question, witness."

Morris remained motionless, staring vacantly into the space in front of him.

"You don't like that question, buddy?" Eddie Moran

was bouncing around behind the bar table like a rabid dog that had broken its chain. He was no longer in court, he was out in the streets, down in the gutter, hurling insults like a ragged urchin. "Try this one on for size: another one of the complainants says the sick bastard that attacked her had a bald head – aren't I correct in saying that head of yours is as bald as a new-born baby's bum?"

"Mr Moran!" His Honour Judge Michael Fraser QC finally snapped. "Sit down!" Eddie Moran was still huffing and puffing, staring daggers at the witness. "Immediately!" Eddie resumed his seat. "Mr Bailiff, remove the jury!" With some relief the jury quickly filed out to the jury room and closed the door behind them. "Constable, arrest Mr Morris immediately! In view of your refusal to answer counsel's questions, I hold you in contempt. You will be held in custody indefinitely until you purge your contempt."

As two police officers led Morris from the court, Eddie Moran scowled at him, daring him to return the stare. He didn't. When the prisoner had left the room, Eddie turned back to see the judge peering angrily at him from the bench.

"Mr Moran! Stand up." Suddenly chastened, Eddie rose promptly to his feet. "If you ever use such language, or behave in that fashion again in my court, I can promise you, you will share the same fate as Mr Morris. Sit down!"

As he sat down Eddie glanced across his shoulder at Bill Keliher sitting in the dock and flicked him a knowing wink.

"Now, Mr Parforth," the judge continued, "I intend to recommend to the Director of Prosecutions that the last witness be prosecuted for perjury."

"Yes, Your Honour."

"I would also recommend that he be investigated closely as a matter of urgency in relation to the instant offences."

"Yes, Your Honour."

"Furthermore, I intend to ask the Independent Commission Against Corruption to investigate the disappearance of his police records."

"Yes, Your Honour."

"In the meantime I suggest the Crown consider its position as to whether this prosecution should continue. I'll adjourn the trial until tomorrow to allow you to take instructions. Mr Moran, you might be good enough to make available to Mr Parforth your copy of Mr Mansell's prison records."

For once in his life Eddie Moran looked slightly sheepish.

"I don't actually have his prison records, Your Honour."

"I'm talking about the ones you referred to in your cross-examination."

"Oh, they're not his records, Your Honour. They relate to another client of mine. We didn't have time to access Mr Mansell's records. I'd just been told what he went to prison for, and I figured that there must be records of it somewhere."

The judge looked slightly stunned, and sat thoughtfully for several seconds before he turned to the bailiff.

"Adjourn the court."

As Michael Fraser QC rose to leave the court, he stopped briefly.

"Mr Moran," he said politely, "we are indebted to you for bringing these matters to the court's attention."

He bowed stiffly, turned and walked quietly from the court.

# CHAPTER TWENTY-EIGHT

The defence lawyer strode into Peter Rosenthal's palatial office with a contemptuous arrogance that was remarkably rude, even for the abrasive Edwin C. Moran. As Bruce Parforth looked on in horror, Eddie walked straight to the Commissioner's desk and dropped uninvited into one of the soft leather client chairs.

"That was a pretty dumb decision you made there, pal!"

Parforth held his breath, waiting for the judge to pick up the telephone and quietly arrange to have Moran thrown out of the building. Not for a moment had he expected the man to behave so boorishly in the office of the Commissioner himself. Moran had politely requested that Parforth endeavour to arrange a conference with Commissioner Rosenthal to discuss the decision that had been taken to persevere with the prosecution of Inspector William Keliher notwithstanding that one of the Crown's major witnesses, Ronald Morris, had been totally discredited. It seemed a reasonable request and Parforth had gladly obliged, informing Commissioner Rosenthal that defence counsel wished to make personal submissions to him on the issue. Being an eminently fair and reasonable administrator, the Commissioner had agreed, as Parforth had known he would.

The decision had not been an easy one in the first place. When Judge Fraser had recommended that the Crown consider its position overnight, Bruce Parforth had made immediate arrangements to meet with Commissioner Rosenthal. He explained the day's events in detail, culminating with the arrest of Morris, and the judge's invitation to the Crown to re-evaluate its stance. Rosenthal was gravely troubled by the news. The prosecution of Bill Keliher was one of the most sensational trials in the state's history, and had become a flagship for the fledgling Commission, demonstrating its commitment to unearth and prosecute the perpetrators of juvenile crime, no matter who they might be. A failure of the prosecution at whatever level and for whatever cause could only damage the Commission. Morris was the most important prosecution witness in the case, the only one allowed to testify who purported to identify the accused as the culprit. Now he had been discredited, not only shown up as a liar but covered in suspicion as the perpetrator of the crimes himself. How could the Crown case survive from here? How could they hope to convince the jury to return a guilty verdict?

Rosenthal had pondered all the issues, questioning Bruce Parforth carefully about exactly what had been said, both in court and afterwards; weighing up what evidence there was to suggest Ron Morris may have been involved in one or more of the offences; considering what evidence was left that pointed to the guilt of the accused. Finally he had decided, reluctantly it seemed, to continue with the trial and leave the matter to the determination of the jury. The prosecution would distance themselves from the evidence of Ronald Morris, but they still had the DNA evidence and they would pare the case back to one of purely scientific identification. When all was said and done, regardless of whether Ron Morris was a convicted criminal, regardless of whether he had lied about his background, and perhaps even regardless of whether he had something to hide concerning the attack on Sandra Hershey, the blood which Melissa Smith drew when she scratched the arm of her assailant was the blood of William Keliher, and that meant he had at least attacked and raped Melissa Smith. Whether the facts of all the other cases were so strikingly similar as to constitute evidence that he had also attacked and raped each of the others was a matter for the jury.

So that was the decision. Tomorrow morning Bruce Parforth would go back into court and tell Judge Fraser that the prosecution had elected to press on. It was a decision Bruce wasn't all that happy with, as he was the one who would have to sell the badly wounded Crown case to the jury. But that was his job, so he went back and broke the news to Eddie Moran.

If Parforth wasn't happy with the decision, Eddie Moran was even less so. He demanded to see the

Commissioner, and now he was perched disrespectfully over his desk, poking holes in the air with his finger and making outlandish and inflammatory insinuations.

"Stephen Rolfe's in the can right now purging his contempt! If this trial goes on he can be brought back! And if he is, sooner or later he might just decide to tell a few home truths, like where he first met you, and what you two have been up to all these years!"

Rosenthal sat silently, his brow knit tightly in a gloomy frown, listening solemnly as the lawyer ranted unabated.

"And if you're relying on that bullshit DNA, I'm going to want you as a witness, because those blood swabs from Melissa Smith were held in your office until the sample was taken from Bill Keliher. That means you're in the gun, pal, and I'm going to want to know all about your grubby tie-up with the McCabe kidnapping case!"

Parforth scoffed at this ludicrous suggestion and he turned to Rosenthal anticipating a similarly outraged reaction. It wasn't there. The judge was sitting bolt upright, his face still a grim, drawn mask.

"What are you talking about?"

"You know what I'm talking about, you pathetic scumbag!" Moran slapped the desk loudly and bared his teeth. "I'm talking about you and Robert Allen, and Stephen Rolfe, and the Brethren, and the whole bloody sick joke! I'm talking about the body of an eight-year-old kid who's just been dug up on the property at Yelgarabbi!"

"What property at Yelgarabbi?"

"The property your grandfather's logging company owned for nearly forty years, that's what fucking property! Had you forgotten about that?" Moran leaned down and flicked the catch on his briefcase and foraged clumsily through its contents as he continued. "Well, you better start trying to remember, pal, because when I get you in that witness box I'm going to want to know all about it!" He yanked a large manilla envelope from the briefcase and removed its contents with two fingers. "Just like I'm going to want to know all about this!"

He was holding up an A4-size laminated enlargement of the dog-eared black and white snapshot Frank Vagianni had discovered in amongst Herbert Montgomery's last known possessions. It showed three young virile men, arm in arm, smiling broadly. Peter Rosenthal was looking grimly at it from across the desk, remembering the faces, the circumstances, a lifetime ago.

"Go ahead!" Moran was lightly shaking it over Rosenthal's expansive desk. "Take a closer look. Don't worry, the original's safely tucked away. It's nicely inscribed on the back, too – 'Garry, Robbie and Peewee'."

The Juvenile Crimes Commissioner leaned forward and took the photograph from the lawyer's grasp. He held it in front of him for a long time, studying it sadly, as if he could change what it depicted just by wishing. Eventually he leaned forward and slid it back across the desk.

"I don't know what you're talking about."

"Don't you? Then I'll spell it out. I'm talking about you and your good buddies Robert Allen and Garry Willet. Don't you recognise your old friends, Peewee?"

The name fell into the silence and hung there as Rosenthal's grey, dead eyes stared blankly back at his accuser. It was a long time before he finally spoke.

"I don't recognise anyone in this photograph."

"Is that right?" Eddie Moran jumped back to his feet. "Well, we'll see what the jury makes of it!" He reached down and delicately lifted the photograph by the top corner in two careful fingers. "You've got to be very careful how you handle shiny surfaces these days, Peewee. They can pick up fingerprints on anything." He slipped the photograph back into the envelope. "You know they never did identify that second set of prints they lifted from the letter Michael McCabe sent home to his parents. I might just have someone throw an expert eye over this photograph to see if any prints on it match up with that letter. What d'you think?"

Peter Rosenthal looked gaunt and pale, his striking presence somehow now reduced to a sad, drooping caricature. Bruce Parforth was gaping at him from across the desk, waiting for some kind of meaningful rejoinder. None came.

Eddie Moran snatched up his briefcase. "I'll find my own way out this time."

\* \* \*

The trial of William James Keliher did not proceed. On the following morning Mr Bruce Parforth, senior prosecutor with the office of the New South Wales Director of Public Prosecutions, told the presiding trial judge Michael Fraser QC that in the light of serious discrepancies revealed in the evidence of Mr Ronald Morris, a witness who was central to the prosecution case, the Director had formed the view that the investigation of Police Inspector William Keliher was seriously flawed, and in the circumstances the Director had elected to discontinue prosecution of the charges. The judge returned the indictment to the prosecutor, who marked with it with the Latin formula 'nolle prosequi', thereby ending the process.

"Inspector Keliher." Michael Fraser QC made a point of referring to his rank. "You are discharged. You may leave the dock whenever is convenient to you."

As the court adjourned Bill Keliher took Eddie Moran by the hand.

"I guess we both passed that test."

"I guess we did." Eddie shook his big hand heartily. "I guess we did."

It wasn't until later in the day that the news broke about the death of Peter Rosenthal, the distinguished academic, barrister, Supreme Court judge, and the first head of the Juvenile Crimes Commission. At first details were patchy. It gradually emerged that he had taken his own life the night before, washing down a bottle of sleeping pills with Glenfiddich whisky behind the locked doors of his JCC office. His body was discovered early the next morning by the startled cleaners.

The acknowledgements of his contribution to the

legal profession and to law enforcement in the state of New South Wales were unusually anonymous and restrained, and rumours were already circulating before the week was out. When state parliament resumed, his name was raised in connection with largely unsupported allegations of a highly secretive network of paedophiles operating within the legal profession. Predictably, an acrimonious controversy erupted, with claims and counter-claims firing back and forth across the house and new facts slowly emerging about the man behind the failed prosecution of Police Inspector Keliher. Finally the government announced that, in the light of the findings made by the Independent Commission Against Corruption into the affairs of one Stephen Arnold Rolfe, based on a meticulous study of archival records and statements taken from various persons including the Protected Witness Dr Milo Forrester, it had commissioned a leading Queen's Counsel to draw Terms of Reference for a broad-ranging inquiry into paedophilia in New South Wales. According to some members of the press the inquiry was tipped to reopen certain aspects of the 1965 McCabe kidnapping case.

The procedural rules for proving identification in criminal cases by use of fingerprint evidence generally accept that fourteen points of similarity are required to be established before a particular print can be said to belong to the same person as the sample print. It took Eddie several weeks to get the police to make the latent fingerprints lifted from the McCabe letter available for comparison by an independent examiner. Three good prints were lifted from the laminated photograph that had been handled by Peter Rosenthal. He found match-ups for two of them with the McCabe letter prints, one with fifteen points and one with seventeen.

\* \* \*

A large crowd was gathered on the grassy hillside overlooking Barrons Landing. St Vincent's Cemetery was ringed by cars as black-suited mourners filed solemnly towards the grave site. Some of them were still residents of Brighton Bay; some had moved away years ago but were back now to pay their last respects to the little town's most famous citizens. Many were constituents of the popular local councillor Faye McCabe; some just patrons of her childcare centre or recipients of her kindness and her friendship. Most had never met either of the deceased, but everybody knew them.

A line of Catholic priests stood on one side of the grave, led in the brief ceremony by Father Paddy Quirk, the parish priest for over thirty years, now long-since retired. Opposite them stood the petite, auburn-haired woman, hand in hand with her oldest and dearest friend, Bill Keliher. She clung bravely to him as two shiny wooden coffins, one the compact coffin of a child, were lowered slowly into the ground.

"Ashes to ashes, dust to dust," Paddy Quirk announced feebly, but with comforting finality.

Faye McCabe stepped forward to the grave's edge and looked down onto the coffins of her only children. They were together again at last. She remembered them sitting on the back stairs of the old house, wrapped in their towels, drinking milk and dunking biscuits in the fading warmth of the western sun. Little Michael, the organiser, the protector, with his arm around his baby sister Catherine. Home, and safe, and happy. As she looked down she saw their happy faces, smiling still. They were her perfect, lovely children, just as she remembered them, just as they would always be.

She reached one hand out and held it closed over the grave. As her vision blurred behind her tears she smiled fondly and whispered just one word.

"Sweethearts."

She opened up her hand and let them fall. A florin, shillings, threepences, and two brown pennies. And last of all the little farthing, cherished, lost, and found again. As they rattled down onto the wood below she said her last goodbye, and stepped away.

\*　　\*　　\*

Frank Vagianni was still wiping away tears and blowing his nose as he followed Slick and Eddie down the hill back to their car. The sun was beating down and Frank could feel it cooking his dark suit.

"God, that was sad." Slick was dabbing one eye daintily, careful not to smudge her eyeliner. Eddie laid a comforting arm around her shoulder.

"Yeah, well, it's kind of a funeral thing, Slick. That's the way they do them."

She laid her head gently on his shoulder. "Get fucked will you, Eddie. You're such a wise guy."

Eddie chuckled softly to himself as they walked on, arm in arm, towards the car. "Hey, you know what?" he said eventually. "Why don't we go back via the blues festival?"

"Yeah!" Slick smiled up at him fondly. "Why don't we."

"What do you think, Frank?"

"They serve piss there?"

"Sure."

"You got me."